ST. MARTIN'S

MINOTAUR
MYSTERIES

PRAISE FOR TOM CORCORAN'S MYSTERIES

BONE ISLAND MAMBO

"Corcoran's insider knowledge makes him a terrific tour guide, and he spins a complex but extremely enjoyable yarn that includes murder, family squabbles, a stolen-car ring, and a warm, folksy sense of community." —*Miami Herald*

"BONE ISLAND MAMBO starts fast, never lets up. Key West's crazies are a hoot, and Tom Corcoran's plot and range of characters add to a series that won't quit. Treat yourself to an exotic setting, laughs, and suspense." —Janet Evanovich, author of HOT SIX

"Tom Corcoran knows the human heart, sure as hell knows how to write a good book, and knows Key West—a setting so real you'll get a sunburn." —Steve Hamilton, author of THE HUNTING WIND

"Vividly written and filled with hilariously eccentric Key West denizens, the novel is as twisty as a mangrove root and as fast moving as the local characters are laissez-faire." —*The Dallas Morning News*

"BONE ISLAND MAMBO gives an atmospheric view of Key West, from a creepy deserted alley to the rush of Caroline Street . . . Melding history with the present, Corcoran preserves Key West for tourists and residents alike." —*Philadelphia News*

"BONE ISLAND MAMBO is Rutledge's third appearance in an excellent series by Tom Corcoran, who moves deep into Carl Hiaasen territory with a story about murder mixed with the continuing development of old Key West." —*Minneapolis Star-Tribune*

"Exciting . . . [A] fast-paced adventure . . . Rutledge leads a fine tour of the area, from the Green Parrot bar to fishing flats in the mangrove forests. The best aspect of this novel is summed up in the line, 'Key West used to be a quaint drinking village with a fishing problem.' Corcoran captures this local atmosphere extremely well." —*Publishers Weekly*

"Corcoran writes in a concise and breezy style, and Alex Rutledge should be attracting more fans to his laid-back lifestyle, which always includes a murder or two." — Otto Penzler, Penzler Pick May 2001

"Corcoran has a real feel for the laissez-faire Key West style, and he knows how to meld island history into his stories . . . The mellow mood guarantees a good time." — *Booklist*

GUMBO LIMBO

"Corcoran lubricates his tangled plot with lashings of rum and beer, and keeps it moving across a shrewdly observed landscape that reeks with authenticity. The gumbo is spicy, the limbo swift in this hot pepper of a novel." — *Publishers Weekly* (Starred Review)

"GUMBO LIMBO . . . is often amusing. Key West, as well, continues to be a terrifically atmospheric setting for intrigue, and Corcoran's wacko cast of characters is colorful. It's nice to be back in the tropics." — *Chicago Tribune*

"In GUMBO LIMBO, Tom Corcoran delivers a well-plotted, atmospheric mystery that even surpasses his superior effort, THE MANGO OPERA. The author brings a vivid imagination and a unique view to the Florida mystery fold. Let's hope Alex Rutledge never runs out of film." — *The Florida Sun Sentinel*

THE MANGO OPERA

"With its sure feel for the Key West that resides beneath the tourist facade and a quirky, hard-edged rhythm pulsing beneath the surface calm, this debut deserves a wide and welcoming audience." — *Publishers Weekly*

"MANGO OPERA leapfrogs over many first-time novels to put Corcoran solidly in the company of the likes of Laurence Shames and Robert Crais. Tom Corcoran is off to a very fast start on what is sure to be a long career as a fine mystery novelist." — *Bookpage*

DON'T MISS THESE ALEX RUTLEDGE MYSTERIES BY TOM CORCORAN

Gumbo Limbo

The Mango Opera

AVAILABLE FROM ST. MARTIN'S/MINOTAUR PAPERBACKS!

AN ALEX RUTLEDGE MYSTERY

BONE ISLAND
MAMBO

TOM CORCORAN

St. Martin's Paperbacks

BONE ISLAND MAMBO

Copyright © 2001 by Tom Corcoran.

Excerpt from *The Octopus Alibi* © 2002 by Tom Corcoran.

All rights reserved. No part of this book may be used or reproduced in any manner whatsoever without written permission except in the case of brief quotations embodied in critical articles or reviews. For information address St. Martin's Press, 175 Fifth Avenue, New York, NY 10010.

ISBN: 0-312-98008-6

Printed in the United States of America

St. Martin's Press hardcover edition / May 2001
St. Martin's Paperbacks edition / August 2002

St. Martin's Paperbacks are published by St. Martin's Press, 175 Fifth Avenue, New York, NY 10010.

10 9 8 7 6 5 4 3 2

ACKNOWLEDGMENTS

Thanks must go to Cindy Thompson, Carolyn Ferguson, Dink Bruce, Mitchell Kaplan, Mark Houlahan, Adrian Hoff, John Boisonault, Carolina Garcia-Aguilera, Ken Snell, Dawn Bailey, Frank Sauer, and Pete Wolverton.

Special thanks to Pat Boyer, Susan Richards Coleman, DeeDee Bartlett, Bill Bartlett, Sandie Herron, Sebastian Corcoran, and Dinah George.

Whether man die in his bed
Or the rifle knocks him dead,
A brief parting from those dear
Is the worst man has to fear.

—William Butler Yeats,
Under Ben Bulben

1

I recognized a Bonnie Raitt song from the seventies, her solid voice, her spine-chilling slide guitar. Without moving my arms or camera, I turned my head left.

Eight feet away and closing. The self-absorbed Heidi Norquist.

Diamond earrings blazed just below the headset's pink foam cushions. Tiny diamonds, for a Sunday-morning jog. Her hair fell to one side, five-toned butterscotch and gold. She stopped advancing but pumped her slender legs, ran in place, paced the music. A loose pink tank top, tight black shorts, sculpted running shoes fresh from the box. Inch-wide neon-pink wrist bands. Next to the Walkman, a small belly-pack—sized, I guessed, for lip gloss, a cell phone, maybe a fifty-dollar bill for pocket change. A hint of trendy, expensive perfume. A discreet gold neck chain. Direct sunlight, no evidence of sweat. Because of the cool January air or spontaneous evaporation?

A million dollars wrapped in a suntan. Or a fine approximation.

Heidi had come to town with Butler Dunwoody, the younger brother of my friend Marnie Dunwoody. The evening we'd met, eight weeks ago, Heidi had impressed me as a woman who'd done time at the mirror, long enough to understand her power, and shape it. Her conversation had plainly mocked Dunwoody. I recall speculating later that she viewed Butler as a handy layover on her journey to more lofty playgrounds. Marnie had assured me that her brother worshiped the young woman's shadow. With the late-morning sun almost straight up and Heidi's slender frame, there wasn't much shadow to consider. I wondered if, given the chance, I might act the fool equal to Butler Dunwoody.

With my wallet, there would never be that chance.

Two cars on Caroline slowed to check her out. A catcall from the second vehicle didn't faze her. "What're you shooting?" She breathed in and out, a separate aerobic exercise.

"Changes on the island." I waved my free arm toward the construction site. The parking lot between the old Carlos Market and a multi-unit rental property had provided access to a wood shop and a sculptor's studio. With the start of construction, each outfit had been offered square footage in the new "complex," complete with an advertising package, common signage, pro-rated insurance and utility bills, and upscale rent. Each had packed it up. A large white sign bolted to the eight-foot fence listed architects, structural engineers, consulting engineers. Underneath it all: APPLEBY-FLORIDA, INC., GENERAL CONTRACTOR. A nearby sign listed four law firms, three local banks as financiers, a security outfit, and a waste-management consultant. The sign did not mention Butler Dunwoody, who I knew was the project developer.

"For the newspaper?" said Heidi.

I laughed. "I don't do news."

She pushed her hair behind one ear, fiddled to park it there. It fell when she removed her finger. Fifty yards away, in the old shrimp-dock area, an offshore sportsman cranked an unmuffled V-8 marine engine, then a second one. Cubic decibels. She fiddled with the hair again, turned her attention to the waterfront.

When the noise died, Heidi faked a coy face. "You from zoning?"

She didn't recognize me. A slap to the ego. I shook my head.

"Some kind of protester?" Her face went harder. She kept jogging, in a tight circle.

The construction site had received heavy news coverage, a call-to-arms to discover how the project had survived variance, had slid through the approval process. The public wanted to know which politicians had sold out. I said, "Nope. No protest."

Heidi jogged to the fence. A red, foot-square DANGER sign loomed above her head. "Why don't you mind your own fucking business?"

My question, too. I stared without speaking, hoping her message would turn around. It did not.

With the first step of her departure sprint, she muttered, "Jerk-off."

I flat-toned, "Have a nice day." For some reason, I snapped a photograph of the woman's departure.

Ten seconds later, a female voice behind me: "That should be a good shot, Alex Rutledge."

I turned. Same flavor, better quality. Julie Kaiser, lovely without undue effort, heiress to half the island. She stopped gracefully on her Rollerblades. She also wore a tank top and shorts. A coral-colored elastic ribbon held her dark brown hair to a neat ponytail. My first impulse was to lift my camera, to document the tan glow on her cheeks, the sparkles in sunlit peach fuzz.

"What was that about?" She gave me a conspirator's grin.

"It's her boyfriend's construction project. She saw me with a camera and stopped to vent her opinion. Her suspicions outran her manners."

"Suspicions?"

"Bad press, I suppose. Zoning pressures, typical hassles."

"Understandable in Key West," she said.

"And a promise for newcomers. Except, with his sister at the *Citizen*, Butler Dunwoody's probably gotten a few breaks with bad press. We know about public opinion. Zoning's negotiable. The banks and the permit people and progress inspectors shape the rules as they go."

Julie looked northward, pondered the waterfront development area. "It happens to my family, too," she said softly.

"But not recently."

"You'd be surprised. The city knows that my father wants to see this succeed. He's been giving advice to Butler Dunwoody. My sister's husband has been a part-time on-site liaison."

Julie's father, Mercer Holloway, had been our representative in Congress for three decades. He'd brought in the military when the Keys' economy most needed help, mothballed the Navy base once tourism regained its strength. With the economy at rock bottom, he had methodically acquired real estate in the Lower Keys. When growth and inflation arrived, his foresight became evident. His white elephants became prime property. He had put Julie and her notoriously unpleasant sister, Suzanne, through college and law school. Divorced before he left Washington, Holloway had retired to Key West to manage his holdings. His son Gram had died four years ago at age twenty-six. Tequila and speedballs, and a widely acknowledged death wish.

"How are things at home?"

Julie shrugged. "Hasn't been great."

I'd never felt comfortable around Julie's husband, Philip Kaiser. After six years at Tulane in the eighties, her undergrad and postgraduate studies, she returned to Key West and began dating him. Within a year they were married.

"It's been a third of your life," I said. "Same old outlook?"

She looked me in the eye. "Philip thinks expressing jealousy is showing his love. He thinks you're hot for my bod."

"I thought you might've settled that before you rang the church bell," I said. "Or else he'd chill out, all this time."

She turned away. "You're not the only one." Her eyes returned to me. "He suspects every man on the island. I thought a long time ago about going to Atlanta, where his folks moved. But he'd have the same attitude there."

"How does he pat you on the ass, with a paddle?"

"It's not quite that bad. He's a good business partner."

"So you put up with it?"

"Philip fears scorpions, poverty, and losing me. Aside from that, he's not a bad person."

A silver Infiniti honked and drove past us. Julie waved. The windshield reflected blue sky. I couldn't see through it, or the tinted side glass.

She changed the subject. "You keeping busy?"

"Paying the bills," I said. "I did eight days in the Exumas, shooting next summer's fashion for some Boston department store. Skinny, snotty models, but fresh fish three meals a day. Then I did a magazine piece up in Alabama, a photo essay on the last year-round waterborne mail route in the country. Beautiful river in Magnolia Springs."

"Did you stay at the Grand Hotel?"

Way out of my price range. "My friend Sam Wheeler, the fishing—"

"I know Sam."

"He's had a camp for years on Weeks Bay, where the Magnolia flows into Mobile Bay. I stayed in his cabin."

"Weren't you doing crime-scene work?"

"Part-time. Not much since last summer. I did a couple minor things for Sheriff Liska in December. The city hasn't called since Liska moved over to the county. I don't think anyone at city hall remembers me. How about you?"

"The last six weeks, I've been slamming deals, thank goodness. I ruined October. I sold a condo to three twenty-four-year-old boys. Twenty percent down on a pricey party pad. Like a three and five zeros. They turned it into a crank factory with an ocean view, making the modern equivalent of bathtub gin. They used the tub to mix methamphetamine. And, stink? The chemicals could have blown the whole complex out to Sand Key."

"They part of the justice system now?"

"I don't know about justice. They're neck-deep in the legal system. We managed to annul the sale. Of course, my commission flew out the window. I'd already spent the money."

I stared at the new version of Caroline Street, the three-story shopping arcade about to fill the last "vacant" lot between William and Duval. I didn't begrudge Julie Kaiser's livelihood, the real estate business. But real estate and co-operative, sometimes crooked city officials had redefined the island since the Nixon years, the buying, selling, and expansions, the tear-downs and the new developments.

"So," she said, "why *are* you taking pictures?"

"My unending documentation. The island. The changes."

Julie looked through the chain link. "By changes, you mean progress?"

"Some people don't use that word."

"When's your exposé hit the papers?"

"The people who'd care already left town."

"Why shoot the pictures?"

"Habit. I've got boxes full, packed away in closets. I keep them for me. It helps me put everything in perspective, the twenty-odd years I've lived here. Someday, off in the future, maybe I'll do a slide show at the San Carlos. A one-night excuse for old-timers to drink wine and laugh."

Julie rolled backward, poised to skate away. "Or else cry. But I want to be there. Put me on your invitation list, okay?" Her departing wave suggested some great secret between us. If one existed, it fell within the realm of ten or twelve years' flirting, a great promise of attraction, and a handful of innocent hello or good-bye kisses at parties or in restaurants.

Ninety seconds later, Julie came back around the block, down Peacon Lane, past swing chairs on porches, railings and cacti, stubby driveways and trash cans. Turning toward Simonton, she grinned and shook her head: "You bastard. You upset that poor girl's exercise regimen. Now she's over by the Laundromat on Eaton, leaning into the wall, intent as all hell, gabbing on her cell phone. Probably her therapist."

* * *

I went back to shooting the new arcade. I repositioned myself two or three times, tried to minimize the maze of overhead wires. With the water table in some locations a foot below the island's pavement, there are no buried electrical cables. I let my mind wander as I shot, to memories of the seventies.

Caroline Street had been seedy territory. Winos in piss-stained trousers slept on benches in front of the shuttered Fisherman's Café. At the east end of the street, people lived in cars and vans buried under mounds of fishnets and nautical gear. And there'd been tough saloons on Caroline: The Big Fleet, an unofficial petty officers' club. The Red Doors Inn, with its all-day smells of stale beer and the previous night's cigarette smoke. There had been Friday-night bloodbaths, shrimpers in drunken, pointless frenzy, city cops on the offense, pot smoke in the air. I'd wandered into the Mascot one night in 1976, when Curly and Lil were onstage. Forty or fifty shrimpers were packed into the tiny bar. Curly had little hair, but a constant smile. He played a beautiful double-neck hollow-body sunburst guitar. With a voice as tough and lovely as Dolly or Reba or Loretta, Lil had belted, "Has anybody here seen Sweet Thing?" Curly's solos rang of Les Paul, with a touch of Scotty Moore. I'd left in a hurry after a staggering fisherman in rolled-down rubber work boots pointed out my huarache sandals to his compadres. They hadn't approved. Time to go.

I'd ventured down Caroline with my camera one Sunday morning in 1977. A derelict had staggered from behind the marine-supply company. Dried blood stuck his hair to his cheek and forehead. His tongue worked a section of gum where a tooth had broken. Convinced that I'd done him the damage, he came at me with a broken beer bottle. I'd lifted my bike in defense. His first slash popped a tire. I swung the bike, bolero-style. It ended there. Two oceangoing brethren intervened, confiscated the wounded man's weapon, walked him back toward the docks.

Historical perspective is a study of contrast. A generation later, the only action on Caroline centered a block east of me. Every sports utility vehicle in South Florida was competing for eleven metered parking slots on the north side of the street. Every angler south of Jacksonville and not on the ocean waited in an outside line for a table at Pepe's. Hair o' the dog higher on the priority list than breakfast omelets.

Despite its lack of visible threat, Caroline Street still felt ominous.

Change is certain in the Island City.

From the direction of Pepe's Café, I felt concussions of sub-aural bass. Rhythmic low tones preceded a black Chevy S-10 pickup truck lowered to within four inches of the pavement. No high notes that I could hear. Opaque doper tinting, a black camper top. The vehicle rolled on bowl-sized, maybe twelve-inch chrome wheels, tires the thickness of licorice twists. Hearselike and ominous, the truck radiated evil. It yanked me from my ten-minute photo jag.

Thumpa-thump-boom. So much for a quiet Sunday morning.

A tourist foursome near B.O.'s Fish Wagon, blue-coiffed seniors in pastel Bermudas, favored the sidewalk edge farthest from the curb. The elderly men squared their shoulders. The women shifted their hands to protect belly-packs, to shield credit cards and cash, a move doomed should the car stop, a door open, a muzzle or blade wiggle in the yellow sunlight. The cockroach grooved past the seniors. The threat lifted, the weight of the ocean had spared a bubble of innocence. Then it slowed to approach me, to pass more deliberately. A row of three-inch-high decals across the pickup truck's rear glass, alternating Confederate flags and Copenhagen snuff logos. In the window's lower left corner a NASCAR competitor's stylized number. A chain-motif license tag frame, also chromed. I thought, Is that gaping hole under the bumper a tailpipe or a sewer pipe?

The truck stopped. An increase in stereo volume as the

passenger-side door opened. Two pasty-skinned specimens exited. Ratty tank-top muscle shirts and identical brush mustaches. One tall, thin oval sunglasses, a Nike beret. One short with a spiraling barbed-wire arm tattoo, his face stupid, frosted with malice. Gold jewelry equal in value to a Third World annual income. I caught a whiff of fresh-burned hashish.

These children were not promoting a fair fight. They had been to punk school, where experts remove conscience and install weaponry. They had grown up ripping chains from tourists' necks on Duval, had expanded their talents clouting BMWs and Acuras up on South Beach. In some other locale, they'd be kneecappers on the docks, or brass-knuck mob flunkies. The only style twist they knew was to slide gold chains before they yanked, to slash neck skin, to leave a wire-thin reminder of that visit to south Florida.

If this social call was aimed at get-rich-quick, the pukes had targeted the right bike—my eight-hundred-dollar Cannondale—but the wrong camera. My Olympus was almost twenty years old. They probably weren't thinking too far into the future. The bicycle would upgrade the truck's stereo. The OM-4 would barely buy an afternoon's buzz.

I learned years ago, aboard sailboats, that stringing cameras around my neck caused their straps to tangle with the lanyards that kept my sunglasses from going overboard. I got in the habit of double-looping camera straps around my right wrist. It cured tangling and kept my gear from going into the drink when a sudden roll forced the use of grab rails. I was about to learn the benefits of wrist looping when the snatch-and-grab boys play games.

The short one moved first; the tall one hung back. Some kind of tag-team strategy. Two sharks chasing a minnow. They'd stupidly given me a fighting chance, if I didn't lose track of the malevolent tall boy in the background.

"You want this?" I said to Shorty. "Take it away." I held the camera body upright, the lens pointed at him. My thumb brushed the shutter button. On impulse I pressed it.

Probably an overexposed, out-of-focus close-up of his
shoulder. Or one of his drug-dead eyes.

Shorty stepped forward. Watery snot glistened on his
upper lip. He stuck out one hand, held the other snug to
his leg. A four-inch pigsticker pointed downward, threw
glints of sunlight. The kid stank like a bucket of onions
and cheap aftershave. His eyes didn't look crazed—just
emotionless—but I felt sure that his long-term prep had
included hurriedly crafted pipes, chemicals and fumes,
clipped straws, and stolen needles.

Where was tourist traffic when you needed it? No pedestrians in and out of the Caroline Street Market? No
Conch Train rolling by? Had some out-of-sight witness already dialed 911? I pictured the sidewalk seniors locked
snug in their LeSabre, making tracks for North Palm Beach.
I smelled bacon on the breeze, drifting down from Pepe's.

Shorty's open hand came closer; his other hand
twitched. I heard clicks from ten feet away: the tall one
setting the blade of a plastic-handled carpet cutter. I was
alone. I hadn't lived my life in constant gang-banger read-
iness. I hadn't gone to dress rehearsal. I would either eat
street and shed blood, or pull off an out-of-character survival move. A few days earlier I'd read a newspaper article
about martial arts schools teaching courses on fighting
dirty. None of it involved graceful, dancelike moves. Most
of the techniques would have gotten you kicked off the
playground, or banished from the team. I tried to recall the
text of the article. Difficult, on short notice.

I baited the hook, stuck out my arm and the camera. The
knife moved upward an inch. Hell. This wasn't a rip-off. I
was a target. Handing over meat was not going to appease
the tiger. As soon as the shitbird thought I was in range,
the sharp metal would swipe at my arm. Then he'd grab
my other hand, pull me in for a deep back puncture, a lung
or a kidney.

To break his concentration, I dropped the camera,
formed a fist with my hand. I swung my forearm in a circle,
like stirring a pot. Shorty focused on the moving fist,

brought his knife to waist level, pointed it at my belly button. He didn't notice the rotating momentum of the Olympus until the camera swung up like a shot, banged his head just forward of his ear. My follow-through put me in perfect position: I kicked him in the nuts. A hard, solid connection between his slightly spread legs. An audible smack.

The tall one was almost on me. I needed Shorty completely out of the game. I sidestepped the carpet cutter and let go a scoop kick. It buckled Shorty's knee. I switched feet and kicked again. The second jab caught his leg broadside. This time I felt and heard his knee go. He toppled, grabbed his partner for support, robbed him of his balance. I swung the camera like a bolo. The tall one's head bounced backward. He grimaced, tried to stand upright, then spit teeth and blood.

The screech was not from the injured men. The low-slung pickup burned rubber in reverse, coming at me, the open passenger-side door flapping like a black wing. The truck skidded to a stop. The driver jumped out, identical attire except for his backward ball cap. He pointed a strange gun. The way he moved tweaked my memory. I knew his name—Bug Thorsby—and family reputation—god-awful. Neither out of synch with the confrontation.

Drawn by the tires' noise, silent onlookers began to gather. The driver understood the need for retreat. He tore off his tank top, draped it over the truck license tag—too late, but not in his mind—and managed to shove his wounded comrades into the truck. As a parting gesture he turned toward me, aimed the pistol at my chest, and fired. I felt the hit, the rush of liquid, pain and a coldness. I stumbled backward. I looked down.

A monkey-puke green splotch on my shirt. He'd hit me with a paint-pellet gun. It hurt like hell. I smelled like cheap salad dressing.

The truck sped away, as did most of the witnesses.

"You okay?" Don Kincaid, from the charter sailboat *Stars and Stripes,* offered me a towel from his motor scooter's basket. A fellow photographer, he worried more about my Olympus than my clothing. The paint-freckled camera was intact. Don told me the license number.

Another bystander, whom I recognized—a regular customer at the Sunbeam Market—offered to call 911 on her cell phone. I shook my head, then noticed the true miracle. In the excitement and action, no one had stolen my Cannondale bicycle.

Kincaid said he had to go. I assured him I was okay. I just needed to catch my breath. I leaned against my bike and looked up the street. I couldn't dodge the feeling that someone had put the kiddie-thugs on me. Julie Kaiser had said she'd seen Heidi Norquist on her cell phone. No sense in that connection, but this was Key West.

The rest of Caroline had shed its turmoil. The Blazers and Expeditions and Cherokees had quit fighting for space. The brunch line at Pepe's was down to the last three, each customer reading a newspaper. The sun shone bright pale yellow. The sky glowed pure blue. The restored Red Doors Inn gleamed with fresh white and vermilion paint. A peaceful Sunday morning in paradise. Someone could argue that the island was improving with age.

I heard a sharp snap, a carpet cutter opening.

There was no one within twenty yards of me.

Just my imagination.

2

A few hours earlier, my morning had begun on a light note. After waking with Teresa Barga in her Shipyard condo, we'd shared wonderful, energetic love, the toothpaste, Cuban coffee, the toothpaste again. Then yellow-label Entenmann's pastries, and the *Miami Herald*. She'd shrugged off my suggestion that we spend the day in a kayak. She wanted the time to herself, to catch up on paperwork. In her eighth month as the Key West Police Department press liaison, she was confirming that the crime rate, and her job load, increased during tourist season. I wasn't happy having to compete with the city for her time on a Sunday. The upside was my admiration for her work ethic, a rare trait in Key West.

Teresa and I had met five months earlier at city hall. She'd been new in town, we'd both been "single" for months. We were attracted by curiosity, humor, and common interests: being on the water and, during bad weather, reading good books. We'd been constant companions since then.

Wearing only a nightshirt, Teresa had walked me to her door, patted my rear end, kissed me. She'd said, "Take care, lover. It's a jungle out there."

I'd boasted, "Show me the vine. I'm a swinger."

She'd laughed. I'm a laugh a minute.

* * *

I rode home from Caroline Street to get rid of my paint-stained shirt. I found my neighbor Cecilia Ayusa, in Dredgers Lane, picking up fallen palm fronds, dead leaves, and litter. She'd always kept a perfect yard. But she had a new compulsion to clean the street. None of the neighbors, including her daughter and granddaughter, Carmen Sosa and Maria Rolley, had mustered the moxie to question her preoccupation. I wondered if she had reason to fear larger judgment, was trying to please the Chief Inspector. Even Castro had hedged his eternal standing by tempering his four-decade suppression of religion. He'd allowed the Pope eight days of secondhand cigar smoke. If tweezing the lane—often two and three times a day—gave Cecilia comfort, that was fine. I hoped she was not holding back news of ill health.

I locked my bike to the mango tree. I peeled off and trashed my ruined shirt. No messages on the machine. I spread a plastic garbage bag across my porcelain porch table and cleaned the camera with vinegar and Q-Tips. My camera strap had been badly nicked by the carpet cutter. I chucked it, strung a new one, and hid my photo gear under the false bottom of a cabinet. I hit the open-air shower, listened to church bells and a neighbor's stereo—early John Prine. The purple paint-ball welt on my chest took me back to Caroline Street. I thought about it, decided not to be a victim, not to slog my flip-flops through self-pity, wallow in victimness. I also pledged revenge. Not simple paybacks, either. I'm easygoing. I shun negativity. But this time, in due time, I wanted cold, refreshing revenge. I also needed to know what had brought on the attack. Choice one was Heidi's phone call. I hadn't looked like a fat-cat tourist, prime meat with a fat wallet and a shiny watch.

Help us take these monsters off our streets.

I found three messages after the shower.

Sam Wheeler: "I need you for twenty minutes at the most. I know you love physical labor. You always stay in touch with the inner animal. I have Caribbean fish chowder as barter bait, and life-affirming cold beer. I'll give you the play-by-play on my Jamaican vacation."

Teresa Barga: "I couldn't work at home, so I came to the office. Just in time for bad boogie. Call my cell."

The last one: "City Dispatcher Faust, one-twenty P.M., Sunday. Detective Sergeant Hayes needs a call soon as possible. Two-nine-nine-five-two-oh-two. That's twenty-nine, nine, fifty-two, oh two. It's a signal five."

I wrote the number, and understood Teresa's distress. A "five" was a homicide. I didn't recognize the detective's name.

The phone rang. I picked up. Marnie Dunwoody identified herself. She was in her car.

I said, "You went to the tropics to chill out?"

". . . and then came back to this lunatic island." Her voice shook. "I've got a message. The watch commander's been trying to find you. Dexter Hayes needs you to photograph a crime scene. I'm on my way right now."

Dexter Hayes? The old "mayor" of Key West's black section had been called Jumbo Chief. "Marnie, what are we talking? Big Dex isn't the police. He was the opposite, until his power dried up."

"Alex, we're talking Dex Junior. Detective Sergeant Hayes. He's been with the city four months."

"I haven't seen Dexito in years. Teresa's never mentioned him."

"He came down from Broward. He was a SWAT Team leader in Boynton Beach, I think. Take my word, he didn't get hired by affirmative action. He's good."

Four months earlier, my previous Key West Police contact, Detective Fred "Chicken Neck" Liska, had been elected Monroe County Sheriff. He'd given me two small jobs since then, when his regular forensic people were busy. But the city hadn't called at all.

"Give me the address," I said to Marnie.

"Caroline Street. My brother's construction site." Her voice trembled. Her emotions let go. "A man was murdered. Butler found the body." She hung up.

Had a body been in there when I was taking pictures?

I returned Sam Wheeler's call to tell him I couldn't help immediately. I wasn't sure he knew about the murder. Also, I wanted him to contact Florida Keys Hospital to find out if anyone had shown up at the emergency room with a smashed face or a broken knee. No answer. Sam was using the power saw or sander.

I scarfed two bananas, gobbled two tablespoons of peanut butter straight from the Jif jar, chugged a tall glass of water. I called it lunch. I pulled my camera satchel from its hidden cubbyhole, snatched a couple three-packs of twenty-four-exposure Kodacolor, grabbed a long-sleeved shirt. The job could go late. A January evening could drop to the high fifties.

I locked the house, rode my motorcycle down Eaton. I felt like stockpiling scenery before viewing a murder victim. Then I thought, Bogus idea. What would I do, trade hand-hewn balustrades for discarded weapons? White ibis for a slashed throat? A queen palm for a fist-sized exit wound?

Baseball players get to average their good and bad days. My first call in months from the Key West Police would launch my new year in the cellar.

City cops had closed the three hundred blocks of William Street and Peacon Lane. I explained myself to the uniformed patrolman at Elizabeth Street. He was an oldtimer, recognized me from other city crime scenes. Something clicked in my thoughts. I asked if he knew Bug Thorsby.

The officer grimaced. "Rotten mango don't roll far from the tree."

I asked if he knew where Bug hung out.

"Little shit'd be out to the Southern Nights, there on Big Coppitt, chasing out-of-town sluts. I got the deputies to pull him outa there once or twice last year. Check it out. He keeps an ice pick in his boot."

"Appreciate it."

The officer shoved aside a sawhorse barricade. A huge

remote-TV truck, its dish to the heavens, ready to snag overhead power lines, tried to follow me around. The cop went apeshit. I didn't stay for the power squabble.

Two squad cars blocked the intersection at Caroline. One faced Greene, the other Simonton. Roof lights strobed in the afternoon sunlight. I spotted Jerry Bovim, Key West's new head detective, in Bermudas and a Hawaiian-print shirt, departing on his vintage Harley. Delegation of duty is not just good management in Key West, it's an art form, a tradition. I saw no sign of technicians from the county medical examiner's office.

I parked the Kawasaki thirty yards up Caroline, next to Teresa Barga's blue motor scooter. So much for her personal-time paperwork. I walked around a silver Mercedes ML-55, another high-ticket sports utility vehicle that would never leave the pavement. Its Florida "Save the Dolphins" license tag read POKEM UP, which I associated with the Pokémon craze of 1999. I'd seen Butler Dunwoody driving an imperfectly restored ketchup-red '61 Ford Galaxie convertible. It too had carried a "Save the Dolphins" vanity plate. Obviously, his Benz. Then I recalled that "poke 'em up," in Florida, referred to the construction industry's goal of erecting buildings wherever it found undefiled land.

I crossed the street, didn't recognize the uniformed cop on duty. I pulled out my KWPD identification card. He showed me through the chain link, not eight feet from the DANGER sign where Heidi had stood when she'd told me to mind my own business. Two more uniforms stood inside, next to a row of four portable toilet stalls. The cops looked semiofficial, barely alert. I assumed they'd been called at home, scrambled for special duty. The stinky portables no doubt a boost to their spirits. They aimed me toward the northeast corner of the framed-out three-story building. Away from the potties, the place smelled of pine sawdust. A walkway of pallets and two-by-sixes lay over clumps of dry dirt, loose rock, fist-sized asphalt chunks from the lot's previous life. The makeshift walkway ended at a fresh concrete slab.

Marnie Dunwoody hurried toward me, a frantic look on her tanned face. She moved closer as if to hug, but instead clutched my upper arm. Almost whispering, she said, "Too awful. I knew the man, real well."

"I'm sorry."

"It's been four years since I dated him. But I can't do this for the paper. It's got to be somebody else's piece. Call us when you're done, okay?"

I nodded. She went away. I walked around a pallet stack and an upended Dumpster. For a moment, time froze. In the shade of a high scaffold I saw, in one take: Teresa—her dark hair pulled to a twist, her face grim and pissed off; Marnie's brother, Butler Dunwoody; Heidi Norquist; Detective Dexter Hayes, Jr.; a uniformed lieutenant; and the city's prince of nepotism, Cootie Ortega. Cootie Ortega was the department's full-time photographer, lab tech, and all-around screw-up. He held an old Nikon and a Polaroid camera.

All but Teresa stared as if I'd kept them waiting for days.

Except for a scowl of distaste, Hayes's face revealed nothing. He said, "Glad you could make it." No other greeting after years of not having seen each other, no offer to shake hands.

"Thanks for thinking of me."

"Your name came up. I just need a few shots here." He handed me a pair of rubber gloves.

"I need shoe socks, not gloves. I'm not going to touch anything but my camera."

He pocketed the gloves.

I remembered Hayes as about five-eight, but he'd grown a couple more inches. He was slender, in khaki pants, a button-down blue oxford-cloth shirt, plain vanilla Reeboks, white socks, sunglasses hung on a cloth lanyard. He reminded me of the actor Gregory Hines. Years ago, Hines had filmed a movie segment in Key West. I'd watched him roller-skate acrobatically down Front Street.

I looked around. Teresa—slightly taller than Dex Hayes—wore pressed blue jeans and a wrinkled cotton blouse, hurry-up professional attire. More clothing than the last time I'd seen her. Dunwoody wore a gray sweatshirt, baggy, bright yellow swim trunks, opaque sunglasses, Blues Brothers–style, a backward ball cap atop disheveled hair. Heidi looked windblown, her hair darker out of the sunlight, her face hardened in shock and fear, though the result suggested fragility. The million-dollar tan not as healthy as before. Her arms were folded across her chest, as if to ward off harm. The self-indulgent power act on hold.

The victim was belly-down on temporary plywood flooring. Not what I expected. No obvious damage, no blood. He wore black ankle-high work boots and a frilly cream-colored nightie—thin straps over his shoulders, most of the garment bunched around his waist. Makeup, rouge, and powder covered his face. Heavy liner around the eye I could see, duct tape across his lips, a panty liner that looked like a clown smile stuck over the tape. A tan webbed belt was snug around his neck. His hands were cuffed behind his back. Whip marks covered his buttocks and upper thighs. A large dark feather stuck out of his ass. A strap-on pecker was next to him on the floor. The kind women wear with women, with Velcro-adjustable nylon belts, chromed D rings, a rainbow-hued dong sized to make men cringe with inadequacy. Crack vials, whole and crunched, on the temporary floor, and small plastic vial stoppers.

"Go ahead," said Dexter Hayes. "Do your thing."

Everyone stared at me.

I said, "Any background notes, might help my approach?"

Hayes shrugged, looked down at a tiny spiral notepad. "Richard Engram. Project manager. No one had seen him since the Friday shift. They don't work weekends. Mr. Dunwoody gave two bankers a tour yesterday. Engram wasn't here. Thirty minutes ago Mr. Dunwoody and Ms. Norquist came in, spent five minutes walking the layout with a prospective tenant, found the body. Called it in twenty-five minutes ago. Other than that, shoot the scene neutral, like you don't know jackshit and need to find clues."

"Which is where you're at?"

"It's the way I work every case. Why taint a scene with suppositions?" He used a forefinger knuckle to scratch his upper lip.

"Like what killed him?"

"This was not a hunting accident. It's not 'Failure to Thrive.' "

Chuckles from Ortega and the lieutenant, at my expense. If it weren't for their smiles, I'd have thought the mood hostile. I didn't want to look at Teresa, to put her on the spot.

I pulled the camera from my shoulder case, fitted the electronic flash, checked my settings. Shit, I thought. I hadn't removed my morning film from the camera. I'd exposed only five frames, but I'd shot them twenty yards from where I stood, smack in front of the site. Screw it, I said to myself. If I swapped rolls right then, I would look unprepared, like an unsure fumbler. Easy enough to have Duffy Lee Hall, my darkroom tech, pull the first neg strip from the packet he'd prepare for the city.

I disliked my audience. I couldn't understand why Detective Hayes had permitted so many people to remain, or why he'd asked me to work before an access alley had been cleared by scene investigators, especially with so many objects on the floor. Even shoe-print lifts were good evidence. Scene contamination could kill a case or make details inadmissible. Even if someone finding the body had rolled the man over, tried resuscitation, the officer in charge needed to preserve remaining crime scene integrity.

I began slightly wide-angle, for scene establishment. After a half dozen shots, I moved closer. Confirmed: No mental preparation cushions the photographer who must capture gruesome details. Alternatively, looking a dead man in the eye is not facing up to death. I walked around him, for different angles. A Rolling Stones gaping-mouth-and-dangling-tongue logo was tattooed low on the far butt cheek. On second perusal, I realized that the tattoo masked a poorly repaired concave scar from a bullet hole.

After maybe two minutes, Dexter Hayes pointed to the plastic stoppers. "Those red tops? That's redneck-quality dope."

"I wouldn't know," I said. "How good is a project manager with a habit like that?"

"When he left work Friday, he was headed for Kelly's. He had a reputation for chasing pretty girls. He told somebody he'd had his eye on a particular waitress. Maybe he thought crack would impress her. Who knows where he went after happy hour."

I tried to figure his line of reasoning. Gossip could offer leads, but he was speculating in left field.

I said, "Did he think cross-dressing would impress her, too?"

"Some guys will do anything to get laid."

"You're getting too scientific for me, Detective."

"Sorry. I hate Sunday murders. Thank goodness the Super Bowl is next week, and not today. Look, pack it up, Rutledge. We got it from here."

I hadn't shot a third of what I knew they needed.

Hayes continued: "Ortega can wrap it up for you. Give him those rolls you just shot. You can head on out."

I'd observed Ortega's screw-ups for years. As if on cue, Cootie went right to work. I could tell by the sound of his camera that his flash wasn't synchronizing with his shutter. His photos would be worthless. For some reason, Dexter Hayes was running this investigation into the toilet. I couldn't bear to look at Teresa, who must realize the folly in play, or at Butler Dunwoody and Heidi, who probably didn't. I extracted the Kodacolor, handed it to Cootie, slowly packed my camera and flash into their satchel pockets.

Having to give film for developing to Ortega, after Marnie's distress and the detective's atrocious handling of the scene, amounted to strike three. I immediately wrote off future work for the Key West Police. I picked up my motorcycle helmet and started for the lumber walkway.

Hayes said, "Better bone up on your skills, Rutledge."

"How so, Detective?"

"Procedures. We'll talk about it some other time."

"No hurry? Maybe after the Super Bowl?"

"Get the fuck out of here."

3

I escaped the construction site's chain-link enclosure. Six onlookers watched from Caroline's south curb—three couples in flowery shirts, woven-frond hats, beads and name tags on necklace strings, tall drink cups in hand. Puzzled party hounds confronted by violence in paradise. I felt the same gravity. I'd avoided ugliness for most of my time in Key West. It had intersected my life too often in the past year. Too often in the past two hours.

I wasn't sure what Dexter Hayes and his forensic team would learn from the scene. I'd found new evidence that crime photography was not my dream vocation. I'd begun moonlighting with it several years back. A few side jobs, helpful income, few hassles. This gig had proved to be a sick game for an unprofessional investigator.

Violence wasn't new to Key West. Sixteenth-century Spanish explorers called the atoll Cayo Hueso—Bone Island. They'd found human skeletons strewn about, evidence of native strife. The first permanent settlement had formed in the 1820s. Since then the island's condition had rolled from tough to impoverished to romantic to lunatic to wealthy. Strife had remained.

A ten-knot north wind had picked up. I rode the Kawasaki toward Sam Wheeler's house at the south end of Elizabeth. Ten days into January, air in the shade cool, but the direct sun hot as April or October. Traffic a zoo, wandering, in slow motion. The main blast of the winter tourist season. Hotels charging more per night than my monthly mortgage payment.

Ironic, I thought, that Dexter Hayes, Jr., had become a detective. His upbringing probably gave him the best possible preparation, but no one would have guessed this outcome. The story I'd heard was that his father had been a juvenile thug in the 1950s, when Bahama Village still was called Jungletown. A stint in a central Florida reform school had cooled Big Dex's jets. He'd returned to Monroe County trained in off-street life skills. He was ready to represent larger brokers as a purveyor of victimless crime. To ensure his position, he also became a one-man neighborhood watch. He launched a career in basic urban fiddles: hookers, numbers, light-duty dope, and two dimly lighted after-hours joints. Equally important was delivering votes and suppressing tourist and sailor muggings. His career's ups and downs had tied into political and economic changes on the island. When his bosses were slick, Big Dex was golden. When the big boys were short, arrest and harassment became occupational hazards.

I hadn't seen Big Dex since a night at the Hukilau in the mid-1990s. The place wasn't crowded—it must've been a weeknight. Coffee Butler had seven Conch housewives at his piano bar, a birthday party whooping it up to "Who Put the Pepper in the Vaseline?" Big Dex had just been released from prison. He was hosting a triple-table of local barflies and players. His two or three years upstate had aged him. I couldn't recall the problem that had brought him down. Probably bolita, the Cuban numbers racket. Anything else would've been a stiffer sentence. At one point a local madam—retired, still young—had entered. She'd beelined for Big Dex. Gushes and hugs. Before she moved away from the table, she'd smooched all the others, too. Former clients.

I recalled Dexter Jr. from the late 1970s, when he was a teenager. Those had been the years when the island had

made its transition from a sleepy tourist outpost worried
about hippies to a smugglers' haven full of boozy spring
break college kids and summer people in motor homes.
Little Dex ran with a group of local kids, the sons of men
in power among whom skin color mattered little. They were
the last Conch boys to scoot around the harbor in open
outboards, small sponging skiffs powered by fifteen-horse
motors. It may have been the last generation to appreciate
Keys traditions and lore and customs. Some of the boys
grew into men like their fathers: car dealers, construction
bosses, bankers, restaurant owners. Some had turned to
drugs—pot and cocaine and Quaaludes. A few had slid to
importation and serious criminal activity. Fewer had become cops.

I'd heard a while back that Dexter Hayes, Jr., had begun
college in Tallahassee, and I recalled having seen a bubble
of intelligence in the kid's face. I'd read it as hope for
something bigger than his father's tainted footsteps. Then
I'd heard, after a couple of years, that he'd flunked out of
law school. I'd lost track of him, hadn't seen him, hadn't
thought of him except that night in 1995, in the Hukilau,
when his father had been kissing a whore.

I last saw Sam Wheeler on Christmas Day. The next morning he and Marnie had driven to Miami, no warnings, no
farewells. They'd flown down to Jamaica. Sam had can-
celed three charter bookings with serious anglers, January
first-week regulars since the eighties. Marnie had put her
Key West Citizen job in peril by giving short notice and
taking vacation without prior approval. But her newspaper
colleagues knew she needed slack. She and Sam had des-
perately needed a break from Marnie's brother and Heidi,
the woman Sam called "Butt's moody lollipop"—in reference to her shape.

I found Sam remodeling the broad porch that bordered
three sides of his one-and-a-half-story Conch cottage. Tools
and tape measures laid out. Dust everywhere. The nervous,
pre-holiday Sam Wheeler had returned to normal calm, his

industry the by-product of a refreshed outlook.

"You survived your time away," I said.

He didn't look up from mitering an eight-foot one-by-two. "I'm a brand-new man."

Sam was out of uniform. Unshaved, a bandanna around his head, shirtless in drawstring cotton shorts and high-top sneaks. A light-tackle guide, he usually wore khaki trousers, long-sleeved denim shirts, deck shoes, a long-billed cap. His tan, in another locale, would be a trucker's tan, though after Jamaica he was dark in places he protected while flats fishing. Enough blond remained to camouflage the gray so typical, these days, of a Vietnam vet. Sam's upper bulk had for years threatened to become paunch, but hadn't succeeded. He wore the horn-rim eyeglasses he rarely showed in public.

I said, "How's Marnie?"

"She called from the office, shell-shocked. Told me about it. She wanted to stay and work. We've been dealing with a better mood since Jamaica, until an hour ago."

I didn't know whether Marnie had told Sam about her relationship with the dead man. I did not want to be a news bearer.

I said, "The yard smells like boiled snapper."

"You'll get your chowder after you earn it." Wheeler gave his chore precise attention. He made a cut, raised the hand saw, carefully set the wood aside. He chose an identical piece from a short stack. I let him concentrate.

Sam's porch had lost its permanent screening during recent hurricanes. He'd planned to install sliders, tracks and bolt holes for interchangeable screens and storm shutters. After two years of trying to find time, he finally was into it. He'd taped a sheet of paper to a table near the front door. He'd sketched elevated storage racks for under the porch, noted the nautical hardware that would hold numbered sections in place. He'd also designed shelving for Marnie's plants, bougainvillea trellises for the porch's corners. Lower Keys' residents should have learned many lessons during the big late-nineties storms. Sam probably was one in a hundred preparing for future bad weather.

He finally quit his concentration. He began to sort the trimmed wood into two stacks.

I said, "You rent a house down there?"

"A bungalow at a big resort. Pay in advance, leave your brain at the door. You buy everything with beads. It's hammocks and umbrella drinks and fresh fruit. Windsurfing, sunset cocktail parties, private hot tubs, birdsongs. A lot of chunked pineapple. Housekeepers beg to clean up, servers wait to fill your plates. For two weeks the employees do everything but change diapers. Better-quality Christmas music, and less of it. How you been?"

"Not bad. Got mugged an hour ago. Next to your future brother-in-law's beautification project."

He sneered at my having named Butler Dunwoody as a possible relative, knew I was joking, let it slide. "Connected to the body inside?"

"Could be, but I doubt it. The murder looked planned and orchestrated. I got jumped by three droolers in a low-roller pickup. The driver was Jemison Thorsby's kid."

Sam took a vintage-looking bastard file to a barely misfitted frame joint. "Bug Thorsby. So much more than just a petty thief. The kind of shit that makes you wish Michelin made condoms instead of tires. One less chubby baby. I assume you didn't notify the police."

I nodded. Key West folks knew Jemison Thorsby's history, his expertise in reweaving the legal net, his proclivity for retaliation. "The weird thing is, they didn't want to rip me off," I said. "They wanted to mess me up, give me some street scars. Who am I to draw contempt?"

"What're you gonna do about it?"

"Invest in hearing-aid companies."

"An earthquake sound system?"

I nodded.

Sam shook his head. "The punks'll never live long enough to get bad hearing. Whatever you decide, I'm a qualified coconspirator. But don't tell Marnie."

"Jemison still fishing commercial?"

"Ever since he got out of Eglin. The captains took a vote. They wouldn't let him back in the Charterboat Association."

"What do you need help with?"

Sam wanted to test-fit his shutters and screens to their tracks. One by one, for almost an hour, we placed the heavy pieces, matched predrilled holes with carriage bolts and wing nuts. Not one section failed to fit in its coded location.

Sam beckoned me to follow him inside. He popped two beers and told me how he'd finish the porch. He'd mentally placed his funky nautical artifacts, stuff he'd found floating or washed onto beaches at Ballast Key, Woman Key, or out in the Snipes. Old wood blocks from shrimp boats, colored Styrofoam floats, antique louvered shutters. Two swings would hang on galvanized chain. He'd collected six mismatched wicker chairs, and four antique-green glass Japanese net floats in macramé slings.

"You don't know how hard it is to find a ceiling fan that turns slowly," he said. "The ones they sell these days, on the lowest setting, they'll blow your Wheaties out of the dish. Set 'em on high, your whole dish scoots off the table." He paused. "What's up? You're staring into a beer bottle."

"I know you'd rather not talk about him, but how did Butler Dunwoody get so far into that project so quickly?"

Sam finished his beer, took a bowl of fish stew from the fridge. "Butler's been sneaking around town for a couple years. He would fly in, stay at the Ramada, take cabs, order pizzas into his room or hang out in restaurants by the airport. He never called Marnie. Claims he didn't want to make waves, or compromise her position with the newspaper."

"But he's bypassed a lifetime of red tape."

"I wondered about that, too. He explained it to me last month, one night before his second drink. About a year ago he hired every lawyer in the phone book, each for a different task. He went to every bank on the island to make deposits and apply for loans and open lines of credit. Made friends with bank board members. One by one, he took four of the five city commissioners fishing. He wanted the city to kiss his ass, and every bank to have a vested interest in his success. He wanted all the attorneys to have conflicts of interest, in case someone tried to sue him. In case someone tried to issue a 'stop work,' or mess with his permits. He did a lot of groundwork through the lawyers."

"Pretty astute for an island newcomer."

"Over the years he'd heard Marnie talk about the old Conchs and their ways. Come to think of it, she said he's been subscribing to the *Citizen* and *Solares Hill* since the mid-nineties. He's done okay, acquainting himself with the system."

"Julie Kaiser told me her old man, Holloway, was on Butler's side, too."

Sam shrugged. "Why am I not surprised?"

Not many first-timers had been so foresighted. The Conchs had survived a hundred and seventy years by knowing who'd come ashore, who'd arrived in town with a bank-roll or a hustle, a load of coal or ice or illegal slaves, a get-rich-quick scheme or a willingness to be plucked. No one could possibly count the people who'd come to the island with loads of money only to be regulated into submission. Wiped out by the town powers. Locals always had understood blue-chip favors, the subtle graft of job opportunities, the delay factor in disguising paybacks, the virtues of dropped criminal proceedings. The victories all had gone to the inspection and taxing authorities, to foreclosures, red tape, and forgotten promises.

For generations a half dozen surnames had shared power. The nineteenth-century roots, the instincts of seamless manipulation, were pure in survival. Unfortunately, since the 1960s, greed had bloomed as the primary motivator. There'd been Hatfield-McCoy range wars, shifts in the power elite. A few newcomers had been allowed to share the booty. Still, few state officials or federal investigators ever penetrated the shady maze.

I said, "Butler confided his battle plan. He must have trusted you."

"We were best pals in early December. In spite of his building project, Marnie was excited about having him in town. So I played along. I mean, I didn't know much about their relationship when they were younger. I was nice to the guy, the first week or so, even when he critiqued my cooking. But I found myself insulting him earlier each evening, so he'd leave sooner."

"It work?"

"Half the time. When it did, Marnie'd look steamed, but she wouldn't say anything. Of course, the *Citizen* got on his case, once he broke ground on Caroline Street. Marnie was embarrassed to go downtown. It got worse the more he drank. I mean, how do you socialize with a guy who calls his woman Baby Girl and Sugarbush in mixed company? One time, in front of his own sister, he called her Heidi Baloney. PC crap aside, it's still a stupid-ass joke. Plus, Marnie's trying to beat her problem, trying not to drink anything at all. Finally one night after they left, after they'd refused a cab ride, Marnie got on the Internet. She bought us two air tickets south."

"Marnie do okay?"

"Wallowed in it. Maximum water time, in or on, and minimum sunburn. The whole trip, not a drop of wine, a total of two rum concoctions. I let that part be her decision, all the way through. She handled it."

"I thought you'd sworn off work on Sunday."

"That's fishing. Chores are different. I never liked weekenders, anyway. A man can't take a day off in the middle of the week, he's not living right. He probably can't afford to fish with me, either."

"That's your modest estimation?"

"If it's true it ain't braggin'. Plus, I'm taking a break on boat maintenance. Captain Turk found us a boy to take care of *Flats Broke* and *Fancy Fool*. The kid's perfect and proper, leaves notes, warns us when corrosion's taking over. Seventeen years old, saving up to buy his own bone-fishing skiff."

"Like that character Fonda played in *92 in the Shade*. The Skelton boy."

"Tell you what, they filmed that thing a year or two before you arrived. You missed one fandango of a party."

A remote telephone handset buzzed. Sam extracted it from a maze of tin snips and masking tape. By the tone of his voice I assumed Marnie was on the other end. After thirty seconds, without expression, he hung up.

"She's a basket case. She's on her way home. I just hope she doesn't stop at Fausto's. She'll want to restock the Napa-Sonoma sauce."

"I'm out of here. You fishing tomorrow?"

Sam nodded. "Thanks for your help."

I rode the island diagonal from Wheeler's to my house via Windsor Lane, the bottle-mirror wall, and Grinnell. No traffic. The path around the cemetery too confusing for three-day visitors. My route had fine architecture, better foliage than the primary streets.

I turned off Fleming, rolled down Dredgers Lane. I coasted into the backyard. I opened the porch's rear screen door as a black Ford F-150 pickup jerked to a stop in front of the house. Silver lettering on the driver's door: TNT SECURITY. The door swung wide. Tommy Tucker, the county's corrupt former sheriff, climbed out and waved to gain my attention.

My day to have the world's ass in my face.

4

I intercepted Tommy Tucker in the yard. I didn't want him on my porch. He swayed toward me, oddly bowlegged, as if holding an invisible beach ball between his knees. His bulk kept his arms from hanging straight down, but he looked more out of shape than obese. An unlighted cigar was clamped in his fat-lipped mouth. With a final step guaranteed to keep the island at sea level, he stopped and stared. Same old charming guy. He wanted me to say the first words.

I had nothing to say.

"You still in freelance, Bubba?" He held the soggy cigar in his teeth while his lips moved to talk. "I got photo work for you."

I had learned the hard way. Most people believed that the "free" part of "freelance" ruled negotiations.

"How about 'Rutledge' instead of 'Bubba,' Mr. Tucker?"

He scratched the back of his neck. "Well, I'm bein' neighborly . . ." His salt-and-pepper hair, swept back with gel, looked unwashed rather than stylish. His pudgy face barely allowed his squinty eyes to function. A wide leather belt supported baggy, olive-toned chinos, with the larger task of containing his belly. Always the cop, Tucker carried a belt-line equipment array: two pagers, a cell phone, a key

case, and a snap case for Mace or pepper spray. I sensed
that his black oxfords concealed steel toes. The red TNTS
logo above his shirt's left breast pocket defined his revised
authority. The American flag shoulder patch was a fine
touch for a man who'd missed being a felon only through
the charity of an overworked county prosecutor. The FDLE
had yet to charge Tucker with his crimes. Talk in town had
the prosecutor falling first, for having let the sheriff slide.

"I wasn't born on the island, sir. Never claimed to be a
Conch."

"I believe that."

"So we can stick to real names, and not sound like old
friends?"

A placating gesture. "Whatever you say."

Five months ago Monroe County Sheriff Tommy Tucker
had been a shoo-in for reelection. His few opponents—all
law enforcement veterans—were untested politicians. His
campaign posters, TV and radio spots, and newspaper touts
had spewed the pompous attitude of a race already won.
Graft distributors anted up brown bags of cash. Suck-ups
and toadies contributed buttons and bumper stickers. A Big
Pine clothing-store owner had printed TT YES ball caps,
effectively securing a steady stream of county purchase orders over the next four years. Tucker's appointees, sensing
job security, ordered new skiffs and pickup trucks. A vic-
tory was as certain as sunshine.

One week before election day, the sheriff's druggie son,
"Little Howie" Tucker, known statewide as a burglar and
thug, murdered his wife and dumped her body in the city
cemetery. He stripped Chloe Tucker's body of eight rings
and three bracelets, fled to Broward County, checked into
a ritzy resort, and hocked the jewelry for a two-night supply
of discotheque pills. Within a day, three "concerned citizens" had interrupted Little Howie's one-man party and delivered him to the police. An investigation by the print
media—that is, by Marnie Dunwoody—and by the
sheriff's own Internal Affairs team confirmed that, as bad
as the kid's record had tallied, it should have been worse.

Sheriff Tucker had been covering his son's ass for years, hushing up busts, "unfounding" and redirecting investigations, squashing cases, and destroying files.

The post-murder publicity had undermined Tommy Tucker's reelection chances. Chicken Neck Liska, the Key West police detective who'd been my main link at the city, launched a last-minute, low-budget effort. He clobbered the incumbent, pulled sixty-four percent of the vote. Little Howie's murder trial had lasted less than two weeks in late November. His sentencing would take place in early February. Consensus held that the punk would ride one more chemical high, courtesy of the governor.

Tommy Tucker had evolved into a rent-a-cop. I tried to picture myself employed by a man who'd disgraced himself.

"I'm kind of booked solid, the next couple months, Mr. Tucker. What type of work you got in mind?"

"Buildings, mostly. Storefronts. Few vacant lots. Arcade interiors, rental properties. Pretty much the whole list of Mercer Holloway holdings."

"This all from a security viewpoint?"

He shook his head. "Investments."

"Subcontracted?"

"It sure ain't."

"Mr. Holloway hired you to deliver a message?"

He scratched his head again. "I never got a chance to say. I always liked your work. Wish you'd have come full-time with the department."

Tucker had a nervous tic. He'd just told his second lie. For the second time, he'd scratched the back of his neck with his left hand. Each time I got to view the brown stain in his armpit.

He let his alleged praise settle, finally shut his mouth.

An hour ago I'd sworn off crime-scene work with the city. Not that they'd called much lately. I knew that I needed to replace lost income. "This photo work, Tucker, do I deal with Mr. Holloway directly, or through you?"

"I been asked to invite you by his office, tomorrow at

three." He handed me a business card engraved with Mercer's elaborate monogram. A single fine-print phone number in the lower right corner.

"Message received. I'll call Mr. Holloway's secretary in the morning, if I can make it."

Tucker thought about it a few seconds. "Suit yourself. You might call in the next ten minutes. Mr. Holloway loves the hell out of quick answers."

"His secretary works Sunday?"

I had asked, by implication, if ex-Sheriff Tucker ran Mercer Holloway's errands on Sunday.

He gummed the cigar. "Mr. Holloway pays well."

"I'm happy to hear that."

He shifted his weight, hitched his belt. He pulled the cigar from his mouth. "Wasn't too many months ago, I signed checks to you. Allowed my detectives to hire your cameras. Now I'm a lowlife?"

He'd been a lowlife for years. I said, "I don't recall voicing a judgment."

"What I told everybody is this," he said. "Wait till your boy goes ass-up bad. Then try to make sensible decisions."

"I'm sure the confusion can wear you down."

His brain took it as a compliment. He said, "Nice to see you again."

I waited. The hand moved upward. The armpit. The scratching.

Tucker waddled back to his shiny truck, hauled himself in. He held his door ajar so he could twist around, stick his head out, put his weight on the poor armrest, watch himself back down the lane to Fleming. I went onto my porch, dropped my cycle helmet on the porcelain-top table, and carried my camera to its hidden cabinet. I needed a pee, a beer, and a nap, in that order.

My brass doorbell rang lightly. I closed up the equipment stash.

No vehicle had replaced Tucker's. It could be only one person. She liked to flick the bell with her fingernail.

"Come in, light of my life."

She'd already opened the screen door. She strolled into the living room wearing what she called her "Sunday sweatpants." Her T-shirt proclaimed, LIFE IS A CABERNET. "My mama's scanner said there was a body on Caroline Street. Did you have to . . ."

She read my eyes.

Carmen Sosa and I have been friends for almost nine years. It has been an evolving relationship; tennis fans know the meaning of "deuce." Carmen's parents, Cecilia and Hector Ayusa, have lived on Dredgers Lane for almost forty years. Carmen grew up in Key West—true Conch, bilingual, bicultural—and twice has been married. Her life's focus is her young daughter, Maria Rolley. Six years ago, not long after Carmen had bought her own place two doors down the lane, she and I had attempted romance. We'd learned that other aspects of friendship outweighed our sexual attraction. We look to each other for common sense and sympathy, mischief and rejuvenation. We swap the personal harassment only close friends enjoy.

She found a glass in the kitchen, opened the fridge to pour water from the filtered pitcher. "You want to talk about something else?" She waggled a beer at me.

I took the bottle, twisted the cap, spun it into the trash. "I worry about what's happening to you, woman. You lose any more weight, Just My Size'll go out of business."

She couldn't hide her pleasure in my having noticed. "I've been walking after work every day. Maria comes to my mama's after school. This other girl from the post office, she and I drive out to Smathers and walk from the parasailing to houseboat row and back. First half against the wind, second half with the wind at our backs."

"This shaping-up have anything to do with lunchtime traffic in the lane?"

"Traffic?"

"I sense denial in your response." I went into the bathroom, half-closed the door. "You've been seen midday lately, with a male friend."

"You're accusing me of nooners?"

"And he looks about twenty-five. Muscular arms, the all-weather look. You're too young for a midlife crisis, my sweetness. You making up for all those times you turned me down?"

"I'm a good girl. I saved it for my first husband. He called me the Extra Virgin. I know, I've told you that before."

I took my beer back to the living room.

Carmen fiddled with the leaves of a fat peace lily. "You'd be proud of me. I met this tourist from central Florida. The guy couldn't have been nicer. He made two mistakes, or I'd have dated him more than once. After our first date he kissed me and said, 'It's been a ton of fun,' which is the wrong thing to say to a weight-sensitive woman. When he walked away I looked at his ass. I noticed the circular-shaped lump in his back pocket."

"Condoms are the sign of a considerate man. Maybe a bit presumptuous, but you should've been relieved."

"It was a Skoal can. End of story."

"So who is this alleged nooner?"

"His name's Nick. He used to work at the post office. Now he works construction. And don't ask. He showers before we—"

"Where does he work?"

"For Marnie's brother. At that atrocious mini-mall he's building. I keep telling him he's contributing to the downfall—"

The phone rang. I raised one finger, told Carmen to hold that thought, and picked it up. "Grand Central Station."

"Liska here. Your cameras nearby?" I could tell he was using a county-issue cell phone.

"Just so happens—"

"Car'll pick you up in . . . seven minutes. Gotta go."

He went. I didn't even hear a click. So much for the nap.

I'd wanted to ask specifics. I comforted myself with the odds against two murders in one day. Not that it hadn't

happened before. Monroe County had seen more than its
share in recent years.

Seven minutes was like two minutes. Barely time to pull
my camera back out of its compartment. Carmen had wandered outside. She called from the yard, "There's a deputy
on Fleming. Probably trying to find Dredgers Lane."

I jumped from the porch, then realized I'd forgotten to
check with the emergency room. The county green-and-
white made a production of backing down the lane. Posi-
tioning is everything. A minute squandered to effect a
dramatic getaway. I took ten seconds to tell Carmen about
my altercation with the boys on Caroline. I asked her to
use my phone, to search for a thug with fewer teeth than
toes, and to leave me a note. She promised to lock the place
when she left.

The deputy swung a land-yacht left onto Fleming, scared
the Coronas out of two moped *touristas*. He ran the blind
corner at White. Probably thought his blue and red strobes
would shield us from being T-boned. I scrunched low in
my seat, snugged the belt another half inch. The climate
control was cranked down to wind-chill level, the fan set
high. Deputy Fennerty's cloying cologne recirculated at
maximum velocity.

Fennerty looked like his own idea of Hollywood's idea
of a cop. He lifted his Ray-Bans to check his computer. I
glanced again. A precision hair-by-hair crew cut. His face
said handsome, the eyes said dullard. He wasn't going to
be chatty.

"How far up the Keys?" I said.

He pointed at the windshield. "Stock Island."

"Oceanside Marina?"

"Squid Row."

Right *there* on the windshield.

We hustled out North Roosevelt. The flashing roof bar
scared dozens of speeders. The deputy favored the fast lane,
managed to clip most of the lane-dividing road turtles with
his left tires. Staccato bips, each adding another degree of

migraine to the pain bubble growing at the back of my neck.

A call came over the police band. The deputy understood the gargling. He keyed his mike. "Passing . . . Morrison's GM dealership. Just passed it."

The voice, clearer now: "Animal Control's almost outa here. Light a fire."

Fennerty mashed the gas. Just as quickly he hit his brakes. Traffic at the Cow Key Channel Bridge was backed up in both turn lanes. Whooping his siren, the deputy swung to the far-right lane, forced his way back left into the line of vehicles going up U.S. 1. He stuffed it over the bridge, bullied his way through the College Road light. He did it again at the next signal, almost swerved into the Chevron Quick Lube, veered onto McDonald, braked, hung a right on Fifth Street, and floored it. Like two-thirds of America's recently licensed drivers, Deputy Fennerty had learned by watching Sunday NASCAR races. Play it fast and tight, walk away from high-speed crashes. If I had eaten a larger lunch, it'd be decorating the dashboard. Liska had better hope the weekly papers didn't investigate his upkeep budget.

Fifth Street was a maze of potholes, ruts, dips, solid litter, and slipshod asphalt patches. Concrete-block sheds bore peeling paint and burglar bars. Mobile homes with mildewed, off-kilter doors and windows squatted behind weed-blown Cyclone fences. Gray laundry hung from drooping cords. The deputy manhandled the shift lever, squealed two more cabin-cruiser turns. He finally found Bernstein Park, the million-dollar sports facility that no one used. He goosed the pedal again, missed his turn-off. He spun a one-eighty in the Rusty Anchor parking lot, threw gravel on four men lurking around a pole-mounted pay phone. He whipped south toward a long line of bulldozed twenty-foot mounds of rubble. After all these years in Key West, my first visit to Shrimp Road.

We skidded, halted in gravel. A crescent of idling vehicles bore audience to a particular pile of trash. Sheriff

Liska's civilian car, his maroon Lexus sedan, was parked
to one side. I swung the cruiser's door and bolted. I felt
like a sailor back on the wharf after a long, brutal storm,
thankful for solid land. The breeze tossed the mangrove
branches west of the road. Stifling air reigned low. It would
help me defrost.

Liska walked toward me. He twirled keys on his index
finger. No cigarette in his hand. His annual New Year's
resolution to cut back gradually usually held until mid-
February. He wore blue jeans with white sneakers and a
white belt. His white satin shirt looked like a piece Elvis
might have thrown from the stage late in his career.
Through the years I'd known him, Chicken Neck had af-
fected an extensive seventies wardrobe. He'd toned it down
since being elected sheriff, had gravitated to a *Northern
Exposure* look. The Lower Keys hosted many eccentrici-
ties. Goofy attire was a minor aberration.

I gave him a "what's-up" look.

"Some shrimper lost his head—"

"Sounds right," I said.

"Not as funny as it sounds. That roscoe over there, the
arm bandages? Says his legal name is Nameless Aimless.
He's our poster boy for twenty-first-century rickets. Aimless found himself sleeping next to a body without a head
when he woke up an hour ago. A wild dog woke him,
chewing on his wrist. Three dogs, total. They'd worked on
the corpse, too. I guess the one dog thought Nameless was
tastier, rum-flavored and all. We had to call SPCA to remove the animals."

A lovely Sunday had become a twofer. "Nameless a suspect?"

"Claims the last thing he recalls, he took drunk at sunrise
on the fantail of *Midnight Creeper*, a steel-hulled trawler
out of Beaufort, South Carolina. Captain Smith Jones, or
else Jones Smith—we can't understand his Geechee accent—verified the drunkenness. The captain figured Aimless'd hurt himself and sue the boat owner. He kicked him
off around ten A.M. But even piss-drunk shrimpers don't

intentionally bunk down with headless dead men."

"So a murderer dropped a body next to a passed-out drunk?"

"Probably. Not much blood on the sofa, no weapon to be found, no head. Even broad daylight, around here, no risk of witnesses. Our victim was stabbed—or speared, the standard deal around the fleet. My guess, he died before decapitation." Liska waved at the huge mounds of trash. "The head could be anywhere in a hundred-yard radius; it'd take us a week to find it. It could be in Miami. It could be in the ocean."

I wanted Liska to keep jabbering, to postpone my photo gig. As he spoke I gazed at a mound that paralleled the pavement a quarter mile to the south. Someone had built a rubbish barrier to block access to the docks. Beneath tall clusters of yellow chalice-vine flowers lay rotted pallets and cable reels, flattened outboard motors, twisted Dumpsters. I saw two collapsed school buses, an upside-down tractor trailer. A rusted Toyota tailgate with TO and TA painted out, YO outlined by chipped reflector tape. Fuchsia bougainvillea grew from the shell of a Winnebago. Evidence of misery and poverty, of quick departures by workboat or sudden arrest. Evidence, too, of vicious storms that had struck the Keys in the late nineties. Mud, marl, tangled fishnets. Lengths of yellow rope dangled from crumbled Styrofoam floats.

A weird, dull silence hung between the mangroves and the mounds. Only rustling shrub tops and the distant rumble of engines at the shrimp docks. The pervasive odors of dog shit, brine, and diesel intruded. In the middle of it all, the rotten velour sofa. On the sofa, the body of a naked, headless man.

"Somebody with a twisted mind," I said.

"The sick shits beheaded the poor fuck. You expect decency after that?"

About the best anyone could expect, judging by the surroundings, was not to be hit by a sniper's rifle, or attacked by more wild dogs.

"Go over there and work fast." Liska motioned to the

sofa. "This spooky-ass place, I feel like I'm walking on unmarked graves. Shrimp Road's the only place in the Keys where I get creeps standing in open sunlight, seventy-five degrees, a Sunday afternoon in January."

I walked toward the sofa. A half dozen deputies and investigators stood by, including Sheriff's Detective Bobbi Lewis. Their expressions, their subdued talk warned me that I faced a gruesome task.

Afternoon light was fading. Mangrove shadows grew long. I paid close attention to my gear. I rigged for fill-flash on manual setting, synched to use ambient light, but less flash on close-up shots. How unlike a dead person, I thought at the time. More object than human, the body with no face excused speculation on the victim's personality, or life. Or postponed speculation. Later I would blame that concept on my shock at viewing such a grotesque spectacle. The mental defense mechanism allowed me to remove myself from the ugliness, the horror, the dogs.

After a roll of "establishing" shots, panoramic, perspective angles to the east, south, west, and north, I loaded another thirty-six exposures and looked around. Beyond the imposing trash barrier, another world, the white superstructures, masts, cranes, the green nets of shrimp boats. Behind me, silent law officers and onlookers who'd strolled over from the shrimp docks, or from the beer bars up the street. Beyond them, thirty feet into a dense hammock, an ocean refugee, a "knight of the road," in a bough-enshrouded single-man tramp camp. A thatch-roofed lean-to, with a rusty bike and a tiny chest of drawers, salvage from the mounds. The sun-browned, dirt-blacked man must exist on charity, on handouts from former trawler-fleet brethren. A sense of foreboding penetrated to my bones. The opposite of trouble looking for a place to happen, this strip of blacktop and mangroves felt primed for intrigue, tuned to violence. I wondered if some spirit had long ago cursed the peninsula, so the land wished now to avenge itself by hosting evil in any form.

I moved to work a few close-ups. The victim's malnourished torso was not tanned except for the arms. Thighs and calves too thin ever to have exercised. A purple, oval-shaped birthmark, or half-birthmark, ran from the top of his right shoulder to the shredded neck skin now curled by drying blood and canine saliva. I went tight to document the half-inch opening in his chest. I shot the stab wound, its proximity to the heart. I got the abdominal scar that told of surgical inexpertise, the jagged lightning tattoo on the inside of his left arm, the odd, deflated scrotum—a testicle removed, perhaps at birth.

All details of a man who'd been alive yesterday.

Finally I finished. Four rolls, thirty-six each, the final roll redundant. I packed my camera bag, looked a final time at those waiting to do their own awful tasks. The sheriff had vanished while I worked. He wasn't the only one spooked by Shrimp Road.

Fennerty motioned me back to his green-and-white.

We drove north, slower than before. A funky station wagon turned into the marina. Four open windows, four shrimpers' arms hung out. The road had been empty. It now looked like downtown. Drunks staggered along the shoulders in white work boots. A new-looking Taurus approached, greaseball at the wheel. I turned to watch it pass and continue south. Two gaunt dudes coasted by on two-wheelers, high handlebars, matching black watch caps. One Fu Manchu, one goatee. We left behind a sea-level landfill, junked cars, cast-off property, debris destroyed by storms, consigned to the hot sun and corrosive sea air, bulldozed aside to let nature do its work.

Nature would be wise to give up on the place. Civilization had done so.

I said, "Plenty of bicycle riders out here."

Fennerty finally made sense: "Not a valid driver's license in the fleet." He pondered the rearview, then added, "Parts of Stock Island, all by themselves, they're enough to make good officers not want to be cops." He lowered his voice, inhaled for self-important emphasis. "Present company included."

A large, industrial forklift rolled by, its empty forks two feet off the pavement. Its driver a fisherman or marina employee with a work shirt the color of sour-green mud. A white oval above the right pocket, a name embroidered on it. The man waved. For an instant he looked familiar, but his waving hand blocked my clear view of his face. He'd been the first person on Stock Island to show friendliness.

I thought again about the Taurus that had passed. I knew better than to trust my memory or concentration at that point in the day. But I could've sworn there was no license tag on the sedan.

5

The house smelled like Antonia's and La Trattoria combined.

My tired eyes registered a refreshing, knee-length, pale-peach sundress, white sneakers, and a backward Air Mango ball cap. For two dozen weeks I'd been in a trance. She could light my fire just brushing her teeth.

Teresa had condiments and bowls and dishes on every flat surface in my kitchen. She stopped her constant motion and looked straight at me. "I don't know why that detective acted so cuckoo. He was in his own world all afternoon. I didn't get free for another hour and a half. I would've cooked at the condo, but you've got these spices . . ."

She was rambling. I said, "I just had to . . ."

She put down the spatula. Caught her breath. "I know. Carmen told me Liska called. I talked to the county switchboard . . ."

"Ugly. Like Stephen King is scripting my life."

"They're all ugly," she said. "But two in one day?"

"Yep. How long has Dexter Hayes worked for the city? I haven't seen him in fifteen years."

She went back to the stove. "He started the week before Liska went to the county."

I inspected more closely. Italian sausage in a skillet, a pot of ratatouille, boiling water, ready for fettuccine. On the counter, olive oil in a tin, a three-foot Cuban bread loaf, a saucer of crumbled goat cheese. Sauvignon Blanc in a pitcher of ice water.

"I thought I told you about this a couple months ago," she said. "He was an undercover lieutenant up in Broward or Palm Beach County. He moved back down here. He and his wife bought a place in New Town. He's got two kids at the Montessori school. His wife, Natalie, stays home. That's about all I know. He gets along okay at the city. He sure was an asshole today." She paused again, then said, "I wish we'd gone kayaking."

Wiped out as I was, I still had the sense not to respond. I put my camera satchel on a chair, picked it up again, put it on the floor, then sat in the chair. "Tell me about Hayes."

She put on her business face—facts only, no emotions—while she tended to her cooking project. "My view, he was right about a few things and wrong about others. He said the body had been dressed elsewhere, then placed at But-ler's construction site. He said there were clues to be found, but someone careful enough to outfit the victim like that wouldn't be leaving fingerprints. He said photographs wouldn't help much. He said old-fashioned detective work, like Sherlock Holmes, would break this case."

"What was he wrong about?"

"His attitude."

"Maybe it's a nervous thing. Maybe he laughs when he's frustrated."

"We were leaving, on the Caroline sidewalk, a young girl, all hysterical, claimed to be the dead man's fiancée. Barely college age, probably less. Very Goth. What is it now, retro punk? She looked dead as the man on the floor."

"How did Hayes take that?"

"It got better. She recognized Hayes, asked if he hadn't been at her house two days ago, questioning Engram, the victim. Something about ripping off a Whitehead Street crack dealer."

"Hayes acknowledge?"

"She said, 'You told Richie, if I balled you, you'd forget

about shit bein' stolen.' So Hayes said, 'For whose benefit is that, ma'am? The people standing here know I don't work that way.' He blew off the accusation."

"Did he ask her how she knew the victim's name?"

Teresa stopped what she was doing, stared at the wall, then shook her head. "No. And one other thing. Someone back inside, one of the coroner's people, mentioned this murder was a lot like that one a couple of years ago, over on William or Elizabeth. A guy tied up, a dildo on the carpet. Hayes acted funny after the guy said it."

"That one ever get solved?"

She shook her head. "Drove Liska nuts before he handed down his files."

"Anyone from the *Citizen* show up, to cover for Marnie?"

"That twerp that looks like Jimmy Olsen with a ring in his eyebrow. He had a pocket digital camera. He actually tried to photograph the body. Hayes almost slapped his head off."

"They teach those newshounds to be aggressive." I took a beer from the refrigerator, then said, "Marnie knew the victim on Caroline. She said she'd dated him a few years ago. I got the impression he'd worked with her brother for quite a while."

"She and Sam, what, less than a year?"

"Almost exactly a year."

"It's rough to lose friends," said Teresa. She gave my arm a squeeze, just as Marnie had done when she'd said she'd known Engram "real well."

A vehicle rolled slowly into the lane. After twenty years I knew my night sounds. This was small, a four-cylinder engine. It stopped not far away, but not precisely in front of my cottage. I leaned back in my chair, caught an angle through the porch screen. Single headlights, close together. I mentally pictured the black cockroach, Bug Thorsby's low-slung pickup. It had been a Chevy S-10, powered by, as far as I knew, a four-cylinder engine. I'd been targeted,

for no known reason. I still could be a target. If so, Bug
had switched off his reverberating stereo.

I whispered, *"Teresa."*

She turned her head to face me.

"Switch off the stove. Take your purse to the bedroom.
You hear any shit, call nine-one-one. Say 'Home invasion.
Help me,' and hang up. Then call Carmen, 'Memory num-
ber two.' You got your pistol?"

Teresa moved quickly. She paused at the bedroom door,
then nodded.

"To defend yourself, *only*. Got it?"

She stared. No answer. She closed the bedroom door.

I went to the screen door. No headlights. No sounds.
Nothing in the lane. No noise from Fleming Street. Not
even the rhythmic tick of a cooling engine. I stepped back
when I heard soft crunches approach. The closest thing I
could use as a weapon was a four-foot length of driftwood.
Probably split if I swung it too hard. I could hear my
damned heart. I could feel the pulse in my forehead. I
looked down. When had I untied my sneaker laces? So
battle-ready. How many pairs of footsteps?

Did it matter, with them in darkness, me on the porch?

Then, as if out of fog, Marnie Dunwoody appeared in
the faint glow of light from behind me. I felt adrenaline
drain from my system. I drooped with relief. I hadn't even
considered that it might be Marnie's Jeep. Her normal pace
in the lane was full-tilt and full-halt. Her time, driver's seat
to my screen door, averaged twelve seconds. She'd be
knocking on the screen before her car door slammed shut.
She was out of character.

Marnie peered through the screen, She jerked back, startled. We were eye-to-eye. She looked catatonic. Her eyes
had no depth. "Sam went to bed." Her voice was hoarse.
"He worked on his porch all day. I can't sleep." The strain
in her voice threw me. I wondered if Sam had had to endure
a long rant. Maybe she'd gone to the end of White Street
Pier and yelled at Hawk Channel for a while. Marnie didn't
have the presence of mind to reach for the doorknob. I

began to open the door, but it wouldn't swing until she stepped back. Limp with relief, I finally got her onto the porch, directed into the living room.

The drama had proved that my promised revenge against Bug and his boys needed to include a defense plan. For some stupid reason, I'd felt content that Teresa and Carmen both owned pistols, probably kept them in their purses. But my best weapon, if I could get to it, was a kitchen knife. The last time I'd kept a gun in the house, a loaner from Sam Wheeler, someone else had shot it to save my life. The man who had fired the gun now was an FBI agent. A pistol was part of his daily attire.

The scare was proof, too, of the power of focus. With Marnie inside the house, my world decompressed; the noises of the neighborhood—crickets, distant traffic—resumed. An air conditioner or two, though the night had a chill to it. I even smelled Bounce as I came in from the porch. Someone in the lane doing laundry.

Teresa exited the bedroom without questioning that I'd been upset. She carried her purse, casually dropped it on a table near the door. She greeted Marnie, expressed sympathy, and calmly insisted that she join us for supper. She gave me a strange, puzzled look, almost a pissed-off look. Then she went to the kitchen and resumed dinner preparations. The light in my brain finally glowed. She'd asked Carmen why she'd been ordered into another room, told to have her gun and the phone ready. Carmen had walked outside, identified the vehicle in front of the house, and explained my problem with the thugs. I'd forgotten to mention the thugs to Teresa. Stupid error.

Now the purse pistol was close at hand. The next vehicle in the lane might not be "friendly."

Smart woman.

Marnie fell into the chair I'd been in. "I'm up shit's creek for leaving the murder scene. The slick from the *Herald* showed up. Someone from their staff called to warn me. They're going to use my name in the piece."

I said, "Because he's your brother?"

"Because a body was found at a controversial construction site."

"That's your fault?"

"They will wonder in print if I've soft-pedaled in the past two months. They'll wonder if I've omitted facts about the permit process that might have given warning about strife, an advance warning that someone could be murdered."

"That's stretching," I said. "No one believes the murder happened at the site."

With a lost look on her face, Marnie yawned. "Words are powerful. So are attitudes. That prick lieutenant kept looking at me. Like, none of it—the costumed body, the construction site—would be there if I hadn't brought my brother to town. As if I had control of my brother."

"Any way to fight back? You getting heat at the paper?" I said.

"They've been great. They haven't diverted assignments. But I want to smooth my boss with a story about the Stock Island thing. The media were not invited to that one. I need your help."

"I've got it memorized," I said.

"Can it wait till afterward?" Teresa offered two dinner trays: food, silverware, paper napkins.

In deference to Marnie's battle with alcohol during the past year, Teresa had put away the Sauvignon Blanc. She offered decaffeinated iced tea and Perrier water. We thought as we ate that Marnie might fall asleep in her chair. Before we'd finished, I too wanted to call it a night.

But Teresa's wonderful food energized Marnie. "I can't do it," she said softly. "I can't bear this cross again. I did it through high school and part of college. I got to this town first. My name's on my byline every day. I've got a reputation for straight reporting. Now Butler's fucking it up, damn his ass."

I offered, "You don't know that for sure."

"People don't want to talk anymore. Information used to come easy. I'm not getting good stories. That's not it.

I'm getting good stories, but I can't develop them. My work feels hollow."

Teresa said, "Why did your brother come here in the first place?"

"He came to visit three or four years ago." Marnie fiddled with the place mat. Rolled its corner, released it. Rolled it again. "His eyes lit up. He saw nothing but opportunity. He saw all these people doing business dressed in Bermuda shorts and T-shirts. He made the mistake every newcomer makes. He figured they were rubes. Didn't give them credit for brains. Right away he started plotting his massive takeover."

"Motivated by . . . ?"

"My brother sees himself as a great tycoon taking double steps up the marble stair to immortality." Marnie kept placing her hand on top of her head, perhaps to hold it in place. "He once said he wanted to be so rich, he could have other people go to wine tastings for him."

"He's always had that nickname?" I said.

"Calling him Butt was against family rules. But in college he joined a fraternity. Their nickname for him was Butt-Woody. One of his old friends still calls him B.W. Just to show you how my brother thinks, he hated the Butt part of the nickname, but loved the Woody part, so he allowed it to stick. He thought it was good for his image. Might help him seduce women. Back then we joked about him. We always said he was a walking billboard, advertising himself. He was full of slogans. He used to boast that he lived on the four Ts: Tequila, Tic-Tacs, Trojans, and Tylenol. He was big on clever lines, like 'bed, bath and behind.' He found new girlfriends before he broke up with the old ones. He called it 'rotating the stock.' One high school girlfriend called him a male chauvinist piglet. She's the one who *tried* to get pregnant."

"So he set his eyes on Key West?"

"He came the long way around. He flunked out of college, went into the Peace Corps, spent a year in Central America, came back and worked construction in Virginia

while he finished college. Then he moved to Jacksonville
and became a contractor. He'd bid on jobs like single town
houses or strip malls, then hire shitkickers out of bars near
the construction sites. Not much of a quality human-
resource program. But he banked money. He reinvested.
He hired good lawyers and accountants, plus laborers who
couldn't get work anywhere else. Now he's investing his
profits in Key West. In my face."

I said, "So, he . . ."

"He made his big arrival. This was before Thanksgiving.
He flies down, buys a Sunday *Citizen*, whips out the real-
estate section. He picks 'The Home of the Week.' You
should see it. It's a Conch-style job next to a man-made
pond at the Golf Club. Three hundred forty-seven grand,
and he made a down payment of all but a hundred and fifty
thou."

"I saw that on the real-estate cable channel," said Teresa.
"The glad handshake with the agent. The pat on the back
from the banker. The paper listed his girlfriend as co-
owner."

"Then, that yacht he's got out at Oceanside. He traded
it for two vacant lots in Annapolis, and he paid three idiots
to bring it down here. They ran it aground twice. He renamed it *Heidi Ho*, like nobody'll get the joke. And he
slapped a bumper sticker on the stern that says, 'Don't
Laugh, It's Paid For.' "

"Thank God you don't share his sense of humor," said
Teresa.

"Then he goes for public opinion," said Marnie. "He
always tries to make a name for himself. The stingy creep
hates Christmas. But he rolled around town in that car with
the hat on."

Teresa and I had seen him, the week before Christmas,
in his bright red Ford convertible, with the long crimson
Santa Claus stocking cap, its puffy cotton-ball tassel whip-
ping in the wind. Teresa had called him the "Fat Cat in the
Hat."

"Naturally, his Navidad was big on borracho and low

on feliz. That's when Sam and I decided to get out of here. We knew he wanted to make a big deal out of New Year's Eve. In the old days he'd throw a premature drunk, two days early, and suffer all day the thirtieth with a sympathy-sucking, knuckle-dragging hangover. Then he'd go into a planning panic so New Year's could be 'perfect.' Our version of perfect was Jamaica."

"You know the odds against get-rich plans on this island," I said.

"I know my little brother. He'll never be as drunk as he appears, or as tired, or as hung over. Sometime during the first few weeks he knows you, he'll let slip his net worth. It'll be a slurred aside to an unrelated story. Sooner or later he will embarrass Heidi by assuring everyone present that she is better in bed than all of his other lovers combined."

"So there's no way," said Teresa, "that you could have insisted he stay away from your town? Or convinced him he could lose it all?"

Marnie shook her head, then shrugged. "I have this weird feeling he's going to come out okay."

Teresa nodded. "This is Key Weird."

I said, "How did you wind up so bogged down by decent manners?"

"And poor? And boring? Luck of the draw. He got my father's genes, I got Mother's. Maybe I'll come out okay, too. If I don't crumble like an old crust of Cuban bread."

"Your brother ever met Dex Hayes before?"

Marnie shook her head. "That man was very strange. Mucho pissy."

"He got that way with the coroner's people, too," said Teresa. "Larry Riley got steamed."

Marnie chuckled. "Detective Hayes may not know it, but he picked the wrong man to piss off. Larry Riley's parents live next door to Chief Salesberry."

"Small town," I said.

"Small island," said Teresa. "The main problem being small people."

"Like Bug Thorsby," I said.

"Oh, shit," said Marnie. "I forgot. Sam said you got mugged."

Teresa said coldly, "Yes. Carmen mentioned something . . ." Her chin receded, her lower lip stuck out. A gray cloud came into her eyes.

I said, "Two against one. I fought dirty, it's over, I'm okay."

I hadn't placated Teresa.

Marnie said, "Sam asked me to tell you, he made a call or two. Jemison Thorsby's working a boat out of Summerland Key. Keeps it docked at that fish house, Big Crab."

"Hell, I forgot to check with the hospital."

"No. What do you need? Can I get it for you?"

"Thanks. I'll just call in the morning."

Teresa stared at me.

"Look," I said, "It's over. Compared to everything else today, it was a minor event."

Marnie saved me: "Speaking of events . . ."

I turned to her. "On Stock Island, one man, unidentified, found on a discarded couch in a trash heap. Naked, scrawny, decapitated. They couldn't find the head. Dead fewer than four hours. Sheriff's officials aren't revealing identity if, in fact, they know it. The crime may have occurred elsewhere. There were no witnesses. What else you want?"

"No dildos or feathers?"

"No."

"No rope or duct tape?"

"No."

"How do you expect us to sell newspapers?"

We froze for a moment, then Teresa laughed first. I laughed, too, but only to acknowledge Marnie's return to form. I had reduced a man's death to forty words or less. Marnie would embellish it with the lingo and adjectives of her craft.

My short summary had brought back the odd chill that Shrimp Road had inspired earlier.

Marnie addressed us both. "I've thought about this all

evening. I can't tell you two what to do, but I'm not telling law enforcement that I knew Richie Engram. It's not a necessary detail. It could complicate things, my working for the news media. The *Citizen* doesn't appreciate reporters who slip into the realm of 'possible suspect.' "

Teresa and I both said okay.

Marnie hugged us both. I'd have offered to drive her home, but she was sober, rejuvenated, more lifelike than she'd been on arriving.

We waited until the sound of the Jeep faded up Fleming. Teresa said, "Can we name this soap *The Mother of Sibling Collisions*?"

"Thank you for sharing dinner. Thank you for cooking in the first place. Thank you for including Marnie."

Later, in bed, Teresa said, "Does she drop in like that when I'm not here?"

"She's a friend. Do you think I'd tell her not to?"

Teresa didn't answer for almost a minute. Then she said, "I wish I had more friends like yours."

6

Teresa had flipped on the air purifier before we went to sleep.

I've never believed that the filter would help me dodge throat-clogging mites and airborne disease. Never counted on its adding a dozen drooling days to the back end of my life. But its hum shielded me from Key West's ambient racket. It masked two A.M. motorcycles on Fleming. I rarely heard the trash trucks or school buses, or electric saws at the crack of dawn.

I hadn't felt Teresa slide out of bed, hadn't heard her leave the house. I woke to an audible pressure drop, a weird silence. No hum indoors, no noise outside. No electric saws. Frequent power failures were part of the island's charm.

I sat up, checked the battery-powered clock. I needed to make a call.

Key West residents discovered the truth about electrically dependent phones during storms in the late 1990s. Cell phones covered them until their batteries died. Then they were out of luck. I'd kept my vintage, basic-black rotary-style when I'd installed two cordless units years ago. I'd adapted a snap plug to its cord. I hoped Duffy Lee Hall had found the same foresight.

He answered on the second ring. "Good morning, Alex

Rutledge. You call this early for only one reason. How many rolls?"

"Caller I.D. in a power failure?"

"I lose power, Alex, I'm out of business. I've got a four-outlet Back-UPS in the darkroom. My Yamaha generator kicks in automatically. A special switch separates me from city power, so I don't pump juice to the outside wires."

An arsonist had burned Duffy Lee's commercial work space six months earlier. An attempt to destroy evidence photos. The negatives had survived. Duffy Lee had been compensated for his loss. He'd used the money to build a darkroom in his home. I depended so much on Hall's talents, if he ever went out of business, I'd consider doing the same.

I said, "Can we do four rolls by noon?"

"I read the paper. I figured you might've gotten called. Bring 'em on." He faked a cough to announce a tongue-in-cheek remark: "I'll add my usual rush charge, fifty percent."

"It'll bump your county taxes in the long run."

"Maybe they'll rebuild the electrical grid."

I hung up and the phone rang.

Chicken Neck Liska, from a cellular: "What time?"

"I told him noon. Why is the high sheriff calling, instead of a detective?"

"Tell him eleven-thirty. I'll see you at eleven-forty. El Siboney, corner of Margaret and—"

"I know."

"La Lechonera used to—"

"I know," I said.

". . . with all the pig statues out front."

"I didn't know you ate there."

"Monday, Wednesday, and Friday."

I made the kind of mistake I'd make only before coffee. I began to make coffee. I'd already poured the first scoop of Bustelo when I looked at the coffee maker's plug in the socket. I put away the coffee, went to get dressed. I looked at the living room ceiling fans and wondered why they weren't turning. Two minutes later I made my third pre-coffee error. I was almost out of the yard on the motorcycle when I thought about the mess on the streets, everyone driving to work. I could make it to Hall's with no traffic signals, but I wasn't sure where I'd need to go after that. I parked the Kawasaki, stuck my helmet on the porch, and unlocked the bicycle.

Duffy Lee lived in the 1400 block of Olivia. His wife had kept the beautiful two-story house after her first marriage ended in the eighties. A large house on a deep lot. Old trees and foliage, dark green Adirondack chairs on the front-and-side veranda. Plenty of room in a spare back bedroom to build a light-tight enclosure. I rode up from White past fences full of purple and red bougainvillea, a purple passion-flower vine, bright yellow palm fronds. Four or five precious parking spaces were occupied by boats on trailers. Something new in the 1300 block: an old bike wedged in a tree, a prosthetic leg affixed to its left pedal. Found-object art or a political statement?

Hall met me at the front door. He offered a full mug. "Black?"

"I always praised your genius," I said.

"Just a mind reader."

"You'd best stay out of there. You dig into my mind today, you'll muck your brain for weeks." I gulped the coffee. It hit my system on the fly.

"I assume this is one of the homicides in the *Citizen*."

"You're in there. At your own risk."

"Both homicides?"

"The one on Stock Island. Don't inspect the prints too closely."

"You said noon. I'll bet you want it earlier."

"You're in there again."

Hall looked at me quizzically. He sensed my stress. "You want me to top off that coffee, Alex? You're welcome to the porch. Listen to the neighbor's parrots. Chill before you face the world."

I shrugged. I had time to kill. I could use some time to think.

"Betsy's at work. I've got yours and three other jobs to process. You've got the place to yourself. Zone out, watch the grass grow."

I accepted, for the Cuban coffee and solitude. I followed Duffy Lee into the kitchen. He disappeared into his darkroom. Outside, I chose a slat chair facing the street.

The lush, shaded yard offered a pure dose of the tropics. Duffy Lee was right. The neighbors' birds gave it an exotic touch. The first Conch Train of the day rambled past, its driver explaining that the sapodilla tree, like the one in Hall's yard, was the source of chicle used to make chewing gum. He drove on, ignoring the rare bottle-gourd tree, the calabash across the street.

I'd never thought that Olivia Street would host rush hour. Its nearness to Garrison Bight dictated the traffic character: charter captains in panel trucks with boat logos painted on their sides, or on mopeds or bicycles; in khaki pants and shirts, long-billed caps, wraparound shades. A funky old sedan passed, its trunk lid removed, the trunk and backseat fashioned into a pickup-truck bed. Then a small refrigerated truck delivering bait. A big hotel van with five or six of what Sam Wheeler called the "natty anglers." More bikes, with high handlebars, ridden by marina laborers in cut-off Levi's and work boots, red sweat-soaker bandannas around their foreheads. A couple of taxis with whining transmissions. The parade lasted ten minutes. I'd lucked into peak viewing time. Then Olivia Street returned to a cool breeze, buzzing air units, birdsongs, muffled noise from neighboring streets.

I couldn't find mental calm. I started to add up facts. The caustic Heidi Norquist encounter. The three-on-one street attack. The construction-site murder, with Dexter Hayes, Jr., giving me the bum's rush. A headless corpse in a surreal setting.

What did it all amount to?

The friction with Dexter Hayes had only confirmed my

fears of the past four months—that my gig with the city had dried up. Okay, things change. The Dunwoody family strife was not my problem. Best to stay out of range wars. I could offer Marnie only sympathy. The body at Butler Dunwoody's construction site was unusual. And the murdered man on Stock Island was standard for the territory—as much as any murder could be "standard."

But there was no linking the separate events. All of it added to zilch.

For two-thirds of my life I've made a point of dodging conflict, traffic jams, idiots, bureaucrats. I don't believe in runs of bad luck, or karma shifts. I don't insist that bad news comes in threes. I've never been superstitious. I sometimes knock on Formica to mock the "knock-on-wood" concept. I have no patience with the idea that bad yesterdays should spoil good tomorrows.

But, damn.

In the past two years I had seen two spates of misfortune. Tragedies and felonies had formed patterns, shaped conspiracies. Worse, they had harmed friends. This run of crap was different. I had no valid suspicions, no far-out logic to connect the dots.

Someone had ordered my mugging. It had been too deliberate, the black pickup stopping next to me, the short one with the jewelry and the barbed-wire tattoo going after my camera. I'd be a fool to think that I'd been chosen at random. Heidi Norquist had been talking on the phone. Had she called Dunwoody, told him I was snooping? Was that reason enough to order an attack?

Marnie had given her brother mixed reviews. A hardworking, money-saving entrepreneur. A morally shallow womanizer. A survivor. A high roller who paid bottom-rung wages to his employees. His life and his business had no connection to me. What bearing could my photographs, or anyone else's photographs, have on the success or failure of his new mini-mall?

No answer to that. But one fact stood out. The unknown

reason for the attack may still exist. Ignoring danger only invites more danger.

My only other concern was Dexter Hayes's attitude. He'd made a point of contacting me, through Marnie and through the city switchboard. He'd asked me to take photos. Then he'd greeted me coldly, fired me halfway through the job. Almost as if he wanted only to watch me work, wanted to observe me. Almost as if I were a murder suspect.

I returned the coffee mug to Hall's kitchen. I went back out, twisted the front door lock, pulled it shut behind me.

7

A dust haze filtered the winter sun, but I could see a signal at White and Truman. Power restored, at least to that corner. I pedaled to a laundry on White, donated thirty-five cents to a maverick phone company. A man—not Mercer Holloway—answered and put me on hold. A flash from the past. The "on-hold" music was a thirty-year-old recording of the Junkanoos, Key West's old Bahamian-style rhythm band. Mercer's secretary came back on. Mr. Holloway would welcome a meeting during the next hour. I told the man I could adjust my busy schedule.

Six minutes later I coasted to Southard's 700 block. I chained the bike to a lamppost in front of Holloway's two-story home. A faded red van backed into a curb space ten feet away. It displayed a Vietnam service ribbon bumper sticker—the yellow band with green and red vertical stripes. The van's vanity license plate read, KHE SANH. Some vanity, I thought. But it offered a moment's consolation. I'd read Michael Herr's *Dispatches* and would never forget its images. If I ever thought I had it rough, in Florida, witnessing the rare death and common betrayals, I could take comfort in never having been to war.

Holloway owned a symmetric, five-bay Classic Revival, one of the few houses in old Key West with its own driveway. It radiated wealth, tradition, nineteenth-century elegance, and mind-boggling upkeep. I had heard Conch Train drivers describe it. Built by a rich shipwreck salvager in the late 1850s of termite-resistant Dade County pine, it had passed, by marriage and death, through five generations bearing three family names. The house and yard had been remodeled in 1972 and again in 1994. The yard showcased twenty palm tree varieties.

Legend held that, in 1998, Mercer Holloway had turned down a huge offer from a Paris cosmetics tycoon. The *Citizen* had quoted Holloway's refusal: "The second-floor toilet is a splendid place to meditate. What do I do with another six mill?"

A flagstone walkway led to four broad wood steps and the north-facing, full-width gallery. A half dozen square columns rose from the painted decking to the steep roof overhang. Dark green hinged shutters flanked peaked window surrounds. A beveled-glass transom crowned the twin glass-paned mahogany front doors.

I rang, heard footfalls on a wood floor, then quiet. A moment later the door swung open. I recognized Donovan Cosgrove, Holloway's son-in-law. Cosgrove had been the Pier House night auditor and desk clerk in the late seventies. He'd proved expert at deciding who was sober enough to drive, who needed a taxi home from the Chart Room. He'd accommodated late-night skinny-dippers by turning off the pool lights and delivering towels. In those days people openly joked that Cosgrove's lifestyle was courtesy of the Pier House. They suggested that the bottom line had leaned a little his way, that his ledger work may have financed the deck behind his home, a vacation or two in Grand Cayman. But he'd never been questioned or caught or fired. He'd moved on to better jobs in the eighties and nineties. Employment with his father-in-law would have been out of choice instead of necessity. The old jokes had been handy rumors to explain the comfort of a successful man who wasn't a pot smuggler.

Donovan greeted me. He was about five-ten, with thinning, sandy-brown hair, horn-rimmed glasses, a plaid short-

sleeved button-down, and a salesman's smile. He'd gained
weight since I last saw him. Given his years on the island,
he had to be about fifty. He looked it. He asked how I'd
been doing.

I shrugged. Asked the same and added, "How's Suzanne?"

"Same old fire-spitting Southern belle. How it's worked
out is a mystery to me."

Suzanne had been in a bad mood for thirty years. People
in Key West had hoped that her years in college, off the
island, might change her. It didn't happen. I don't know
how she'd managed to attract a husband. Donovan Cosgrove was a patient man.

Donovan exited through double doors to my left. The
foyer was a simple, almost square room, with subdued decor. Three tall, thin tables along yellow tongue-and-groove
walls; brass sconces, white woodwork, custom cornice
molding. A well-used Oriental rug atop polished hardwood.
On the west wall a vintage Detroit Lithographic color print,
a hundred-year-old photograph of Greene Street and the
U.S. Government Coaling Station, shot from the peak of
old city hall. A note stuck to its frame: *Julie to bank.* The
note written on yellowed stationery from the old El Mirador
Motel.

The first floor of the house had been redesigned, turned
into offices. The door to the right, held open by the rusted
fluke of an ancient anchor, led to what had been a sitting
room. Now, if I guessed correctly, it was Donovan Cosgrove's office: tall, dark cherry file cabinets, a long, low
table with stacks of papers, each crowned by an antique
glass paperweight, a cherry desk, a medium-height blond
leather chair, a single straightback chair for visitors, a vase
with fresh-cut flowers.

I snagged a glimpse down the center hallway: a sunroom
with glass-top tables, miniature palms in ceramic planters,
white wicker furniture with poufy cushions, their striking
tropical print upholstery just shy of gaudy.

Donovan invited me into Mercer Holloway's office, then

excused himself. Holloway, in dark slacks and a pink, long-sleeved dress shirt, stood at a front window. Reflected light caught in his silver hair as he peered through the oak blinds. "Day after day, that dirty red van. Big wart in front of my house. Dead center, the middle of my view." His gravely voice hinted at a Southern accent. He drew out his words: "Ugly business in the papers this morning, these murders. But they missed the biggest facts. Am I the only person in this town who's realized that similar whatever they're called—methods of operation—were used to kill other people in the past several years?"

"I hear that a coroner's investigator saw a similarity on Caroline Street. The victim in drag, dildos around him. The other, I don't know."

"It wasn't that many years ago," he said. "A beheading, the body and head found hundreds of miles apart. Except last time they found the head first. This time it's the body. Anyway, my point is, this town's become a bad mixture of Woodstock and a modern hobo jungle. Alternate lifestyles galore. Right out my front window, in particular."

"The island changed thirty years ago, Mr. Holloway. When the Navy left."

His head turned. His stern expression promised a reprimand. But Mercer knew what I knew. If he had to choose between not accepting back talk from an employee and admitting I was right, he was stuck. I had yet to accept his job offer. And I was right.

"Some of us," he said sharply, "hoped Key West might grow out of its stupid and awkward adolescence."

"Some people have paid dearly to stop the clock."

He jabbed his finger at the window. "One man's succeeded. The Vietnam stickers all over that hippie truck, that man's living in the past."

"I've never had a quarrel with you, sir, but people in this town think the same of Mercer Holloway."

"Rather than argue the point, sir," said Holloway, "I'll point out what I've accomplished."

"Did you spend the first four months of 1968 getting

your ass blown to bits on some remote Asian hilltop?"

"Okay. You know the guy who owns that red truck, is that it?"

"Nope. Nice place you've got here. Who owns it, the Red Chinese?"

I waited out his silence. My half of the argument was ended.

It worked. He'd blown off his steam. He shrugged off the debate, stepped closer to offer a handshake. "You're right. Let's talk about photography."

Mercer Holloway, long ago, had established himself in the Keys. He saw himself as a figurehead, much as he hoped his fellow citizens regarded him. He always looked the part of his self-image, a cross between a Fortune 500 chief executive officer and a prime-time television evangelist. I'd never seen him wear shorts or a shirt without a collar. Until that moment, in his own office, I'd never seen him alone.

Locals considered Holloway eccentric. I once heard a city commissioner call him a philanderer, then correct himself and call him a plain old pussy hound. He was known as a favor broker with a caustic wit. He was capable of hair-trigger and arbitrary decisions. He was famous for spooky wee-hour ramblings. He considered everyone competition: an opponent in a political race, another contract bidder, or—no secret to his family—someone in a race to make the next pretty tourist woman. Folks wondered why his divorce hadn't happened three decades earlier. Yet, off the island, he owned the reputation of an invincible bureaucrat: moral, fair, more honest and square-shooting than most politicians.

Holloway offered me one of two identical leather chairs. He waited until I sat, then took his own seat behind the large mahogany table that was his desk. It held a compact speakerphone, two short stacks of papers, and forty square feet of empty space. "First off," he said, "I'd like this chat, for business reasons, to be confidential. Can we start together on that page?"

"We can."

"I need pictures of a select assortment of properties. I assume you're up to speed on architectural work."

"I've done it. I own a lens specifically designed for it."

"Good. The technical stuff, that's all up to you. You're the craftsman. I'll want curb views, significant architectural detail, all outside entrances and, in some buildings, interior main foyers. Once you're familiar with the scope of the job, we'll want aerial shots, too." He stood and began to pace the office. A century ago it had been the formal room where its owners had greeted, entertained visitors. Six antique glass-enclosed barristers' bookcases along the walls held law tomes and pottery. One held a collection of Keys-related novels and reference books. I noted the pre-war WPA guide to the island with its wonderful black-and-white photographs. On a short, wide table behind the desk sat a laptop computer—open, not running. Next to it an antique Seth Thomas clock, and a foot-wide glass bowl full of jelly beans.

"It's been twenty years since we pulled together an overall appraisal," said Holloway. "I'm not getting any younger. I need to make changes, revise a number of trusts. And I need your quality of photography. We'll provide a list, you devise your own work schedule, a day and time for each property on our list. You with me so far?"

I nodded.

"We'll arrange for the city to move aside ugly power lines, for however long you need. You want security, you got off-duty cops taking orders from you. You need a crane, we rent a crane. You want to work from the top of a van, we lease a van, build you a roof platform. Matter of fact, we'll lease one for the project, you outfit it, drive it, take it home at night. It'll be your van, however long you want. You need to stop traffic on a street in town, a couple hours? Done. You got camera trouble, a little glitch? We replace your camera, brand new, yours to keep. You understand how we do business?"

He lifted a china cup from its saucer and sipped his

coffee. He winced, stood, walked to a window behind his desk, lifted the bottom section, and spit his mouthful of coffee onto an exquisite bougainvillea. "Cold," he said. "Tasted like motor oil. Bitter oil, at that." He shut the window, used his hand to wipe a few splatter drops from the sill. "Any questions?"

"Tommy Tucker."

"My vice president in charge of making things happen?"

I stood to leave. I'd adapted to quirks and inconsistencies, job to job. But the scope of Holloway's offer, his attitudes and choice of associates, had just asked more of me than snapping pictures.

Holloway read my disgust. He backpedaled quickly, returned to his seat, used calming hand gestures to urge me back into the chair. Benefit of the doubt, I sat.

"Okay, I understand," he said. "I'm not blind to public opinion. Tommy Tucker's a liability." He swiveled his chair toward a window. "Understand, Mr. Rutledge, that I'm showing loyalty to a childhood friend." He focused his eyes on a distant point, looking into the past. "His nickname when we were kids was Bacon Fat. We and two or three other kids were too young for the Swamp Gang, as the cool boys were known. We were inseparable friends. Back in the salt marsh, or on the jetties. Or on North Beach, before North Beach was lost to development. Then we went our separate ways. I chased votes, he chased criminals. But he helped me often, when he had the power to grant favors." Mercer turned again to face me. "The man's unemployable in the Lower Keys. He may have broken rules, but he wasn't a thief. He's not a wealthy man. I loaned him a few bucks to start his own little business, the security thing. Look at it as one-third paybacks, two-thirds charity. If he never pays me back . . ." He tried to read my face, to see if his argument had flown well. "You okay with that?"

An acceptable Key West explanation. "So far," I said.

"I've been a lucky man, Mr. Rutledge. You will learn in the next few weeks that I've accumulated what I call 'opportunities.' Property appraisers look upon them as 'tax targets,' and that's a large reason for what we're doing. I intend to challenge a few arbitrary valuations. That much I owe my heirs, although I go by Warren Buffett's concept of letting children fend for themselves. They're capable. I don't want to deprive them of the joys of making their own fortunes. I just don't want to be screwed big by small officials."

He wanted a reaction. I had no opinion.

He pulled a packet of papers from the stack closest to him. "I've assigned priorities. There'll be three groups. Group One is typed out here for you. Again, not to offend, I'll stress the need to keep this confidential." He held out a pen. "If you could just read and sign this form we've prepared . . ."

I didn't reach for the pen. "You have my word."

Suzanne Cosgrove—Holloway's daughter, Donovan's wife—barged into the office from an adjoining room. Too thin to be healthy, a black pantsuit, a pixie cut to her dark brown hair. She glanced at me, snapped her head as if she'd viewed fresh roadkill, and snatched a file folder from the desk.

"You've known my girls for years, haven't you?" said Holloway. "Alex Rutledge, dear."

She wouldn't face me. "I know who he is."

"How are you today?" I said.

"Not so fucking good," spat Suzanne.

"You'll be pleased to know," said Holloway, "that Suzanne's sister Julie recommended your skill with the camera."

Suzanne was already out the door she'd entered.

Holloway said, "Much as we are not permitted to pick our families, we're not allowed to choose their moods."

I had an opinion, but no need to share it.

"Anyone asks, while you're working, your response will be, 'Insurance documentation,' and that is it. Those two words, only. We okay with that?"

I nodded an "okay."

"Let me add one more thing. This relates to our discussion of changes in Key West. We have plans that will benefit this island in the future. It won't be gentrification, and it won't ignore history. My personal view is that it'll be so good, even the tree-huggers and zero-growth nuts and letters-to-the-editor windbags will bow down and thank us. Your photography will add to our effort. I beg you to take me at my word. Ease your mind about my view of things."

My mind was not eased. One way or another, Holloway had given me plenty of reasons to bag the job, to express gratitude at his having asked, to turn down his offer. Dealing with bad clients, while infrequent, was part of freelance photography: ad-agency account execs, publishers' art directors, record company reps, even models' agents. With Key West being home turf, my misgivings focused on personal aspects. Still, the money would come in handy. I was on the fence.

My mind kept going back to when I'd called from White Street, when Donovan Cosgrove had put me on hold. Anyone who still owned an old Junkanoos album couldn't be all bad. And someone who perpetuated the music by installing it in his phone system . . .

I said, "We'll do this one of two ways, Mr. Holloway. You set up an account at Conch Photo so I can stock up as I go. Or I'll buy the supplies I need and add a fifteen percent surcharge for extending credit."

"As luck has it, I own Conch Photo. Do what's easiest for you. Why don't you check that list tonight? We'll start scheduling first thing in the morning."

Holloway made no move to show me to the door. I saw no one in the hall and foyer, no sign of Donovan in his office. The red van was gone from the parking space out front. I unlocked the bike, rolled off the sidewalk, glanced up Holloway's driveway. A silver Infiniti sedan with tinted windows. The one that had driven down Caroline Street twenty-two hours earlier, when I'd been chatting with Julie Kaiser. Just before Bug Thorsby's social call.

*   *   *

I found Duffy Lee Hall stroked out in the chair I'd occupied on his porch. Eyes closed, legs stretched, a contented expression. I had just come from an orderly, expensive palm tree exhibit. The Halls' neighborhood foliage existed because it had sprouted there and no one had hacked it down. I'd have loved to spend the afternoon back on the porch, even with the hourly Conch Train. I had eight minutes to meet Liska.

Hall heard me park my bicycle.

"You're set to go," he said. "I was in the darkroom, I kept thinking of you out here. I came out to take a break. I just watched the garbage men for the first time in years."

"A cultural experience."

"Maybe not. When did the trash trucks lose their sense of humor?"

I hesitated a moment, then understood. For years the garbage trucks in Key West bore the signs WE CATER WEDDINGS and FREE SNOW REMOVAL.

"You're right. No extra services."

"The town has changed," said Hall. He handed me two bags—one held the negatives, which I always kept in my files—and an invoice. "Thanks for warning me not to look at the photos."

"Awful?"

"Not so bad. No blank face looking back at you." He looked away. "It's always dead eyes that see too far into my soul."

8

Pure Key West: parked near El Siboney Restaurant, a red Volvo with a red-and-black Harley-Davidson decal on its rear window. Was a Harley the other vehicle, or the owner's alma mater? Pedaling up Catherine, a gray-haired man with wood crutches hung on hooks at the bike's front sprocket and at its handlebars. A huge parrot was perched atop one crutch's armpit cushion. The bike rider sang in perfect falsetto, "Those oldies but goodies reminds me of you . . ."

Sheriff Fred Liska had angled his maroon Lexus into a slot out front. The air smelled of fried plantains and garlic used to season yuca. I chained my bike to a *USA Today* vending box. Inside the front door, more concentrated scents: steam from cooking olive oil, roasted chicken. Also a space problem. I waited for three people to pay their checks. A Cuban woman finally noticed me as a fresh face.

I said, "El Jefe?"

She smirked, and hiked her thumb toward the dining room on my left.

Liska sat alone at a four-top with a café con leche, a Presidente beer, and iced tea in a thick tumbler so big a child couldn't lift it. The *Key West Citizen*, read and re-folded, was set aside. Also two packs of Marlboro Lights, held back-to-back by clear packaging tape. He wore a blue flannel shirt over a red T-shirt. Chicken Neck suddenly was issuing a left-handed punk statement, expensive clothes worn sloppily. I'd noticed it five weeks earlier. I hadn't thought he'd change when he took over as sheriff. After all, he was an island icon, accepted as eccentric, acknowledged as one of the best investigators in police department history. He'd long ago been forgiven his vast collection of seventies disco-era clothing. Evidence proved that his new job had inspired a jump in fashion.

I placed the packet of proof sheets and five-by-sevens on the table. A waitress, without speaking, dropped a set of silverware in a tiny white paper envelope, then vanished. I took the seat opposite Liska. He tapped his index finger on the packet, looked me in the eye.

I said, "What?"

"I've been down this channel before. Put the negatives in there, too."

"I no longer own my own work?"

"I hate lawyers," he said.

"They exist." I helped myself to a chunk of buttered Cuban bread.

"I know, I know. The negs are your property unless you've signed a prior, written, work-for-hire contract. I just want to hold 'em."

"They'll show up in the newspaper," I said. "I'll never see a cent . . ."

"When did they ever?"

"Never," I said. "But why risk our lovely relationship with the potential for disagreement?"

"A case out West, the prosecutor had photos and no negs. The defense alleged that the prints had been digitally manipulated, which sounds dirty but fun. The judge pitched the case out of court. So, you suffer a fire at your cottage, I squander how many murder investigations?"

"Trust me, Sheriff. I've got fireproof storage. Goddamn, it's weird to call you 'Sheriff.' "

"Your praise takes odd forms. Look, some idiot spills coffee in my file cabinet, ruins these prints the day you drive your Japanese motorcycle into a tree. What do I do, petition your estate for my evidence negatives? How come you're driving a Kawasaki, anyway? That rice burner doesn't match your all-American Shelby Mustang image."

"Some writer gave it to me to pay off a debt. I'd have never collected the cash, so I took it. Where in Detroit did they make your Lexus?"

He tapped his finger on the bag again.

I'd have been within my rights to keep the negs. But I'd never made—or lost—a penny by doing so. "They're my property, right?"

He nodded. "They'll be bagged and tagged. With a sign-out slip."

I extracted Duffy Lee's second bag from my shirt pocket. "I just kept them to screw with you, anyway."

Liska didn't laugh.

I knew the waitress drill at El Siboney. Middle-aged women, all sisters or cousins or friends since childhood. One walks to your table while carrying on a mile-a-minute Cuban conversation with all the others. For an instant there is a lull in the talk. She will look you in the eye. You must give her your whole order. Take too long, the chatter in Spanish resumes. You wait until the next lull to order. If a tourist has questions about the food, the waitress develops an urgent need to be elsewhere. She motions, Wait a sec, be back in a minute. A long, long minute. So you learn by watching, or learn the hard way. Once you know, you order quickly. You say your main dish and side dish in Spanish, order your drink in English. She will say, "Thank you, honey," and beeline for the swinging door to the kitchen.

Liska ordered arroz con pollo. I ordered ropa vieja. Old clothes.

I said, "Where do you eat on Tuesdays and Thursdays?"

"My desk. A lady in the office goes to Publix, brings back tossed salads, Caesars, the usual rabbit food. Man's gotta watch his wasteland—I mean waistline—this day and age."

"Why me, yesterday?" I said.

"We found a headless body and thought of you."

"Your praise . . . Well, now we're even." I stupidly up-ped the ante: "Did you ever reconcile with your ex-wife?"

The moment I said it, I wished I hadn't.

Liska kept rolling. "In a minute or two I'm going to ask a favor. So for now I'll forget you said that. We got the Marathon doofus to drive down. The ants on the body spooked old Lester. Kept looking behind himself, like the head might appear. He ducked into the mangroves to barf, right into some bum's campsite. Lester was too afraid to barf. That's when I called you, got a busy signal. A minute later you had the good fortune to answer. We put Lester Forsythe in his car and sent him back up the road."

Liska paused while the waitress put my iced tea on the table, then said, "You made an appearance at Caroline Street."

"Abbreviated."

"I heard that, too. What, exactly, went down?"

"This the favor?"

He nodded. "That's why I said 'exactly.' "

I told the chronology, the list of those in attendance, a description of the body, Hayes's flakiness.

"It's identical to one I had a year ago," he said. "Damn near identical."

Holloway hadn't been the only person in town to notice the similarity. It made sense that Chicken Neck'd see it.

I said, "That wasn't one that I photographed."

"Right. The FDLE swooped in. Their boys did the scene-scoping. Right down to fingerprints off the toilet-flush handle. Then they handed it back to me. Or most of it. I never closed the case. The little I've heard, I'm told it's been passed along to young Dexter."

The waitress placed Liska's meal before him: chicken and yellow rice, chunks of chorizo sausage, green olives, pork, a side dish of plantains. She replaced the empty red plastic basket with another—a stack of buttered Cuban bread. My plate came second.

I said, "Why here, three days a week?"

"Look around."

Cuban housewives, aging hippies, a few business owners. In a corner, his face half-hidden in the *Herald* sports
section, Captain Turk, who kept the *Flats Broke,* a light-
tackle charter skiff, next to Sam Wheeler's *Fancy Fool* at
the Bight.

"Don't ask me why, 'cause I don't know," said Liska.
"Cops don't eat here. Men or women, nobody city, nobody
county. Even on their days off. It's a secret sanctuary, with
eats. A midday mental oasis."

"Pressure so soon? You've been in office how many
weeks?"

"My first pledge, when I took the office, was to check
out county units named with an acronym. In my experience,
acronyms are money sponges. Politicians love to fund acronyms. They never react when you tell them all that cash
went to FAST or CATCH or STOMP or FUNK. They say,
'What's FAST?' and you say Fugitive Apprehension Strike
Team. End of question. Ka-ching with the money, lots of
zeros. Now I'm boss. I know. Automatic funding means
automatic loafing. It so happens, the Fugitive Apprehension
Strike Team is a good operation, underfunded. But FUNK?
The Friendly Urban Neighborhood Kops? Tell me why they
gave away a thousand dollars' worth of Jamaican-flag-
colored balloons. Make friends with black kids? I mean,
where's 'urban' in the Keys? And, no shit, they had a Special Homicide Investigative Team. Figure out that one."

Liska's story reminded me of Sam Wheeler's story about
a Psy-Ops office in Saigon. Someone had had the idea of
handing out red-white-and-blue rubber balls to Vietnamese
kids, an effort to build loyalty to the invading forces. The
kids didn't want them. Psychological Operations Headquarters was awash in cardboard boxes full of rubber balls.
The desk jockeys invented a game. They painted numbers
on wastebaskets, put them around their desks. They took
turns throwing the balls into the slow-moving ceiling fans,
having them ricochet into the cans. Different cans were
worth different points. They worked on timing, and veloc-

ity, and angles. They wagered huge amounts of money. They did it for months on end, then returned to the States wearing combat theater service ribbons.

I looked at five empty plates on the table. Chicken Neck Liska had the metabolism of a high-torque blender.

I said: "You don't eat at your desk twice a week."

"You're right. I get to Bobalu's fairly often."

"Do I dare ask about the cigarette packs taped together?"

"My New Year's resolution. I start each day with a fixed number, which, this week, means fifty-one. This is my daily ration, this kit. I reduce the count in the packs by one cigarette per week. By July it'll be one pack, a year from now I'll be clean. Next year I can resolve to stop chewing on my steering wheel."

"Something else is bothering you."

"You bet," said Liska. "First we got Caroline Street, like my case from a year ago."

"Okay."

"Yesterday afternoon," he said, "a headless body. Ring a bell?"

"Now that you mention it."

"Two years ago we found that head behind Searstown. The body turned up in Dade. Ice-cold case, closed-casket funeral. Damn fucking strange, two in one day like two I never solved."

"I don't believe in coincidence."

"We'll know for sure if a body wrapped in plastic shows up at Bahia Honda."

I shuddered. Nine months earlier the body of a friend of mine, an ex-lover, was dumped in a beachside hammock up the Keys. Fortunately, that case had been solved. Liska knew my connection to the dead woman. I couldn't believe he'd zap me with the memory.

"Now we're even for the wife remark," he said.

I gave him that point. "Ever bust Bug Thorsby?"

"Barracuda shit in the ocean?"

"Do me a favor? Or yourself, depending on how it works out. Run his prints back through AFIS? But don't include his vital data. Put them through as unknowns."

"You used to be undetectable on the radar screen. You lived a damn calm life until when, about a year ago? You've been in the barrel since then. Now you're a blip the size of a fucking Humvee. You're asking law enforcement favors when you should be minimizing your echo."

"None of it's been my doing or my choice."

He stared at me. "Anything else you need to tell me?"

"Yep. You've got a stolen-car ring moving vehicles out of Stock Island."

"Shipping 'em out of there?"

"Or warehousing, repainting. I don't know. Whatever they do."

"Where are they hiding 'em, down in the abandoned coal mines?"

"You asked."

He tapped a knuckle on the newspaper. "I've got skin and bones to worry about. Dead humans. Plastic and metal come later."

Liska shocked me. He picked up both tabs.

9

I pedaled into a fifteen-knot north wind, stair-stepped side streets, wove my way through traffic. Working off a late breakfast—shredded beef, yellow rice, black beans, two pints of tea. I'd gained five by eating one pound of food. Disorienting scenery, sharp glare, a tint to the foliage. I tasted grit in the air, smelled exhaust fumes floating down from Fort Myers. I'd hoped that the wind might have ignored the embargo, blown the haze to Cuba.

I thought, The dirty yellow fog may be self-induced.

I'd delivered prints and film to Liska. After I invoiced Monroe County, with an extra whack for working Sunday, the Stock Island decapitate-and-drop job was over for me. Gone, behind me.

Every day in January two events coincided. The glut of today's visitors arrived by vehicle from Miami. And the first wave of yesterday's tourists—after shaking hangovers and recoiling at the price of gas—started back up the Overseas Highway. The two flocks crossed paths at Truman and White just after lunch hour. One beer truck turning left could jam traffic back to Bahia Honda. I stayed away. I rode Francis past the cemetery to avoid the noontime traffic jam.

I found Heidi Norquist in front of the house, sleeping in a silver Jaguar XKR convertible. The cloth top was up, the

windows down. Her pink headphones hung from the rearview mirror. A pink pastel knit shirt. Today's gold chain a
fraction wider than yesterday's. A glistening drool at the
side of her mouth informed me that she wasn't feigning
slumber.

I wasn't going to wake her. She looked peaceful. I didn't
have the energy to deal with the flip side of her charm.

I wanted to shower, then walk to Sunbeam Market to
buy the *Key West Citizen* and *Miami Herald*. The *Citizen*'s
page-two Crime Report usually was worth the price of the
paper. I wanted to see the front page this time, to see how
they'd handled the murder on Caroline.

A subdued voice on the message machine: "Hi, this is
Heidi Norquist. I'm falling asleep in my car, in case you
didn't recognize me, so this is probably the best way to
reach you. First, I'd like to apologize for yesterday, but I
can do that to your face, when we talk. Second, would you
please wake me up? Pound on the fender, or something.
Even if you don't want to talk to me, I've got a two o'clock
hair appointment that I don't want to miss."

She had a solid one-hour nap ahead of her.

Mornings tend to cool temperatures in winter months.
Cold air in the outdoor shower, while invigorating, inspires
quickness. It had been weeks since I'd enjoyed midday
comfort in the rain locker. It made me wish I'd replaced
the exterior stereo speakers that long ago had rotted. I could
stand Miles Davis under the mango tree, or something more
lively—Buena Vista Social Club, or Mac Rebennack's
New Orleans–style whorehouse piano. The early-afternoon
sunlight gave elegant tones to limbs and fronds, shadow
angles and reflections I seldom saw. The constant breeze
kept it in motion. As minutes passed, the haze faded. Just
as I suspected: a personal problem.

This was my second shower since taking pictures on
Stock Island—I'd done a major hose-down after dining
with Teresa and Marnie, but hadn't felt as though I'd fully
washed the filth. This time did the trick. I was thankful to
have the mess twenty hours behind me. I've always said

that I couldn't have been a schoolteacher, a restaurateur, or
a police officer. The stress on good days would eat me. No
telling how I'd cope with the bad, but this was a fine sample. Years ago I had gravitated to my laid-back tropical
lifestyle, my no-boss, no-bureaucrats job with mental survival in mind . . .

I kicked open the stall door so damp air could escape,
toweled off, dried my hair, stepped into my flip-flops. I
swung open the rear-porch door. Heidi sat there, facing
away, perched so close to a chair edge I feared her petite
ass would go floorward in an instant. No padding to cushion the drop. She tickled her upper lip with a bottle of Jolt
Cola. I wrapped the towel before she swiveled and nodded
hello.

Blue jeans, barefoot, the belly-pack. Red-tinted skin
from yesterday's jog. Her first words were to ask to use the
bathroom. She trailed a cloud of high-ticket scent as she
walked through the living room. She faked having to get
her bearings to find the john door, scoped out my furnish-
ings, the wall decorations, the books. She left the bathroom
door open. I realized she'd gone in there to brush her teeth.

I went to the bedroom and pulled on shorts. I envisioned
Butt Dunwoody and Teresa Barga simultaneously arriving,
ringing the bell. Odd fear gripped me; I considered a plau-
sible explanation for Heidi's presence. Why do I dread social strife more than an attack by teenaged hoods?

Heidi began talking before she was through spitting out
toothpaste, half-shouting so her voice would carry: "I
couldn't sleep last night. I kept thinking . . ." She exited the
bathroom, wiping her mouth with the back of her hand,
then tucking her toothbrush into her belly-pack. ". . . the
way you looked at me when you came down there to photograph Mr. Engram's body . . ."

"The way I looked at you?"

"He doesn't recall his reaction," she said to the wall.
Then, to me, "Yes."

We faced each other in my living room, ten feet apart,
a slowly rotating ceiling fan between us. "Enlighten me."

"When you were taking pictures, when I skated by and asked you to stop. Didn't you think I was unpleasant?"

Get her out of here. "Yes, you were unpleasant."

"Oh, good, he's normal. Did you wonder why?"

"Assholes are everywhere."

"You don't know . . . Oh, fuck it. I can't control your opinion. Never mind." She began to pace the floor. "After Butler found Mr. Engram, the detective, the bossy black man, made everyone wait until the photographer arrived. You showed up. I didn't know you worked for the police. You stared at me as if you knew, or you thought you . . . because I told you to go away from the construction . . . Do you think I knew Mr. Engram was in there dead?"

"Crossed my mind."

She stopped pacing, threw her arms up. "He thinks I knew."

I said, "Something else crossed my mind."

She stared at a framed Tom Szuter drawing on the west wall. "What?"

"That maybe you wondered why I was hanging around. That maybe you asked someone to hurry me away."

She inhaled deeply. "I may look like a stereotype, Mr. Rutledge. Butler Dunwoody, my partner, doesn't help my image. He likes people to think that I exist only for his pleasure. No other reason. But here's the deal. I'm not just a receptacle for his unit. I know murderers don't hang around victims taking snapshots. Even the weird ones in movies take only one picture, then get the hell out. Come to think of it, Butler's more my possession than I am his."

"The word 'partner' has two meanings."

"Think of both."

I gestured to offer her a chair, then sat in my oversized bamboo rocker. "Where you from, originally?"

"Wisconsin. Farm country, dairies. Boring with a capital *B*. That stands for Beer." She began to sit but chose to keep pacing.

"On Sunday you were listening to a Bonnie Raitt CD

that was released about the time you were born. How did you—"

"I had six older brothers and sisters. Same mom, four different fathers. Lots of influences around the house. I liked Bonnie's sense of independence."

I said, "Fun time, growing up?"

"I stayed busy. I dated older guys in high school. They all owned cars."

"Reasonable criterion."

"Even an ugly car is a warmer place for sex than a frozen hayfield."

"Sounds like paradise," I said.

"We did the best we could. I was basically trailer trash."

"And you broke free."

"Yes. I did it myself. I got straight-A grades, a partial scholarship to the University of Michigan, an off-campus job, a marketing management degree. I left school owing twenty-two thousand in student loans. But everyone told me I'd succeed in the business world. They told me I had savvy and 'money hair,' the color of hair you see in the wealthy parts of big cities."

My motorcycle helmet lay on a chair near the door. She patted it and said, "One of my old boyfriends had a Harley. He'd take me riding. Man, I loved that, but it broke down every time we rode. What kind is yours?"

"Somebody paid off a debt, gave me an old Kawasaki 400."

She sneered. "Not all that classy."

"It wasn't my choice. If someone builds a strip mall in Wisconsin, does anybody complain?"

"People don't have to drive so far for haircuts and beer and chip dip."

"You miss it?" I said.

"Did you read the paper yesterday? The wind chill Friday was thirty-eight below. A truck stopped on a bridge and froze in place. They found people in their cars, stiff and blue."

"Key West covers less than six square miles."

She pushed her hair behind one ear. It fell loose immediately. "How long have you been here?"

"Since 1975."

"What month?" she said. "That's the year my best friend was born."

Slap me in the head with your youthfulness. "My point is, on an island this small, every change is big."

The hair thing again. "Didn't I say I wasn't fucking stupid?"

The charm.

She said, "The whole island suffered an electrical failure this morning. Isn't it quiet when the pool pumps quit?"

"Did you meet Butler in college?"

"I met him three years ago. His partner hired me to run their office. A week later the partner sold his half of the company to Butler. They'd just developed an eighteen-home subdivision south of Jacksonville. I figured my job was out the door, too. Turned out, I became Butler's top salesperson. I learned the game. I kicked ass. I was the best closer in St. John's County."

"So you're expert at getting to the point?"

"I'm there. In the end, on my commissions and a couple investments, and after the development company got tangled up in two lawsuits, I made more money than Butler Dunwoody. That's why I'm so interested in success in Key West."

"It was your downstroke?"

"And it's poorly leveraged. It's a situation of win okay, lose big. Do you think I killed that man?"

"I have no idea. I don't know a single fact about it, except the man's name and what we saw down there. I've got no reason to talk about any of it, and tomorrow's another day."

"So you're happy to shut down your brain and have no opinions at all?"

"As far as the pictures I take, I try not to dwell on them. The police have their jobs to do. I did mine. I have my opinion about construction of instant shopping arcades in

Old Town. But my opinion will not stop your project."

"Right you are."

"A lot of people have gone bust on this island. You should pay attention to everything. Don't rent to anyone selling socks or long-sleeved shirts or ice scrapers. If you make a fortune, you should think about tearing down your building in ten years. Be the Queen of Altruism. Plant mangroves, or some other protected species."

"Donate the building to the Audubon Society?"

"Sure. A deduction. Make enough money to retire early, allow somebody else to return the land to its original state. What a concept."

Matter-of-fact: "Yes, it is. I've enjoyed your company, Alex. I should come by more often. My boyfriend is surrounded by smarmy, suck-ass sycophants."

Who taught her to talk, Spiro Agnew? "I wouldn't know."

"Do you want me to come back after I get my hair done?"

A nooner on a silver platter? Fool if I don't, fool if I do. I said, "I'm sure that's a bad idea."

"He's got a sense of humor, but he's a wimp?"

I said, "I've been dating a fine woman for the past five months. I don't want that to change."

"I didn't think that mattered in this town."

"Let's say my mother told me never to eat fish in a strange restaurant on a Monday."

"That's actually funny. I like it better than your first answer. Anyway, my proposition was conjecture. You passed the test. You're not like the other ones. I swear, ten thousand slimeballs in this town."

"I know."

She looked me in the eye. "You know what?"

"The proposition, by your word, conjecture. By my word, horseshit."

"How so?"

"Putting big money into a venture with few guarantees. You did it out of love. No other reason."

"You're not so fucking dumb yourself."

My brass doorbell clanged. I walked to the porch. Anybody but a schoolteacher, a restaurateur, or . . .

Dexter Hayes, Jr., at the screen, wearing Ray-Bans. A phone in one hand, a manila five-by-seven envelope in the other. A yellow button-down shirt, olive trousers, the Reeboks he wore twenty-four hours earlier. And an expression of curiosity.

I said, "You just missed our analysis of your crime scene."

Hayes's pager beeped at him. He ignored it. He wasn't lost for words so much as waiting for someone else to fill silence.

Heidi did it. "Gotta go," she said. "Nice to see you, Mr. Hayes." She came around me, hit the door handle, almost knocked the detective off the stoop.

"Have a nice day," I said, for the second time in two days.

Hayes, still silent, moved backward so the young woman could leave. I stepped outside. Hayes extracted a photo from the envelope, turned, held it up so we could view it as we watched Heidi Norquist slip into her Jaguar.

It was my photograph of Heidi skating away from me on Caroline Street. "Perfect likeness," said Dexter Hayes.

I said, "Damn near identical."

10

Dexter Hayes, Jr., handed me a manila KWPD "Internal Use" packet. My exterior shots of Butler Dunwoody's construction site.

"You could've stuck these in the mail."

"What now," he said. "I'm a delivery boy?"

"Okay," I said. "I ran a stop sign on my bicycle this morning."

He looked at me like I was fresh bird mess on his windshield.

"Or did you come to apologize and offer me back my job?"

He shook his head, checked out my porch, focused through the screens, eye-jumped plant to plant. "Even Ortega told me I was out of line yesterday. That fuckup'd have trouble noticing if somebody shit in his hat."

A detective sorry for unprofessional conduct? That would make him unlike any Key West cop I'd ever known. He'd come for a different reason. The photos placed me at a crime scene prior to a body's discovery. The photo of Heidi, and Hayes's timely arrival, connected me to Dunwoody's girlfriend before and after the body's discovery. I needed to watch my step.

"I accept your apology," I said. "I'd like an explanation."

"I can't get into the specifics of a murder investigation."

I was being patronized. Or I was a suspect. I said, "Gotcha."

He stepped back. "That look, Rutledge. I've seen contempt before."

I didn't doubt that. Racism aside, the man had grown up the son of Big Dex Hayes. Island attitudes—official and otherwise—regarding his father's business pursuits had, with passing time, swung from amused tolerance to adamant reform. A "community leader" had been sent to jail. His son, Dexter Hayes, Jr., had taken crap I could never imagine.

"Don't misread me. I'm thinking a cop might not have done his job."

He bought a few seconds of time, rubbed his lip with his index finger knuckle. "How so?"

"That viewing gallery when I came to take pictures. Butler Dunwoody found the body. That's no reason for him or his girlfriend to be hanging around for scene analysis. Not to mention the newspaper reporter and the department liaison officer."

"Your girlfriend."

"Right," I said. "Teresa's a spokesperson. She's not a scene tech."

"I expect she studied site analysis at the University of Florida. That'd be a three-hundred-level course."

"And she probably aced it. I'm talking job description, not expertise."

"Each of which, in your case, is in question."

My job description had never been put in writing.

I said, "You got your criminology degree?"

"Same curriculum as Ms. Barga," said Hayes. "A few years back."

"And plenty of in-your-face experience on the dangerous streets?"

"That's right. Up close and personal."

"And I don't know shit about what I'm doing. Is that

what you're saying? Or was that just a bullshit act for the audience?"

Hayes breathed deeply, swelled his chest, began to expel air through his pursed lips. Buying time. "Tell me about procedures, Rutledge."

"The Justice Department's *National Guidelines for Death Investigation*? I've got a copy in my camera bag. I review it every ninety days. Scene entry and evaluation. Body documentation, jurisdiction, written docs—for medical history and scene exit. The recommended equipment list. I've checked out Polaroid's Web site. I've read the forensic photo section of the Field Evidence Tech course outline from Cal State, Long Beach. I own way more than the minimum equipment. I maintain it for cleanliness, accuracy, and longevity. I've always got a supply of rubber gloves and shoe socks. I've also—"

"I don't act for any damned audience, Rutledge. In your vast experience of judging bullshit, how did you see that tableau at the scene? Or maybe I should ask, How did you sniff out the scene? Smell like shit?"

It hadn't smelled like that, which confirmed what we already knew—that the death had not happened there. "How did the murderer gain access to the construction site, Hayes? If there wasn't full-time security, I'd have to guess the perimeter was locked."

"You bet," he said. "That's good thinking. You paid attention both times you were over there."

"What's the good answer?"

"The victim's own keys. He was the foreman."

Hayes had worked this back around to my presence at the site, my presumed connection to Heidi. "Tell me about these photos." He pointed at the envelope in my hand. "Do these connect you to a murder, or do we have a coincidence?"

"I've been taking pictures for years. Keys people, buildings, cars, signs, boats, bikes. Should I be grateful you're not holding a Miranda crib card?"

Disbelief with a touch of disgust in Hayes's eyes. I couldn't blame him.

"This beeper'll page backup, if you feel slighted."

"Don't ask me why," I said. "I've saved them all. I've got shots of old city hall, when they renovated it. I've got Dorothy Raymer walking her German shepherd past the cupola when it was sitting in the middle of Ann Street. I've got one of Love-22 on top of his red-white-and-blue bus at Mallory Square, at sunset, handing out twenty-two-dollar bills. The ones the feds hassled him about. There's one from the mid-seventies, of Bobby Brown, the day he lost the election. He's holding a phony newspaper with the headline 'Wm. Freeman Charged with Impersonating Sheriff.' I've got a portrait of Cigarette Willie, the old bum who used to sleep on the bench at Simonton and Eaton. The bench is gone, too. I've even got the Conch Train, on July 4, 1976, decorated for the Bicentennial. One of the first pictures I ever took on the island."

He scowled, unconvinced.

I said, "Why does somebody climb a mountain? Why do race drivers try to go faster? People gamble. People kill. I press the camera button."

"Anyway," he said, "your film came out fine. Ortega's camera went south on us. All he got were half-frame photos."

"Not the camera's fault. Would you like to know why?"

He stared. I began to explain the camera's inability to synchronize with shutter speeds above one-sixtieth of a second in some models, one-hundred-twenty-fifth in others.

He waved me to a stop. "You didn't tell me you got painted gang colors."

How the hell did Hayes know that?

He read my mind. "I narrowed it down to a few arms, and twisted."

I didn't believe that, either. But no matter how Hayes had found out, he was stacking up chips. "Let me ask you, Dexter. If you were a civilian who got accosted by Bug Thorsby, would you bother reporting it?"

Hayes nodded, in thought. "I didn't know it was Little Bug. You probably did the right thing. I used to know his scummy father. Every high school has a bully, every town its pet felon. The one-man crime wave finally got his."

"It took twenty years for the system to send Jemison Thorsby away. He got out in less than four. I heard he earned fat money at Union Correctional lecturing inmates on witness intimidation."

"Hell with that. My father was up there then. Thorsby got turned out and shanked at least twice. He's got one scar I know from his collarbone to his belly button. I expect he came home with a chip on his shoulder the size of Sand Key."

We still stood outside the porch, staring at trees as though they held our interest, kicking blades of grass. "Well, Jemison's handed down the legacy," I said. "Bug's a good copycat, or else he found inspiration in his butthole buddies. Why are you back in Key West, Dexter? You trying to clear your family's name?"

"Shit. Anybody ever gave a damn about my family left town, run away by property taxes."

"They still know Big Dex Hayes's reputation."

"Nobody knows how it went. Hookers and gambling. The town tolerated it. The powers did every damn thing to keep him in business. Made my life hell, especially after the point when other kids and I were old enough to know what was going down. People'd see my old man's three-inch bankroll, think I was growing up in some fairy tale. Wrong. But that's the way it goes."

I knew he was right. A generation ago, a law officer of Dexter's rank could jeopardize his career by messing with Big Dex. These days basic corruption drew more attention, more attorneys, but less shame.

"Let me ask you this," said Hayes. "You thinking of settling the score with Bug?"

"You're leading up to something, Detective. I hope you're almost there."

"Go ahead and answer that question."

"I'm not going to sink to his level, unless I'm forced to, but the old wheel comes around. Let's say, if my timing is right, maybe I can help Bug win a ticket upstate, get his chance to meet some fraternity brothers in Starke."

"I'll bet you get that chance. You're a hotshot. Word gets around. You've done a lot of work for us and the county the last few years, you maybe think you've earned your wings . . . made your bones?"

He was working his way back to Heidi. I said, "I've been there for the paycheck. Not recognition. If I'd wanted a career, I'd have gone to the academy. That's not my deal."

"I agree. I don't know whether you're a troublemaker or a lucky son of a bitch. You're a picture taker. I don't know if you pay your bills, change your underwear, bullshit your closest friends, or call your mother on holidays. And I don't care. What concerns me directly is I know you're not a child molester, you don't beat up women, and you act like a grown-up during daylight hours. You've made your contributions. But you're not a cop, you aren't James Bond or *Spenser for Hire*. You're not a detective. You're not a sworn officer of the law."

Hayes's monologue was clever, designed to boost me up, knock me down, and put me in my place. But I had no designs on his job, no ambitions to be a crime stopper. I wanted the life I had enjoyed for many years to continue for another fifteen or twenty, without ugliness or tragedy. I said, "I'm with you on all the above, no argument." Then I added, "I'm still guessing you've come back to settle some scores of your own. I may not be the only one to think that."

"Maybe they'll see it that way. I came here to get my wife and babies off the goddamned Gold Coast. You got fatal accidents once an hour up there. The schools are armed camps. The mobile homes they call classrooms, they look like armed trailer camps. More uniforms at junior high than at the malls. Ironic as hell, isn't it? I came back to Key West for quality of life."

"The ironic part is your being worried about safety, the job you do."

"Look, Rutledge. If it ever comes down to court, testimony for me and the prosecutor to win conviction, I don't want your so-called knowledge, that cute booklet in your bag, to get shoved down my throat. You want to work for me, you need to take courses. Do it on the Internet, however, but write it down, tell me what you're taking. Keep me posted on your progress."

"Fair enough."

Hayes walked to a tall bush at the edge of my property, fluffed out the branches. "My mama, bless her soul, always used to say, 'Croton bushes are like Conch kids. They'll grow up fine, even if you don't take care of 'em.' "

I said, "Didn't work for Bug Thorsby."

"He don't count. That family came here from Alabama. By the way, you'll be proud to know you made history yesterday. My liaison at the county tells me AFIS kicked back a fingerprints hit, that headless man you photographed. The pisser is, I've got to coordinate on a joint investigation. But you made history. You photographed two dead Richard Engrams in one day."

"Same name?"

"Same social, same date of birth. There's probably a place for you down at Ripley's Believe It or Not! They'll mold a wax effigy of you in there. The way they design faces, it should look just like you right now. Stunned and empty-headed."

"Sounds like an investigator's problem, Dexter. I'm just the photographer, remember?"

"Right." He did his knuckle thing on the upper lip. "It sure as hell connects the two murders. One last question."

"I wish I believed that," I said.

"A couple of minutes ago you used the word *copycat*. Any reason, your choice of words?"

Someone had matched Mercer Holloway's line of thought.

"No, but I know what you mean. Are they your cases?"

"Used to be Liska's." A quick, almost imperceptible nod. "See you later."

"Now I got one last question, Dexter."

He turned.

"Actually, two," I said. "You mentioned your mama. You said, 'Bless her soul.' I never heard that she passed away."

He thought for a minute. "My mother is still alive and she is increasingly guided by divine voices. What's the last question?"

"Like I said, I accept your apology. But I'm looking for a reason why you were such an asshole yesterday."

"And now it's your turn? Look. You weren't the photographer. You were a suspect."

As I'd thought. "Am I still a suspect?"

"Follow me here. I'm new on the job. I'm trying to step aside from my father's shadow. I'm following Liska's act at the city, which is tough. And I intend to be good. Yes, Rutledge, you're still a suspect. Don't feel special. Everyone's a fucking suspect."

Hayes walked toward his plain white four-door Chevy Lumina. My small yard looked barren without Heidi Norquist's Jaguar convertible. The antique thermometer on the porch read seventy-four degrees. Hayes looked back as he eased into his car. His final glance made me flash to what Heidi had said about wind-chill factor. Hayes dialed a number before he put it in gear. He rolled out of the lane, slouched near the center of the front seat, the cell phone jammed to his ear.

Reporting on his progress? Linking me to Caroline Street?

I walked up the wood stairs to my porch and thumbed through the five photos in the manila envelope. The big white APPLEBY-FLORIDA, INC., GENERAL CONTRACTOR sign. Was that the name of Heidi's corporation, or Butler's? The other sign listed the muscle, the lawyers and the bankers. Small world. The security company name hadn't rung a bell

when I'd taken the picture: TNT Security was Tommy
Tucker's operation.

A horn honked. "Hey, Rutledge." Dexter Hayes had returned, backed his car down the lane. He beckoned me to
his passenger-side window.

"What's up?" I said.

"Your friend Marnie Dunwoody? She walked out of the
Citizen building on Northside Drive. She found an oversized Ziploc bag on the floor of her Jeep. The plastic was
fogged by freezable gel packs, but she made out the contents when she saw a human ear. You want to make a quick
buck?"

"I don't do portrait work."

Hayes turned human for an instant: "I don't blame you.
This is right up Cootie Ortega's alley." He put it in drive
and chirped the tires.

No question now. Butler Dunwoody was drawing the
crap, and anyone who got close to him or his project was
fair game for one form or another of terrorism and violence.
Time for a simple solution. Fly to Atlanta, take Sam and
Marnie and Teresa, check into a cheap motel for a week or
two.

I returned to the porch, dropped the packet of photos I'd
been perusing. I called Sam to ask about Marnie, how she
was taking the shock of finding the severed head.

No answer. The perfect time not to leave a message.

Back on the porch, imagining Marnie's reaction, I mindlessly shuffled the photos. My hands were sweating. Maybe
that was why the last two pictures in the stack had stuck
together. I peeled them apart. I'd forgotten about the one
on the bottom. It was the shot I'd taken without sighting
or focusing as the shorter thug had moved toward me, just
before the dude behind him had snapped open his carpet
cutter. The blur was exactly as I'd imagined it. Parts of
Shorty's chin and shoulder, overexposed, mottled. Sparkles
off his necklaces, his gold hoop earring. By some stroke of
fate, the focus was perfect in the background. At the right
edge of the frame, the torso of the taller one, from his waist

to eye level. The hand with the carpet cutter was not in the shot. The man's skinny belly showed under his shirt hem, and . . .

. . . a purplish-red, oval-shaped birthmark ran from under his shirt collar to a point behind his right ear. The carpet cutter's birthmark.

Maybe the same ear Marnie had seen through the fogged Ziploc bag.

11

Some people are born in love with cars. Some people don't know motors from meat hooks. Teresa's enthusiasm peaked when she bought a Shimano motor scooter that matched her blue Pontiac Grand Am. She couldn't understand why I owned a shabby beater.

I've always believed that an eye-catcher attracts two things. Thieves and cops. In town I use my bike and my motorcycle. I remove the car from its padlocked garage only for trips off the island, and only when the motorcycle won't do. Teresa regarded my high-performance Shelby GT-350H as I hoped others would: an ugly '66 Mustang fastback with sun-bleached primer paint, warped bumpers, perforated upholstery, no hubcaps. It took a vacant road session on Middle Torch Key one clear October morning— high-speed corner-cutting, acceleration, deceleration, and braking—and an explanation of the Shelby's value, the reason for my "collectible" insurance, to win her appreciation for my fox in dog's clothing.

I needed to escape two days' weirdness on the rock, blow carbon out of the Shelby's valves. I hoped that distance from the island might help me sort events I'd assumed were unrelated. Events I now knew to be unexplainably linked. Blanking out questions that lacked immediate answers, I spent an hour with the Shelby, draining and refilling coolant, and checking levels at the dipstick, battery cells, and master cylinder. Then I drove six blocks to the Chevron on White Street—one of the last free-air pumps in Florida—to top off the pressure in my blackwalls.

A navy-blue Ford Expedition pulled to a gas pump fifteen feet from the air and water station. Connecticut plates. A bumper sticker: AL GORE INVENTED THE INTERNET. MY WIFE INVENTED MONEY. A burly, red-bearded tourist climbed out, told me he'd give me three thousand dollars for my old Mustang. He looked ready to whip out his wallet on the spot. I thanked him, declined his kind offer, not letting on that three grand represented a fraction of the car's value.

"How about thirty thousand?" he said.

He knew. We shared a laugh. He asked about the engine's originality, and hoped I still had, stored away somewhere, the special Magnum wheels and scooped factory hood.

He said, "Good idea, that paint."

Teresa usually worked late, claimed her efficiency tripled when the office emptied after five P.M. I dialed her direct line at five-twenty. She picked up.

I said, "You've heard about Marnie?"

"I've heard."

"Have you talked to her?"

"For thirty seconds. She took it okay at first, but then it got to her. She's ticked off because she got attitude from the police officers. Same shit she told us about. Like it wouldn't have happened if her brother hadn't come to town. She's home, sleeping."

"You want paybacks for cooking last night? Dinner at Mangrove's?"

"I've had an awful day. Not as bad as Marnie's. You're offering to drive?"

"Gassed up and ready," I said.

"Give me time to go home and change. Can you wait forty minutes?"

"This night's for you. Take forty-five."

"I think we've got a lot to talk about."

"I've got a lot to think about. But I want to wait until morning."

We couldn't have picked a better night to drive Highway 1. No bumper jumpers on Stock Island. No road racers past Boca Chica Naval Air Station, no turtles on Big Coppitt. The day's wind had laid down. Cotton-ball clouds glowed, the moon only two days from full. Conversation could not compete with wind noise through the car windows. Teresa looked content, though I knew she had questions. I faced two dilemmas. I'd told her that the mugging had been a minor event. With my discovery that the headless victim had been my attacker, my white lie bloomed into blatant deception. The other problem was, if I revealed the connection, she'd be on the spot. I knew her morals. She'd feel obligated to inform her colleagues at the city.

Somewhere around Bay Point, she reached across the center hump and patted my leg. That, in itself, said a thousand words.

Mangrove Mama's is a funky spot on the bay side, fifty feet west of mile marker 20 at the top of Sugarloaf. I turned left into the parking area, noting a slight pull in the left front brake. I stopped next to a glassed-in phone booth under a lamppost, a narrow cone of light to fend off breakins and attract bugs. In daylight my car did both on its own. I clicked my key chain button, the only technology stroke on the Shelby. The V-8's mechanical fuel pump had crapped out weeks ago. I'd installed an electric pump, rerouted the gas line to the carburetor, and attached a remote-activated cutoff switch to the new electrical pump. If a thief hot-wired the ignition, the engine would turn over. Fuel-starved, it never would start. Peace of mind.

We were greeted inside by a young woman wearing a striking, form-fitting cocktail dress. I felt Teresa's chill of disapproval. The pixie hostess looked seventeen, the face of an angel, the eyes of a harlot. Her black dress fit like skin. We followed her to a table. To placate my jealous lover, I kept my eyes diverted. Teresa picked a chair facing the restaurant's open patio. I faced the restaurant's central area and greeters' podium.

I said, "Policing my thoughts?"

No answer.

The restaurant's stereo was perfect: "Love the One You're With."

"Trade seats?" I said.

Teresa studied her menu. "Four things," she said. "Eye candy is rarely sweet. She's cute but not beautiful. Somewhere, for some reason, somebody hates her guts. And your conscience is my best friend."

"You possess a wondrous mind."

"You will choose your entree quickly. I'm hungry. I could eat a tree."

We ordered wine. After the server had returned, poured Cabernet, I told Teresa about Mercer Holloway's employment offer.

She said, "That many properties?"

"Over the years he picked them up. People died, families left town, landlords screwed up their lives, went to prison for smuggling. He was no dunce. He looked into the future. He bought cheap, he paid his taxes."

"I've heard Paulie talk about him. He's cut a lot of corners, too."

Teresa's stepfather, Paul Cottrell, had been the city's zoning inspector for most of the time I'd lived in Key West. He knew the history of every building on the island, rules bent, variances granted, the politics behind approvals.

"You've got a problem with Holloway's offer?" said Teresa.

"I wonder if I'm whoring myself, or hosing my photography career. I'm helping a rampant capitalist hurry Key West to a point of being unlivable."

"Malthus had an idea or two about that," she said.

"I thought you majored in criminology."

Teresa narrowed her eyes. "I've read the occasional book."

"Malthus worried about population outrunning food supply," I said. "I'm worried about humans overwhelming square footage."

"It's going to happen, one way or another. People've been trying to stop it for thirty years. Your taking pictures won't make a difference. If his checks don't bounce, do the work. At least you don't have to travel. I can have you around more than usual."

"There you go, being logical again."

The hostess passed our table, ushering a couple to the outside patio. A song lyric popped to mind: "Half woman, half child, she drove him half wild." I told myself not to look. I failed to heed my advice.

"She's as ripe as an avocado in a rainstorm," said Teresa. "If I had to make up her story, she's in love with a jerk, he spends her earnings on dope and sports gambling. I'll bet you fifty we come back in two months, she'll have a new glow on her face and a pregnant belly out to here. A month later she'll be gone. We'll never see her again."

The song also had said, "In the tropics, they come and they go."

I said, "You never bet unless you're sure to win."

"It's like that old lawyers' rule."

"Never ask a question to which you don't know the answer."

"You're smart about some things, Alex, dense about others. If it averages out to eighty-twenty, you're my dream date."

We toasted to that. The server brought our main course, broiled grouper for Teresa, poached snapper for me. Sometimes I wonder about waiting all day to consume a costly meal that disappears from your plate in less than ten minutes. I took a bite, then wondered how I could live without it.

The server tried to sell after-dinner liqueurs, oversized desserts. We chose to drive home and attack the French vanilla in my freezer.

I paid the bill, told myself not to check Lolita as we departed. I made it.

Four steps outside the restaurant door, Teresa stopped. She grabbed my forearm. "What's wrong with your car?"

The Shelby's front wheels were angled oddly. I hurried to the driver's side door. The lock had been forced. Strands of wiring hung loose below the dash. The thief had made a mess, but my fuel-shutoff "insurance" had paid off. I flashed to the burly tourist in the huge SUV. No way. Since the stock market surge of the Clinton years, Republican car thieves were few. It had been someone else. I was surprised that I hadn't heard the engine cranking, trying to catch. I spent a minute looking around the parking area. No other cars looked damaged. Mine had been the only target. Perhaps it had been judged an easy target because of its age, its easy-access ignition, its lack of a locking steering column. Perhaps the target had been me, not the car.

Me and my paranoia.

By the glow of the lamppost, stripping insulation with my penknife, I restrung the color-coded wires. The motor cranked and ran fine. I backed the Shelby, then eased forward to the main road.

New problem. While I waited for passing traffic, a car appeared behind me. Thin, beam-directed halogen headlamps. I sensed something amiss. I'd had a clear view of the restaurant's front door. No one but the two of us had left in the previous ten minutes. There was an entrance by the bar, behind the patio, but the bar had closed a half hour earlier. I'd seen the lights dim, watched the bartender walk to the office with her cash drawer.

I turned left when I pulled onto the highway. If there was going to be a problem, going north gave me more evasion options than heading to Key West. I accelerated normally in first and second gears. The strange headlights came our way but hung back.

"Alex, what are you doing?"

I said, "Guy wants to put his nose up my butt."

"So, let him pass. This is not the best place to play macho."

"He doesn't want to go around. I think it's whoever tried to steal it."

I gave the Shelby more oomph in third past a LIGHTS ON FOR SAFETY sign and sped over the Bow Channel Bridge. I was doing fifty-five—ten over the limit—past the sheriff's department substation on Cudjoe Key. A Shelby is not quiet at that speed. Three cruisers and a van in the rear parking area. No deputies in the lot. If things got ugly, there was no time for help, anyway.

Suddenly the headlights in the mirror were two car lengths behind us. I stuffed my gas foot.

Teresa twisted in her seat to look. "Maybe it's kids who want to race."

The tailgater flashed his brights, then flicked his headlights. I thought back. I hadn't recognized anyone in the restaurant. I couldn't think of any reason to stop. If he'd wanted information, he could have approached me—without a weapon—in Mangrove's parking lot.

Screw his intentions. He wanted no witnesses. Once we chatted, I'd be toast and Teresa would be in the wrong place at the wrong time.

Fear is good, as long as it doesn't cloud judgment.

"Is your gun in your purse?"

She hesitated. "It's locked up at home."

I added ten miles per hour to our speed. I was tracking thirty over Cudjoe's posted forty-five limit. The vehicle drew closer. A prolonged chase could only end ugly. I knew there was no way to outrun him on a public-access two-lane with nowhere to turn that didn't dead-end at the ocean.

"Tighten your seat belt."

A flutter of concern in her voice: "I did that already. It's tight."

"Tighten it till it hurts."

"It hurts."

No oncoming traffic. No radar-toting FHP sedans that,

any other time, are common as rental ragtops. The headlights quit flashing, but the car moved to tailgate, weaving
slightly, maybe prepping to pass. I was in fourth, adding
speed, probably over ninety-five, but I wasn't going to look
down to check. I felt a tap, a light nerf on the rear bumper.
A moment later the car pulled out to pass. Bingo, oncoming, a big van flipping his high beams. My butt buddy
slowed, tucked in behind me. The van's horn was constant,
grating, doing Doppler like a southbound locomotive.

I rounded a right-curving bend, spotted a car about to
pull out of a side road. The perfect setup for a T-bone, with
us the meat. I slowed an instant, ensured that the car had
seen us. My drop-in speed gave the chasing car its chance.
He jerked into the southbound lane. He began to edge
alongside.

I glanced over my shoulder. A dark, four-door late-
model import. Prelude or Altima. Maybe a Sentra. Who
discerns differences? They all end in vowels. A south-side
street lamp illuminated the sedan. Its passenger's hand was
out the window. It wasn't just his hand. The sight of the
gun almost brought up my fish dinner. I heard a soft pop,
a loud rap on the Shelby's floor pan.

The bastard was trying to shoot my rear tire.

"Unbuckle, Teresa," I said loudly. "You're on the floor."

She yelled, muffled, "Yes, I am!"

I turned my head for an instant. She was still buckled
in. She'd leaned to fit her head under the dash.

I looked left. The sedan was alongside. I slammed the
brakes, dropped enough speed to dump the shifter into
third. The engine didn't like it. I juked the wheel, then
floored it. The Shelby shifted sideways, then a little forward, like dancing the mambo. The other car attempted to
slow, to match my speed, but my move put me directly
behind him. A Maxima. I kissed its rear bumper and used
the Shelby's torque to push it faster. We smacked when I
upshifted. Probably didn't scratch the newer car—my two-
hundred-dollar front bumper wasn't made for minimized
damage. The crunching noises got worse when I slipped

left, forced the other car right. His right front wheel caught the pavement's edge. I lifted my gas foot. Teresa sat up straight, watched the Maxima begin a slow clockwise spin onto the shoulder.

The other driver was good: he had the wisdom not to counter rotation by steering into the skid. To do so would have caused the Maxima to roll, to ball up like a pita sandwich. The driver turned his wheel right, hurried the spin, left the road backwards, doing at least sixty. The gun waver would survive unhurt, or die. No need to check on their welfare.

I heard two gunshots. They weren't dead yet.

I was surprised the Maxima had kept up with the Shelby. I should've read its license number.

"You okay?" I said.

No answer.

Ahead, opposite a grocery store, was Blimp Road, access to Fat Albert, the government spy balloon that monitors Cuba. The feds had used the tethered blimp for thirty years to monitor Communist entertainment, ship-to-shore, air traffic control, television, and military radio. Blimp Road is a ruler-straight two-lane. Streetlights line the first fifty yards. After that, total darkness.

In case the other team survived their off-road excursion, I wanted extra insurance. I hung a left, late-braking, moving too quickly. The left front brake caliper snagged, pushed the car to the outside of the turn. I slid across the narrow service road, scrubbed off speed, just missed a utility pole, swapped paint with a landscaping outfit's security fence.

I faced two miles of deteriorated pavement. Gravel shoulders on both sides, with grass interspersed. Beyond the roadbed, sparse mangroves, open areas. No other vehicles on the road. I accelerated rapidly to sixty-five, then eased off, maintained speed. I doused the headlights, a try for concealment in case the Maxima pursued us. Moonlight on swampy water flashed past, a river in the opposite direction. An optical illusion: the roadway appeared to be well below sea level. I knew it wasn't too far above. Four inches lower, I'd be aquaplaning, leaving twin rooster-tail wakes.

"Be my backup eyes." I raised my voice to counter wind and road noise. "Anything you think you see—an alligator, a wild dog, anything—yell out."

Teresa faced forward, steeled, not happy, not complaining. A sour brine scent filled the car. Focus, I thought. Focus.

The first half mile's rough surface gave to smoother, still imperfect concrete. Lights popped into my rearview. The halogens' beam angle lifted as the other car accelerated. The lights swung side-to-side—anxiousness or a blown tire. Front-wheel-drive cars suffer torque-steering, but don't fishtail.

I suddenly realized I'd blown it. I could have U-turned, gone back to the sheriff's substation. Instead, I'd run away to a dead end. The only way to depart Blimp Road was by retracing my path.

Within ten seconds I knew they'd blown it, too. If the Maxima driver had been familiar with the area, he'd have understood that my only escape was a bicycle trail. He would have only to sit in darkness, near the highway, and wait for me. But he rolled on, his headlights moving perceptibly closer. If my luck and timing held out, he'd be sorry he'd bothered to chase. If things went the other way, there was always the bike trail. I bumped the mirror upward so the halogens wouldn't spoil my night vision.

In a vintage Mustang, you step on the brake, the pedal-swing arm trips a switch, and the brake lights come on. I knew that the halogens already had found the reflectors molded into my taillamp lenses. But distance is difficult to judge at night, and I wanted every advantage. I reached between my feet, kept my eyes above the dashboard. I fumbled with the swing arm, found two insulated wires leading into the switch. I pulled gently. Nothing happened. I yanked. A wire fell loose. No sparks, no short circuit, no red glow behind the Shelby. I couldn't tap the brake pedal to assure myself of success. I'd find out soon enough.

We passed the westbound cutoff to Waste Management's Cudjoe Key Station—the one-mile point, if my memory was working. Farther along, to the right, we passed a hiking path cut into the refuge area. I didn't want to spend hours fleeing on foot, in darkness, especially if people with weapons chased us.

"Tell me when you see a vertical sign with letters on it. Yell it out."

The lights in the mirror approached rapidly. The guy was past eighty, maybe close to a hundred. He'd be on my bumper in twenty seconds.

An instant later Teresa shouted: "The sign!" A six-foot post, red reflector, and vertical lettering: CKAFS. Whatever that meant.

I was into the last hundred yards. My next cue was the government's half-hidden "authorized vehicles only" access road on the left. Then a sign: NO MOLESTING OF CRAWFISH TRAPS.

This, I thought, could go horribly wrong.

I stabbed the brakes to drop speed, spun the steering wheel left, gave it the gas for a movie turn. The right front disc brake caliper grabbed early. Steve McQueen, please be with me. I hit the right shoulder, a twelve-foot-wide gravel turn-off area. Two trash drums loomed forty feet away. The Shelby did a quick one-eighty. We faced the Maxima's rapidly approaching headlights. I jammed my foot on the brake pedal. Gravel showered the Shelby's inner fenders and floor pan. The tire treads shuddered. Momentum skidded us backward and across the road. We hit a wide spot on the far shoulder. I feared for a moment that he would aim for me. The Shelby grabbed traction as the Maxima flashed past, its nose down, its headlights pulsing with the action of its anti-lock brakes. I heard three gunshots, then another. No pings on the car. Mangrove limbs scraped the Shelby's trunk and rear bumper as we crunched to a stop.

I'd come closer to the water's edge than I'd intended. I'd also let the Shelby's engine stall.

The noise from the Maxima didn't last long. When it hit

gravel at the road's end, its high-tech brake system couldn't keep it from its destination. We heard a springy thud as the sedan's undercarriage hit the top edge of the boat ramp, the downslope that extended eight feet past the tideline. I'd expected the next sound to be a splash, not a crash. But it sounded like a two-car collision. The bursting air bags echoed off the mangroves, rumbled into the empty night. Only a small splash, then sizzling, then quiet.

I felt a cloud of marl dust enter the car, smelled shoreline odors mixed with burned rubber and my toasted clutch.

I said, "Welcome to the Great White Heron National Wildlife Refuge. We blew some carbon out of the motor. Oughta run better now."

Teresa whispered, "I was just kidding, wanting to eat a tree. Isn't this where you wanted to go kayaking on Sunday?"

"Don't you wish we had?"

I twisted the key. A low, slow moan from the starter motor—my classic's weak link. My triple-A dues weren't up-to-date. After six or seven agonizing seconds it cranked the overheated motor enough to catch ignition. I pushed the lever into first, silently apologized to the vehicle once again for mistreatment. I flipped on my headlights and started south.

"You want to stop at Mangrove Mama's for a drink?" I said.

Teresa laughed, then began to cry. Then she just as quickly quit.

I slowed for the stop at U.S. 1. A sheriff's cruiser veered off the highway's northbound lane, hit the brakes, lighted its red-and-blue roof bar. The deputies must have heard the Shelby pass the substation. Or the gunshots.

I pulled to the shoulder. Cooperation is my watchword. Candor is my command. Especially when I've just suckered two pistol-toting maniacs into six feet of salt water. A dash-mounted laptop glowed, lit the deputy's effort to handle his power window and his spotlight at the same time. The window descended in three start-stop stages. The spot swiveled.

"You gonna turn that on and night-blind us all?" I shouted.

The light remained dark. "Whatcha doin' out here, sir?"

"Kissin' my girlfriend. We're going home to Key West to finish the job."

"Car come by here, moving fast?"

"Yessir. Two of them, bumper-taggin'. That's why we're leaving."

"Your car smells like it's been workin' out, too. You been down here burnin' doughnuts on private property?"

"This old thing, it overheats just idling."

"Your antifreeze smells like fried brake pads." He flung open his door, played a flashlight on my front wheel. "I need to see paperwork."

If I dropped Liska's name, he'd never believe me. "How about a character reference? Detective Bobbi Lewis."

He climbed out of his car. Eight feet tall. "Everybody knows somebody."

"I work for the department. I did the evidence shots, that body on Stock Island yesterday."

He tested me. "With the bullet through the forehead?"

I passed his test: "There wasn't a forehead attached." I also turned the table: "What do you know about a gunshot wound?"

He stared at me.

I said, "Pretty damn quiet down the road, there."

He stared some more, tried to memorize the Mustang. He barked, "Get your ass outa here."

I did so. I turned south on U.S. 1 and rolled by the Freeman Substation doing forty-four in the forty-five zone. Two cruisers scrambled as we passed, exited the parking area, whipped north off Drost Drive.

"They're delivering towels and dry clothing for the marksmen."

Teresa was silent a minute, then said, "I'm trying to recall what I learned in college. About the point where self-defense becomes attempted murder. You did good with that car chase. You also did good with the deputy."

"Creative solutions for complicated problems."

"Now you've got a bigger problem," she said.

"How so?"

"You either tell me what's going on, or your antifreeze is going to smell like fried brake pads."

12

I drove into Key West, monitored the rearview. If the Maxima's occupants had been saved by air bags and made it to shore, they could cause problems. A cell phone to summon friends, if the phone had survived the salt water. Or a wild fiction for the deputy. Some bullshit to shift the blame. I didn't want to talk my way around another blue-and-red flasher.

I was hiding from bad guys and good guys. I didn't understand any of it.

Inside of two days I'd been street-jumped, chased in my car, and shot at. Scumbags with loud music and cheap blades had marked me. Jerk-offs with a medium-caliber gun had drenched me in sweat, pock-marked the Shelby's left side-frame rail. I hadn't gone looking for trouble. Both times trouble had come straight to me.

On the other hand, I'd made us perfect victims for an imperfect crime. The Caroline Street mess should have put me on notice. But I'd gone out in public when lying low would have been wiser. And I'd taken Teresa with me. We'd been lucky. Our pursuers could've used silencers, shot us in Mangrove Mama's parking lot. Quieter, sliced our throats. Less messy, snugged our windpipes with heavy monofilament or nylon rope. The shooter could have aimed for my head instead of my rear tire. Instead—for want of an action word—they had *messed* with us.

The head in Marnie's Jeep had confirmed that the violence was focused on driving away Butler Dunwoody. I couldn't guess how messing with me, or stealing my car, could stop a construction project. Meanwhile, two men had died, one of them a scumbag. Two more people could have died but for someone's deficient killing skills. Not that Teresa and I wished them higher scores.

I wished I'd had the sense not to expose her to a threat.

I assumed that the sanctity of my house was as threatened as my ass. I didn't want either of us to spend the night on Dredgers Lane. But I wanted my car out of sight.

I drove up Fleming, quietly coasted into the guests-only lot at the Eden House, the inn adjacent to the lane. No open spaces. Is it double-parking when you block six cars at once?

"Lock yourself in. If anyone shows, pretend you're passed out," I said. "I'll be back in two minutes."

She gave me a cold look.

"Is that okay?" I said.

She opened the car door, stepped out. "Crap's been going on for thirty-six hours, Alex. This is the first time you've asked my opinion." She closed the door. She was coming with me.

I'd asked her opinion of Dexter Hayes's actions at the Caroline Street murder scene. Bad time to argue the point. I still didn't want to tell her about the purple birthmark, the connection between my Caroline Street muggers and the body on the dumped sofa.

A cold front had blown itself south of Lake Okeechobee. The midday norther now had a bite to it. It took us three minutes to scope Dredgers Lane on foot. The lane looked safe, my house unmolested. Sure as hell, we returned to a minivan owner who wanted to kick my butt. Poor son of a bitch probably on his dream vacation, tapping out the MasterCard, trying to get some squeeze, having to make a midnight run for Pampers. Teresa shivered, acted drunk, bitched about no rooms at the inn. After inspecting my expression up close, the van owner backed down.

I lease the garage behind Carmen Sosa's house in the lane. Her four-year-old Saturn gets parked in open weather, next to her porch. But my rental cash makes up for young Maria's long-gone daddy's failure to make child-support payments. With the Shelby's minimal exhaust system, I try not to come and go after Carmen's and Maria's bedtimes. I'd considered spending the night at Teresa's condo, parking the Shelby there, behind the Shipyard security gates. Who's kidding whom? The swinging gates are cued by coded keypad; every pizza and package and grocery delivery service, every garbage and recycling-truck driver, every taxi driver had this month's code. Not that it matters. Anyone can walk into the parking area by sidewalk. The gates open automatically for any vehicle departing. I'd left my car there all night only once and hadn't slept well.

I coasted to the dead end, hid the Shelby, secured its garage. A night light in Carmen's bedroom. Her friend in for a visit. He must have parked out on Fleming. I pondered the call I needed to make while Teresa and I walked to my yard. I wasn't quite prepared to enter my house without making sure no one waited inside.

I stashed the Shelby's distributor cap in the Weber grill. Then I peed in the bushes. Teresa, not to be outdone, squatted and peed next to the mango tree. Something about team spirit and cool weather . . .

I wasn't accustomed to thinking like a commando. I faked it. Anyone waiting would have heard the Shelby return. They'd have jumped us while I was locking up. Or watering the foliage. Maybe they knew more about stealth and preferred to wait until I entered the house. Should I go flat on the porch floor, reach up, twist the door handle, hope that the gunfire went high? Or walk on in? I wasn't going to find the carpet cutter's head next to the kitchen sink.

I hand-signaled Teresa. She understood. We went in opposite directions, walked the perimeter a second time, checked each window. There was no way to enter without two keys or causing damage. We found no damage. I waved her away from me, unlocked the door, walked in, flipped the lights. I waited for the bullet I'd never hear.

I didn't hear a thing. I waved Teresa inside and dialed the phone.

A drowsy voice: "Do you know what fucking time it is?"

A mental picture: Liska in a pitch-black bedroom, knocking over an ashtray, grasping the Caller ID module.

I said, "It's important."

"A problem worth waking me, this hour of night? I'm nine-one-one? I've been asleep all of forty minutes."

"Your deputies are pulling bad people out of the water at the north end of Blimp Road. Find out who they are before you release them."

"Who are they, your Stock Island car thieves?"

"They tried to steal mine."

"This is a great midnight chat."

"I can explain in the morning. They shot at me, if that matters."

"Like I said, nine-one-one." He clicked off.

Bad planning.

I'd lost Double Jeopardy. First, I'd pissed off the sheriff. Second, it was better than fifty-fifty that Chicken Neck would check with the deputies. If someone was injured, he'd send his boys after me as a witness. If anyone had been shot—God forbid, a deputy—they'd find a prosecutor to charge me as an accessory. Even if it was just two wet renegades, they'd want to know my connection. They'd check my house and, on Liska's direction, Teresa's condo. They'd detain me until the crack-of-dawn office hours. I needed more sleep than that. I didn't want to drain the checking account to the favor of a bondsman. Or open-endorse the deed to my house so I could walk free by lunchtime.

I called Sam. Marnie answered on the third ring. Immediate concern in her voice. I told her about the chase. I asked her to keep her ears open about a car in the water, but not to connect me to it. She handed off the phone. I told Sam I'd get a room at Eden House.

"I've got a guest room right here," he said.

"If they can find Marnie's Jeep, they can find your house. You might want to think that way."

"Strength in numbers."

"I don't want to drag a menace to your place."

He grunted, paused, then said, "You need a day on the water. Good for your health."

I found the phone number for Eden House. I recognized Helen's drowsy voice. She told me they were booked up. I thought again about strength in numbers. I called Sam to warn him about incoming house guests. Asked for a ten-minute moratorium on shooting at shadows.

I called a taxi, asked for a pickup in front of Eden House. Then I dug out a foul-weather jacket for Teresa and walked her to the cab. She said she'd stop at her condo, to pick up her toothbrush and work clothes for the morning.

I asked her to start carrying her purse pistol.

Back at the house I grabbed a flannel shirt and a flashlight, and unlocked the Cannondale. I beam-reached Southard, let the breeze push me down Simonton to the Atlantic side. People struggled toward me on bicycles and mopeds, bundled in heavy coats, locked into their own worlds. I passed a woman on a motor scooter who'd mastered the art of dragging on a cigarette while doing twenty into a fifteen-knot headwind.

Funny how outerwear suggests biographies during cold weather in Key West. The last time many residents had worn a protective coat had been the first day they'd hit the Florida line. They refused to buy new ones, given rare cold snaps and no wish to travel northward during winter. Old-fashioned varsity jackets, fat thermal parkas, foul-weather gear, preppy zip-ups, fraternity logos—was that Rastafarian once a Sigma Nu?—plaid woolen coats, Irish knit pullovers. Dozens of hooded sweatshirts. Once a year the Goodwill sold out of coats. Not that real-world style ever ranked high among locals' concerns . . .

In the dim light of Sam's rarely used extra bedroom—
a twenty-five-watt bedside lamp, the dappling of a neighbor's yard light through foliage—I saw a vacant glaze in
Teresa's eyes. Fatigue, plus her thoughts about what had
happened on Blimp Road. As I undressed for bed she
moved close to me. It wasn't pure affection. It was the
jitters. On other occasions each article of removed clothing
marked another wee act of love, another rung up the ladder
to our pleasing. This time our moves were mechanical.

We both wore T-shirts in bed, nothing else. We held on
tightly, absorbing each other at first for security more than
passion. We took comfort in the knowledge of chance, the
momentary belief that our problems were small jokes in the
big world when we held each other. We talked with our
breathing, adjusted pillows, brushed the sheets thigh-to-
thigh, minute after minute, before relaxation took over, before we shut out everything not us. Our closeness slowly
became passion, touches became tranquility. Teresa moved
on top, set the rhythm, slowed, wanted something else but
the bed was too small and we were almost there, and then
she was there and she gave me trembling permission to join
her, to melt together, to keep the big world outside the door,
away from the bedsheet, out of our minds.

I was almost asleep when Teresa smoothed my damp
hair. She mumbled, "The way you drove tonight? Promise
me that you knew how it would end."

"I had a plan, and it worked out okay."

"Just tell me you knew."

"I knew."

"You've got something to tell me?"

"Can it wait until morning?"

She grasped my upper arm like a ship's lifeline. "Fine."

When you hear a woman say "Fine," in a certain tone,
you'd better get ready to pay one, in some form or another.

13

I slept lightly in spite of the lovemaking. I heard noises—
structural creaks, footsteps in Sam's yard, whispers of
home invaders. Palm fronds ticked the tin roof. I woke
before dawn after a truck on South shook the neighborhood.
Two guttural Harleys followed. Cats prowled and whined.

The road chase replayed itself in my mind. I wished that
the deputy had not shown up. I wished that I'd been alone.
I'd have found a way to slip back to the boat ramp, hide
between the mosquitoes and random bullets, find out who'd
been so eager to chat. Find out why they'd wanted to swipe
my car.

One solid fact. No one was after my money, if they
knew anything about me. Financial truth was nigh. I'd love
to turn him down, tell Mercer Holloway that I had a conflict. But I needed a boost. A freelancer living off the sav-
ings account needs career repair. Then again, location shots
are difficult for a man hiding from cops and felons. For
health and cash-flow reasons, I needed to stop the crap,
soon.

Teresa stirred when I got out of bed. Her eyes asked a
question.

I asked my own: "Did you tell anyone we were going
to Mangrove's for dinner?"

She shook her head.

"I'm going to get a paper. I'll call you at work."

She pursed her lips for a good-bye kiss. We spent a minute holding each other before I left.

I pulled on my jeans, tucked in my flannel shirt. It would be colder at dawn than it had been at midnight. I borrowed a windbreaker from Sam's pegboard. Even my bicycle felt creaky in the cold, made sounds similar to cat howls. I knew that the submerged car couldn't have made the papers' deadlines. But I wanted to check the *Herald* for news about the deaths of Richard Engram and Richard Engram.

I didn't have pocket change for the vending flip-downs. Valladares's newsstand—Key West's daybreak cultural center—wouldn't open for twenty more minutes. I seized the moment. How often does anyone get the chance to ride the center line of Duval?

Key West at sunrise is closest to the island of twenty-five years ago. Smells of hot Cuban bread and night-blooming vines. Air fresh with the salt tang of onshore breezes before being weighted by exhaust fumes. Muted pre-dawn grays turning into pastels fuzzy with the humidity that will blow away in the first daylight hour. A few people were up early. A few staggered home from a long night of it.

A lemming-like tourist line had crowded Duval's top end. Folks got up early for this. They could stay in their cars, glance at the Gulf of Mexico, turn left, continue on their way. No chance of spray or ocean scent soiling their vacation duds. One after another they found the dead end, U-turned through huge puddles. They thought it was rain-water. They did not understand high tide and low pavement. The salty seawater would take two years to cause its havoc. The tourists would forget about puddles. They would blame the car makers for faulty brake rotors and rotten shock absorbers.

Inside the Pier House, I got change from the desk clerk, bought a paper. The lobby smelled of eucalyptus and stale coffee. A nervous couple waited for an airport taxi, checked and rechecked their watches. They asked the desk clerk to confirm the van. The tropical sojourn had failed to chill their inner turmoil.

I sifted for the Keys section, found two follow-up articles. No names—"pending notification of next of kin." No incident details beyond "foul play" and "under investigation." Authorities refused to release causes of death after Monday's autopsies by Medical Examiner Larry Riley. Sheriff Fred Liska "declined comment on rumors or leaks at this time." No mention of the head found in Marnie's Jeep.

The lobby's French doors swung open. Butler Dunwoody and two men in suits—therefore not locals—entered the lobby. Dunwoody stopped, shook my hand. He sent the men ahead, told them to follow signs to the beachside restaurant. No introductions. He'd see them in a minute. Butler eyeballed the desk clerk, then asked to speak with me in the motel's atrium.

"Your photography . . ." He studied the water fountain, the broad philodendrons. He avoided facing me. "I need building progress documents for the big city bankers. After that ugly deal Sunday, all the rules changed."

"Thanks for asking. I'm booked the next several weeks."

He nodded, refused to show disappointment. "Crazy island you live on, Rutledge. I always heard in college that the farther you drove down the Keys, the smaller the islands became, the narrower the bridges. Somebody said I'd know I hit Key West when I found twenty naked people smoking weed around a sun-faded stop sign at the end of the pavement. I spent all day yesterday on city business, arguing with a woman who spoke no English. I mean, permits? Builders in Florida don't ask permission. They ask forgiveness."

"Those women speak English as well as you do," I said. "If she stuck to Spanish, you'd already pissed her off."

"This is stuff Engram handled for me. I explained to the zoning man, time is of the essence. Let's straighten out this bogus dispute on fence height. He says to me, 'I'm sixty-two. My only hurry in this world is to move my boongie

out of the path of a choo-choo train. And there ain't one
here.' That's the mentality I'm up against. Sweet Jesus."

"It's a bitch to get on their wavelength, Dunwoody.
Sometimes even the townies complain. Not being from
here, you need to watch your back."

A family of four walked past in shorts and T-shirts. Ca-
nadians, unaware that every Key West resident was bun-
dling up against the chill. Dunwoody delayed our chat until
they'd entered the lobby.

"I thought I was on the right course," he said. "I'd heard
stories about classic business failures on the island, how the
machine could grind you up, suck your money. It'd all happen so clever, you couldn't blame any single person or
official office. Leave you standing, thinking, I'm lucky to
still have my shorts. The people in power call you 'amigo'
and 'bubba.' They build houses on Key Haven and boats
in Lauderdale. They sit around the Yacht Club packing in
prime rib and twice-stuffed potatoes, and they won't let me
join. I heard about, what, three or four commuter airline
companies in the seventies? Air Sunshine and a couple others. I heard tales of fifteen bistros, cafés, future five-star
restaurants. Airplane tours of the Tortugas, electric car
rental outfits, you name it. All I'm doing, I'm knocking up
a three-story, traditional-design shopping arcade."

I said, "Some people don't see it as innocuous."

He looked at me, nodded. "Some people think I'm an
asshole, too."

"You begging an argument?"

"Look, I'm still alive, still working. Unlike my right-
hand man. Tell you what. I've got to comply with the Monroe County Comprehensive Plan, the county's Rate of
Growth Ordinance, the Utility Board's Advisory Committee, the Monroe County Tourist Development Council,
Florida Keys Audubon, and the City Board of Adjustment.
That's just part of the list. Hell, I could be building nuclear
warheads in a lean-to and not have to deal with so many
damn rules, so much petty oversight. These people are try-

ing to preserve their island by passing laws. Laws never changed the mind of a community."

"They're meant to change the actions of newcomers," I said. "For fifty years in the middle of the last century, poverty preserved the island. When money showed up, the laws came right behind."

"So you claim a state of poverty's ideal?"

I said, "There's an excuse the real estate people use, that land tends to find its 'highest and best' use. But I see it like this: When hard cash and greed meet at closing, some piece of turf's headed downhill."

He shook his head. "Let me tell you something. I've been saving this up. You're the lucky listener who gets to hear it first. Before I tore up that parking lot to build my building, before I closed on the property, I did my homework. I memorized the title abstract. I went to the library and got the local historian to help me research the land. It will pain you to learn that, in 1952, someone tore down a lovely piece of architecture to pave that lot. Before the destruction of that building, which had fallen into disuse as a sponge-storage shed and flop hotel, another building had occupied the land. That one had been designed by a boat builder named Sweeting out of Green Turtle Key in the Bahamas. It was damaged in the hurricanes of 1909 and 1910. Its owner decided to level it rather than repair it. Before that, a three-story building identical to the one that's still at Caroline and Peacon Lane—on the southeast corner—was owned by a ship chandler and barrel maker named Allen. That one burned in 1886, when the city's steam fire truck was getting repaired in New York. The fire started at Fleming and Duval and worked its way northwest to Whitehead and Greene and northeast to my lot. All those changes happened on a single piece of property.

"So I ask you, who's the bad guy? The one who tears down? Or the one who builds? I just happen to be in line to build right now."

I kept my mouth shut. I admired his absorption of history.

"Would you like this island so much if *nothing* ever changed? Like a song repeating itself three hundred and sixty-five times a year? Like every time you turned on your TV, you watched reruns of *Hee Haw*?"

He'd made good points. I didn't try to interrupt.

"I'm unpopular," he said. "I know that. I'm flamboyant. My mannerisms get me ridiculed. I came to town, I wanted to turn a vacant lot into a source of income for me and my future tenants. I thought I could add some spirit to Old Town. Change is inevitable. And any change brings criticism. It goes with the territory. Wasn't there a city commissioner who learned that change is unstoppable? After he left office, he went back to his profession—he was a builder, too—and worked on the same principle. If people are going to build, money's going to come in. Why not have it be a guy with a sense of taste? Why shouldn't I earn a profit, instead of the other guy? It's the American way."

"You're a patriot, no argument."

"And here I am, treated like a damn carpetbagger. My architect tried to mimic some old island designs. The building codes wouldn't let him. That's typical of the crap I see every day. The only person saving my sanity is Mercer Holloway. You know the man?"

"Everybody in town knows Holloway." Dunwoody would find out sooner or later: "That's who hired me for the next two or three weeks."

He stared at me, nodded as his thoughts went inward.

I heard a shrill beep. Butler Dunwoody reached behind his back, pulled out a cell phone the size of an audiocassette. He said, "Right." Then, "Put him on." He listened a while longer, then asked, "What time was that?" He closed the phone without saying good-bye.

"You had a visitor yesterday," he said. "Lady in a Jag ragtop?"

Oh, boy. I hesitated, then nodded.

"Fuck, man. You're standing right here, telling me to

watch my back with the bureaucrats. And you're stabbing me in the gut."

"You don't have to worry about Heidi."

"I know that. I may not be her best memory, but I'm the best deal she'll ever have. You, on the other hand . . . Jesus." Butt Dunwoody spun away. He punched numbers into his phone as he hurried to the beach restaurant.

I leaned against the cement-block wall next to the Chart Room, listened to the hypnotizing fountain, stared at the pool area. I wondered how men like Dunwoody and Philip Kaiser made it day to day, coexisted with their inner fears and jealousies. On the other hand, Dunwoody, with his history speech, had not come off as a robber baron, or the sexist sauce abuser Sam and Marnie had described. He'd come off a planner and thinker. A good builder. Or a top-notch criminal.

Suddenly, Donovan Cosgrove, Holloway's son-in-law, emerged from the west entrance to the pool-bordering walkway. He approached Dunwoody, shook hands, continued with him to the restaurant. An odd pairing. But Julie Kaiser had told me that Cosgrove was acting as her father's on-site liaison. Maybe helping to calm the bankers.

Someone already had swiped my newspaper from the Pier House lobby. I used the courtesy phone. No answer at Sam's house. No answer at Teresa's office. No messages on my machine. I dialed Carmen Sosa's number. In the background, when she picked up, salsa music full blast. The primary sign of her morning-afters, not hung over, but waking after a romantic encounter.

I said, "You're not at work?"

"I couldn't wake up. I called in sick."

"Lovesick?"

"Bet your ass. I'm a brand-new woman."

"Any two-toned four-doors in the lane this morning?"

"Two at once, until ten minutes ago. One city and one county. They were out there, kickin' dirt, gabbin', playing their police radios on high volume. One's still out there.

The county guy. He's got a kid on Maria's Little League team. You rob a bank, my sweet man?"

The city? Liska had asked for help? "Worse. I ticked off our new sheriff."

"Was that his girlfriend's sleek roadster by your house yesterday?"

I said, "Did you come home with your cabana boy?"

"I came somewhere. Heaven, I think. Once at noon, twice last night. You wanna make something of it?"

"He ratted me out to his boss."

"Don't tell me. Not with that bimbo you bitched about . . ."

"No, Carmen," I said. "Not what you think."

"What I think doesn't matter, my love."

"You be home a while longer?"

"You know my rule—after the Bone Island Mambo, I wake up and dance the tango. I've barely begun. The bottoms of my slippers aren't even warm yet. Please stay out of trouble."

It took me four minutes to reach Cobo Pharmacy—less than a half block from the lane. I called from the coin phone on the store's front wall, donated thirty-five cents to Phoenix Telecom LLC, wherever they are. You can bet they're not in Key West. Out of breath, Carmen said, "All clear."

It took less than two minutes to lock the Cannondale, change my shirt, chug a quart of OJ, grab my camera bag, extra film, my helmet, and Mercer Holloway's list of prospective photo sites. I heard the momentary whoop of a police siren on Fleming. It alarmed me until I ran three rational thoughts in a row. Probably urging some motorist to move from the Eden House loading zone, to quit blocking traffic. No new messages on the machine.

Time to haul ass on the Kawasaki.

Near the door I saw the envelope I'd probably stepped on coming in. Tommy Tucker's TNT Security letterhead on cheap bond. He'd slid it under the left-side French door that I never opened. A check from Mercer Holloway. Twenty-five hundred dollars. No note.

I rode south on White Street. I had no idea what to do or where to go. I obeyed the speed limit. I recalled a man saying that the only people who drive the speed limit in Broward and Dade are on parole. A traffic slip will send a violator back to the cement for another year. I couldn't unload my road rage. An empty yellow antifreeze jug blew out of a pickup truck's bed, made a hollow slap against my helmet. I smelled Cuban coffee, bacon on a grill. I wanted some but didn't want to stop moving.

My mind drifted to Teresa's words at Mangrove Mama's. I'd worried that, by working for Holloway, attaching myself to what he represented, I'd be part of the island's growth problem, and not part of its solution. She'd suggested that my photography was not going to make a difference. In pattern with the previous hundred and seventy years, the island would change anyway.

She was right. Change is inevitable.

But the *flavor* of change is within our control.

There'd been a time when motor vehicles could meander to the end of White Street Pier. A driver could park, walk to the south wall, be the closest American to Cuba. It always has been a fine place for solitude. Folks there, fishermen and sightseers, would leave you alone to think. To ponder the crap that trespasses paradise. The county remodeled the pier a few years ago, created a pedestrian bridge to the old center pier section. The county commissioners claimed it would better appeal to tourists. But no one could ignore the fact that a prominent politician lived in the condo just east of the pier, and that Mother Nature insisted on depositing noxious seaweed on the condo's beach. The remodeling included a spillway so the tides could reduce the buildup of stinky flotsam. Lucky break for the politician.

These days you must come on foot or bicycle. I parked the Kawasaki in a slot near the West Martello Garden Center. I carried my helmet past the AIDS memorial, crossed the new bridge, and hiked to pier's end. The farther from land, the less lee effect. At the broad pierhead apron, the wind, which had clocked slightly west, cut through Sam's jacket. I've never known why fifty-five in Key West feels colder than twenty-five in Ohio. I felt new hunger and wished I'd stopped at Pepe's or Harpoon Harry's.

I looked at the south edge of the island. From a hundred yards off the coast, the place looked almost the same as it had when I'd arrived during the Carter administration. Builders had completed the four-unit condo, much to the disappointment of growth opponents. The "indigenous park" at White and Atlantic—once a large open area where weekly flea markets thrived—had been paved, turned into a parking lot decorated with a token cluster of native shrubs. A little green to please the protesters of asphalt. On a tree-shaded grassy field opposite that corner, an elderly man and his wife had operated a miniature train on weekends, sold rides to children for the coins in their pockets. That acreage had been annexed and fenced by Higgs Beach County Park. Another new condo, the Beach Club, squatted up east. To the west was the storm-ruined Higgs Beach Pier and Henry Flagler's Casa Marina Hotel, shuttered in the 1950s, restored in the seventies by Marriott. Then the building called Southernmost House, though it wasn't. From my angle, given the passing of time, not much had gone away.

Such vantage points were harder to find each year.

I pulled out Mercer Holloway's Group One property list, put my back to the breeze so the pages wouldn't rip. A strange assortment of buildings: retail shops, an apartment complex, a bank on the boulevard. No definition beyond, I assumed, Mercer Holloway's name on the deeds. He'd said that he disagreed with his tax assessments. But he'd claimed that "tree-huggers and zero-growth nuts will thank us." He'd said that the island would reap "future benefits."

A career politician had begged me to take him at his word.

I suffered my second stroke of paranoia for the morning: a siren carried down White Street with the wind. It sounded like the siren was heading right for me. Then a fire engine appeared, turned up Flagler.

I gazed to sea for several minutes. A shrimp boat had anchored to the southeast, its gear laid out port and starboard to stabilize the craft for better daytime snoozing. A handsome, wooden-sparred ketch ran with the wind and against the Hawk Channel current. Full main, working jib, a single reef in the mizzen. She trailed an inflatable runabout. The sight took me back to a sail transit I'd made with Sam Wheeler in the mid-eighties, a delivery to Bimini, a favor for a fishing client. Another case of going blind into a situation without preview of events that would spin out of control. A crisis where a trustworthy companion had saved the day.

Holloway's concept, whatever it was, might be wonderful for all involved. It also might be the boondoggle of the millennium, the scam to beat all. One thing came to mind. He'd said of his daughters, "I don't want to deprive them of the joys of making their own fortunes." The line suggested a limit to each daughter's inheritance.

Whatever happened, my name would be attached. I wanted the income. I wanted to know more.

The Sunrise Rotary Club's elegant compass rose told me I was located at 24° 32.724' north by 81° 47.009' west. I didn't know where I stood with my conscience, my reputation, my bank balance, or the law. I wanted a nap on the sun-warmed concrete. I walked the bridge off the apron, passed two men straddling their stopped bicycles, reading victims' names embossed on the AIDS memorial. Tears streamed down their faces.

Like the man who'd stonewalled Dunwoody, I was in no hurry to make decisions. No hurry to do anything except remove myself from craziness, from the past two days' gruesome events. I hadn't been to Epcot in years. I needed a quiet few days in Cedar Key, or a couple of nights slumming the bars on St. Pete Beach. My psyche required a therapeutic maxing of credit cards.

For some stupid reason I drove the Kawasaki back into Key West.

14

I slowed at Peary Court, where Palm Avenue's utility-pole forest intersects Eisenhower. I wanted to search the far end of Charterboat Row for *Fancy Fool*, Wheeler's bare-bones flats boat. I needed to connect with Sam for advice. I rode the turf Mercer Holloway had claimed was his North Beach childhood playground. The little I'd read about North Beach had described cork and sea-grape trees, patch mangrove, sea oats, pristine sandy beach. Holloway had reminisced about the days before it was "lost in development." By my calculations, he would have to be ninety to have played there. I could not imagine how the man could honor the past—Junkanoo music, antique lithographs, fond memories, the house he maintained—and at the same time ambush the future.

I started up Garrison Bight's bridge. Most of the charter boats bobbed in their slips. Captains reclined in canvas sling chairs, in groups, gazing around the parking strip, bullshitting, spitting downwind. Mates aboard the bigger yachts pretended to spruce topside while scoping the sidewalks for possible customers. Even with the chill January air, the day marked an odd lull for the charter fleet. I guessed that Wheeler would be out with a client, some permit chaser or bonefisherman who'd booked the same week every year for years. Given the shallow currents favored by those fish and the difficulty in finding fish in roiled water, a northwest wind would make it a short day.

At bridge peak I looked south. Bingo. Wheeler, alone, in his sixteen-foot Maverick Mirage, coasted toward me, leaving the Bight's dockage basin. I hit the cycle's squawky horn as Sam glided under the west end. I didn't catch his ear. Then I stopped in a hurry. Traffic had backed up from the Roosevelt signal—a tourist-season normality in recent years. I saw no activity at the dockmaster's office, one or two people at the cube-shaped public rest room. No need to double-check for police cruisers. My mental radar already was tuned to that frequency. I waited for a break in traffic, crossed the double-yellow, and jumped the curb into the municipal dock parking area. Sam nudged his throttle between marker 29 and the red 30 triangle, then saw me walking Dolphin Pier, angled over, beckoned me aboard.

I pointed to my illegally parked Kawasaki. Sam pointed northward. Our mutual friend, Carl Wirthwein, owned a home on the spit next to the yacht club. Problem solved, and an invitation to the backcountry. I returned to the bridge, waited in line for the light, hurried up Roosevelt, swung left onto Hilton Haven. The narrow peninsula had been created during the island's first major facelift, the heralded arrival of Henry Flagler's Florida East Coast Railway. By dredging and filling, engineers had built a peninsula for the railway straight to Key West Harbor. The hurricane of September 1935 had shut down the rails, and these days the fill to either side of the bay-access cut offered perfect weather protection for the Bight.

I left the motorcycle alongside a jasmine trellis in Wirthwein's carport. *Fancy Fool* bobbed a few yards off his short dock. Sam's flat-bottomed skiff was pure utility, with little freeboard, designed for shoal water where schooling fish offer their challenge to light-tackle enthusiasts. Anglers invest plenty in equipment and guides. With rare exceptions, they release fish after battle. The pastime was reputed to be more addictive than sex or drugs. I'd always been a better spectator.

Sam nudged the dock with his port bow so I could step aboard.

I noticed no fishing gear. "How's it going, Captain?"

He looked over the top of his sunglasses. "Da boat she float. You?"

"I keep getting bottle caps that say, 'Sorry, try again.' Key West used to be a quaint drinking village with a fishing problem."

"Been a long, strange year. All two weeks of it."

"Getting weirder," I said.

"You missed a great breakfast in my kitchen this morning. Staff Sergeant Pissoff and Corporal Malcontent. They were being extra polite about sharing the bagel cutter and butter knife."

"Too many lightning bolts in the front yard?"

"Sunday the crap was in your lap," he said. "Yesterday it reached everyone else."

"I've been wasting time, dodging the threat."

"Instead of?"

"Instead of trying to figure what's behind it all."

Sam idled out of the Bight, then kicked the ninety-horse Yamaha up to 3,500 revs. *Fancy Fool* came instantly to a plane, put astern the Sigsbee Park backyards of Navy Officer Housing. Sam dropped the engine speed. We slapped along wavetops, into the wind, north into Florida Bay. Aiming for mangrove islands in the Lower Harbor Keys, we wove between backcountry markers, old wood stakes topped with Day-Glo-painted triangles. We passed an old purloined stop sign, now faded, covered with guano. We skirted hammocks, ran past Cayo Agua. Startled birds flushed. Cormorants like jet fighters went for max speed at shallow altitude, then lifted for safety and perspective. Frigate birds patrolled, stood guard aloft. White seabirds played in the fresh breeze. More glare than detail reflected off the choppy water, kept us from a clear view of the bay bottom.

The view took me back to a picnic in the Mud Keys four months earlier. Teresa and I had been dating only two or three weeks, dancing around our relationship, fascinated by the strength of our fast attraction. While wary of instant romance, we didn't want to threaten the momentum. We'd accepted an invitation to explore the Mud Keys aboard *The Conch*, the boxy pontoon boat owned by my amigo Dink Bruce. A day-cruising masterpiece, *The Conch* resembles a four-poster bed with a forty-horse outboard, two lawn chairs, and a ladder to the sundeck on the canopy. Years ago Charles Kuralt cruised aboard her, wrote about it in a best-selling book. You decline a Dink Bruce offer at your own peril. A local woman once turned down an afternoon in the lakes with the excuse that it was her only day for laundry. He never asked her again. More than social rebuke, a need for solitude had motivated our acceptance.

Four of us—Dink and his companion, and Teresa and I—rode *The Conch*. Marnie and Sam joined us in *Fancy Fool*. They brought along a CD blaster with an assortment of jazz albums—Branford Marsalis, Paul Desmond, and an old favorite of mine, Donald Fagen's *The Nightfly*. We beat the humidity by taking frequent dips in the water. The bugs never found us. Teresa and I checked each other for sunburn, kept the humor rolling, put on flippers and snorkled, explored meandering channels. Her eyes widened at the sight of a ray, only five feet below us, its wings almost touching the mangrove roots. Small fish checked us out. We swam behind a thick hammock, still could hear the peaceful music. Someone loudly accused us of spawning.

Later, at my house, we'd made love before showering, then again after washing away salt and sun lotion. The day had secured the link between us.

Just beyond the small hammock called Fish Hawk Key, Sam slowed, cut the ignition, and let *Fancy Fool* drift. In no hurry, he went forward, pulled a small stockless anchor from a compact well, and chucked it into four feet of water.

I looked around, then saw Sam's reason for stopping. A mile to the northeast, a guide poled his skiff into the wind as an angler on the bow cast in our direction. Wheeler's sense of nautical courtesy was as strident as any of his waterborne traits—knot bending, neatness, storage, maintenance. His home was just as meticulous. His only failing was his refusal to clean or sell his ancient Ford Bronco. Friends allowed him the eccentricity.

Sam flipped opened a live-bait well. He pulled out two ice-cold beers. "Top off that coffee?"

I accepted, but my stomach reminded me that I'd skipped food. I tilted the bottle toward the other skiff.

Sam said, "Captain Turk's *Flats Broke*. Fishing a local man. Holloway's son-in-law. The real estate guy."

It must be Philip Kaiser. "You'd think somebody local would pick better weather."

Sam lifted his beer in toast. "We didn't, and you needed this. You looked more windblown on the dock than you do now."

"I needed to get out of town. I'm a wanted man."

"Not by your girlfriend. She thinks you're holding out some great clue."

"I am."

We sat back and watched the fishermen. I described the car chase and the relation of the slayings to previous murders. I unloaded my secret, the photo-proved connection between the deaths on Caroline Street and Stock Island.

"I knew the copycat part," he said. "It'll make the paper tomorrow morning. They got an anonymous tip. Marnie got the assignment to follow up. She learned that someone else in the office was prepping a piece on the city's unsolved murder cases. She wondered if the tipster was the person who dropped the stinky, blue-faced head in her car."

I parked that detail. Holloway or Liska or Hayes could've tipped.

"The FDLE took her Jeep," Sam added. "Told her to pray hard that they didn't find evidence. One man let slip a remark about 'weeks of pain-in-the-butt storage.' They wanted sample fingerprints from anyone who's been in the vehicle the past six weeks. Hell, Marnie loaned it to a girl in the office when we went south."

"Teresa said she was doing okay with it all."

"The head, no problem. Why they picked her Jeep, that's a biggie."

"Butt and I interacted this morning. The boy's got two flip sides. He's an entrepreneur with an eye for detail, and he's an island-history buff. Also, he doesn't trust his lady friend."

"He's a sloppy drunk and a fool with his money," said Sam. "He's heavy into nostalgia, and he knows good carpentry. You give him a reason not to trust her?"

I shook my head, waved off the idea of monkey business. "Did you know he's tied into Mercer Holloway?"

"Politicians are wonderful people. Retired politicians, every last one of them, are mysteriously successful. He could do worse."

I brought up Holloway's offer, and my misgivings. "There's a catch to it all," I added. "I'm taking this moral stance, imposing standards on people. The developers are no different from Henry Flagler. He tore up the place, dredging and filling, brought in his money, he was given a hero's welcome. The place is more crowded these days. That's the difference."

"That's why the standards are different."

"But I'm not a native defending the homeland. In an ecological sense, I'm a newcomer, too. My roots don't go deep in the coral rock."

"Tell me about roots. I come from a long history of dead ends."

"Your father? You never said much . . ."

"Born loser," said Sam. "Broken spoke in the wheel of progress. The anti-Renaissance man. Up north, Muncie, my folks got married, he was a milkman. They phased out milkmen. He got a job selling Packards and, sure as hell, Packard went out of business. Went over to the Edsel dealership, slick as you please. Came to Florida to try something new. Packed everything worth keeping into a Chevy panel truck, along with a bag of hard-boiled eggs and thermos of coffee, and made the long drive. Moved me and my mother to the swamp. He told everyone he knew that he was going to be a surgeon. Then he'd laugh and say, 'Tree surgeon, get it?' A real maverick."

I'd never heard Sam talk about his family this way. The topic always had been off-limits, like discussion of heroics that had earned his military battle decorations. "You've got sisters, right?"

Sam peered over the gunwale at propeller ruts in the bay bottom. "I grew up with three little sisters. My father thought he was cute. They were born after we came south. He made my mother call them Florence, Lorie, and Ida. Put together, the names spelled Florida. Good thing they all were girls. Two are married, live back up north. Lorie disappeared. Back in the eighties."

"They must've been young when you went to the Far East."

"Oh, yeah. Grade school. There I was, a pump jockey in Andytown, which then was the Everglades. The intersection of Florida 84 and U.S. 27, out by that man-made wonder of sluice, the North New River Canal. Pumping gas was one of only two jobs in Andytown. The other job was pumping gas. You might say my future looked brighter in the Cambodian jungle." Sam laughed to himself. "Those stories about boys who went off to 'Nam, did a year, then came home? They'd knock on their parents' door and a stranger would answer it? The parents had moved away, and the letter with their new address hadn't reached the grunt in-country. Well, I came back to Andytown, not only to no parents, but the whole damned village was gone. Obliterated by a freeway interchange, Interstate 75, at the start of Alligator Alley. Not even the *real* Alligator Alley. All of it paved and landscaped. Like those cities up North that ceased to exist when valleys were turned into reservoirs. I look back, I think that was the main reason I re-upped, stayed on active duty, and went the long twenty with Uncle Sugar. No place to call home."

I said, "Where would you live if you left Key West? Alabama?"

"My cabin up there's too small to be any kind of permanent place. I guess I'd drive north through Florida until I saw the first road sign that says 'Bridge May Freeze in Cold Weather.' That hard freeze line is my imaginary fence. I'd find that sign, I'd turn around, come back fifty miles, and find a home. But hell, I don't know for sure where I'd go."

"I assume you found your parents."

"What was left of the old man. I think the remote life got to him. Nothing in the boonies to jostle his mind. He suffered . . . I don't know what to call it. A hermit's senility, I guess. Some people thrive on it, like that photographer up there, Clyde Butcher. The man's a genius. He must live for the isolation. I've always figured my old man died to prove he could finally do something right. My mother moved to Hallandale, learned to be a keypunch operator. One more occupation by the wayside. Then she became a typesetter at the Fort Lauderdale *Sun-Sentinel*. Computers killed that job, too. Like she'd caught the bug from my father, got phased out of life. She said she got to see Ronald Reagan elected. It made her happy about something before she croaked. She put up with a lot. She gave me a good childhood before we came south."

Our chat lapsed into silence. I wondered how someone with Sam's background had evolved into the man I'd known for fifteen years, a little more. Career men I'd known in the service, the "lifers," had tended to be refugees from rural America. For many, their military years had insulated them even farther from the mainstream. But here was a man whose thought patterns went beyond linear, a man who provided me week-to-week common sense, who liked to play devil's advocate with consistent, clear thinking. The man who, long ago, had saved my life during a storm in the Gulf Stream, and who claimed to this day that I had saved his. He'd rarely discussed the past, and for damned sure never used it as a crutch.

Sam said, "So someone who mugged you is now dead."

"Must've been killed within two hours of attacking me."

"And his head appeared in my woman's Jeep."

I juggled the facts. "Someone's sick game is pointing fingers at me."

"And at Marnie and Butler, too," said Sam. "Can we bank on the fact that you didn't do anything like tell a witness or the sheriff or a detective that you wanted to find Bug?"

Oh, shit.

Sam read my forehead furrows. "What was your exact wording?"

"Trying to remember."

"Who got to hear it?"

"Dexter Hayes, Junior."

We were drawn to the sound of Captain Turk's engine. Turk and Kaiser stood at the center console. *Flats Broke* popped quickly to a plane and began to circle toward us, avoiding shallows in the center basin.

Sam pointed to the northwest. "Look what he's running from. We need to boogie. We're going to get our asses kicked." Four hundred feet above the water, under a high scattering of stratocumulus, a smudged-charcoal storm pushed southward at thirty-five or forty knots. A strip of white weather, like frosting on a gray countertop, loomed ten miles farther off. "These usually happen in late spring," added Sam. "Time to go drink beer on the porch."

Flats Broke approached from the east. Captain Turk slowed fifty yards off so his wake wash could dissipate, not pitch *Fancy Fool*. Philip Kaiser, with the thick neck and stocky build of an ex-jock, stood even with Turk's five-ten and matched his muscular bulk. He showed only slight graying near his sideburns. I wondered if he'd given his hair store-bought help. He wore bleached Levi's and ratty Topsider sneaks, a threadbare denim shirt. In the spooky light, his skin had an olive tone. He'd let his hair go long, perhaps to mask encroaching baldness.

"Thanks for hanging off," called Turk. "You didn't miss much."

"Bullshit," yelled Sam. "I saw you hook and release two

fish in twenty minutes. Bet a hundred bucks, you'll be right there in the morning."

In spite of what Julie had said about Kaiser's viewing me as a threat, he nodded to acknowledge me. "Don't usually see you without your camera," he said.

"Day off for everybody." I thrust my arm toward the scenery around us.

"Half day for me." He scowled. "I'll take it. I understand you've got some old pictures of the Island City."

"A few, boxed away."

"Love to see 'em someday." His face radiated patronage. "You're going to work with my father-in-law?"

"I'm not sure yet."

"What's he got you doing?"

Why wouldn't Kaiser already know that? I shrugged as if I didn't know. "That's why I'm not sure."

He said, "Watch yourself. He's a crafty old coot."

Odd that a man of his success and civic stature could feel threatened by his wife's friends. People respected Philip Kaiser, enjoyed his company. He'd always been part of the in-crowd, tuned in to island humor, running off in groups to Miami Dolphins or Heat games, conversant in topics common to gatherings of bachelors, power brokers, the newly wedded. He'd rarely used foul language. He was reputed to be scrupulous in business dealings. Being Holloway's son-in-law had put him in positions of favor. I'd heard that he had gone out of his way to be fair to associates, to include in sure-bet real estate deals friends who'd needed help.

Turk checked the sky. "First to the dock gets Mud Keys in the morning."

Sam laughed. "Turk, you just lost a hundred bucks."

The *Flats Broke* idled away from us, aimed across shallow water to the meandering channel, down-tilted its engine, accelerated to speed.

"Philip Kaiser is an odd one." Sam twisted his ignition key. The motor popped and rumbled.

"I'm used to his shit. Anyone who knows Julie is the enemy."

"He's one of them? They never get it, do they? They spend years driving away competition, wind up driving away the spouse."

"Or whuppin' on the spouse," I said.

"Maybe so. Being an ex-policeman, he'd've gotten away with it."

I'd forgotten. Years ago Kaiser had been a cop. "What're you talking?"

"Abuse cases. Except they don't cover each other now like they used to. I guess a lot of them are second-generation law enforcement. They watched their mothers absorb rage. Or their personal attorneys have wised them up."

The weather came quickly, with violent gusts but little rain. Under dark clouds the water became an ugly gray. Away from clouds, the sun reflected the bay as a mirror, directly in our faces with disorienting brilliance. Running with the wind in *Fancy Fool*, there were moments when the motor's exhaust wafted about and we spoke at normal, closed-vehicle voice levels. Then buffeting would put us to silence, toss salt spray across the bare decks, make our eyes water behind our dark glasses. About the time we reached Garrison Bight, the strange dry squall passed. Straggling clouds, smoke puffs, moved southward, lifted a thousand feet. The water behind us became a milky pale green. The sun gained a new yellow tone, with more intensity. Sailboats at anchor between Fleming Key and Sigsbee nosed into the wind.

Sam idled toward the Hilton Haven peninsula to drop me off. "For the most part," he said, "I'm normal. I vote. I don't hoard old newspapers. I have never pawned my shoes to buy beer."

"Your point is?"

"Getting to it."

"Go direct," I said. "My fatigue won't allow layered communications."

"You're worried about two things. Violence and job ethics. You need the money, stop worrying about the job. Take it. Take the money. Worry about the violence, the connections, why you're riding a tangent to it all. It's come around to me, too; the package in Marnie's Jeep. I told you I'd be a willing coconspirator. This is no time to ignore warnings."

"They keep sneaking up on me."

"We had a saying in-country, back then. When a battle's inevitable, don't wait for it to come to you. Take your fight to the field. You sometimes get to do it your way. Take the offensive."

"If I dabble in the field, I might end up in jail."

"What'd Mark Knopfler say?"

I'd heard this one before, on a Dire Straits album. " 'Sometimes you're the windshield, and sometimes you're the bug.' You wanna shake six hands?"

"What'd Alejandro Escovedo say?"

That one I didn't know. "He's a singer?"

"Bunch of good albums. On one he said, 'You feed a dog a bloody bone, he's your friend for the rest of your life.' "

I stepped onto Wirthwein's dock, peered around the side of his house to make sure the Kawasaki was still there. I said, "The longer you live, the more people you knew. We're supposed to live longer than dogs."

Sam shook his head. "Not in the Bloody Bone League."

"Stay in touch. Any more tips for a man on the offensive?"

He pointed. "Remember the sign on the seawall."

I looked.

LEAVE NO WAKE.

15

I exited east onto Roosevelt from the Hilton Haven residential strip. Two sheriff's department cruisers passed going west, one in each lane, a rolling roadblock. Deputy Fennerty, in the far car, didn't look. Billy "No Jokes" Bohner, in the closer car, turned to scope me. I had last seen Bohner, an officious bully, six months earlier. I knew that turning his head was a major effort, not to be ignored. If Liska had put a BOLO on me, Billy would love to be the matchmaker. He'd loop my wrists with circulation-robbing restraints, escort me to his boss, urge me to hurry with the rubber stick. He was that sweet a guy.

A quarter-mile east I ducked left into the Hampton Inn. I found a parking slot in the sea of white Sebrings and green Mustang convertibles. With luck I'd dodge the flashers if Deputy Bohner chose to illuminate North Roosevelt. There was another reason to be there. With the standard glassed-in phone booth fading into the past, motel lobbies offered the best weather-sheltered, semiprivate coin phones in the Sunshine State.

I walked past the registration desk, put a lost look on my face so I'd look like I belonged there. The icy A/C ensured my shocked expression. I found two wall booths in a hallway with writing shelves, piped-in music, the noise of a housekeeping vacuum in the background. One phone

in use. A young man in khakis and a knit sports shirt. Next
to him, an open briefcase full of white pill bottles, medical
implements in plastic bags. Years ago they'd have been ups
and downs, straight from the boat. Dealers back then were
brazen enough to spread out their wares in plain view.
These days sales associates market the real thing: antide-
pressants for residents of paradise.

I checked home. Six messages. No pencil or paper.

First message: a hangup.

Sheriff Fred "Chicken Neck" Liska: "If you screw me
over, you better plan on living out of the country, in poverty. Make it Haiti. That's the only place I won't go to beat
your ass. Call me. Do I need to spell it for you?"

Spell "Haiti" or "screw"?

Donovan Cosgrove: "Alex, we're hoping to work with
you this morning. Please call or come by before eight-
thirty. Mr. Holloway will be meeting with a man from the
Ford dealership. He'll have several vans to pick from. Also,
we noticed you haven't ordered supplies from Conch Photo.
We assume you made other arrangements."

Blew that one. Had Cosgrove left that message before
or after his meeting with Butler Dunwoody?

Teresa: "My neck hurts from that pillow. My eyes hurt
from when you stopped your car so fast. The minute you
get this, call and tell me why Dexter Hayes is treating me
like dog shit."

Dexter Hayes, Jr.: "A gentle guy like you, Mr. Rutledge.
Your name came up this morning at the year's first meeting
of the Monroe County Violent Crimes Task Force. Do you
have knowledge about violent crimes to share with me? If
so, please call my office, my home, or my pager. You have
my card. I'm in the book."

Dexter hadn't given me a card. Sheriff Liska was pivot
man for the VCTF, no doubt had attended the meeting.
He'd probably told about my midnight phone call. His turn
to redefine our professional relationship. Or shit-can it.

Teresa: "It's nine forty-five. The least you could do, with
the wind out of the north, is lunch at Louie's. Pay me back

for a rotten night's sleep on a saggy mattress with no explanation."

I didn't need pencil and paper. I needed a new address, a new job, a new girlfriend, and a handful of GET OUT OF JAIL FREE cards. I sat in the motel lobby, in neutral territory, to think things through. I had no faith in my ability to remember details. A day ago Marnie had become part of the mess. Twelve hours ago I confirmed that I was a target. Four hours ago I learned that the cops wanted me, too. Liska had puzzle pieces two, four, and six. Dexter Hayes had three, five, and seven. I held the keystone, the tie-in of Bug Thorsby's attack team to the mutilated corpse. If Hayes and Liska discovered the link, it would take fewer than five minutes for them to deduce my guilt. Even if I had an alibi. Even if the crime had yet to be defined. It would take them longer to decide which could claim me. Maybe they'd have me drawn and quartered—with a lawyer present—then divvy the severed parts.

Sam had suggested taking the offensive. I'd never gone wrong taking his counsel. Spur of the moment, I could think of only one way to hide from the law. That meant disguising myself as a tourist and riding the Conch Train for the next eight hours. I was down to only one other move. A ride up the Keys. It promised nothing but fresh air and scenery. And maybe some answers to questions, if the deputies didn't have my Kawasaki's tag number.

I slid out of the Hampton deep freeze. The motel had not always been there. I'd attended a county fair in that same location, in the 1970s. I recall riding a Ferris wheel to its top, watching a regatta in the harbor. Back to the southeast there'd been the miniature golf course, a near-empty HoJo motel. Farther in that direction, Kentucky Fried Chicken, and Searstown with fewer than twenty cars in front of the old Winn-Dixie. I'd watched a Cessna 150 looping touch-and-gos with the airport landing pattern to itself. To the south and west, a view of the island's old section, from Glynn Archer to the lighthouse to City Electric's smokestacks. A peaceful island begging for business, praying for tourists in the pits of the gas crisis.

The pendulum of prosperity swings both ways. In good times it crowds the highways. I should have known.

Traffic up to Summerland Key was a zoo. No time to enjoy the scenery north of Big Coppitt. One-day visitors, the timid who vacation in Marathon and brave the wilds of Duval only in daylight. Motor homes headed back to the mainland, away from the skinny streets at road's end. Delivery trucks from Hialeah that sprint the round trip twice a week and treat the Overseas Highway like Daytona International Speedway. Lights on for safety. Sales reps with totes full of stainless steel fasteners, or glow-in-the-dark condoms. Sly junior execs out of Coconut Grove who've played hooky from work, zipped to the island to chase women for a day. They're hurrying home for supper with the wife and kids.

I saw a way out of it all. Ten seagulls sat on the Shark Channel seawall at Big Coppitt. I could perch there with them, blow off my worries, watch the crazy traffic pass.

Brochures hint at a leisurely drive. I spent fifty minutes accelerating and braking, hurrying and waiting. I should have gotten pissed, U-turned, gone back into town. Or stuck with the gulls.

No one out front at Big Crab Fish House. Three dirt devils danced in the scuffed marl that posed as a parking lot. Cellophane trash and old receipts blew in circles. A coffee-colored mongrel raised its leg, watered the rear tire of an old GMC pickup. I peered through a dirt-crusted window. No one in the office. Nothing in there but a lawn chair, humming flies, and a trash can full of fast-food containers. A fuzz of dirt over everything.

A true backdoor operation.

Four spindly sea-grape trees and a sad line of unkempt croton and aralia ringed the property. A fifties-vintage mobile home park snugged the dry dockage. This was not a gated community, not the Family Motor Coach Association. The old trailers must have belonged to pioneer caravanners who'd croaked at the ocean's edge and bequeathed the homesteads, the twelve-by-twenty concrete slabs. I wondered how the relics had survived the 1998 hurricane. I wondered how special it was to inherit a corroded box.

I noted an odd absence of birds. Maybe they'd all found their way to neighborhood dinner tables.

I wandered around back. The dog ran when I neared, cowered behind the root structure of a stumped-out tree. Four LIVE BAIT signs, no evidence of vending efforts.

Five ugly dudes stood around a beached lapstrake lobster boat, twenty yards distant. Dirty, with strangely shaped facial hair. Goatees, untrimmed Vandykes, drooping mustaches, long Elvis sideburns. In the John Prine vernacular, "illegal smiles." Two of the mulletheads rolled their own coffin nails. One held a wrench larger than my forearm. Another tapped a rolled, greasy towel into his open palm. He wasn't holding a billy club, but he was thinking one. None of them looked my way. Each was aware of every step I took.

I had sudden second thoughts about asking after Jemison Thorsby. I began to calculate the time it would take to reach the Kawasaki, crank the motor, rip down the highway before the Happy Crew laid hands on me, offered to help me find truth in pain. But that wasn't the definition of "being on the offensive." And I didn't want to provide that much entertainment.

Beyond the torn screening of a dockmaster's cubicle, a warped sixty-foot dock drooped seaward. Driftwood repairs atop low-budget materials atop flimsier repairs. At the top of the pier an unpainted equipment shed, two wooden fish-filleting platforms, one eight-foot garden hose. At the end of the dock a man was stacking slat-built traps on a beamy workboat's afterdeck. I thought I recognized him. The sun was in my eyes. I'd seen Thorsby's picture in the newspaper, seen him in person twice, many years ago. Once at night, in a bar, trying to pick a fight with a treasure diver. Once in daylight, from a distance, being ejected from Oceanside Marina. Better to approach the man on the boat,

I thought, than the home team down the beach.

I'd taken four steps onto the weather-beaten wharf when a knife whizzed past my ear. It thwanged into the equipment shed. It had missed my face by less than a foot. By its angle in the wood, it had come from the Boy Scouts. Instead of looking their way, telegraphing fear, I inspected the weapon, touched my finger to it. A custom throwing knife: a leather-wrapped handle, a scroll design on the blade. It had made an eerie, crisp sound as it flew past my head, an elongated version of a bug hitting an electric zapper. You never hear the one that gets you. I was happy to have heard this one.

"Gawd dog. Too friggin' bad there's no witness." Thorsby walked down the dock. "That was a close call, 'less you consider how good his aim is."

Jemison Thorsby look sun-dried. His furrowed skin resembled a desert wash. He was probably six-one, slender, with the oversized pecs and neck and shoulders of an ex-con who'd done fifteen hours of push-ups each day to kill time in the joint. But he'd added a gut and poor posture since gaining his freedom. His receding chin and bushy mustache made him look like a beaver. His eyes were orange puddles, his pupils pencil dots. He wore ankle-high work boots, olive-drab overalls from a uniform supply house. A patch on the upper section read JEMMY. Jemison had gone to Hair Club for Men and the School of Bad Advice. The hair on his forehead looked to have been transplanted from someone's pubes. The toupee was thick and dark. It failed, in texture and tone, to match the pubic hair. Why an ex-con boat captain so concerned himself with grooming was beyond me. I didn't really care.

I also didn't care why someone had thrown a knife at my head. Why get into details? I heard my own freedom behind me: whining tires, diesel stacks at full cry, the rhythm of trucks and cars hurrying on U.S. 1. Someone didn't like me. Why not just get on the motorcycle and leave?

Thorsby turned to face his henchmen. A stripe down his

back, the oils of perspiration. "You boys think this pussy'll ever come back to visit?"

That was the funniest thing any of them had heard all week. They were unanimous in their response.

He smiled. His teeth looked like the history of the gutter. "Any you grunts wanna buy that motorbike he drove down here? Take it a test drive?"

"Fuckin'-A, yes!" said one of the doctoral candidates.

Thorsby waved him off. "Shit, Elcock, they suspend your fuckin' license so often, that judge downtown, he sold it to a Cuban."

The second funniest line they'd heard in a while, except for Elcock.

Thorsby turned back to me. His stance spoke the perfect indifference of a lifelong screwup. "I seen you around," he said. "Don't know your name. I know who you are, know who you hang with. This dock, it's 'invitation only.' You don't come around here. You do your business out front, whatever. You stay off my dock, the rest of your life. Or we'll shorten it. Got my breeze?"

Thorsby got his own. The west wind gusted, his toupee jibed. If he hadn't acted quickly, the mop would have flown away.

I reached behind my head, yanked the throwing knife out of the shed. "I've got some business with your boy, Bug."

Jemison's face tightened to a scowl. "I divorced that son of a whore." His voice developed a phlegm rattle. "You find his shitty ass, whoever you are, you piss in his boot. Tell him it's a love letter from his hateful daddy."

"That's about the same message I wanted to give him."

"Whatever your grief, it ain't nothing like he give me. I hope you find him. Now get the fuck gone, 'fore that motorbike falls off the dock."

So much for a family conspiracy.

I didn't want to get close enough to Thorsby to hand him the knife. I held it by its handle, let the blade swing to point downward. I dropped it. I wanted it to stick straight up-and-down in the dock. In the instant after I released it, I knew my error. If the weapon fell between slats, or struck a nail head and chipped its point, or fell sideways into the water, I'd be mincemeat. I held my breath for the longest fraction of a second I'd ever known. With a slight tap, to my relief, the knife entered a pine plank six inches from my foot. It lodged itself and remained upright.

Time to exit.

I walked back to the Kawasaki. I calculated with each step my chance of making the highway should Jemison Thorsby change his mind, sic his yard bitches on the intruder. Ninety seconds later I was crossing Kemp Channel Bridge in the long line of late-day tourist arrivals, wondering what the hell kind of *Twilight Zone* drama had filled the past five minutes.

I also wondered what I'd hoped for. An amicable tête-à-tête with Bug? A little talk out of earshot from his remaining partner, to offer sympathy for the loss of his carpet trimmer? An admission of guilt, the name of his sponsor, if one existed? A truce, while we worked out the conflict?

My long shot hadn't paid off. I'd almost cashed my own check. I probably needed another twelve hours' sack time, a feast of broccoli and asparagus, a spinach salad sprinkled with vitamin B-12 pills.

For the second time that day I jammed my brakes. I missed rear-ending a halted line of eight or ten cars and SUVs. Someone up ahead turning left. I'd been thinking too hard about my dead-end dilemma. Not enough about now. The spike of adrenaline and heart rate prompted me to try an old trick to dispel the problem from my mind: change the subject, go for the overview. I turned my thoughts to traffic, the highway, the route ahead.

That didn't work, either.

I mentally previewed my trek back to town as far ahead as the four-lane around Boca Chica Naval Air Station, then three miles farther. The image of Stock Island turned my thoughts to the tramp in his bush camp. I wondered if

Liska's investigators had covered all their bases.

It meant another long shot, but less traffic, less personal danger. And a chance to nail the last clue that might help me.

16

Shrimp Road hadn't changed in two days. A spooky emptiness lay over the rubble and deserted pavement like pervasive evil, like the waiting for something that might never arrive, but if it did you'd regret it forever. Out of sight, far away, someone rode a two-stroke dirt bike. The staccato engine would fade, become loud, then drop away, become loud again. I wondered if the rider was testing plowed-over tabletops and gnarly berms, the canted valleys of the garbage dump, flying wheelies above coiled chain-link fence, performing spin-turns on trash dunes, bottoming out in the pallets.

Free to ride. We all find freedom in different ways.

My search took me beyond piles of dead Australian pines, rusted-out refrigerator compressors, truck wheels and loose tires where the pavement curves to Robbie's Marina. I found broken, rusty bikes and a dingy pair of metal-wheeled roller skates. Rear-window louvers from an old Camaro. The tramp had moved his lean-to away from the road, deeper into the mangrove hammock. A tropical hobo's version of a little grass shack. A normal person's budget Caribbean vacation gone horribly wrong.

I parked in the roadside gravel, hung my helmet on the twist grip, looked again, up the side road. No signs of life. Nothing there but the tattered *Lady Caribe I*, waiting out

red tape and repairs to become, in one man's dreams, a car
ferry to Havana. The vessel's name and surrounding paint
had faded to reveal its previous name, the *Lucy Maud
Montgomery*. A shrimp boat's diesel rumbled in the docks.
The dirt bike sounded closer, still playing.

I called hello.

No answer, but a rustling in the vegetation, the frantic
scramble of someone hiding, or concealing an item of
value. This was not stealth, not a jungle warrior blending
into the environment. It was quiet panic, a bird protecting
the nest. I tried to think of an opener, a gambit to break
the ice. Not wanting to impose myself, to demand a response so dear as the truth, I said: "What's your name,
buddy?"

More rustling in the mangroves. He'd worked out this
defense drill in his head, but not in practice.

"I'm not looking for trouble here," I said.

No answer. I took a few steps into the hard dirt. I looked
straight down. A lame attempt at a trip wire. If I'd kicked
it, I'd have rattled a bouquet of tin cans suspended from a
bush branch. A backwoods early-warning system.

I said loudly: "Hello in there?"

Nothing.

"I'm not a cop. I'm not looking for refugee Cubans."

A muffled, "Fuck off. Go away."

"I'm not gonna do that," I said. "What's your name?"

"The Feck."

"It's what?"

A quarrelsome, odd, high-pitched voice: "The Feck.
What d'you want?"

"Just askin' your name, buddy. Need to shoot the shit a
minute."

"I ain't got food. Nothin' like that."

"Buddy, I'm not hungry," I lied. "I ate good this morning. You heard how I got here. What could I steal from
you I can take away on a motorcycle?" I stopped talking,
let him think about it.

The sales pitch worked. After about thirty seconds the

hobo made his appearance. A short, dark-skinned man, Latin or a veteran of the outdoors, no immediate way to tell. Stringy dark hair hung from a Budweiser cap that had faded to pink, then grimed to four dull shades of brown. An oversized shirt of indeterminate color, sleeves rolled to his elbows. Even his beard stubble lacked spirit. He waved some bugs away from his face. "I'm Wiley Fecko. The street calls me the Feck."

No trace of Spanish accent. The pigmentation either sunburn or years of accumulated dirt. Whatever there'd been of Wiley Fecko, there wasn't much left. Frail, malnourished, he was in danger of being lifted aloft by a wind gust. His wrists and forearms matched the circumference of a flashlight. His neck dripped with extra skin.

I said, "I'm Rutledge."

From twenty feet away he looked me over. "How you get money?"

"I take pictures."

He squinted, continued to size me up. "Who from?"

The mind-set: It's not gainful if it's not a scam.

"I'm a photographer. People pay me. I use a camera to take pictures."

Fecko had lost so many teeth, his gums and lower jaw had shrunk. His lips canted inward. "Saw one yesterday, over in the road."

I checked a trash heap behind me. "A picture?"

Wiley stared, new concern on his wizened face. He waved away the bugs, then enunciated so I'd get his drift: "A picture taker."

He'd meant me. On Sunday, with the deputies. Don't push this too hard. "Was he taking pictures of the road?"

"Nope, corpse. Or most of a corpse. Lots of police hanging out. All of 'em afraid to look right at that dead man. Most of 'em too ashamed of their spit and polish to look at me."

Right to the point. Fecko was no softie.

"Did the police ask you questions?"

Fecko shook his head. His mannerisms became those of

a small kid being naughty, his furtive, distracting move-
ments made not to duck punishment but to minimize pain.
"I'd tried to talk to one, you know. He tell me to get on
back, tell me I stink like Knights Key. He got some prissy
cologne, I don't tell him he stink like a French whore. Look
like he shined his face with a floor buffer."

Knights Key, the island at the north end of the Seven-
Mile Bridge, often smells of rotting seaweed and plankton.
Permanent halitosis.

"What were you trying to tell him?"

" 'Bout the funeral parlor truck leaving them goods in
the open. Probably charged the kin for a pine box and a
hole. But they ripped 'em. They left that dead man in the
hot sun. Ugly black birds startin' to think, Here's supper."

"Funeral truck?"

"Black truck, fancied up. Kinda like your minority au-
tomobiles. I'm not a prejudice guy, you know, but it's a
description."

Bug Thorsby's truck? When I was scrambling around
the house, getting ready to shoot Dexter Hayes's pictures
on Caroline Street, I'd had an image of Bug's pickup truck
pulling up to the emergency room entrance at Florida Keys
Memorial. That's why I'd asked Carmen to follow up, to
call the hospital. I'd wanted to identify the man with the
busted face and teeth, the man now a murder victim. She
couldn't get a name because the man never made it to the
hospital.

Had the victim's teammates beheaded him because he'd
failed to cause me pain? Was he punished for weakness in
battle? Or was it so he couldn't be identified? Was Bug
Thorsby that cold? Would he kill to avoid being linked to
a mugging?

He'd shoot his toe to cure an ingrown nail.

Why not shoot me, instead?

I suddenly was aware of an idling chain saw. I wondered
for a moment if someone still was cutting tree trunks felled
by old storms, but that made little sense. The instant I
smelled raw gasoline, I knew what I'd heard. A loud burst

of high-pitched exhaust racket cut the silence. I felt dread,
I knew—

My Kawasaki exploded with a percussive *woof.* I felt
the blast against my back, heard the bike crunch as it toppled onto the pavement's edge. With a rapid series of pop-
clutch shifts, the dirt bike made its departure. I crouched in
expectation: a moment later the tank exploded, then one of
the tires, then the other tire. The complete package. The
stench of scorched petroleum hit my nose, acrid fumes of
melting plastic, burning rubber. Fecko had fallen straight
to a sitting position, flat on his butt, mouth agape. I waited
for movement, to make sure he hadn't been struck by a
piece of shrapnel. He moved. He was fine. I stayed where
I was. I couldn't bear to witness what I knew was happening. The torch had split, faded up the road. I wasn't going
to identify or nab anyone. My only reaction was to feel my
pockets.

Shit. No coins for a phone call.

Inside of two days and six hours, two men's lives had
ended and I'd been either the unfortunate victim of repeated, random vandalism, or I'd received my third unde-
fined warning. Would the spinning marble fall into my slot,
or was I immune? Bigger question: If the motorcycle's destruction had been planned, was Wiley Fecko in danger for
my having been at his campsite?

Another ear-busting blast. I almost dived, ate dirt. From
the west this time, a Navy fighter swooping on final approach to Boca Chica, crackling, spitting, shaking the
ground. Hot pilots in training. Another jet came, close-
stationed. A ribbon of ivory-toned condensate streamed
from its port wing tip. The third jet followed, then faded
fast. Again, in their wake, the huge quiet. Did campers in
the mangroves put up with this racket every day?

"Fecko, I need your help."

No Fecko. Between the road explosion and the thunder
above, Wiley had beat feet. I needed to chase him like a
wounded deer, not to dispatch him humanely, but to rescue
his emaciated butt from whomever.

I hoped Fecko didn't ask me to identify the enemy.

My first steps through his camp were careful ones. I didn't know whether he'd booby-trapped it, or had dug a latrine, or kept a box of trained snakes. I noted that he owned a balloon-tire bicycle, with two flats, no chain, and a mildewed seat. A tin cup and metal plate, hooked together by a twisted coat hanger. A stack of aluminum frames, maybe eighteen by twenty-four, motel art–sized, without glass or art. A collection of stuffed black garbage bags. No telling what they held. Wiley Fecko's mini-museum of vintage trash, items discarded fifteen or twenty years ago: an RCA Victor 45-rpm record changer with a plastic one-inch center post. A mildew-encrusted vinyl carrying case, full of sun-warped eight-track tapes. His bed: the broken-sponge composite of carpet underlayment. A cache of unopened Vienna Sausage tins, Frito wrappers, and empty wine bottles. Fecko had shoplifted screw-top vintages. I grabbed a bottle to carry. I wasn't sure why. Maybe I'd have to fend off attacking bats, or one of Fecko's soul mates, an opossum, a rabid armadillo.

I gained distance from the crackling fire, stopped to listen. Wiley was not a master of escape and evasion. It wasn't a stepped-on twig that got him, but labored wheezing. I found him less than twenty yards away, on his ass in a patch of sand, swatting away gnats, rubbing his ankle. His eyes were those of the cowering, pissing dog I'd seen an hour earlier at Big Crab Fish House.

I said, "I want you to come with me."

"I ain't goin' nowhere."

"Someone might try to kill you."

He swatted. "I can live with that."

"Humor is good." I held up the bottle. "You into grape?"

He grinned, almost leered at his weakness. "Artificial energy. I was nine or ten, hiding under the trailer, beer-buzzed. My grandmother told me I'd turn into a drunk. I should've took her warnin' way back then."

"You saw something happen the other day. Something

a few bad people would rather not hear mentioned in a court of law."

A hint of fear in his fogged eyes. "Tell 'em I didn't see jack."

"When do I do that? The next time I see 'em at Fast Buck Freddie's?"

"Whatever."

"Lemme see if I got this right, Fecko. You want to drink your next pint through your mouth, or bypass that? You want the express route down your neck? You can do it just like that man the funeral dudes left on the sofa. No tongue to get in the way, no swallowing. They might be kind to you, use a clean hacksaw blade instead of a dull rusty one. Unless a chain saw did it . . ."

He withered. "There's people back in here. I go away, they rip me off."

"How 'bout you go with me now, we come back in a couple days, I replace anything that's missing?"

He swatted, then shook his head. "Certain things, gotta carry 'em out."

"Whatever you say, man."

I will learn not to issue blanket statements.

Fecko took fifteen minutes to inventory his belongings. I waited for a fire truck, a sheriff's department cruiser, or a curious passer-by to stop and ask about the smoldering Kawasaki. Maybe a shrimper in the dockyard, the caretaker aboard the *Lady Caribe I*. Maybe someone in Bernstein Park heard the bang. Nobody came to the party. I felt as isolated as Wiley. To the rest of the world, the explosion had been one hand clapping.

When he'd finally sorted the contents of his garbage bags, the contents of which I had no desire to examine, I asked if I could help carry anything.

"Whew," he said in his strange high-pitched voice. "You could use a bath, my man. That reminds me. I gotta take my shower."

"A shower?"

"Bring it with me, or some jackoff'll rip me for it."

Wiley Fecko possessed the innocence of a man too addled to imagine duplicity. Or else he strove for that ideal. He'd also developed the resourcefulness of an ocean-transit sailor. His shower was a contraption formed of a coral-colored douche bag, a hot-water bottle, a plastic funnel, and a maze of fifteen feet of translucent surgical tubing. Silver duct tape held all the parts together. I looked closely. Fecko had gotten his hands on a funnelator.

The first funnelator I'd ever seen had been aboard a sailboat in Antigua, during a photo assignment for *Outside* magazine. Two sailboats had shown up with them. The captains of four other yachts that I knew of had paid air-express rates—before FedEx—to have proper components sent to Nelson's Dockyard. Funnelators were, quite simply, water-balloon launchers. Rigged correctly, with the surgical tubing lashed to pelican hooks and those hooks affixed to vertical stays, the funnel could be armed with a fat water balloon, pulled backward to the far gunwale, to the full stretch of elastic tubing, and released. The resultant payload, aimed with precision, fired with skill, could fly forty or fifty yards and put another sailboat's whole cockpit awash. The liquid bomb became ceremonial, instant tradition, an irreverent, oceangoing party joke. Captains felt it a point of honor to return fire. Half the racing fleet scrambled to obtain rubber, plastic, and tape, no matter the shipping cost. Fecko, somehow, had found one that a sailor had discarded. He'd also had the cleverness to add the douche bag and water bottle that, filled with water and hung from high branches in direct sunlight, would create a hot-water shower.

The man was no dummy. I began to understand that he lived in the weeds by choice, for reasons that meant much to him.

We walked toward the road called, ironically, Fifth Avenue. I balanced a stuffed garbage bag on the flat-tire bicycle I'd volunteered to push. Atop the bag the toilet seat and lid, a toaster and a neon beer lamp. Items important to Fecko in his camp without electricity. Fecko limped along clutching a metal folding chair. With his free hand he continued to shoo no-see-ums.

The trio of jets returned for another approach on Boca Chica's runway. A chopper chugged westward four hundred feet above us. Paranoia runs deep. I felt like a refugee in exodus, traversing a conflict zone, running from enemy gunships. This chopper was not a military unit. A silver sheriff's department star on its hull. I didn't expect it to check out the still-smoking cycle.

It didn't.

I thought, No more Kawasaki, no more imported motorcycle. The recovery of my all-American image would please Liska. He'd be pleased to know that I'd joined the new breed, the American victim. Free to walk.

We passed the site where purple birthmark found his ultimate freedom.

"Got friends in Key West?" I said.

Fecko's thin hair fluttered as he walked. "Don't reckon."

"Not a single one, somebody to connect with?"

"My friends, mostly, they DBF."

I'd heard of DBA—the Dis-Barred Attorneys club. But not DBF.

"That's a street slang," explained Wiley. "Dead by forty."

I had three problems. Panhandling shouldn't have been one. I defined humility; I assumed Wiley Fecko had the ability. But we lacked prospects.

Problem two, if I called Teresa Barga, even though her Grand Am was five or six years old, a survivor of her college years and eight months on the chuckholed streets of Cayo Hueso, there was no way she would allow Wiley Fecko inside her car. Finally, I didn't know what to do with the Feck once I got him inside city limits. I may have been humanitarian of the week, dragging him out of the bush to save his life, but I didn't want a houseguest. If I dropped him on Duval to join the buggy brigade, the residentially challenged old-pro bums, they'd chew him up and forget to spit him out.

"Maybe this'll be the first step to getting you out of the woods," I said.

"I'll go back here," said Fecko. "I know you mean well, but I have a pretty damned good sense of destiny."

At the intersection of Shrimp Road and Fifth, I looked left, saw a deputy parked in the shade near the entrance to Bernstein Park. The deputy had his head down—maybe paperwork, maybe a snooze. What kind of vigilance? My taxes pay that man's salary. Maybe I could tap on the cruiser's window, get change for a buck. Maybe not. I'd have to explain the toilet seat and the neon beer lamp.

I steered Fecko to the right. We headed for the pole-mounted pay phone in front of the Rusty Anchor. I dug once more into my pocket, hoping that by some miracle I'd find coins for a phone call.

"Little short?" said Fecko.

"No change, no ride."

"You got money where you stay?"

I took out my wallet, showed him twenties, tens, and fives.

Fecko grabbed his heart. I thought he'd cave in his chest. "Jesus, man," he said. "Never show that to a man in hard times." He checked the street, walked down the side of the restaurant, found a rusty coat hanger in the weeds. He looked around again to see if he was being observed. He pulled the cap off a cylindrical fence post, the chain link that surrounds All Animal Clinic, stuck in the hanger, pulled out a Baggie. He unwrapped it as he walked toward the phone. He placed two coins in my palm, took out a small device, unlocked the square coin-box access door.

"Make your first call."

"Amazing."

"Use it, don't abuse it. They never catch on."

"How'd you . . . ?"

He swiped at his filthy clothing with the backs of his hands. "I wasn't always like this. I was a sparkling kid, a young man. I had jobs and wives and children. I had a future. I climbed Mount Whitney. I owned a Morris Minor and a Triumph Bonneville motorcycle. I could take that cycle apart and put it back together blindfolded. My last job was at BellSouth. I kept a token of their appreciation."

Survival.

I paid the machine, dialed Teresa's office. In the time it took to be routed to voice mail, I observed Fecko's battle with gnats. They hadn't bothered me. I realized there were no gnats, probably hadn't been any gnats. The bugs were characters in Fecko's continuing nervous tic. I hung up, recycled the coins, called Teresa's condo. Got her.

"Look, I'm sorry about lunch."

"Me too," she said. Unpleased.

"I've got a huge favor to ask." I tried to sound desperate. "I'm stranded on Stock Island, and I've got company."

"I don't want to know her name."

"It's a gentleman who may have info on the decapitation murder."

"You playing detective?"

"Somebody's got to do it. But I need to warn you. He's running short on hygiene. Have you got access to the city's car?"

"Your ride will arrive shortly. Wear dark glasses and change your name. I'll explain when I see you."

I thanked her. My next call was to the house. Three messages. The first from Marnie Dunwoody: "The car in the water? I did what you asked. I didn't connect your name to it. Near as I can tell, no one else did, either. It was an old Nissan Maxima, showed on a hot list, stolen in Boynton Beach. Here's the nut. It was swiped from Dexter Hayes's ex-partner in the police department up there. The new captain of the Boynton SWAT Team. Dexter's in a rage. I'm not sure it's because of that. Sam says to keep your sails high and the wind on your quarter. Thanks again for supper the other night. Talk to you later."

Another love note from Liska: "Your silence is deadly. Once a month I reevaluate my friendships. It's part of politics. I already forgot your name."

Finally, Mercer Holloway. "Alex, I hoped we'd pitch in

to get this done on schedule. Are you still in town, or have you run off for a week in Cuba? I've called a man in Tampa who'll get me a quote by noon tomorrow. You're still my first choice. Please contact Donovan if you wish to participate. If you choose otherwise, I would recommend you don't cash that check."

I called local information—what luxury, a freebie—got the number for Schooner Wharf. I called there and asked for Dubbie Tanner. It sounded as if the bartender—a woman whose voice I didn't recognize—did not want to admit Dubbie was at the bar. I began to describe him . . .

"Hold on." It was more of a grunt, like "Hldn."

"Jeb Bush for President, Campaign Headquarters."

Dubbie Tanner lived out of the trunk of his old Chevy. He badgered both tourists and locals for free beer. He lied about pirate exploits and alleged family wealth to suggest marriage and thereby seduce women from foreign countries. He picked clothing from Dumpsters in Old Town. I was probably the only person in Key West who knew that W. B. "Dubbie" Tanner, over the past fifteen years, had established himself as one of the foremost children's book authors in the country. He was living on pennies, stashing royalties. He was expert on SEP-IRAs, small-cap, no-load growth funds, communications and biotech start-ups, and high-speed server networks.

I identified myself to him.

"Gettin' fuckin' chummy, callin' on the damned phone, aren't you? All you ever want is favors. Least you could do is venture down here to the low-rent part of town, scoot a few frosted mugs my way. But, no. You're dialing me up on your cordless, nine-hundred megahertz, fifty-channel unit while my mouth is dry like an upside-down canoe. What'd'ya want?"

I spoke in general terms—Wiley Fecko had moved closer, was listening in. Tanner got my drift, picked up on the fact that I had an audience.

"Tell you what you do. I'll need twenty-seven bucks for the hotel room."

"Hotel?"

"City jail. I'll sluice him down with bar gin, take him to Front Street, right across from the Aquarium, get him to stumble against a beat cop, breathe on him, cuss in front of a few tourists. Get him grabbed for petty vagrancy."

"I'm not sure that's what we need."

"Hey, look, brother. He'll get a ride to the city, they'll delouse and bathe him. They'll wash his clothes, give him a haircut and two meals. He'll come out a new man. The twenty-seven's for court costs, so he can stay in good standing. We can do it again in six weeks."

These street-life boys weren't bucking the system. They were playing it like a well-tuned fiddle.

I said, "Where can I meet you?"

"Corner of Einstein and Franklin." Tanner hung up. The coins, for the fifth time, dropped into my palm.

A taxi cruised Fifth Avenue, looking for its fare. I handed the coins to Fecko. "Stay here and stash these," I said.

I separated myself from Fecko, hurried away, brushing my shirt as if to unload the bad luck in which Wiley dwelled. I hailed the cabbie, gave him a thankful expression for appearing, for saving me from the bum. The driver regarded me strangely, then saw Fecko dragging his belongings, trying not to be left behind in the parking lot. The driver got the picture. He stopped. I opened the rear door of the cab and positioned myself halfway inside so he couldn't pull away. I stalled, argued, threw a twenty over the seat back and dropped the name of Darren, the cab company's owner. I threatened to have the whole company busted for breaking federal discrimination laws. I knew Darren when he was a teenager, driving the only airport limo in town—a van with eight seats.

Pissed, confused, the cabbie popped his trunk. He refused to help Fecko load his junk. I didn't want Wiley to have to make two lumbering trips. But I was afraid to get all the way in and close the door so the cab could roll closer to the Rusty Anchor. At least the driver didn't attempt a getaway with my feet on the pavement. Finally the useless bike was hooked to the trunk-mounted bicycle rack. Fecko got in the other side of the car. He handed me the plastic bag that held the coins and key. It would be my job to re-stash them.

I leaned over the seat back and whispered, "If you try to drive past that deputy up there, you may as well kiss your ass adios. Take my word."

"I recognize you." The driver gave me the hard eye in his mirror. "Your name's Rutledge. The city's looking for your sorry butt. You need to toss me another sawbuck and sit low in the seat."

17

"This time of year, sunset's early." The cabdriver spittle-sprayed his dash as he spoke. The windshield fog was turning into a science experiment. If he'd showered since New Year's, he'd omitted shampoo. I wanted to think that the seats were stained with saddle soap. He sped down Truman, clocking forty.

"Lucky you," he said. "In darkness you can hide your face."

Lucky was out of town.

I didn't want this dunce to get pulled over. He'd use me as a blue chip. He could do burnouts on Front Street, screeching turns off Duval. He'd hand my ass to the city, cool the ticket, slide with a warning. I burrowed lower in my seat. The taxi's mildewed vinyl fought the good fight. But it came in second place. Fecko's stench of malnutrition had combined with drive-thru burgers and onions I'd bought so I wouldn't fade and Wiley wouldn't croak on us. I was ripe as a dropping tide. Windows down didn't help. I couldn't blame the cabbie for wanting us out of his hack promptly. I handed him another twenty and asked for less throttle.

We passed a local writer leading a flock of intent-looking folk down the sidewalk. A walking tour of famous authors' homes, part of the annual Key West literary seminar. The followers wore badges in clear plastic holders, carried book bags and small notebooks. A few college students in the group, but many were mature granola types, the core of the *Harper's* and *The New Yorker* subscription lists. Their clothing ran the gamut from punk-perforated jeans to denim shirts and tweed sport jackets. They peered into a classic house on Eaton as if expecting to see someone in there, typing on an ancient Underwood, doing final revisions to *Horn of Africa*, or *To Have and Have Not*, or *Panama*.

I'd heard it for years: "The corner of Einstein and Franklin." It was not an intersection. It was a social hub. The kind of place writers hung out, instead of being at home, facing the monitor, writing.

Wall decor in Key West bars is haphazard and irreverent. The national chain restaurants have their clean antiques, spit-and-polish relics, cornball nostalgia. A sign in the Green Parrot demands "No Whining!" Customers have filled the bar on Whitehead with donations: street signs from other towns, out-of-state license plates, placards from defunct businesses, various artworks. It's an open-air drinker's bar, in the top tier of the island's survivors. The Parrot's all-day, all-night clientele ranges from down-and-out booze-hounds to attorneys from the courthouse across the street. It's mostly blue-collar—male and female—and shop owners. The bartenders work inside a central rectangle. At the room's northwest corner, on adjoining walls, hang the portraits of two major intellectuals of their times.

The taxi stopped on Southard for the signal at Whitehead. I jumped out, heard Stevie Ray Vaughan's wailing *Voodoo Chile* before my third step. Dubbie Tanner was right where he said he would be: in the Parrot, wedged between Albert Einstein and Benjamin Franklin. The beer hawk was perched on a stool. His talons clutched a can of Bud Light. Vicki Roush, the bartender, had just placed a shot glass full of copper-colored liquor next to the Bud. I snatched the shot and tossed it back—nasty, sweet Southern

Comfort—then slapped down a five. Vicki grabbed the bill, stuffed it in the tip jar. A sparkling thanks in her eye for my coaxing Tanner outside. Dubbie's ragged T-shirt read STILL WASTED AFTER ALL THESE YEARS. I got him into the taxi's backseat as the light changed, and slid him two twenties. The cab driver went right, drove toward the sunset. Fecko's thirst for wine was about to be quenched.

I walked two blocks west to Teresa Barga's condo. I kept to the shadows, pretended to scratch my face when cars passed.

Teresa doused her hall light, flipped on the outside sconce, edged to the door with her hand in her briefcase. She checked to make sure I was alone, then let me in. "Ooh. Would you like to take a shower?"

I deserved to be forced by pistol into cleanliness. "I've taken a boat ride, a wild-goose chase, and a dose of Good Samaritan. Yes, I would like to shower."

"Good. You can stay."

"What's with 'Wear dark glasses and change your name'?"

"I'm sorry. I was mocking your drama and high intrigue. After I said it, I thought this time I pushed too hard. But, please, go easy on yourself. You're not a fugitive. Liska's called off his dogs."

"What about whoever tried to run us off the road? Whoever firebombed my Kawasaki two hours ago?"

"Not true."

"It's a cinder. My helmet looks like somebody's brain on drugs. How do you know that Liska's chilled out?"

"He bought me lunch at the Half Shell. I told him what happened last night. Down to the last detail."

Liska had blown off my story at midnight. "He believed you?"

Audible tightening of the jaw. Wrong question.

"Is there anything else," I said, "besides Liska canceling the hunt?"

She put on a stubborn face. "You've got something to tell me?"

"Are you in a hurry?"

"You bet," she said. "And I want two things. What you've been holding back, and why you've been doing it."

"How about first I tell why? Then you decide if you want more."

"Red flag. Man patronizes woman."

I couldn't lose my reluctance.

She said, "Tell me about getting mugged on Sunday."

"Dexter put you up to this?"

Huffy vibes again. "You and I live together in separate houses. We're not a secret at the city. Nobody puts me up to anything. Especially with you."

"Has Dexter brought up my name?"

"He's kept it straight. He asked how to get in touch with you. I think that's it."

I told her about the carpet cutter's birthmark and the blurry photo.

Slam dunk. She finally changed her expression. "So they're connected?"

"Only through me."

She thought it over. "You were afraid I'd feel compelled to tell Dexter?"

I shrugged, nodded.

"That was the only right answer," she said. "Here's the thing. I'd feel split in two directions only if I thought you'd done something wrong."

"Somebody told him those guys jumped me."

"My lips are sealed."

"Outside the house, you mean?"

She smiled and leaned forward. I didn't dare hug her, but I leaned in for a fat kiss.

"Southern Comfort?" she said. "Oh, yuck."

I took a beer to the shower. I had to drink it quickly— her hot water was about twenty degrees hotter than mine. I stayed in as long as I could stand it. Then I found a pair of Bermuda shorts and a once-worn Hawaiian-style sport shirt that I'd left in Teresa's closet weeks ago.

She'd put my smelly clothing in plastic, tied a knot in the bag, set it near the door. I sat in her living room and started my second beer.

She held a yellow legal pad full of notes. "Six things." She checked her list. "Liska said the man on Stock Island, the fake Richard Engram, they strangled him before they stabbed him and before they took his head."

Strangulation is retribution. My suspicions confirmed, at least to me. They'd killed him for both reasons: punishment, and to mask his identity.

She continued: "The real Richard Engram, Dexter got a confirming fax from the man's high school in Jacksonville, the man's senior picture. Engram grew up there. No one had knowledge of his being anything but a rampant heterosexual. No cross-dressing, no closet gay scene. He'd worked with Dunwoody for four years, was a cosigner on the company checking account."

"Okay."

She continued, "The two identical names, Richard Engram, without inside access, there's almost no way anyone could've rigged the FCIC database with false identification. By inside access, they mean someone who works with the FDLE's computers in Tallahassee. Anyway, four different agencies are looking into it."

"I hope Liska doesn't believe that shit's true. It could've been one of those agencies, trying to fight crime their own special way. The FDLE has tricks up its sleeve, giving fake names to informants. They lie to serve justice. Some prosecutor caught the FBI and the Highway Patrol in Tampa a couple years back, not telling the whole truth. To protect undercover cops, they set up drug runners for probable cause. They'd install a kill switch in some bastard's ignition, shut him down on the Interstate. A trooper would stop, supposedly to help. He'd decide that the vehicle driver was being 'evasive,' or 'furtive,' or some other specious trait that'd prompt him to call for 'assistance.' They'd bring in drug-sniffing dogs, the bust would go down. Those guys didn't care how they did it. I'm all for busting drug traffickers. But I'm a great fan of the Constitution, too. Cops like that are just like criminals. They've probably been pushing the truth for years. Or holding it back and not calling it lying. Seeing things that haven't happened, putting words in people's mouths, forgetting details that might save a guy's butt. The main reason they're like the bad guys is they never think they'll get caught."

Teresa said, "A little blabber energy from that beer?"

"I tend to ramble. Only when I'm tired."

She backed off. "No, you're right. A couple of college courses, they drilled it into us: Play it straight, because sooner or later . . . So, the state's forensic people used a portable argon laser, a light that exposes hairs and fibers in fabrics. The duct tape, the panty liner, and the fancy nightie Engram wore all held industrial fibers. They're trying to find a match in their library of samples. It could be the man was killed on a unique carpet. Or on foot-cushioning floor mats, in a shop where a concrete floor is padded to conform to OSHA standards."

"I'm impressed," I said. "Sure didn't seem like Hayes was headed toward a real investigation."

"Surprised some people at the station, too."

I said, "Do his colleagues see him as a flake?"

"Not that bad. I get the feeling he hasn't proved himself. He hasn't solved a big one or been involved in a tense situation, to show his courage."

"Which means he better watch his back."

"Finally, the Nissan Maxima that chased us? Did you get your messages? Marnie said she told your machine it was stolen from Dexter's ex-partner in Boynton Beach. Dexter got the county to release it to him. He was trying to get it transported to Key West this afternoon or in the morning."

"Is that all?"

"I saved this for last. You just missed our former sheriff, Tommy Tucker. He came here looking for you."

"I don't like that he came here."

"Me too. He came to ask you to accept Butler Dunwoody's offer of work. Claims Mercer Holloway's willing to share your services."

"Was that all?" I said.

"That was it. He left right away."

"Two things you should know, to put that in perspective. Heidi showed up at my house yesterday, to proclaim her innocence in the real Engram's death. Don't ask me why. I told her, 'Sure, whatever,' and sent her on her way. This morning, I went into the Pier House to buy a paper. I ran into Dunwoody. He asked me to shoot construction-progress pictures. I told him I was booked. His phone rang, and he listened while somebody talked. Then he asked me if Heidi had visited me. I said yes. He got pissed. Now, suddenly, I'm forgiven?"

She lowered her voice. "Is that all Heidi wanted?"

"Yep."

Relief in her eyes. "Next time we should live in a small town."

I said, "Next time they should go to a bigger one."

"So, where are we now?"

"In a vicious circle. Logic says that someone's trying to screw with Butler, to drive away his project. But he and Holloway are hand-in-hand. Maybe the crap's aimed at Holloway, too. Maybe I should just sell the cameras and take up carpentry."

Teresa's phone rang, postponed her response. She picked up, said "Okay" five or six times, then put it down. She was pissed. "I've got to go."

"Who was that?"

"Dexter. They need me at the station. Something's going down. The news people are already there."

"What is it?"

"He was too hurried to say. He's so weird."

"If Liska called off his dogs, why did a cabbie tell me the city was looking for me?"

"I suppose Hayes agreed to help the county find you.

Before Liska called it off. It's easier to put out the word than it is to retract it."

"Why do cabbies know about BOLOs?"

"Favors for favors. The old Key West tradition. Cabs are all over town. The cops need extra eyes, the taxis need fewer tickets. The police help with drunk passengers, people who bolt their fares, all that."

Our conversation ended. She was gone in two minutes.

I found the keys to Teresa's motor scooter, considered another beer, and chose the beer. There was the problem of returning the scooter. Sooner or later I would have to walk eight blocks between her place and Dredgers Lane. I could enjoy my new freedom right away. I called Sam and Marnie's house. No answer. I finished the beer, thought for a minute about how I could collect an insurance settlement for my crispy cycle. I found a large plastic cup, poured in another beer, grabbed my dirty laundry, began the hike home. I blanked all dilemmas from my mind. I hoped that some wondrous revelation would fight its way to freedom. Some tidbit would pop into my brain, give me the insight, the connections to make sense of two murders, three attacks, and Key West politics.

Then I thought, Screw politics. I'd never make sense of that.

I came up with zip. Twelve minutes of blank.

Julie Kaiser exited the library on Fleming, walked under a streetlight. She wore Levi's and a rare sight in Key West, a plain white T-shirt. No slogan, no advertising. Class act.

"You're seeing me at my worst," she said. "The part of my job I least like."

She held three books. The top one bore the title *How Things Work in Your Home*. She set them on the rear fender of her white Honda Accord.

"I thought you only did sales," I said.

She shook her head but smiled. "Property-management fees are like free money. Going into the weekend with broken water heaters and appliances is the bitch."

"You're a do-it-yourselfer?"

"The prima-donna repair people on this island, you need reservations. It's worse than getting a table at Antonia's. My father always told me, 'Study hard, get perfect grades, or you'll wind up a plumber.' I've got two postgraduate degrees. I have to pay plumbers seventy-five bucks an hour. I get attitudes about it."

"Philip doesn't do dishwashers?"

"Not so much in the past few weeks. When Philip got into real estate, he liked the one-on-one with people. I know I said he was a good partner. But lately he's into building PowerPoint presentations. And traveling around the state to promote our business. He's not so much hands-on as he once was. Anyway, I got a stove with two burners whatever . . . burned out. I can handle it. I hear you're dodging my father's phone calls."

"Thanks for recommending me."

"Thanks for considering. I don't know how my sister stands to be around him all day. I love him dearly, but he thinks being a bad-ass is the way to do things."

"I figured Donovan was around all day."

"Well, Donovan. He talked his way into working for my father about four years ago. He's done a great job. Sometimes, though, I think Suzanne sticks around to keep an eye on him."

"Your father's been pleasant to me, and I still haven't said no. He claims his property plans will be good for Key West."

Julie inhaled deeply, got a distant look in her eye. She looked up Fleming at a bicyclist riding against traffic. "What I know of it, it'll be positive. At least for Key West." She gathered up the books, walked to the driver's side of the Honda. "Gotta go."

An hour and a half after sundown, and Cecilia Ayusa was in the lane with a broom and a dustpan. Carmen arguing with her, pointing out the futility of perfection when every tree on the island sheds blooms, branches, fronds, buds, leaves, or pods. Reason meant little to Cecilia. Carmen's father, Hector, had long ago given up. In every other aspect of her life, Cecilia was normal. She had a thing about litter in the lane.

Carmen walked me to the porch, then came inside. "I've got new excitement in my life," she said. "But nothing like yours."

"Did those deputies hang in the lane?"

"The city cars came and went, too. Until about one-thirty."

"Why weren't you at work? Did you already tell me that?"

"Yes," said Carmen. "I called in sick."

"Lovesick, right?"

Carmen grinned like the Cheshire cat in *Alice in Wonderland.*

"And your mother, with her project?"

"She keeps talking about church. It's the old Catholic guilt. I'm starting to believe her biggest problem is worrying about my love life."

"The frequency, the timing, or the participant count?"

"Up yours, my sweetness."

A knock at the door. The phone rang. I didn't want to deal with either one. I peered around the corner. Detective Dexter Hayes, Jr., a wary look on his face. The streetlight illuminated two stern-looking KWPD uniformed cops. They stood back, between the porch door and a blue-and-white squad car.

I let the phone ring. The machine would get it. Probably Teresa on the phone, calling to warn me.

"Rutledge, you look surprised to see me." Hayes turned to the other men. "Rutledge looks surprised to see us."

"I see you at my door, Dexter, it's a phone call at three A.M. Can't be anything good."

"We'd like you to come down to the station. Shoot the breeze about what you might have seen on Caroline Street—"

"When you were scuttling the crime scene?"

"—and the car chase up the Keys."

"We can sit here on the step and talk, if you want."

"I'd like to include some other people," he said, "so they can get up to speed on your take."

"I'll tell you right now, it won't be hard to translate. Sunday morning, I was taking pictures along Caroline Street. You saw the pictures. I didn't see anything strange or out of place. The car chase, if you talked to Sheriff Liska, you know as much as I do. I got chased, there were two men in the other car, a Maxima. One of them shot at me. I more or less outran 'em."

Hayes stared at me. He was onstage, performing for the men in uniform.

I tried again to shift the subject: "Okay, I'll give you that point, Dexter. In Key West nothing's strange or out of place . . ."

He said, "You want to quit the horse crap?"

"You got a specific question?"

He smirked. "Exact wrong thing to say, Rutledge. Specific questions get only part of the truth. You sound like a lawyer defending a guilty client."

How many minutes ago had I expounded on cops and lies of omission? The detective was right. I was guilty of horse crap.

Hayes jacked his thumb at the squad car, the motion no casual gesture, but a concise statement. "We'd like you to come down to the city."

The last thing I wanted to do was ride six blocks in a locked-cage backseat. "Meet you there in fifteen."

He half-turned toward the uniforms. They shifted to full-huff, ready-for-action stances. Primed for action. Fullbacks made larger by Kevlar undershirts, waiting for the snap. Hayes looked me cold in the eyes. "We'd like it now."

"I'll ride my bicycle. You won't have to bring me home."

"Walk to the car, Rutledge."

I glanced at Carmen, then peered over Hayes's shoulder. He said, "You lose something?"

"I'm looking for the film crew, Dexter. The lights and sound and honey wagons. I'm waiting for the 'Bad Boys' theme song, in full stereo."

"Mr. Rutledge, you have the right to remain silent . . ."

They're pissed because I haven't told them anything. Now I have the right to shut my mouth?

The uniforms came in a hurry. Placating hand language at first, until one yanked cuffs from behind his back. The bastards spread me against the outside wall of my house, patted me down as Hayes read aloud his three-by-five Miranda card. I checked over my shoulder. Carmen Sosa stood in the porch shadows, tears in her eyes, hands to her face in silent disbelief. I asked her to lock the house and call Sam. Water the plants if I wasn't back in a week. The suggestive power of words: I suddenly needed to urinate.

One officer—C. TISDELL on his name tag—claw-pinched my upper arm, quick-walked me to the squad car. He pushed the top of my head downward so I wouldn't bump my skull, the move learned from a thousand newscasts and crime "reenactments." Its best use was not in protecting a suspect from harm but in marking superiority. The molded-plastic enclosure they called a backseat stank of puke and dried shit. Urine was champ. Lysol was out of the running. In the street-lamp glow I viewed a mural of blood smears and tooth marks and stains. Cops build routine to counter intended suicide by door-edge head-banging. They never consider suffocation.

Tisdell powered a right onto Francis to make my slick-seat ride more comfortable. I skidded sideways, banged against the left-side door. They got a chuckle, I got a panic stop at Southard. I caromed forward.

He went right. I was going to Angela Street, the station locals called "the city," instead of the Stock Island county-managed lockup. If a bad situation can show a good sign, that was it.

The cop in front of me: "Damn quiet back there."

I said, "I'm memorizing."

"Memorize this," said Tisdell.

He clipped an elevated sewer-hole cover, bounced us all. I descended, ass bone to a hard seat. I wondered how many police officers, in this era of allegations and litigation, had redirected their pent-up angers to abusing equipment.

My face hit mesh grate when Tisdell braked hard in the Simonton Street parking garage. I felt a snap at the bridge of my nose, a knot beginning on my forehead. I didn't yell in pain. If I sustained viewable injury, the only way for the boys in blue to dodge a civil rights beef would be to claim I resisted arrest. That'd be another grand to a bondsman, and who knows what extra court penalties. Things get complicated quickly. A friend once tossed a glass of water in some land developer's face, got sentenced to anger-management classes, fifty hours of community service. He was lucky he didn't have to wear an ankle bracelet. Water's a tough commodity in the Keys.

Sure as hell, Tisdell's partner palmed my head as he hoisted me out. Don't want head lumps in addition to avoidable facial injuries. Dexter Hayes had followed in another vehicle. The three men marched me through double doors. One of them with a stranglehold on my elbow. The place hadn't been a bona fide jail for years. It still smelled of old perspiration, disinfectant, ear wax, rotten socks, and drain odors. I'd heard jail smell called the stink of humiliation.

They turned me over to a desk jockey for booking. The clerk checked out my Hawaiian shirt, sneered to telegraph his fashion opinion. Hayes spit out an array of charges. The ones I noticed most were evidence tampering, obstruction of justice, and suspicion of accessory to murder.

Hayes wandered down a hallway, checked a bulletin board, pulled out his message pager. He turned, caught my eye and said, "Don't think for a minute that you're staying here, Rutledge. You'll love your room at the county. It's a modern facility, but it's furnished in early-American steel. Don't spend too much time in the showers, eh, buddy?"

"Who did I murder, Dexter? Let me in on it."

Hayes shuffled a wad of message slips. "First you ask a

city cop where to find Bug Thorsby. Brilliant. Then you tell me sooner or later Bug'd get a visit from the wheel of fortune." Dexter drew a large air circle, a wheel's path to clarify his words. "We found Bug in the trunk of the Maxima." He pinched his nose. "What a treat. We don't have proof yet that you choked him to death, but we've got what the coroner's investigator called 'ocular petechiae,' and a black Olympus camera strap in an evidence bag. Paint-ball residue on it, fingerprints, the whole magillah."

I'd tossed the strap in my outdoor trash can.

Dexter added: "There were fresh scrape marks on the rear bumper cover of that car, like it got pushed into the ocean. We'll get a search warrant to inspect that hot rod that's registered in your name. Bottom line, Rutledge, you waxed his ass, or he died spontaneously of terminal bloodshot eyes."

I'd escaped the car chase, but the action still had gone to the other guy.

Out of the quicksand, the answer to one question:

If they'd succeeded in stealing my Shelby, Bug Thorsby's body would have been found in my trunk instead of the Maxima's.

"You're talking stuff that happened in the county. Why am I at the city?"

"Professional courtesy. Liska's due here in ten."

18

The duty grunt aimed his camera, told me to face it. I shivered in the tax-supported meat-locker air. "Stand on the damn X," he said. "Face me." Stupid voice tone. Vocabulary and sentence length reduced to lowest common IQ: "Look at my hand." Bang, bang. "Point your toes at the wall. Stare at the red spot. Make this easy. Eyes open wider. Keep staring."

He'd revoked my right to blink. The spot was orange, the twin strobes angled for least-flattering light. Let's talk Dostoyevsky, *Darkness at Noon, Native Son*. What do you say we debate reasonable and prudent assumption of evidence destruction? Or circumstantial presumption of horseshit. I'll write a book. *The History of South Florida Justice*. A six-page pamphlet.

Mug shots in newspapers make new jailbirds look depressed, deranged. Friends will review my expression, make comments reserved for funerals: "Doesn't he look natural?" I recalled the blurred portrait that illustrated a Jerry Jeff Walker album cover in the early 1970s. The cut line had credited Joe Santana, Key West Jail. I asked if Joe was still around. No one answered.

Did I have a lawyer? I said the cuffs had been so tight, my allotted call would be to my doctor. They said okay.

This wasn't going to be an audition for Letterman. These people had heard it all.

A few years ago, *Aperture* magazine ran a feature about a historian who found antique glass-plate negatives, photos taken of prisoners in Marysville, California, from 1900 to 1908. Front shots of all, but the woman photographer had angled her subjects for three-quarter views instead of perfect profiles. The angles revealed more character than straight ahead or straight into the ear. The traits were not reassuring. Even then, felons looked guilty as hell.

A morbidly obese clerk took me to an eight-by-eight interview room next to the double-door entrance. We edged past six other handcuffed detainees waiting for paperwork. Grovelers, fist-clenching methamphetamine wrecks, indolent human skittles. One with a lumpy head, mouth swollen shut. Two avoided eye contact. The others scoped my threat potential. One laughed to himself. We passed a notice board, a sign-up sheet for "security" opportunities—the department's officially sanctioned moonlighting gigs—and a wall-mounted rack of message cubbyholes. I heard someone say not to bother with fingerprints. Rutledge was a department part-timer, or used to be. They already had me on file.

The clerk barked by rote: "Face the wall. Hands up to chin level."

I nodded. He attached my cuffs to a D-ring in the wall. He left me hooked up to stare at the scarred bulkhead, to guess what would come next. I stood there listening to foreign noises—cops horsing around, swapping after-hours gripes. It must have been shift-change time. Officers who stopped to pull message slips poked their heads through the open door, checked me out. Crew cut, bald, crew cut, bald. Demented-looking or baby-faced, though a few resembled male models of slight intellect. No reactions, no emotions. Each trailed aftershave. Oldies but goodies. Old Spice, English Leather, Aqua Velva. Mennen Skin Bracer prevailed. I'd figured the brand had withered out of existence after their main customer, my father, had died.

I thought, Teresa's in the building. Does she know I've been arrested? Or has she been asked to steer clear? The air-conditioning began to sink in. I felt a shiver in my legs. I tasted post-nasal drip the flavor of blood.

Nothing would settle in my mind. I felt dizzy, wondered if kissing the mesh divider in the cop car hadn't done something to my head. I knew one thing for certain. Hayes's message on my answering machine asking me to share "knowledge about violent crimes" had been a ploy to get me downtown so they could bust me. Save the city's time and money by having me arrive under my own steam.

A slurring drunk in the hallway pled his case to the booking personnel: "All I axed her was an esplanation. All I axed, a simple esplanation. No. She don't tell me. No, she don't."

"So you hit her."

"I thought her mouth was stuck."

I'd begun to find devil imagery in the cement-floor scrape marks when Marnie Dunwoody showed up. She wore go-to-office clothing. At least one thing had worked right. I didn't know whether Dexter had realized it, but my asking Carmen to call Sam also had meant, "Call Marnie," with the hope that she was up to reporting. I was innocent. I wanted an attorney. I wanted the media to know I'd been falsely apprehended in a three-against-one bust. I wanted to invoke the power of the press, the horsepower of public opinion. I wanted to leverage victimness.

Maybe it wouldn't work that way. She looked at me like at a punk busted for shoplifting Trojans. She looked alert, not suffering from having received her weird gift twenty-seven hours earlier. "How the hell did we get into this?"

I said, "A string of weird shit? Coincidence?"

"Sam told me that in your confusion you'd grab the short straw first. He said to remind you that you don't believe in coincidence. Especially after Teresa's story this morning, 'living her own Bruce Willis film.' "

"Thank you, Sam."

"Then why?" she said.

"Somebody made it happen."

"Working at the paper, I'm an easy target. What's your excuse?"

"Who doesn't like Alex Rutledge? I am liked. Even my ex-girlfriends still like me. I'm that kind of guy. No one wants to do me bodily harm."

"You want to rethink that, Mr. Teflon? Sam said he had this discussion with you once before, about people wanting revenge. A loan you failed to repay. A drunk you kicked out of a bar when you worked on Duval."

I shook my head.

Marnie pinched her nose. "I don't come in here that often. You put every smell in a horse race, bet on piss to win. Kind of a poetic match for the paint scheme. What do they call this, burnt grapefruit?"

"They're going to transport me to the county stockade."

She laughed. "Commonly called the Go-to-Hell Motel."

"The Trashmore Lodge."

"The Felony Suites."

"Discomfort Inn."

She said, "You're looking for humor in the situation."

"I'm looking for daylight. How's your sense of humor?"

"That surprise in my car yesterday? There's a saying in the news biz—'print paybacks'—but it means a revenge too fabricated, too small. I want honest, messy, painful revenge. I want that weasel to beg forgiveness that will never arrive."

I said, "Please don't repeat that to anyone here or at work."

"Thank you for taking me at my word."

"Where's the press liaison officer?"

"Banished, for now. There may be procedural difficulties. No one knows I'm in here with you. I'm not supposed to be in this part of the building with a weapon in my purse."

"Why banished?" I said. "Dexter's personal politics?"

"Something about your not being newsworthy. And, yes, Dexter. Maybe because the Maxima belongs to his friend.

Speaking of which, after the car was pulled from the water, the county never notified the media."

"Why would they keep a lid on it?"

She shrugged. "I didn't want to push the fact that I already knew."

Had they tried to set me up? I could believe Dexter, but not Liska.

A commotion began outside the door, multiple voices. An only-in-Key-West conversation: aggressive arguing, one side ninety-percent rapid-fire Spanish, the English side of it peppered with Spanish epithets. Woven into the confusion was Hayes's unpracticed attempt at the Conch-Cuban idiom. He'd lost his touch. The two other voices weren't giving ground.

Marnie said, "That may be your secret weapon."

"I just heard the name of the county prosecutor."

"When Carmen called the house, Sam asked if he should call one of the Spottswoods or Nathan Eden. Carmen said he could save you money if he called Mercer Holloway."

Major Key West Rule: In legal matters, money saved is ground lost.

I said, "How 'bout we call Nathan, too? For insurance."

"You want to be rude?"

"Does this place smell like good manners?"

"I'll make a call," said Marnie. "See if anyone's home." A low-pitched buzz came from her purse. "Weird timing." She checked the LED readout, handed me the phone. Teresa's greeting was too civil, too matter-of-fact. She was steamed, willing to communicate the fact, but wanting to hold herself in check for the sake of information.

I said, "I should call Sheriff Liska, ask him to redefine 'not a fugitive.'"

Marnie put her finger to her lips, told me to keep my voice down.

Teresa hesitated. She hadn't called for criticism. She finally said, "Mercer Holloway found out about your arrest. He sent his son-in-law to the city. He had some kind of voucher, a guarantee for your bond."

"You mean Donovan Cosgrove, right?"

"The one who's not married to Julie."

I said, "Suzanne's husband is Donovan Cosgrove."

"He's the one."

"If I tried to calculate the motivation for that move, my brain'd switch off like a dead computer."

"Don't turn him down," she said. "Anything's better than getting caught in the system."

"I get out, I go to the house, some crazy man will shoot me though a window. Sam was talking earlier today about having no place to call home."

"You buy that pessimism at Walgreen's?"

Through the phone, a face slap that I needed. Teresa was right. Inside the slam I was powerless. If our pursuers wanted me hurt or dead, jail was the easiest place to subcontract the job.

She backpedaled: "You get out, we'll drive to Marathon and check into the Faro Blanco. We'll rent *The Fugitive* and hole up for a couple days."

"How about we stay in town and defend the fort?"

She said, "You call it, we'll both play it."

"I love you, too."

Marnie had been gone fewer than five minutes when Dexter Hayes, Jr., carried a folding chair and a thin red file folder into the cubicle. He set up the chair and sat. For a minute or two he said nothing. His face told me he was pondering frustration or disgust. Finally he said, "Howzit, so far?"

"Might've been a more pleasant ride in the dog catcher's truck."

"Be glad you're inside. It's pouring out there."

"Like a Conch pissing on a flat law book?"

He almost laughed. He pulled the chair closer, to within three feet of me. "How could you say such a thing?"

"I wish you'd told those shitbirds in the squad car that you were only pulling my chain."

"They wanted to give your face some street character,

Rutledge. Why are you even suggesting I might play games?"

"Teresa Barga told Liska every detail of that car chase. You say I pushed the Maxima into the drink. That wasn't part of her story. Why isn't she in here, manacled to the wall? You say I bumped off Bug Thorsby. When the hell yesterday did I have time to do that? I spent the morning with Holloway, the lunch hour with the sheriff, and I entertained you in the afternoon."

"Sunday night?"

"Ask Teresa."

"You were in the Navy, right?"

"You're saying I should've learned about rousts in the service?"

"Aside from enemy attack, what's the worst can happen on a Navy ship?"

I said, "Ordnance explosion."

"Second worst?"

"We're having a casual chitchat while my arms are chained to the wall. You think I'd find it in my best interest to overpower you and escape?"

Hayes looked disgusted. "I go by the rules. Second worst thing in the Navy?"

"Three things are tied," I said. "Collision resulting in a punctured hull below the waterline, a loss of power or steering in a storm situation, and shipboard fire."

"Which an ordnance explosion would cause . . ."

"Usually."

"So," he said, "you're trained to fight fires?"

"I knew what I needed to know. I'm not sure how much stayed in my brain after all these years."

"What type of fire extinguisher goes to what kind of fire, the color codes, the triangles and shit?"

"Right," I said. "All that. I'd need a brush-up course."

"Because the guy who died on Caroline, Mr. Engram from Jacksonville, Florida, the cause of death was not the belt around his neck. He suffocated because somebody jammed an extinguisher down his throat, fired it for a while, and corked the chemicals by ramming down three D-cell batteries. They held those in place with a big chunk of raisin pumpernickel and then the duct tape. And you saw the panty liner."

"Pretty well organized, that murderer," I said. "Think somebody planned it ahead of time, or did they grab on impulse, whatever was handy?"

"I was going to ask you."

"Get off it, Dexito. You're fishing without bait. What're you going to do, bust everybody on the island who's ever owned an extinguisher? Collect twenty thousand alibis, distill your list down to two hundred idiots with empty canisters? Use intuition to find the one sick schmuck who did it?"

Hayes wasn't humored. His expression spoke his instant belief: my glib response suggested a cover-up. I still was holding back.

Which was true.

I tried to think what harm could be done to myself, to Teresa, to anyone else like Wiley Fecko or Marnie or Heidi the silent investor, if I revealed the Engram-Engram tie-in. I took too long to ponder it.

"Here's the deal," said Hayes. "Mr. Donovan Cosgrove sashayed in here with a stack of bond guarantees. He also mentioned my boss's lap-dancing mistress, which most of us thought was a well-kept secret. Ten years ago it might not have been a problem. With a town full of self-righteous newspaper readers, times change. A good boss is hard to find in this profession. I've talked to Sheriff Liska. For all I know, you're in his hip pocket. Anyway, for now, you walk. With 'for now' underlined."

I said, "I hear the sound of a turning table."

"Let's put it this way. Cosgrove may have changed my tactics, but not my opinion. I've got a strong feeling that you know something I want to know. And the county wants to discuss the car that went in the water, to the best of your knowledge, with two people in it. You didn't attempt a rescue."

"They had a gun. My Mustang's not equipped with flo-
tation devices."

"That doesn't mean shit. You had a gun, too."

"Not true."

He threw a disbelieving look. "You didn't check your
girlfriend's purse?"

Teresa had said she'd left her pistol at home. Maybe
she'd told Dexter a different story. I couldn't recall if her
job required carrying while off duty, or demanded that she
not carry. Time to dodge the topic.

"If you analyzed that camera strap for paint-ball residue,
then you also checked my garbage can and found the same
residue."

Dexter let it ride a moment, then nodded.

"And you did it without a warrant."

He nodded again. He'd taken a risk. He'd been trying
to convince himself of my innocence, not my guilt.

"Have you cross-referenced the copycat cases?"

"Inside this building, we call them 'Liska's Revenge.' "

"Progress?"

He wasn't sure he wanted to chum-up enough to discuss
it. "They're not the same perps. That's all we know."

"Mind if I look at some files?"

"Shit," he said. "Now I'm sure you're stiffing me."

"Good. We're one step closer to negotiation."

"I guess the dog catcher'll take you to Stock Island."

I looked him cold in the eyes. Waited for his move.

He posed a disgusted look on his face, sat back, crossed
his arms. "I'm source agnostic. I don't care who rats out
bad guys. This better be golden."

"What do I get to see?"

"You want the three already copied, or the three other
unsolved?"

"The others first," I said. "Maybe all of them."

"My office, my presence, outside business hours. No
photocopies, no handwritten notes, no press leaks."

"You get up early?"

"I'm here by seven-fifteen."

I permitted Hayes's roust to pay off. I said, "The head belonged to one of Bug Thorsby's partners. The ones who came at me with a knife and a carpet razor."

He looked at me without changing his face, but measuring my ability to fight off two- or three-against-one. "Somebody call and tell you this?"

I explained the blurred photo in the stack he'd returned to me.

"How many in this gang, total?"

"Bug stayed in his truck. Two other starlets tried to play mumblety-peg."

"Two? You walked from that?"

"Appreciate the compliment, Detective. You want to arm-wrestle, see who's more of a man here?"

"Ducking blades," he said, "there's usually a nick, a little bleeding. All they sliced was your camera strap? What were you holding?"

"My fucking breath."

"You just amended our negotiation, Rutledge. You'll be here awhile. Plan on window-shopping computerized mug shots until you hit pay dirt. We need the third man. You find him. After that maybe you can review a few files."

Hayes delivered me to a part-time, third-floor info tech who knew more about local area networks than law enforcement. Hayes went home to eat dinner. I was on my own. I spent almost two hours in front of a huge monitor before identifying the short one who'd smelled of onions and marijuana, the boy who'd waved a dagger until I'd kicked his balls up to his rib cage. His photograph showed more than the cold, empty eyes I'd viewed in person. Malice and calculated evil, his own revenge for perceived wrongs—probably from birth—radiated from the computer screen.

Robbie Carpona, age twenty-four, had not specialized. He'd committed enough crimes to earn merit badges in multiple categories, though his arrest record did not suggest an ability to avoid arrest. Armed robbery (firearm), battery on a detention-facility officer; aggravated battery; driving

while license revoked (habitual); possession of methamphetamine; possession of cocaine; issuing or obtaining
property with a worthless check (restitution); grand theft of
a motor vehicle; carrying a concealed firearm (adjudication
withheld); felony petit theft; resisting a law enforcement
officer with violence (sentenced, to time served); violation
of probation (three counts); fraudulent use of a credit card;
showing obscene material to a minor (community control
followed by eighteen months' probation). The attacker I'd
called "Shorty" had served a grand total of twenty-three
months in jail. Talk about paying a light price. For the past
four years, the police departments of Key West and Hamilton, Ohio, had shared info on Carpona's activities.

A standard one-liner noted a sealed juvenile record.

I went to the steel cabinets that lined the room's west
wall, helped myself to the crime records files. The first
folder I pulled from Carpona's accordion-style jacket in-
dicated he had been robbing the cradle, too. Three years
ago he moved two sixteen-year-old runaway Iowa girls into
his mobile home on Big Coppitt Key. He'd run an errand
and returned to find his landlord in a three-way sex scene
with the jailbait. After he'd beaten the landlord with a halogen lamp stand and trashed the man's classic Corvair
model 700 sedan, he'd swiped a service station's tow truck
and pulled his residence off its slab. The mobile home vanished. It was never seen again. Carpona had stolen his own
house.

I returned to the computerized mug shots. It took twenty
more minutes to find Freddy Tropici. Long, stringy hair in
the photo, a bold notation about the purple birthmark. Tropici was a military brat, a small-timer, a one-time police
informant. That last notation made clear the liability, explained the beheading.

Hayes strolled in spooning Cherry Garcia out of a pint
container. He wore Bermuda shorts and a T-shirt that read:
LICENSE APPLIED FOR. He leaned over my shoulder,
checked Freddy Tropici. "I was coached on this piece of
talent. The creep sold his own blood and lived by petty

thievery until he learned a new trick. He was stealing weapons in Monroe County, selling them at official 'no-questions-asked' Miami-Dade County gun buy-backs. Clever guy, Tropici."

I pointed to the Carpona file.

"We know this doofus, too," he said. "His eyes look electric, don't they? Sits around his trailer over here on Simonton pickin' his nose, pickin' his ass, pickin' his Lotto numbers. The jackpot goes over twenty million, he's out ripping off neighbors to buy lottery tickets. I was still in high school and he was, maybe, eleven. He tried to rape a girl in a stadium rest room. Boy'd steal flowers from his own funeral. Can't happen soon enough."

"Ask him if he wants to kill me, okay?"

"I'll loan him the blade," he said. "Wait. I take that back. We need you to photograph the head, Rutledge. Ortega's on vacation in Atlantic City. We tried to hire your pal Kincaid. He told us he'd rather shoot a shark's tonsils."

"It takes a certain mental numbness," I said.

"I saw some of that tonight, downstairs."

"My cameras are broken. If it's false arrest, do I get a free ride home?"

"Don't push when you're on a ledge. You'll tip backward and fall."

"I'll see you in the morning."

"I'll save you a trip," said Dexter. "There's the unsolved man in drag and the unsolved beheading. Those match Engram and Tropici. Then there was a hanging, a strangulation, a throat slashing, and a bullet to the head."

"Can you give me one detail per occasion?"

"What do you know about solving crimes?"

"What do I know about any damned thing?" I said. "What do I know about clouds? I look up, I know it's about to rain. Maybe I can't name an exact type of cloud, but I can tell you where I've put my umbrella. I'm working on common sense. What the Navy called 'preventive maintenance.' "

Dexter thought for a moment. "The hanging, a man

named Toth, from a tree in his backyard. If the guy took himself out, somebody came along and stole the stool. The victim with the auxiliary smile, his Adam's apple hung out like a dog's tongue—Liska's own words. It was a *Psycho*-like thing. Killed in a shower. The woman shot through her head, ear to ear with a twenty-two, lived long enough to call nine-one-one from a pay phone. Told the operator she didn't feel well."

"Give me a bonus track," I said. "Describe the strangulation."

"A lamp cord around the neck. Found the guy in his car, parked overtime at a Smathers Beach meter. Had a dime-store straw hat tilted down, like he was sleeping. Does that save you a couple hours' work?"

"The last one does for both of us. Loosely speaking, it copies Bug Thorsby's demise."

Hayes inhaled, sat back, closed his eyes. Once more he stroked his upper lip with the knuckle, as if he'd once had an unruly mustache. He hadn't put it together. But now it was obvious. The pattern was solid. His problems had escalated.

"These killings," I said. "Were all the details revealed to the press?"

"I don't know. I wasn't here."

"Dexter, you're lucky I didn't confess to three murders and tack on a few more. Gaps in my time line, inconsistencies, phony motivation, a sprinkling of details only a perp could know. Imagine your workload this weekend. No time for the Super Bowl. No time for Ben and Jerry's."

"Up yours, too." He stood and bolted.

I walked outside to brackish post-rain air. In the municipal garage's lower level, diesel fumes spit by an outbound Greyhound smelled of freedom. I never thought a wanging moped would sound so good. A taxi blasted a gutter puddle and spoke to my soul of the real world. A palm frond's flutter, a crime light's glow, an uneven sidewalk each jerked me from the bureaucratic morass, away from my jailhouse mind-set, pulled me back to Key West.

I wondered why I'd considered a trip to Marathon, or hiding in a motel room. Or, yesterday, riding to Epcot or Cedar Key. I began dodging puddles on Southard, in no hurry, paced by deafening drips of moisture from foliage, inspired by fecundity, absorbed by the night.

19

My quaint cottage in the picturesque Old Island lane had become, in my mind, a twice-fought battleground. I pictured barbed wire strung from burned stake to broken post, smoke wisps rising from craters under the mango tree. Constant cloud cover, frigid humidity, raw dirt in clumps or thick puddles. Spent weapons, forgotten guns scattered, upturned helmets half-full of rain. Cordite stink, powdery residue on horizontal surfaces. For the second time in two days I slid the perimeter, traversed the croton bush no-man's-land. I pulled the clip-on flashlight from my bicycle handlebars, scouted sand spur terrain for opposing forces, inspected access portals for signs of intrusion.

No footprints under the windows. No jimmy marks, no screen frames askew.

I doused the light, felt tranquility in the puke-sepia glow from Fleming.

I'd intended to march into the house, damn the dangers, take command. But Robbie Carpona might be stroked out on my couch, his feet on the glass-topped table, meditating in the dark, waiting to expand our new friendship. He could be cleaning his fingernails with his four-inch pigsticker, focusing his criminal brain on my future happiness. Dodging land mines placed by the neighbor's springer spaniel, I retreated. I crossed the lane to the home of Hector Ayusa. I went for firepower and company.

Hector—Carmen Sosa's father—had retired after thirty-two years at City Electric. He'd been a dedicated employee. By the utility's count, Hector had been struck by lightning more often than he'd been caught sleeping on the job. His main assignment in recent years had been his granddaughter, Maria Rolley. Hector also prided himself in personal enforcement of law and order on Dredgers Lane.

Hector came to his front door in threadbare suit trousers, suspenders, bare feet. The tank-top-style undershirt did little to contain his midsection. A museum-quality cowlick sprouted at his thin hair's peak. He held a .45 in one hand, a bottle of Spanish brandy in the other. Firepower and firewater. I feared for the springer's life. I changed my mind about needing help. I told Hector that I'd cased the joint. My house was safe for entry. No one waited to cap me, or to bust me for crimes committed, imagined or real. I had no need for an escort.

Hector wanted to come along, just the same. He argued in English, but with pure Cuban mannerisms. When he described his thinking, he pointed to his forehead. When he told me what he'd seen, he pointed to one eye. He'd heard something, he pointed to his ear. If he wanted to clarify meaning, or tell what he'd said, he pointed to his mouth. I wanted to point to his ass, tell him to go sit down.

"I'll walk you across the lane," he said.

"I'll be fine, Hector."

"Lotta bums in this island. We got to help each other."

Continuing the conversation could only make it worse. I finally broke away. I crossed the lane, walked onto my porch, reached for my keys. They were still in the police property envelope that I'd jammed into my pocket on my way to freedom. I fished them out, took a chance.

No explosions, no flashing knives. I could tell by the cleanser smells that Carmen Sosa had scrubbed my kitchen sink. I keep an orderly house. She's a fanatic. She'd left a note on the counter:

If you get home tonight, which Mercer Holloway promises you will, welcome home, you evil man. Someone has watered your parched plants, especially the poor bromeliad which doesn't need as much in winter months, but it needs some. *You haven't been to your P.O. box since last Thursday, so I pulled this stack of mail. My papa is checking your house once an hour until he goes to bed. If you hear him outside, don't freak out.*

Love,
Britney Spears

I shoved my clothing into the garbage bag I'd toted from Teresa's place. No telling how many mutant infectious strains my pants had collected from the cop cruiser. If I kept up my wandering ways, perhaps I could requisition Superfund monies for laundry soap. I opened the refrigerator, checked the vegetable bin. Two beers. In my state of depletion, one would be too few and two would be more than enough. I took a chance and opened both.

Something bugged me. Having shed the mystery of whether I might be jumped or rearrested on returning home, my mind loosened up, wanted to say something. I pestered myself for the right answer until I finally formed the right question. After all the friction, after busting me with great pride, causing me to get my forehead flattened against the mesh divider in Officer Tisdell's prowler, why had Hayes suddenly shown a change of heart?

I'd been conned by a cop. I wasn't the only one holding back info.

The phone rang. How did it know?

Sheriff Liska said, "You just can't get enough of Stock Island."

"I'm saving to retire there. To hell with Marco Island and Longboat Key."

"Why is that, Rutledge?"

"No street-work dust, no loud Harleys. And cheap real

estate, unspoiled by zoning restrictions. You get used to the
F-18s."

"We found the crispy critter. Did the rigmarole with
your license tag."

"I figured."

"Story to go with it?" he said.

"I'm working up a version for my insurance company."

"We can help you there, if you help us. Get you some
cash, next time buy a Blazer."

"Not funny," I said.

"Wait'll you see the towing company's bill for burned
hulk removal."

"Thanks for cutting me loose."

"I guess you've had a long night."

"Does Robbie Carpona ride a dirt bike?"

"He told me about Carpona, too. Look, you may be a
free man, but parts of your story are still coming up lame."

" 'Bout time I heard a discouraging word. So many people wanted to help me tonight, I felt like Happy Henry in
the Barrel. Now I know how a politician feels around lob-
byists."

"We'll be in touch." I heard no click. He was gone.

I called Teresa's number, got her machine. I said, "I'm
free, at the house. Maybe you knew that, or knew I was
going to be free. Anyway, give me a call. I've been worried
about you, and I wanted to tell you I'm sorry for causing
you embarrassment at the—"

Teresa said, "At least you could say it in person."

I spun around. She stood on my porch in an orange tank
top and spray-on biking shorts. The glow from the kitchen
illuminated perspiration on her face and shoulders.

"Anyway," she said, "to answer your question. You
didn't embarrass me except on behalf of my employers."

I hung it up. "Hey, it's the city."

"You don't see what I see, every day." Teresa leaned
against the door frame. "Believe it or not, since I've been
here—what, seven months?—the Key West Police Department's played by the book. Tonight, no. Procedures got

chucked in the ocean. Standard rules of apprehension and
booking went adios with the wind. Dexter Hayes was trying
to prove something or learn something or fuck with me or
fuck with you, but it was screwy. And he knew Marnie was
in that interview room with you. I got the impression he
figured whatever she did, it'd help his little cause."

She was running out of steam, depleted, profoundly un-
happy. I didn't want her to quit, or cop a pissant attitude
about her job. Until now she'd been proud of her position,
confident among male co-workers, and eager. I wanted Teresa to blame her exhaustion on her bike ride.

"You're in good shape. How did you get this way riding
eight blocks?"

"I rode to Houseboat Row," she said. "But I wanted to
check in, tell you what was on my mind."

She'd made a six-mile round-trip. It had been profound
job frustration.

"Want a beer? Glass of chilled white?" I moved forward
to hug her.

She stepped back. "My turn to need a shower. Someone
bumped your face?" She reached for my beer bottle, upended it for a commendable slug.

"I smell like my fellow prisoners," I said. "I'll join you."

"You're so romantic. Give me two minutes to wash my
hair."

I reached for the kitchen wall, flipped the remote switch
for my outdoor shower stall's fifteen-watt night-light. I
turned back around. Teresa stood there in her tank top and
panties. I watched her peel off her shirt. I'd have to start a
program of rehabilitation. She topped my long list of reasons never to risk freedom, never to go to jail.

"Bring me a towel?" She did something at her hip with
both thumbs. Her panties slid past her bottom, down to her
ankles. She stepped out with one foot. With the other she
kicked upward, Rockette-style. The underwear went airborne. She grabbed them from the air, curtsied to beg ap-
plause, and went out the back screen door. I applauded.

I was carrying a fresh towel from the closet when she

stepped back onto the porch, ladylike, all-biz, oblivious to her own nakedness. "What is this contraption out here?" She crooked her finger. I followed.

She opened the shower door. Dubbie Tanner, who knew my house, had stashed Wiley Fecko's belongings in my shower stall. Three garbage bags, scuffed and split, leaking odors and artifacts. Wiley's funnelator, his homemade shower with its hoses and douche bag and water bottle, lay atop it all.

"New tub toys, Alex?"

"I can explain everything, dear."

"You can put it by the curb. The city picks up twice a week."

"It belongs to Fecko, that homeless witness from Stock Island."

"He's staying here?"

I nodded. "I gave him my room. The least I could do."

"Thank God."

"Because I gave up my room?"

"Because now I know you're bullshitting." She looked into the shower. "I've lost my bathing mood. I want to go look at the ocean again."

A bike ride. Waves. Horizon. Perspective. A unique concept.

"Maybe," she said, "you could buy him a spray bottle of Febreze."

Teresa borrowed bathing trunks and a long-sleeved T from Lulu's Sunset Grill that I'd brought back from the photo job in Magnolia Springs, Alabama. She grabbed a ball cap from Robicheaux's Dock & Bait Shop in New Iberia, Louisiana. She was primed for the Gulf Coast, but headed for the island's south side.

It has been years since Fausto's bought Gulfstream Market, but it's still strange to see that sign on White Street. We skirted rainwater puddled at the curbs, hogged center lane, thankful for light traffic. A cloud of garlic hung near Mo's Restaurant. A city cruiser approached, slowed. We lighted our flashlights to comply with the law. The cruiser kept rolling. We dodged the citation. When you've just beat an attempted murder rap, you don't want to get tripped up by the small stuff.

"Tomorrow's the full moon." She pointed upward.

"It's pulling me southward."

The end of White Street Pier, for the second time in a day. This time with less mental turmoil. Bright moonlight painted the pier's concrete pale violet and cast sharp, geometric shadows. Two women on Conch cruisers—old English three-speeds with milk-crate baskets and high handlebars—rode circles on the apron. They were half in the bag, laughing at each other, sharing a joke. Their care-freedom was another Key West resource endangered by growth and change. They spun a few more laps before they pedaled lazily up the pier. Teresa and I leaned our bikes against the southwest-corner seawall. I locked them to a handrail.

I said, "Talked to Marnie?"

"She's changing her tune. She's starting to get testy about her brother's bad press. It's not like his project is a major encroachment. After all these years of development, he's like the straw that broke the camel's back." She paused, then said, "Can we not talk about it right now? Can we forget politics and crime and revenge and graft and crazies?"

"Yes, we can."

We stood quietly, stared at the faint hazy band where water met the sky. Teresa snuggled against me. The line of weather that had passed while I was in handcuffs moved slowly to Cuba. Sparse lightning danced above moonlit cloud tops. Bright yellow reflections played on waves. The northwest wind carried muffled island sounds—a moped chorus, a distant car horn, shrieks and laughter from Higgs Beach. But none as loud as the soothing play of water at the pier posts. Matching the waves' rhythm, Teresa shifted her hips, began to sway against my thigh.

I put my nose against the back of her neck. "Seashore bump and grind?"

"A magical dance to ward off evil."

"It might shield you from violence, but not from sin."

"I love it when you talk dirty."

I put my hand under her shirt hem, moved it upward. "Muddy fingers."

"Tell me more."

"Old motor oil."

Her hand went between us, behind her back. She moved it downward.

"Perhaps we should face the beach," I said. "We'll know who's arriving."

"You look that way." She turned, faced me, opened my shorts as she spun me around, then pushed my hips to sit me on the cement bulkhead. "I want to come looking at the Gulf Stream."

I lifted her onto my lap. She pulled aside the bathing suit's center seam and uttered a soft groan. "Let's try to hold still as long as we can," she said.

"Umm, I can't guarantee . . ."

"Joke," she said, giggling, moving so her breasts rubbed my chest. "But if you could wait for me twice, I'd be ten times happier."

I wanted to give her that much, but I wasn't going to count sheep or think about car wrecks so I could slow down nature. I listened to waves slapping under the pier apron. The night was trying to be peaceful. I looked back at the shoreline, the two-hundred-yard view I'd scoped fifteen hours earlier when I'd worried about a siren headed my way. Now only crime lights and one more moped on Atlantic Boulevard.

Me and my paranoia.

My thinking about the morning helped me deliver Teresa's first gift. I joined her from that point on, thoughts focused, my hands caressing slick perspiration on her back. When she held me tighter, quivered, whimpered, I wondered if her eyes were open to watch waves.

After several minutes, after catching her breath, she pushed herself off me, looked around, stripped off the shirt and bathing trunks. "I've never made love on White Street Pier. Never been naked, either."

"Don't take off your shoes," I said. "There's always broken glass."

"Can't hurt me. I could walk on hot coals."

A few minutes later we walked our bikes down the pier. "Funny," she said. "My stepfather was on the dedication committee for this new construction. I wonder what he'd think about our initiation."

"I doubt we're the first."

"Yes, but he looks at me sometimes."

"He's an old Conch."

"He's a slime. Don't tell my mother I said it."

Three young dudes pedaled their bikes toward us. By body language I could tell they were sneering, up to no good. Future Bug Thorsbys, I thought. I was not in the mood for trouble. One angled toward us, got close enough to try something. I steeled myself to deliver a bad surprise. Suddenly the kid said, "Evening, ma'am," and rolled on.

Teresa chuckled. "His father's an assistant county prosecutor."

I thought, Me and my paranoia.

Back at the house my answering machine awaited us: "Mercer Holloway here, Alex." At midnight his voice morning-cheerful. "After your ordeal this evening, I'm guessing you need a treat. Will you and Ms. Barga please join us for late brunch or early lunch at Blue Heaven? If I don't hear regrets, make it twelve-fifteen. You would do us all a favor if you brought a camera and a roll of film. Souvenirs are too seldom gathered these days."

The man was quick to play his chips.

I lifted the phone, said into the receiver, "Thank you, Mr. Holloway. I was just saying to Ms. Barga that brunch at Blue Heaven would beat takeout from Fausto's deli."

"You really want to?" Teresa was naked again, on the porch, with a towel slung over her shoulder. She slowly shook her head. "I don't get you."

"You said yourself that my pictures wouldn't harm the

island. I want to hear what he's got to say. Why pass a free lunch?"

She looked puzzled, with a touch of disgust on her face.

I said, "You like to read mysteries, right?"

We both knew the answer. She stared at me for part two.

I said, "He's in cahoots with Butler Dunwoody. Maybe a clue to solving the murders will jump out as you munch your pencil-thin asparagus gratinée."

She said nothing. She remained standing there.

She was waiting for specific action.

I went to the shower and moved Fecko's belongings to the locked shed where I stored my lawn mower. I gave her two minutes, then joined her.

20

Muffled thunder rumbled across the island. A dim flash of lightning woke us. Faint daylight outlined the blinds. The strange silence, one more time. The digital time blinked 00:00.

Another power failure. I hoped the subways weren't stuck.

Teresa checked the clock, threw off the sheet, hit the floor running. A fine sight. She hadn't brought office clothes. She'd have to go home before going to work. I boosted myself from bed, trudged barefoot into the living room, opened the door. Humid air wafted from the porch. I went to the kitchen, in dim light began coffee. Yard palms looked blue instead of green. My head felt full of sluggish blood, like a whiskey hangover. Probably from bouncing off the police car's metal interior grate. Even the birds sang a depressed song. It would be a long, wet morning.

Then I remembered. No power, no coffee.

I'd left myself a note: "Holloway—Blue Heaven." Mercer would pressure me again to photograph his "opportunities." A real photo job might remove my mind from other crap. Maybe I could request that he post Tommy Tucker as my personal security guard. I thought back to Butler Dunwoody's description of his property's history. A closer knowledge of Mercer's holdings might make it easier to accept his offer.

Thunder rolled again, more distant. Carmen's car left the lane. Teresa entered the kitchen dialing my cordless handset. I looked at the phone. She looked at it, put it to her ear, hung it up.

I said, "What time does your stepfather get to work?"

"He leaves at seven. He does breakfast at Harpoon Harry's until seven-forty. If it's not raining he walks into the zoning office at exactly seven fifty-nine. If it's raining, he's one minute late."

"I need an appointment?"

"Not if you carry a bag of doughnuts and a café con leche."

I plugged in the old rotary for her. "Can he get me into the tax appraiser's files?"

"Take a pint of Añejo for Cheap Juan Mendez," she said.

"Can I take the rum straight to Mendez? Bypass your stepfather?"

"I recommend it." She checked a stack of papers. "What's all this?"

"Carmen picked up my mail for me."

"Look at these postmarks," she said. "Have you paid bills this month?"

"It's a question of time."

She looked at the stack and back at me. "Is it a question of money?"

"Do me one thing?" I said.

She answered with a half-awake quizzical expression.

"Think about the afternoon before we went up the Keys for dinner," I said. "Try to remember if you told anyone where we were going."

She called for a cab, then poked her head through the porch door. "Okay. If I talked about it, I can't recall who or why."

The rain had let up enough for her to wait on Fleming for the taxi. She kissed me good-bye. "Did the concrete scuff your bottom?"

It took me two beats too long to understand.

"Remember, White Street Pier? The moonlight? A naked lady?"

I saved my ass, caught it on the fly: "The seawall texture was that of a mild loofah sponge. Refreshing to the epidermal, a reminder of reality, yet a small factor of my happiness package."

"I'm getting strong signals on my detector."

"I woke up with fifteen things on my mind."

"If you want," she said, "I'll call Holloway and accept his kind invitation." Teresa walked down the lane laughing.

I wanted to catch Wheeler before he left for the dock. I dialed Marnie's cell phone. When she answered, I said, "Thank you for whatever."

"I don't usually make jailhouse calls," she said. "They told me when I left that you'd walk before midnight. Do you want him? He's opening the door."

"Yes, but I have one more question for you."

She snagged Sam, then came back on. "You're going to ask a favor."

"Two, now that I think about it. Any scuttlebutt about Dexter Hayes in the skirt-chasing category?"

"He's married."

"I know," I said. "I mean, like hitting on suspects or people he meets on the job?"

"I pay absolutely no attention to that kind of stuff."

"Could you?"

"For two days, maximum. Then I shut it off. What else?"

"I need details on six unsolved city murders, three of which have been copied this week."

"Three?"

"Last night."

"Oh. I didn't even think . . ." She paused. "Joe Hooks is working up a long piece on them, supposed to run in early February. A follow-up to the police-chief controversy."

"Any chance of getting copies of everything the *Citizen* ran on scene descriptions, what the police revealed to the press?"

"I like this kind of favor, Alex Rutledge. I promised myself a lazy day. Shoveling newspaper into a copier is the mindless task I need. Here's the captain."

Sam, out of breath: "I'm out of here."

"Client?"

"If he doesn't wimp out by the weather."

"Can you ask around, see if Jemison Thorsby's really catching fish?"

"As opposed to . . ."

"The endless list of South Florida alternatives."

Sam said, "Do we already know the answer?"

"In general, but not specifics. How's he paying bills? Who's he dealing with? Who's on his team?"

"Have a nice day and be a good American." He hung up.

Cecilia Ayusa's broom whisked in the lane. I should buy the Ayusas a cable subscription. She could check the Weather Channel before wasting her cleanup efforts. I walked out slowly. I didn't want to jolt her out of her dream state. I waited for her to notice me. She carried a paper sack and a dustpan.

"Who these bums in the lane?" she said.

"The police, you mean?"

"No, the bums bums. I kick them away, they say your name, they got to make a delivery. Got a old hot-water bottle, I don't want to say what else. Got trash bags, I think, all the caca this week, dead bodies in those plastic bags." She stooped to snag a solo leaf. "Hector, he gone to Budde's to get his sticky-paper notepads. He think I remember my whole life, he put the notes everyplace in my house. I got notes on a bathroom sink. Notes on my bed."

Cecilia found a pack of dry berries, leaned to sweep them into the dustpan. Before she'd dropped them into the bag, a gust of wind had replaced them with leaves and litter. I didn't tell her.

At eight fifty-nine I stopped at the Tropical Package Store on Fleming. Then I rode down Bahama to the tax assessor's office on Southard. I chained my bike to a rack in front of the bank.

Johnny "Cheap Juan" Mendez, the county tax appraiser, worked out of a leased storefront. Mendez stood five-six, had the scrappy look of someone who'd had to fight back most of his life. He spoke into the telephone at his secretary's desk, lifted his chin to greet me. Every time he spoke, he sneered. An aerial photograph of Fort Jefferson at the Dry Tortugas hung on the west wall. The only other objects in the room were the desk, an adjustable-height chair, an armchair, a circular discount-store clock, and a tiny table stacked with outdated copies of *Modern Maturity* and *Time*. Oppressive fluorescent lighting threw a yellow-green tint. A radio played in the next office, boring "beautiful," music, adjusted for minimum treble. I could smell Mendez's breath from across the room, a deadly combo of cigarettes and black coffee.

Mendez half-recognized me. We'd seen each other in various offices and departments for years. Never socially. I put the Bacardi Añejo on his desk, made my request.

Mendez led me to a poorly lighted room packed with floor-to-ceiling file racks. A mote fog fought four low-watt incandescent bulbs. Money saved in illumination was being spent to drive a window-mounted air conditioner. It struggled to suck air through a filter that, through the plastic grille, looked like bear fur. It stank as if a cat had sprayed the exterior part of the A/C, and the spray had blown in ripe. The climate control was a fruitless attempt to make up for failures betrayed by odors of damp cardboard, paper, and carpeting soaked by rain leaks or condenser distillate.

Mendez didn't mind my being in there, but he wanted out. The rum had eliminated any curiosity he might have had regarding my intentions. He left me to what he called my como se llama.

Six rows of shelving, narrow aisles. There had been half-assed attempts at uniformity in box sizing and labeling. It took an hour to acquaint myself with the filing system, the seven different plat-book groups: by date, then by lot number. Nothing was alphabetical. I had to figure out arcane real-estate stuff like easements, foreclosures, and chattels in order to make sense of the deed histories. By eleven o'clock I'd worked halfway through Holloway's "Group One" list.

Three corporations owned the properties. Chrysalis-Manifest Partners had begun acquiring in 1964 and had made its last purchase in 1983. The Sut-Ho-Dor Corporation made its first buys in 1971. In 1982 Sut-Ho-Dor sold several properties to Chrysalis-Manifest, and several to Holloway Holdings, Inc. One other property acquired by Holloway Holdings was the old El Mirador Hotel, popular from the fifties until the late seventies. The place had been called Key Breeze Suites in years since then. It never had benefited from a knock-down-and-build like the Hibiscus, or from renovations like the Atlantic Shores. Sut-Ho-Dor's only holding since then had been at 544 Southard. Of the three corporations, only Holloway Holdings, Inc., had bought property after 1983.

After two hours I'd learned nothing but company names. Transactions earlier than the sixties meant nothing to me, and there was no way to tell how the properties had been used. Butler Dunwoody must have done some kick-ass research to come up with his information.

"Howzit go?" Cheap Juan was back. He stood in the doorway. He'd been testing the rum. He wobbled.

I thanked Cheap Juan Mendez for his permission to peruse the files.

It had rained but the sun was back out. I stood on the sidewalk, thought a moment. I checked the front of the building. It was 544 Southard. Sut-Ho-Dor Corporation owned the building.

I went back inside. "Mr. Mendez," I said. "Who collects the rent checks on this building?"

"The city, it pay direct," he said. "I got a leak, I call that real-estate lady, Mrs. Kaiser. That daughter of that Holloway man who went to Washington."

"Julie Kaiser?"

"Best on this island, you bet your ass. She send her husband with a tool box, every time. She's a nice lady."

21

I sat in late-morning sunlight on Teresa's condo porch steps. No breeze at all. Every cubic foot of air stuck in its own space. A fat bumblebee flew figure eights above my head. Ignored me, ignored the flowers, kept flying the figure eights. A vagabond rooster wandered the parking asphalt, pecked at pebbles and buds that had fallen from an acacia, hoping for a corn kernel. He crowed, probably in protest.

I hear you, pal.

Teresa's car turned into the driveway. She punched the entry keypad, waited for the twelve-foot iron security gate to swing slowly. She cruised in, windows down, her hair fluttering. Barenaked Ladies loud on the stereo. I knew the lyric. Angst beyond my imagination. A loser shaves his girl's name into his hair, but misspells it. I thought I had it rough.

Teresa parked, rolled her windows, left a gap. She wore tan chinos and a polo shirt, a *Red Sky at Night* ball cap. She kissed my cheekbone, unlocked her condo door. I heard her briefcase drop onto the hall table. I followed her in, waited while she used the bathroom. A paperback book sat on her kitchen counter. *A Cool Breeze on the Underground*. I'd never seen it before.

She rolled her bicycle backward to the porch. "You

could have been in the shade. You were sitting out here sweating."

"I was airing myself out. Cheap Juan's storage room started growing on me."

"Home-grown Astroturf?"

"Don't step on my green suede shoes."

She said, "The tax files give you anything you wanted?"

"Not much. I'll tell you later."

We rode three short blocks down Thomas. Blue Heaven, at the corner of Petronia, was central to Key West's black section. In the 1990s the intersection suffered a period of open crack cocaine sales. Expensive white powder from Duval Street had become cheap. The true ground zero was Virginia and Whitehead, where loitering was "proof evident, presumption great" of dope dealing. Naturally, there was a pecking order in the loitering process. I had heard that one regular peddler openly claimed to the cops to be marketing rocks as big as the Ritz. Vigilance and investment, what had become multiracial gentrification, had returned Petronia-Thomas to civility.

Blue Heaven is a four-star throwback to five stages of island history. Its current incarnation—a pink-and-pastel-blue restaurant, bake shop, open-air backyard bar—calls to mind peace signs, flowers woven into hair, the era of alcoholic vegetarians, back-to-the-country doobie tokers. The dining patio is filled with almond and Spanish lime trees, surrounded by an unpainted six-foot fence. It's frequented by neighborhood animals, domestic and fowl. The food and wait staff are first-rate. Everything else is laid-back Caribbean.

We locked our bicycles to a galvanized security rack in front of a fifteen-foot cactus. Half the other bicycles were retrocruisers—modern-day white-walled balloon tires, half-acre seats. Most of the others had high-rise handlebars and rusted frames. One or two were polka-dotted in primary colors atop geometric patterns. Rolling exhibits by vehicle artist Captain Outrageous. We walked around back. Every table was full. Vultures hung at the outside bar, made small talk with the early drinkers, waited to pounce at the maître d's faintest beckon. One of the owners, Rick Hatch, saw us, grinned and pointed to the second-floor porch. Our host had arrived early.

Holloway's recorded invitation had said to join "us," without identifying the others he'd asked along. I had guessed there would be immediate family members. I was greeted by my first positive surprise in four days. Next to Mercer Holloway sat Flo Franklin, the grande dame of Key West. Down-to-earth and elegant, Flo was the sparkly, silver-haired widow of Willy Franklin, for decades kingpin of Key West's shrimp- and fish-house industries. Flo wore a traditional red shawl over a black bolero vest, a white linen shirt and dark skirt. She held her Bloody Mary aside. We exchanged hugs and air kisses. Expensive old-lady perfume wafted into my eyes.

A small red button on her vest: CUTER? YOUNGER? PERKY? JUST SAY NO.

I recalled seeing her one day twenty years ago in the post office. She'd asked how my friend Jimmy Buffett was doing. I told her I thought his career might have staying power, that he'd just recorded *Son of a Son of a Sailor* and bought himself a Porsche 928. Her eyes had lit up. She'd said, "Oh, yes, Alex. I owned a little red Maserati for years. Even when the top's not down, even going slowly, those cars will make your hair stand on end." Since then I'd always held a wonderful image of Flo zipping about the provincial island, long before my time, in her exotic Italian sports roadster.

I introduced Teresa and explained her mother's marriage to Paulie Cottrell.

Flo smiled broadly, perfectly poised, and said in aristocratic tones, "Worse things have happened." Her smile so captivating, her manner so charming, that no one else caught her drift.

While Flo engaged Teresa, Mercer Holloway took me aside, told me all was forgiven—my delays, my failures to respond to messages. He understood that I'd been stressed since the weekend, noted that I hadn't attempted to cash his check. Holloway looked spiffed up in a blue dress shirt with a straight white collar, khaki trousers, expensive loafers with no socks, a tan-colored drink in a rocks glass. His full head of hair, slightly long, an elegant gray, was slicked back. Almost as if he was dolled up for a photo.

He'd asked me to bring a camera. I'd forgotten the request on hearing the message, forgotten on purpose. I handed him the envelope I'd brought along. It held the twenty-five-hundred-dollar check.

"So you're turning down my offer?"

"No," I said. "I'm returning your check before we talk here. We resume our talk on level ground."

"You should have been a lawyer."

"You should have been a beatnik."

He said, "Not in a million years."

"You got my point."

I heard voices on the porch ladder, checked over the rail. Philip and Julie Kaiser climbed ahead of Donovan and Suzanne Cosgrove. The sisters wore tropical business attire. Donovan looked ten years older than his brother-in-law. Butler Dunwoody and Heidi Norquist appeared, drinks in hand. I hadn't seen them on the way in. They must have been on the far side of the outside bar. Dunwoody wore an authentic Panama hat. He looked to the balcony, saw me, then stomped up the stairs. In cadence, in a booming mock sea-shanty voice, he sang, "I brought my bimbo to dance the mambo, this island life is for me!" He spilled his Collins-looking drink on his wrist. Damned cheerful for someone who'd lost a primary employee only seventy-two hours ago.

Embarrassed, Heidi tried to defuse it: "Always the social climber."

I introduced Teresa to those she didn't know. Not a soul but Mercer and Flo Franklin looked happy to be there. Everyone else smiled, with near-total awkwardness. Chewing on lower lips, checking for bugs in drinks. A server took another drink order. One brought hors d'oeuvres to the table. A third poured Pellegrino. I knew they cut off breakfast at eleven forty-five. I'd had my mind and stomach set on Seafood Benedict. A jerk chicken sandwich would have to do. Ten places set at the table. We weren't waiting for anyone else.

Stilted small talk buzzed. Philip Kaiser remarked on the convertible that Dunwoody had parked on Thomas Street. He wondered if it wasn't a risky spot for an old beauty. "It'll catch a thief's eye," said Kaiser, "in spite of its age."

"Bad topic." Heidi's sunny face went away. She glared at Philip Kaiser.

Kaiser went silent, pulled back, looked to Dunwoody for an explanation. He didn't understand his gaffe.

Dunwoody explained: "Her Jaguar roadster went bye-bye last night. First time we've ever left it outside. We didn't hear a thing. They must've rolled it down the driveway. They had at least five hours before we discovered it. By now it's on a boat to South America. Or in a chop shop in South Miami."

Kaiser took the high road: "I'm sorry to hear that. Sorry to have brought up the subject. I sure like your old Ford."

Butler said, " 'Bout to get rid of it, anyway. You can tell a car's getting old when you can't fit any more fast-food napkins in the glove box."

Teresa nudged me. Her Pontiac Grand Am's glove compartment always held mounds of leftover paper napkins.

Mercer was back to me. "You brought a camera?"

I shook my head. "Sorry, forgot."

"I was hoping for a happy family group shot. We're so seldom together anymore. Maybe the restaurant has one we can borrow."

I didn't want to create a Holloway family memento. "No chance of asking everyone out to Olan Mills, the Nation's Studio?"

My humor fell flat. Mercer's hospitality face went to pissed off. Teresa stepped closer. She'd overheard. She tapped Holloway on the arm, opened her small handbag, extracted a silver clamshell point-and-shoot, her "drunk-proof" Olympus Zoom 80. I'd always enjoyed using the small camera. Press the button, decent quality. I still didn't want to play the game.

Mercer ignored my scowl. He shifted Teresa's camera from her hand to mine, patted my shoulder. "Ply your trade in the open air, young man. Better for you than sitting in a jail cell. Or rooting around a stuffy tax assessor's office all morning."

He turned, began to position his daughters and their husbands.

Cheap Juan knew which side of the butter his bread was on. He'd told on me. And Mercer had a point. He'd sent Donovan Cosgrove to pull my ass out of a sling. I owed him more than just shooting a picture.

Holloway arranged the pose. Vanity ruled. The women complained about their outfits. The brothers-in-law wanted to comb their hair. I took a dozen snaps, got it done. Mercer and Flo looked majestic. Heidi looked saucy. Julie looked classy. Suzanne Cosgrove didn't smile a single time.

After a minute of seat selection, we settled at the table, passed plates of finger food. The tree above us dripped rainwater, spotted our shoulders. Holloway made a fuss about draping his cotton sweater over Flo Franklin's shoulders. Philip Kaiser broke the conversational ice. He raised his drink in salute. "This fine atmosphere, the elegant nature," he said, gazing at the old trees in the yard.

Butler Dunwoody responded, lifted his glass. "Here's to a picturesque setting. The whole place vibrates with history."

Kaiser agreed. "You're absolutely right. It's not bad for a place that used to be a minority whorehouse." He turned to Julie and asked pointedly, "Did Daddy Big Dex own this place, or just run it for his white bosses?"

Suzanne Cosgrove said, "Nice question for your wife in public."

Julie turned to her sister. "You'll keep your goddamned mouth shut."

Suzanne leaned forward. "Right, skinny bitch. You worried about secrets in this town?"

Julie put on a cold face. "You haven't had one since that biker in ninth grade."

"Because you let me have sloppy seconds."

Julie turned to her father. "Sissy's rampaging, Father. She forgot to take her pill today."

Suzanne forced a laugh. "You're such a great sister. Your dysfunctions always make me feel better about myself."

Teresa's hand moved to mine. She pressed her fingers into my palm and squeezed hard. Our secret code: Let's head for the door.

"Heidi," said Butler, "it's your turn. This looks like fun."

"I don't fight in restaurants." Heidi turned to the warring sisters. "Why don't you take it outside, you silly preppie hosebags?"

It took less than thirty seconds. The luncheon turned into a free-for-all. A glass of Chardonnay flew, along with a feminine-sounding "Motherfucker," a loud "Son of a bitch" from Donovan Cosgrove. A plate of Portobello mushrooms sailed. Mercer Holloway stood shouting. Flo Franklin grabbed her drink before losing it, then went under the table. Most drinks and appetizers went airborne. Goblets broke. Several plates shattered on the wood deck.

I'd pushed back from the table, held up my napkin to shield Teresa from debris. Suzanne had taken the first major hit. Philip Kaiser and Donovan Cosgrove had rushed around the table to defend her. It ended as abruptly as it had begun. Action froze at ground level. I half-expected an ovation from a hidden audience. Julie Kaiser, who had not started the words war but had thrown at least three strikes, sat isolated, anger and guilt on her face. Tears and cream-colored sauce and red wine dripped from her chin. Servers rushed up the wood stairs with towels. One carried Dunwoody's hat. The expensive Panama had been knocked over the railing.

Almost on cue, Suzanne Cosgrove's phone rang. She

made a production of holding out her hand—"time out" in the ball game—wiping debris from her hands and face, carefully extracting the phone from her purse. We don't want salad oil on our fine leather. She leaned away from the table, sure we could hear her side of the conversation. "Yes?" she said. "Was anyone hurt? Who saw it happen? Thank you, I'll tell him."

She thumbed the END button, turned toward her father. "The police are going to the house, Daddy. Someone shot a gun. It made a hole in your door."

Holloway crouched to help Flo Franklin back into her seat. "Arguments happen," he said. "Bad manners can be excused. Gunfire in my residence is not acceptable. I am sorry. Our social gathering is over."

Donovan stood, grabbed the fat set of keys he'd placed on the table. "I'll take care of it, Mercer."

Softly, out of the side of his mouth, Holloway muttered, "I doubt it."

Teresa's cell phone rang. The city was calling.

"Matter of fact," said Mercer more loudly, "please give the Infiniti keys to Mr. Rutledge. I'm sure he wouldn't mind seeing Mrs. Franklin to her home. I'll go with one of you."

"Happy to help," I said.

Philip and Donovan, knowing they'd miss lunch, attacked scattered hors d'oeuvres before departing. Teresa had walked down the stairway to take her call. She met me at ground level, offered Flo another escort elbow. Butler and Heidi preceded us to the Petronia gateway. Heidi didn't care who heard her: "She looks like J. Crew and her stupid sister looks like Land's End and they both smell like hotel soap."

I looked right. Flo frowned. Teresa fought back a smile, adjusting her opinion of Heidi. I asked Teresa to walk with us to the Infiniti sedan and to dial my answering machine.

One message. Sheriff's Detective Bobbi Lewis: "Please call back."

Teresa hugged Flo good-bye, told me she'd leave my bike chained to the rack.

Flo Franklin and I discussed my photo travels until we reached Johnson Street. Finally she mentioned the food fight. "Suzanne's such a spirited gal. I remember the day she was married. It rained and I thought, This is a bad sign. For all I know, Alex, her Donovan is a bundle of fun underneath the veneer. But a dullard on the outside. I wonder how she keeps her sanity."

"No offense, but ever since high school I've wondered if she still had it."

"Well, who knows. Maybe they're good for each other. Maybe he's a star in their relations. Lord knows my Willy made up for his faults that way."

On one hand, more than I needed to know about Willy and Flo. On the other hand, talk about a spirited gal . . .

Flo Franklin's driveway, at the corner of Johnson and Grinnell, opened to both streets. I pulled off Grinnell, stopped under the entrance portico.

"When we went into that restaurant, I left my handbag in the trunk," she said. "I hope it hasn't spilled."

I pulled the keys from the ignition, popped the remote button on the key ring. Her purse had spilled onto the trunk-floor carpet. Several items had rolled toward the front of the car. I leaned in to help her scoop them up.

"I need that little ticket stub," she said. "But I don't believe that feather is mine." She pointed to a dark recess. "I thank you for your kindness. Would you like some iced tea?"

I slammed the trunk, shook my head. "Thanks. I've got to get going."

"Alex, dear, what happened to your face?"

"I bumped my nose on a piece of metal."

"You young people. I was afraid it was the other way around. Send me a postcard from your next exotic port of call."

I promised I would.

I didn't want to return the car immediately to Holloway.

If the police were at his house, Southard might be blocked off anyway. I wanted to park it out of the way while I thought about the feather stuck to the trunk carpeting.

I wasn't an expert on feather shapes or rarity or commonness. I knew nothing about microscopic yarn and fiber identification. I knew only that, to my untrained eyes, I'd found my first solid clue in four days. The feather was identical to one that a murderer had inserted in Richard Engram's ass.

22

I unlocked my house to a furious message light and a ringing phone. Bad signs, like the rain at Donovan Cosgrove's wedding.

I picked up, beat the machine for the grab.

Teresa, from her cell phone: "You're not going to believe the mess down here. Dexter's turned into an all-biz, by-the-book dervish. Strict rules and procedures."

"Why now?"

"Hear him? He's screaming at a scene tech to stay off the front walk so he won't foul the grid. He's tried to call you four or five times. This is my third try."

"He'll accuse me of this crime, too."

"No. The bullet shattered the beveled glass in Holloway's front door. It went down the hall, across the patio and pool, into the rear neighbor's house. It hit a carpenter in the ass. The 'starboard-side gluteus maximus,' as Marnie's going to print it."

A perfect opportunity for the city's ace crime scene photographer. "Ortega's not there?"

"He stepped in dog shit on the sidewalk and tracked it down Holloway's hallway. He took a few pictures. Cootie has left the building."

"How about Suzanne Oil and Julie Water?"

"Separated by distance and their husbands."

"What do I do, photograph the trajectory?"

"I don't know. The wounded man's already gone to the hospital. Mercer's off the deep end. Dexter's got nothing nice to say to anyone. Marnie's pissed because Holloway wants no mention in the paper. Told her she'd lose the advertising of anyone who rents store space from his company."

"And I should walk into this circus?"

"It's income," she said. "And you're tough. Gotta go."

I'd left the Infiniti on Margaret between Fleming and Eaton, in a "residential permit" space. I wanted to show Dexter the feather before I returned the car to Holloway. I extracted my photo satchel from its stash, relocked the house. I had no bicycle, no motorcycle. I began the four-block hike. Cracked sidewalks, a decent breeze. Birds lively in song—doves and parrots loudest—swooping about. Civil war among the jays. None of the morning rain clouds.

I made a detour. I wanted one more look at Holloway's Infiniti.

I played with the chance that Mercer was behind the murders. With three copies of previous murders, someone involved in one slaying was linked to all three. Holloway was supposed to be guiding Butler Dunwoody, to ensure the Caroline Street project's success. But Richard Engram's demise guaranteed bad publicity and the loss of a key employee.

Five questions: Had Julie Kaiser known who was driving the Infiniti down Caroline on Sunday? Had Engram's corpse been in the trunk, dressed and ready for delivery? Had Holloway—or the driver, if it wasn't Holloway—sent Bug Thorsby to scare me away, so a body placement could be done without a witness, or without the Infiniti's inclusion in a random photo? Had Julie known about the body—in the trunk or already inside the construction site? Had Heidi Norquist known that a body was en route when she rudely invited me to hit the trail?

If Holloway was involved, he'd had at least one helper. Someone who'd fired a shot at his empty house.

Had Dexter located Robbie Carpona?

Poor Heidi would be distressed to learn that I'd reconsidered her role.

I opened the Infiniti's trunk lid. I could learn nothing from the feather. I pulled out a camera, spooled a twenty-four-exposure roll, attached the mini-flash, snapped a dozen with three different lenses. I slammed the trunk, opened the front passenger door, then the glove box. The registration and insurance card were in a white envelope. The car belonged to Donovan Cosgrove, 1800 Atlantic Boulevard.

Donovan's ocean view could cloud up soon.

This time I remembered to remove the film from my camera.

A police roadblock diverted Southard's traffic but allowed pedestrians to pass. They'd also wrapped Holloway's yard with CRIME SCENE—DO NOT CROSS yellow tape, shuffled a crowd of onlookers to the north sidewalk. The first officer I met was Tisdell, the co-arresting squad car driver who'd taught me negative lessons about road hazard avoidance and the virtues of seat-belt use. Tisdell waved me off like batting a moth. I stood my ground, waited for someone to appear with the power to overrule.

I didn't have to wait long. Dexter Hayes stepped to Holloway's broad front porch. He bellowed, "Your sergeant was ordered to let that man pass, Officer."

Tisdell stood aside, lifted the yellow tape for me. "Como mierda," he said softly. I wasn't expert at Spanish. I thought he'd said, "I eat shit." He'd meant it the other way around. He wasn't Cuban. He wasn't a Conch. He'd learned the phrase from a local for just this occasion. A local with a sense of humor.

"Sounds like a nutrition issue," I said.

"Your mother."

I let it slide. The wheel goes around.

Hayes descended the steps as I approached. "You owe me this one."

"You want a picture of broken glass?"

"You're the expert. You always act like a miracle

worker. So perform a miracle. Help me solve this crime."

I said, "It's a bullet through a door. It's not somebody's head."

"It's firing into a residence, shitbird. The shooter couldn't know if anyone was home or not. It's attempted murder."

Point won, though his sudden dedication baffled me. I had no choice but to walk the trajectory, attempt to determine the shooter's location. A passing vehicle. I knew that much. No one's stupid enough to commit a walk-by.

I said, "I think I found some evidence, the Caroline Street thing."

Hayes clenched his teeth. I thought his eyes might burst into flames. "Do me one favor," he hissed. "Do this first. Think of nothing but this problem. Anything you've got, we'll discuss the minute we're done."

"This might not wait."

"Wanna bet?"

I stared at him. Stubborn shit. He stared back.

"Want to walk me through," I said, "so they know I belong in there?"

We passed through the foyer. I looked through Holloway's open office door. Mercer peered out a front window. Philip Kaiser and Suzanne Cosgrove sat in the twin chairs that faced Mercer's broad desk. Tommy Tucker sat in the chair behind Holloway's desk, praying to a can of Diet Pepsi. Glum faces. No life in the party. No one said hello.

Hayes led me to the open patio. Donovan Cosgrove and Julie Kaiser sat on cushioned teak slat chairs, sipping tall drinks. Making up for lost alcohol at Blue Heaven. Julie offered a grim, ironic smile, like folks affect at funerals. Donovan looked distraught, rubbed his face with an open hand. Distraught, I thought. Too distraught. Was Mercer's emissary to Dunwoody's project propping up the job with one hand and squashing it with the other? Then whacking his hired thugs to eliminate witnesses?

I turned to look out the front door. A clear view of the front walkway. A half dozen people on the north sidewalk.

I recognized one fellow. The *Citizen* photographer had been banished from the premises.

"You want to hurry, every little chance you get?" said Hayes.

The city investigative team had placed a ten-foot double stepladder over the rear lattice fence and croton hedge. After Hayes steadied his feet on the far side, I handed him the camera bag and followed. The police had blown the yellow-tape budget in the neighbor's yard. The landscaped yard and rear of the home-in-renovation were great examples of hidden Key West luxury. I heard children playing, a Dan Fogelberg song in the house next door.

"He was in there." Dexter pointed to a glass-enclosed sunroom that overlooked a small ice-blue pool. Two sets of French doors had been swung open. A working platform lay on two substantial sawhorses. Off to the side, a large table saw, an industrial band saw, and an upright belt sander. I walked inside, immediately noticed a stain on the fresh parquet floor.

I said, "The poor guy bled on his own work."

The instant I spoke, I knew Hayes would zap me with a wise retort.

No answer. I looked. Hayes had gone back over the ladder.

A dark red oval, a foot-long blood smear. What did I know about bullet velocities, the effects of wind and weight on trajectories? If I stood behind the bloodstain, looked at Holloway's house, the croton hedge blocked direct sight down the central hallway. I positioned the wounded carpenter's three-rung aluminum stepladder. I saw over the hedge, across the patio, down the hall. I barely made out light coming from the busted-out front door. I pushed the stepladder about eight inches to the left. This time perfect line of sight. The view no different from what I'd seen from the patio end of the hallway.

I was pissed. I couldn't think of a reason for Hayes to want me there. My presence, my photos were unnecessary. Dexter Hayes was scamming me. I'd arrived with a Big

Clue. He'd blown me off, sent me to the neighbor's house.

Play it out his way. For now.

I shot a sequence of photos with a 28mm wide lens, a standard 50mm, a "mild" 100mm telephoto, and a 300mm long lens. It occurred to me that the shooter might not have had a clean shot directly down the hall. I shifted the step-ladder as far to the right as I could and still see daylight through the front door. I took that angle with the two longer lenses, then repeated it with the ladder pushed to the left extreme. The limiting factor was not the front door. It was the opening at the rear of the hall, at the patio.

I hadn't even shot a whole roll of color print film. I played the game, took out my tape recorder, verbally documented time of day, camera, and lenses.

I hung my camera bag over my shoulder, climbed the double ladder. No sign of Donovan on Mercer's patio. But off to the yard's east side, next to a sputtering circular fountain, Dexter Hayes and Julie Kaiser had their heads together. She looked down, was shaking her head; Hayes wrote in a small notepad. He heard me descend the ladder, quickly ended their chat. Julie added the traditional Conch code words, "How's your mother, Dexter?"

"My mother is . . ." He looked at me. "She's doing okay."

I said, "Talk to you out front, Detective?"

We walked the hallway. Mercer Holloway stood in the foyer, expounding to officials and family members. Teresa and Marnie stood in the front row. "The town's downhill," he said. "It's become an open-air asylum for alcoholics and weirdos who failed at being less weird up north. Let the weekly papers explain this crap. They spend so damn much ink trying to replace political professionals with amateurs. They should start ignoring old-fashioned graft and lambaste violence."

No one said a word. Mercer was coming off weirdly. But I suspected that many of those assembled agreed with him.

"You don't know where to look for these types?" he

bellowed. "Try all the basic colors. The Red Doors, the Green Parrot, the Blue Heaven. For all I know there's an Orange Peekhole! A Yellow Submarine! They're porking each other in the torpedo tubes! Go ask 'em why I got artillery flying through my home."

Philip Kaiser took control, began to usher Mercer back into his office. Kaiser turned to Marnie. "That remark about the papers doesn't mean he's changed his mind about having his name bandied about."

"The *Citizen* doesn't bandy, Mr. Kaiser. We're a *daily*. We report. Look at the crowd out there. There's going to be talk."

"There's always talk on this island. There's always talk to take the place of yesterday's news. But talk isn't the public record, or the archives, or whatever they do these days on the Internet."

She said, "You're fooling yourself if you think talk won't come get you."

In the confusion, I finally regained Hayes's attention. He pointed to the driveway, began to slide in that direction. We wound up closer to the street than the house. I gave him a plastic canister, the film I'd just removed from my camera.

Dexter started it: "Do you sometimes wish you could be Bob?"

"I don't recall that wish. Any particular Bob?"

Dexter pointed at a street barricade next to a sewer excavation. A faded stencil on the crossbar read: BOB'S BARRICADES. "Bob shows up on time one day, then goes home. He gets paid fees every day of the project. He doesn't take daily crap, he doesn't have to write bullshit reports, risk his life, work shitty hours. Old Bob's got the deal. Who's that other guy? Paul's Portable Potties? He delivers temporary bathrooms. He sends his minimum-wage flunkies out to retrieve and empty them once a week, collects his money at the mailbox. It's your hidden economy. It's a simple life. Don't you wish for it?"

"That's what you want?" I said. "Maybe Bob and Paul

spend years eating potato chips, sitting in front of the television. Porking themselves up to high blood pressure and oversized hearts. Kings of the couchies. Or maybe one of them's in a wheelchair, invented this leasing businesses because he can't be out and about. In that case this enterprise is a triumph. Maybe it's not such a cushy gig. Somebody's got to keep track of all those barricades, all those expensive shitters. Did you ever find Robbie Carpona?"

"Not answering his phone. Tell me about your world-class clue."

Dexter's face was wet with perspiration. I realized mine was, too. Just then a cloud blocked the sun, gave us a moment's respite. I explained the Blue Heaven luncheon. I listed those present. I shortened the food fight, and mentioned the cell call to Suzanne. I finished with driving Flo Franklin home in the Infiniti. I described the spilled purse. I told him that the feather in the trunk matched the one stuck in Richard Engram's asshole.

Dexter nodded. He stared at the roadwork.

I'd expected more excitement. A loud hoot, or jumping jacks.

I was pissed. "You know your job," I said. "You know what's important and what's not. I've got this image of you sifting every murder scene for the last possible clue. I've got this mental picture of you checking every one of Paul's Portable Potties at Dunwoody's site, picking through the piss and shit to see if a murderer dropped evidence down the bucket. I'm going to store that image of you in my memory. I'll call it up, every time I hear your name."

Hayes's jaw tightened. He said nothing. He walked to a decrepit moped, pedaled it ten feet to jump-start the motor, and rode away.

Teresa and Marnie walked up to me. They'd been hanging back, not wanting to interrupt. Marnie handed me a file pocket. The photocopies of news files on the unsolved murders.

Teresa said, "Dexter acted today like he should've acted Sunday. He got his deal backward."

Donovan Cosgrove approached. "Helluva deal," he said.
I said, "One way to put it."
"Where'd you leave the car, Alex?" he said.
"It's over in the city garage."
"How did it get there?"
"I stopped to see if the city needed my services. A cop drove me home for my camera."
"Okay," said Cosgrove.
"But I left the keys at the house."
He pulled a key ring from his pocket. "No problem, Alex. I'll get it in a few minutes. Drop the keys off anytime."

23

I stared at Holloway's north-facing house, tried to collect my thoughts. Classic island architecture, symbol of the revered past, a manicured prize of today's opulence. The sun never had shone directly on its front porch.

Philip Kaiser leaned out of the door, surveyed the splintered frame of the blown-out window, then ducked back inside. Another job for the carpenter with the bullet in his butt. Fix that flaw in a hurry, write a check. Keep the peace, the tradition. Maintain that family image.

I borrowed Teresa's cell phone and called Detective Bobbi Lewis. She and I knew each other, spoke on the same frequency. We chatted fewer than forty seconds. I gave her the tag number for the silver Infiniti. She said she'd meet me on Margaret Street in about twelve minutes.

"Walk with me back inside," I said to Teresa and Marnie. Their faces said they wanted to read my mind, figure out my sullen mood. If I tried to explain, I'd lose my line of logic. I'd thank them later.

No one challenged us. A uniformed lieutenant stood just inside Donovan Cosgrove's office. Tucker and Suzanne still sat in Holloway's office. Tommy Tucker's eyes like knife slits in a mango. A fresh haircut, a twice-worn shirt. Suzanne had generated a dark cloud that hovered just above her head. No one else in sight. Classical music drifted from the second floor, battled static and chatter from the lieutenant's radio.

I left the women in the foyer—to give me a break from the cop—and went to the end of the hall. Dexter, in his frenzy, had missed two items of evidence. I found a hole in the narrow space between the right-side wall and the woodwork around the patio door. Right where I'd guessed it'd be. I found another hole in the exact opposite spot, adjacent to the left wall. It took a half minute to rig my 50-mm lens, my small flash with its homemade bubble-wrap diffuser, a fresh roll of film. I shot eight photographs, packed my gear, returned to the foyer. I directed the lieutenant to what I'd found. I hoped he'd follow up, find the projectiles in identifiable shape, deduce that the shooter had taken time to fire at least three, maybe more shots at slightly different angles. A smart investigator might even believe that there'd been a moving target, a shadow behind the fancy glass door.

A smart investigator might guess that Tommy Tucker had failed to reveal important information.

I asked Marnie to have Sam call me when he had a moment to spare. I suggested to Teresa that, since we'd missed lunch, we might have an early supper at Camille's. She smiled, shrugged, and smiled again.

Detective Lewis was waiting for me on Margaret. She's about five-eight, carries herself with authority. Too many citizens think that female officers lack the will to be forceful, especially attractive women who've managed to retain femininity on the job. I would hate to be a man who made that mistake with Bobbi Lewis. She wore dark slacks and a pale gray polo shirt with an imprinted badge. A pager and cell phone on her belt, a spiral pad and pen stuck in her belly-pack. She'd brought a muscular young assistant with faded jeans, a loose cotton sport shirt, a backward ball cap, and a video camera. He'd begun taping as I rounded the corner at Fleming. I wondered who'd review the lead-in, wondered if my body language spoke of confidence or flakiness.

Right down to business: "How did you come into possession of the car?" said Lewis.

I explained Mercer's request, his handing me the keys.

She held out a slip of paper, a memo form embossed with a green badge. "We've got the owner as Mr. Donovan Cosgrove," she said. "Was he present when his father-in-law, Mr. Mercer Holloway, asked you to drive the car?"

I nodded.

She waved her hand at the video rig. "Do me a favor. Answer me verbally so Robin can get his audio. Was Mr. Cosgrove present?"

"Yes."

"Did he see Mercer Holloway hand you the keys to this Infiniti?"

"I don't know. He was there, but he could've been distracted. He could have been looking away, talking with someone."

"Was there any doubt in your mind that Mr. Holloway had the authority to lend you Mr. Cosgrove's car?"

I said, "No doubt at all."

"Please open the trunk," she said. "Show me what you found in there."

We continued the charade so that Lewis could establish her right to be snooping, create an evidence trail, generate an admissible video file. She did not touch the feather, but instructed the young man to zoom for a close-up, then pull back to reestablish location. She went to her unmarked sedan, got what looked like a black plastic body bag, had me assist her in removing the entire carpet from the trunk, rolling it, sliding it into the bag. She placed the bag in her vehicle's trunk and directed the assistant to cease taping.

"Fingerprints from inside?" I said.

"Too late. You've driven the car, and—what, three days?—who knows how many other people have been inside, driving or as passengers. We'll test the trunk mat for blood and hair and all that. Even with a series of matches, it'll prove only that the car was used in a murder, but not who used it. Some asshole lawyer wants to step to the edge, he could claim only the trunk mat was associated with the murder, and there's no proof that it was in this car at the time of the crime."

My big clue was small potatoes.

Bobbi Lewis turned so the video kid couldn't hear her speak. "Why was your motorcycle burned next to Wiley Fecko's camp?"

"I wanted to ask if he'd seen anyone drop off the headless wonder."

"You found him sober?" she said. "I tried three times."

"He didn't tell me you'd been there."

"Please believe that we're everywhere on Stock Island. From the classy side to the suicide, night and day. Necessity. We've got the whole place wired for sound, so to speak."

"The day you found the body, that deputy, Fennerty, told me that Stock Island was enough to make anyone not be a cop."

Lewis laughed. "If it wasn't for Stock Island, Deputy Fennerty wouldn't have a life. Where's Fecko now?"

"He identified Bug Thorsby's truck. I took him downtown, gave him to a gentleman of the street for safekeeping. I was afraid Fecko would tell the wrong people what he'd seen."

"Where's he stashed?"

"His first stop was Mallory Square."

"Get him drunk, get him the Deluxe Wash? Windshield bugs, spray wax, ashtrays, and vacuum?"

I nodded.

"You called from Holloway's. Did the city find anything?"

"They're lucky they found the house," I said. "Dex Hayes wanted to do it right, but he brought his attitude."

"Dexter's made mistakes lately," said Lewis. "The kid's trying to be an old-fashioned Conch detective. He's forgotten how many old-fashioned Conch detectives retired early or went to prison. He may work out okay. But it'll take time." She stepped between two cars to let a U-Haul truck roll by.

"What do you think?" she said. "Are all the snuffs connected?"

"Only via me, the Caroline Street geography of the body, and the attack. And a link between Dunwoody and Holloway in the Caroline site progress. Is that enough?"

"Enough for you or me, but not for a judge. Assume this whole mess is one big mess. What was your first big clue?"

"Bug Thorsby . . ."

"Who's now dead. What was your second big clue?"

"Linking Bug to the headless wonder."

"A young man also gone to history," she said. "Your third?"

"The feather."

"So maybe somebody wants this guy Dunwoody to fail." She'd done her homework. "Okay," I said.

"If he fails, who gets hurt the most?"

"His girlfriend, Heidi Norquist, confided to me she's a heavy investor."

"So we take a macro view, assume everything's a big package. All these crimes are being committed to hurt Ms. Norquist?"

"I don't know," I said. "There may have been a multipurpose script. The copycat nature of the cases is making Liska look bad. Dexter, too, but not as bad as Liska. Somebody wanted to mess with me and Marnie Dunwoody. Somebody thought the boy-thugs were expendable."

"Maybe they weren't thugs," she said with a straight face. "Maybe they were New York photo critics."

Not only did she have a sense of humor, but a sense of history. She'd paraphrased Tennessee Williams's sardonic quote from his 1979 mugging in Key West. He'd blamed drama critics.

I said, "Heidi's fancy Jaguar disappeared from her driveway last night."

Lewis shook her head. "Where's she live?"

"Town house at the Golf Course. Any talk about a car-theft ring, maybe working out of Stock Island?"

"There's been talk. I have to ask myself, How the hell does a theft ring work with one road off the Keys? I'm not saying I'm not interested, because we've lost more cars than a normal quarter. But right now I've got more important concerns." Detective Lewis thought for about ten seconds, then shook her head. She pulled a business card and a ball-point pen from her belly-pack. She wrote a five-digit number on the card. "For you, only."

She'd given me the last five numbers of her home phone. In the seventies you could drop the two and nine when you dialed locally. Longtime Key West residents still never used the first two numbers in conversation.

"Where to with the car?" she said. "Return it to Mr. Cosgrove?"

I explained that I'd trampled the truth.

"Go ahead," she said. "Take it down to Simonton Street. Make up another story. Don't tell him we'll see him to-morrow. Thanks for your help."

"How do I explain the lost trunk carpet?"

Bobbi Lewis said, "It ran away with the spoon?"

An old Keys law-enforcement joke about missing cocaine.

I drove to the city lot. I met Cosgrove as he was walking from the upper deck, peering among the used-up cars in the city's maintenance fleet. I did a song and dance about reaching the car first, having to hurry film to the processor. I apologized for making him wait.

He wasn't buying. There wasn't much he could do about it.

Except snuff me.

I shut my mouth and got the hell out of there. I walked to Blue Heaven, drank a beer, gabbed with the bartender as he prepped for the pre-supper rush. The staff still was talking about the noon-hour food fight. I decided against more beers at restaurant prices, retrieved my bicycle, rode down to Southard, then east. By the time I reached Jeana's, the market opposite the Green Parrot, the sweet beer taste in my mouth had me wishing for more. My stumbling memory told me there was no beer in my fridge.

I locked the bike, went inside, took a six-pack from the glass-front cooler. A barrel-chested man, maybe thirty, arms big around as my legs, ponytail, stood at the deli counter waiting while a harried server crafted a Cuban Mix sandwich. The tattoos on his arms had faded, shifted in time. They looked like blue-black seaweed, dedicated to "Betsy" on one forearm and "Liz" on the other. The back of his shirt read PAUL'S PORTABLE POTTIES. I decided to order a snack for myself.

"How's business?" I said.

"Don't ask if I had a shitty day." The name embroidered on his shirt was NORBY. "I didn't, but the jokes get old."

"No joke, I'm curious about your leasing and servicing schedules."

"What you want to know?"

I guessed at the proper terminology, to prove I was serious. "How do you figure the unit count for a site? How often do you swap them out for upkeep and sanitizing?"

Norby checked progress on his sandwich, put an analytical look on his face. "Can count goes straight ratio with head count, expected traffic. The variables are alcohol and female users. More booze, more ladies, more units, as you called them. We call them shitters. Exchanges for drainage and steam-cleaning, we go by an average daily temperature chart on the computer. Summertime, we obviously got more to do."

"So this time of year," I said, "say, a construction site with eighteen men on the job . . ."

"We could go once a week. We got six of those right now. I pull one every day, Monday through Saturday. Today I did that motel renovation on United. Tomorrow, I'm not sure. On Saturday I get the new gift-shop arcade there on Caroline."

"I saw that place. Rode my bike past there the other

morning. How'd you get those portables through the chain-link fence?"

"They've got an access gate around back. Through the trailer court, so they can receive building materials and all."

"So you go down Elizabeth, into the trailer court, then . . . ?"

"You got it, buddy."

I nodded, mimicked the man's analytical expression. His food arrived. He'd already paid for it. He left without another word.

I'd lost my appetite. I slid to the front counter and bought the beer.

I biked down Whitehead to Fleming and turned toward home. The thirst hit me as I passed the lemonade vendor at Duval. I went another forty yards, swung left on Bahama, stopped at the trash bin behind the Key West Island Book Store. It wasn't a full-tilt chug, but the beer vanished in about twenty seconds. I dropped the empty in the bin, almost fell asleep at the wheel as I rode home. One question kept me awake. Why had my motorcycle died while I'd been allowed to live?

"Why can't I find a normal man who just wants to date for a while? Every goddamned one of them wants to get serious right away." Carmen followed me in my front door, stood in the living room while I hid my camera bag in its special spot. She'd been on her mother's porch, home from work fewer than five minutes.

I said, "Should've stuck with me when you had the chance."

"Oh, right. My father would have marched you to the altar at the point of his pistol. But, hell, these men either want to mooch off me, or tell me how to discipline Maria—which usually means find ways to keep her seen but not heard, or get a house together. Or change their life to suit me, or get jealous if I have friends. Or they turn into utter slobs after about the second time we sleep together, laughing at burps, forgetting to bathe. Or they want me to do their laundry. They want me to get my tubes tied, or they want me to have a baby. Whatever happened to dinner and the movies?"

"You're saying this construction guy hasn't worked out."

"He's in stage four."

Carmen's men go through seven stages. One: This guy's pretty cool. Two: He knows all the right things to do. Three: He might be all right. Four: I don't know what the deal is with him. Five: What's-his-name came by last night. Six: I've about had it with this dude. And seven: Guess what time Butthole called me? Over the past few years the standard elapsed time, levels one through seven, has been fifteen weeks. The times between men have been much longer.

"From now on," she said, "the only men in my life are going to be Chuck, Bill, John, Mark, and Bob."

"Do I know . . ."

"I'm going to chuck my junk mail, pay my bills, go to the john, mark my calendar, and bob for fucking apples."

I laughed, then offered her a beer from the six-pack. "What year did you graduate from high school?"

She twisted off the bottle cap. "Did we stop talking about my love life?"

"Were you in the same class as the Holloway girls?"

"Is that where you took pictures? I saw the street blocked. My mother said someone got shot. She heard it on her scanner. She's either sweeping the lane or glued to her scanner."

I told Carmen the basics. "Back to my question."

"I think Suzanne was a year or two older than me. Julie was in my class."

"Talk."

"Oooh-wee. Talk about a defensive little witch. Talk about a girl who was lucky her family had money. That little honey was drawn to trouble."

"Which little honey?" I said.

"Suzanne Holloway. Suzanne Cosgrove, now. Oh, Alex, stories we could tell."

"Test me for shockability."

"Oh, let's see . . . Should we start with the married man? Her senior-year married man?"

"Start there."

"You know how, every year, there's somebody or some couple who's the new kid in town? Everybody suddenly adores them, invites them over, meets them for drinks. This guy and his wife, supposedly wealthy up-north types, come on vacation a few times, wind up buying a house on Washington Street west of White, massive bucks. She rents a shop on Duval, starts selling knickknacks nobody needs. Called the shop Lollipops and Pralines, which is clue enough. Might as well call it Nobody Needs This Junk. So the husband, he's traipsing around town, 'looking for a place to invest.' Both of them are hanging in the bars, leaving their kid with not one but two Haitian nannies, so the nannies can watch the kid around the clock if they have to. A regular training camp for dysfunctional futures."

"How does this guy meet a high school girl?"

"Bop Brown's Jazzy Joint, on Petronia."

"What's Suzanne . . . what's either of them doing in there?"

Carmen shook her head, rolled her eyes. "Anyway, they get hooked up, so to speak, but one Sunday afternoon the guy—I think his last name was Griffiths—supposedly takes his kid to Astro City to play on the slide. A cop busts him with Suzanne performing—isn't that a great word for it, like it's a routine with curtain calls?—doing oral sex in the parking lot behind the grocery where Discount Auto Parts is now. Romantic as hell, by the Dumpsters. The kid's asleep in the backseat. Suzanne's performing, a cop knocks on the window. Oops. Needless to say, Mercer Holloway put a lid on it. But lids have a way of popping off on this island."

"Was she underage?"

"I doubt it. Probably too young for the Jazzy Joint, but

not to screw. So, needless to say, the blowee and his wife
blew town. Left the nannies behind like abandoned house
pets. I heard they wound up heading and grading shrimp
in one of Willy Franklin's plants."

"How about Julie?"

"How about that jerk cop who stood in your yard the
other night and arrested you?"

"Dexter Hayes, Jr.?"

"Oh, that's the jerk I mean. The very one."

"He and Julie?"

"The whole bit. Hugs in study hall. Public displays of
horny. Pregnancy scares—at least two. Melodrama to beat
the Cubanitas. He was a senior and she was a junior. He
was a lucky boy. Just to make sure he left town, Mercer
Holloway had his company give young Dexter a four-year
scholarship to the University of Florida. Gotta keep that
community service going strong. Even got him a summer
job in Broward County, I think."

Detective Hayes had been frantic to find clues at Holloway's home, but lackadaisical at the body-drop scene inside Butler Dunwoody's construction site.

"He was one of two lucky boys," continued Carmen.

"Who else?"

"Philip Kaiser. His family had money when he was a
kid, but they lost it when he was in high school. Once he
married Julie, cash was no problem."

I twisted the cap off another beer, put the last three in
the fridge. I looked out at the high palms swaying, branches
tossing in the light breeze. I thought about fortunes that had
come and gone on the island. I suddenly felt lucky to have
known a constant state of "barely enough" for as long as
I'd lived there. In a sense, I was just like Norby. He was
transporting and setting up crappers, dumping and steam-
cleaning, fending off bad jokes. I ran around, job site to
job site, worrying about employment security, praying for
checks to come in the mail. I needed to get myself a uniform shirt with my name on a patch, like Norby the potty

supervisor. Like Jemison Thorsby. Like the guy driving the forklift on Stock Island last Sunday.

Oh, shit. Why hadn't I put that together? Thorsby had been driving the forklift. He'd waved, but not to be friendly. He'd waved to hide his face.

I said, "Carmen, what's that horrible noise?"

"The people across from me bought new wind chimes. I didn't get much sleep last night."

"We'll steal them tonight."

"Sometimes you say things that make me regret not marrying you years ago."

The phone rang. Sam Wheeler: "What'll happen next?"

"I don't know," I said. "It's focused on Dunwoody, and nobody's dropped a skull in his fancy convertible. Nobody's shot a bullet into his front door. Maybe he's the bad guy."

Sam said, "We've got all the evidence we need to convict Dunwoody of being an asshole. From an objective juror's viewpoint, I sure as hell don't know. But I'll say this. Marnie's got a lifetime of evidence and good judgment ninety-nine percent of the time. She brought up the subject two or three days ago. She said that people would start to suspect her brother. She said, in spite of his bluster and his aggressive business ways, in spite of her personal bias, he's nothing but a puppy dog. Ask me what else is new."

"What else?"

"Do we need any more?"

"We need to sit on the porch and drink beer," I said.

"See you in a half hour."

I hung up, began to walk away. The phone rang.

Teresa, calling from her condo. "Did you borrow my car?"

"I had no intention of borrowing it."

"It's not here." Her voice shook. I heard sniffles. "Someone else borrowed it."

"Call the Highway Patrol, and call Bobbi Lewis at the county. Also call the Marathon substation, ask for Deputy Saunders. Use my name."

Shaky: "Okay." She hung up.

My thoughts echoed Bobbi Lewis's question. Why would anyone steal cars with only one road to the mainland?

Jemison Thorsby had been driving a forklift. With oversized hatches, the right hoist, cars could be put aboard shrimp boats. How did they keep them from being damaged once they went into the hold?

The phone rang. Teresa's voice had hardened. "They stole my gun, too."

24

The black mood of our early supper at Camille's spoiled the food flavor and the company of Sam Wheeler and Marnie Dunwoody. We waited for our meals, wedged into a corner table next to the front window. It looked like Freaks and Families Night on Duval. Suburban moms dodged transvestites, chubby bikers took care not to trample the kids. Teresa told us that she'd requested a middle-shift city cop to take her statement on the missing Grand Am and nine-millimeter pistol. Officer Chris Ericson sounded like the polar opposite of our boy Tisdell. He'd pointed out that the typical complaint, week to week, was the naked man in a tree. But this week they'd had more murders than drug pops. He'd assured her that she lived in weird times. Her losses were not her fault. He'd left her feeling two percent better about losing her car, having her home tossed. His words had helped.

Marnie informed us that her boss at the *Citizen* had taken the high road. He'd decided to run the Holloway bullet-damage piece. It would run below the fold because three county commissioners had been seen lunching in a motor home next to a movie shoot. The report suggested that the men had violated the Florida "Sunshine Law," a thirty-year-old statute requiring all meetings of elected officials to be open and public. Unprinted speculation at the *Citizen* held that the commissioners' greater risk lay in the fact that they'd hung around to scope a "partial nudity" scene that required multiple retakes and jogging.

Sam declined for all of us when the server offered coffee and dessert. He handed her a fifty, asked her to keep the change. I promised next time would be my nickel. Sam and Marnie had parked in a metered spot on Simonton, had dropped in eight quarters to be safe. They still worried they'd get a parking award from the tickets-for-profit brigade. We walked east on Angela, found shadows under a tree. Sam slid a Walther pistol from under his shirt, handed it to Teresa. A loaner, for peace of mind. It went into her purse. Sam and Marnie continued east. Teresa and I walked the opposite direction, back to her condo. The evening had turned cool. Even the light breeze kicked up street dust.

Teresa said, "Did you hear someone call your name?"

"Constantly, the past four days. It echoes."

"Seriously . . ."

With the Duval traffic and sidewalk crowd noise, I was surprised she'd noticed anything. Then I heard the strained, gravelly voice. Wiley Fecko? I turned, didn't recognize him at first. Mercer Holloway, dazed, disheveled, seated alone on Mangoes's patio. Not the puffed-up tyrant who, hours earlier, had railed against the press and the police. He looked ten years older than he had at Blue Heaven.

"Join me?" he said. There were two extra chairs at his table. The only vacant chairs on the patio.

I stood where I was. "Thanks, we just ate."

"A nightcap, then? Help me finish this pizza?"

He looked fried. His hair was uncombed, his shirt wrinkled. He'd bad-mouthed boozers and weirdos in his mid-afternoon tirade. Now he looked as odd as any downtown street dweller. He was inviting us in for a drink.

Mangoes had turned on their exterior radiant heaters. Looked inviting.

Okay, I thought. He can't murder us in an open-air restaurant. I wanted to view him from a new angle, lightly pick his mind on the subject of Donovan Cosgrove.

I looked at Teresa. I hadn't turned him down. She must have known that I was curious about something.

"I don't mind," she said.

"You don't have to sit through this. Go home if you want to," I said. "I'll be over in a while. Not long."

She shook her head. "I'm not ready to be there alone."

The greeter made a big deal about leading us to Mercer's table, handing us menus, summoning a server with a water pitcher. Teresa wanted only the glass of water. I almost ordered a Corona. I'd been Honest Alex eight hours earlier, given back the man's twenty-five-hundred-dollar check. I ordered a cognac and a chocolate dessert. Holloway didn't flinch. The server removed an empty Cabernet bottle. Holloway asked for another.

A ground-hugging compact sedan cruised Duval, its stereo thud strong enough to shake the streetlights. Then two Harleys with straight-pipes, then two more Harleys not so loud. I half-expected to see Bug Thorsby's black truck roll by. Where was that truck?

Holloway said, "Believe these crowds? A joke in the early seventies said the Chamber of Commerce had a man on the Seven-Mile Bridge who'd call ahead. He'd warn the Duval Street merchants if a southbound tourist was spotted."

"Key West got discovered," I said. "But so did every city in America. The highways are jammed, real estate's up—"

"You can tell the world's overpopulated." Holloway was on a roll. He'd be doing the interrupting, not me. "People going for groceries risk their kids' lives for a fifty-yard advantage in traffic," he said. "They tempt fate trying to make a yellow light. It's a universal death wish. The earth exercising its own checks and balances." He looked at the sidewalk. "The Conch Train used to cost a buck."

I didn't go back that far, but I remembered it being two or three dollars. "We used to ride for the fun of it," I said. "Cheap way to kill an afternoon. Get a little buzz, take a ride—especially when Rex was driving—sit in the last car and goof on the scenery. We'd learn something new every time. Back when my body would tolerate a flat-back bench seat."

The server arrived with the wine. He began the ritual of showing the label, cutting the foil, pulling out an antiquated "traditional" corkscrew. Holloway asked Teresa if she wanted a glass, then asked the server to quit the act, just open it and pour. When the man had left, Holloway said, "They make you sit and watch so they can justify a twenty percent tip for ninety seconds of work. It's like a real-estate broker sending a forty-dollar bouquet after collecting a fifty-thousand-dollar commission. I'll pay a sawbuck tip, but only if I don't have to sit through the show."

He sipped wine, then said, "What did you expect of this town when you first arrived, Alex?"

"I liked it fine the way it was."

He turned to Teresa. "And you, Ms. Barga?"

"I liked it fine the way it was."

"Let the record show," said Holloway, "that these two people did not get to Key West on the same day. Do you mind my asking how many years apart were your first days in town?"

Teresa said, "More than twenty."

"And you saw change during those twenty years, Alex?" I nodded.

"Did you expect not to see change?"

"Everything changes. I wanted change to suit my tastes."

"So, it's a question of taste instead of inevitability?"

Point well made. I nodded. I also liked the fact that he'd included Teresa in the conversation. Her bum mood had shut her up. But his willingness to ask for her input had put a trace of spark back in her face.

"That historical museum at Mallory Square," he said. "I went in there—for eight dollars. They've got actors playing the parts of pioneer fishermen and wreckers. There was this broad-chested, burly, bearded guy trying hard but talking with a contrived accent and archaic lingo. In all my years I never met an overweight fisherman. They were ninety-

nine percent muscle, and they were all too skinny. Those
old coots who used to sit around the Fisherman's Café, the
old salts who'd spent their lives on the ocean looked worse
off than the winos that came later. You could fit six of them
in a rain barrel."

Mercer paused, leaned toward me. "I know what you
think of me. You think we've got a finger in every pie,
we've fixed everything with our fabulous riches. But you
must remember that, as a family, we've always been like
this island. We've been under economic attack from every
newcomer with a half-baked dream. The island hit its real
low point in the thirties. The federal government came to
run this town. Since then, the people who've stuck it out
have sworn that no one would ever again take away that
power. That's why you hear about strange alliances fighting
outside money growth. We're not connivers. We're survi-
valists. We're guarding the fort. We're not padding our
wallets. Our proprietary approach is not greed. It's cover-
your-ass, for the benefit of children and grandchildren. The
endangered species on this island are old-time residents.
Half of them have fled to Ocala, run off by noise and dirt
and taxes. The rest are wealthy and powerful, or else des-
titute and getting worse. I made a decision, years back, to
be ruthless, to do anything it took. But my goal is not evil."

I said, "Where does Butler Dunwoody fall on the scale
of carpetbaggers to fort defenders?"

"Dunwoody's new in town. He's trying to buck generations of players. Those players are always successful unless intramural squabbles escalate."

"Do these successes always require the other guy to
fail?"

"You bet," he said. "It's a small island."

"Do they require murder?"

"Never. And he's a special breed. He's the kind we
need. Do you know what was going to happen to that parking lot he's building on?"

"Under your rule of inevitability," I said, "I'd be a fool
to imagine it might remain 'as is.' "

"Some idiot had an idea he could buy up that trailer court behind the property, extend a building all the way to the Bight boardwalk, put in a giant combination brewery, de-sal plant, and aquarian museum. Supposedly had big Texas money to back him, some movie star to be a five percent owner for the sake of name power. Why these people think they can crap on the pavement like a stray dog, I do not know. Excuse my language, Ms. Barga."

Teresa leaned forward. "Crap is a tame word for what you're describing, Mr. Holloway."

I said, "So what'll happen to the buildings I'm supposed to photograph?"

"Those buildings will not be gentrified. They won't be part of a palm-tree Epcot. Nobody's going to have to pay admission to soak up the past in my Key West. Some people in this town are peddling history they got for free, selling it with Florida-resident discounts and package deals."

I thought: It takes a worried man to sing a worried song. Whatever my guilt in acceptance of growth, tempered by my not having been born here, wrapped in nostalgia for the seventies, Mercer was right. Everyone's first day in Key West is a visit to paradise. Every morning I wake up here, I thank fortune and my priorities for not having to wake up to snow chains and dead batteries, slush, bare trees, urban sprawl, and the foul moods of those who must endure it all.

I said, "All that you've just said, and you're helping Dunwoody?"

Mercer refilled his empty wineglass. "Live by the sword, die by the sword," he said. "The profit motive made America great. But competition must be based on 'Do unto others . . .' The profit motive warped by greed has inspired some of the most awful human tragedies of our time. I decided a year ago that Dunwoody's motive wasn't warped by greed."

"Monday morning you said something like, 'We aren't permitted to pick our families, and we're not allowed to choose their moods.' Do Suzanne and Julie view progress with your sense of history?"

"I love my daughters, faults and all. You can't help but love your children, unless they're mass murderers or Unabombers or whatever. But even then, I might love them anyway. Thank goodness, I'll never have to know. But my big mistake, long ago, was my choice of wife. I was in love with two women at the same time. I had to make a choice. One was the daughter of drunken parents. Her upbringing was a shamble of strife and what we'd call high-class poverty. The other young woman had a traditional family, salt of the earth, hardworking father, homemaker mother. I saw my future in the mothers. My parents were boozers. I'd had enough of drunks. I didn't want to live with a drunk. I picked the girl who promised me pleasant calm. Unfortunately, she became a drunk, and she tore my political scene to shreds. I divorced her. The woman I cast aside is married to a future Senatorial candidate.

"I also paid the rich man's tithe, straight out of a Greek tragedy. It's happened to other men. Mel Fisher paid the price, twenty-five, almost thirty years ago, searching for gold and silver and emeralds. Bill Cosby, too. I lost my son four years ago next month. That event stole any happiness I might have found at the end of my life. The old people are supposed to die first. No amount of success or wealth can make up for that kind of loss."

Once again, point well made.

"I can't say much more about these property trusts, Rutledge," he said. "But I know you're worried about a taint of your professional reputation. I'll tell you this. The town will reap benefits. Think what you want, but it won't be a black mark."

Teresa said, "I'm going to have to excuse myself."

She looked beat. Her hair looked beat. Even her clothes looked beat.

Holloway attempted a pleasant smile. It almost turned into a yawn. "I wish I were younger and could stay out all night. It's time for me to walk home, too."

We did our thank-yous. Holloway sent us on our way. We walked down Angela, hugged the pavement's edge where there was no sidewalk. A tipsy bicyclist wobbled toward us, veered just before colliding.

I came away from Mangoes believing in Mercer Holloway's brilliance. His genius was directed. He was expert at molding history to match his personal goals. I was no closer to knowing if his pompous wizardry propelled altruism or murder.

History is full of tyrants who deeply believed their goals were good.

"He's an odd man," Teresa said suddenly. "If one person is behind all these murders and attacks, it's Mercer Holloway."

"Why do you say that?"

"I've never heard so much bullshit in my life. He's guilty of something."

"Aren't we all?" I said.

"People like Holloway have ways to make things happen, and they're never directly involved. We could argue that he's not the bad person, but this sure is revolving around him."

"So power's the pivot point for trouble?"

"Money, power, volatile family scene. He matches all the stats I've ever read."

"You might be right," I said. "That bit at the table was like a salesman's presentation. Too perfect."

My gut told me that Donovan Cosgrove's stock had risen.

When we reached Teresa's condo she said, "You're going to hate me. I don't think I could sleep a wink in here. Can we go to your house?"

We spent a half hour in the condo while she retrieved messages—about eight condolence calls; the word had spread about her car—and gathered clothes she could wear in the morning. Then we risked a traffic citation, rode double on her blue motor scooter to Dredgers Lane. She wore the helmet to fool the fuzz if they saw us from behind. I shut it off on Fleming under the three modern crime lights between Grinnell and Francis, and I rolled it from there. All I could hear were the tires in the gravel and Teresa's footsteps ahead of me. The odd stillness in the lane reminded me of a power drop. Not quite as silent, but the same effect. Everything closer to your skin, thoughts booming inside your head.

At six A.M. the phone rang. Teresa moaned. She had it right. Couldn't be anything good.

Dexter Hayes said: "I need your help, man. I can't even start to tell you. I'm sorry about yesterday afternoon. Bring your stuff down to Mercer's. The poor man's dead. He hung himself in the back patio."

I spread the blinds, looked outside. Barely sunup. "Five minutes," I said.

He tactfully added, "If you can get a message to Ms. Barga quicker than I can, I'd appreciate that, too."

25

I arrived at Holloway's home ten minutes after Dexter Hayes's call. Three minutes later the bus unloaded: two county commissioners, Mayor Steve Gomez and two other city commissioners, and a minister wanting to claim Mercer Holloway as a devoted, generous church member. A photographer from the *Citizen* and two reporters from the *Miami Herald* showed. Then, more quietly, Sheriff Fred "Chicken Neck" Liska, Detective Bobbi Lewis, and Lewis's video assistant, in the same grunge clothes he'd worn the previous afternoon.

No family members in sight.

Ex-Sheriff Tucker, ace security expert, had discovered Mercer Holloway's body. Tucker had slept in the house, on the second floor, and had wakened at daybreak. I'd seen Tommy Tucker when I arrived, sitting alone in a police van with the passenger-side door open, in wrinkled pants and a tank-top undershirt, sipping a Mountain Dew, staring at nothing. Tucker looked guilty as hell. Guilty of letting the worst happen on his watch.

Dexter told me not to approach the body. He wanted only general shots: the patio, the rear fence, the ladder on its side. The same ladder I'd used to scale the rear hedge fifteen hours earlier. Mercer was dressed in the clothing he'd worn at Mangoes, the trousers now soiled, his feet bare. Stains on the flagstone and the narrow, symbolic path of antique ballast stone. A vehicle tow-strap hung from a twelve-foot-high branch of gumbo limbo. The force of his drop, his dead weight, had stretched Mercer's neck two or three inches. I looked close enough to see the half-shut eyes, his weird grimace, his tongue, his expression of massive regret.

I'd shot maybe eight pictures before Dexter hand-motioned me to put the camera away. I dropped it in my satchel, stood aside, my back to the foliage, as the Florida Department of Law Enforcement investigative team blew into the yard. Four in dark pants, black sneaks, CRIME SCENE pullovers, radio mikes snapped to their shoulders. Varsity wrestling in ninja jammies. Two of them, not eight feet from each other, conversed by walkie-talkie. Their commanding officer declared the patio "secured," demanded that anyone not "authorized" vacate the premises. The modern military gives us these wizards. On our way out, we passed four more incoming: Medical Examiner Larry Riley, his chief investigator, and two assistants.

Outside, I watched Liska's Lexus turn the corner of Elizabeth, roll northward. My best guess: breakfast at Harpoon Harry's.

Dexter and I both knew the zinger, the one small detail. And Liska would know, too. Holloway had kicked the stepladder out from under himself to commit suicide. No one had stolen the ladder.

Hayes told me he'd reached Teresa's cell phone, told her that he didn't need her on scene, apologized for waking her early. He asked me to hang a minute, then huddled on the front lawn with Bobbi Lewis. I could tell they were pissed at the FDLE, but policies of all three agencies dictated seniority. In some city cases, the county sheriff will elect to command a scene. In a few murder cases the FDLE will do so. It was the manner of pick and choose—especially when headlines were at stake—that brought interagency conflict. The death of ex-Congressman Holloway guaranteed high-profile headlines.

When their discussion ended, Detective Lewis hurried away while Hayes strode toward me. "The man changed my life completely," he said. "Now I'm politicked out of investigating his death."

"Teresa and I ran into him last night," I said. "We had a drink at Mangoes."

"Tell me he was normal," said the detective. "Please tell me that."

"That was my impression. Defiant, pompous, talked our ears off."

"Elderly white men in Florida commit suicide more often than teenagers. They feel that 'vague loss of joy,' and they go the hemlock route."

"I've read about that," I said. "It's when they lose control, usually over their health."

"What'd you talk about?"

"Changes on the island," I said. "Power struggles."

"Was he drunk?"

"No, just drinking."

"His appearance?"

I said, "Kind of sloppy."

"Did he mention his son?"

I nodded.

"Then he was depressed."

"He didn't bring up the subject. He mentioned him only because I asked about his relationships with family members."

"Why a question like that?"

"I asked a bunch of questions. I wanted to mentally eliminate him as the source of this week's nastiness."

Dexter's jaw tightened. "Did you succeed?"

Play this easy, I thought. Go gently. "I couldn't decide. But the hanging, there's the similarity to the Toth case."

"And the people in there are trampling the scene," said Hayes. "I tried to explain the copycat theory. One guy laughed out loud."

"I learned yesterday how he'd helped you with college."

Hayes tried not to act surprised.

I said, "It's rough to lose friends." I realized as I said them that they were the exact words Teresa had expressed to Marnie on Sunday night. It's hard to be original before the day begins.

Dexter looked down the street, toward Simonton, mentally took himself farther away. "I bit myself in the ass," he said, "when I told you to buzz off with your clue."

Bobbi Lewis had told him about the feather.

"It wasn't as slick as I thought," I said. "Doesn't much prove anything."

"They're going to talk to Donovan Cosgrove in the next hour or so. You got any other ideas?"

"Detective Lewis tell you about Wiley Fecko?" I said.

"The weed sleeper? Yeah. I got to him before we cut him loose, ran some mug shots past him. He identified Bug Thorsby but not Robbie Carpona. Bug had a helper we don't know about, when he dropped Freddy Tropici's body on that sofa. Maybe one of his daddy's wharf rats from up on Summerland."

I said, "Tell me about Gram Holloway."

Dexter shook his head. "The boy's dead. I'm not going to walk on that grave."

Liska, on Sunday, had mentioned "walking on graves." Must have become a standard cop expression. We both were talking in echoes.

"How about I walk on it?" I said. "You just say 'yes' or 'no.' "

Hayes started to walk away. "Sounds like out of a movie."

I tried it anyway. "Was he a loser?"

"Yep."

"Druggie?" I said.

"Yep."

"Close to his family?"

"Enough to jingle the purse. Year or two before he died, the idiot declared bankruptcy."

"Close to his sisters?"

"No," he said. "He embarrassed them, and vice versa.

They were yuppie, he was street. Julie once told me she got tired of waiting for him to grow up."

"You ever go to law school?" I said.

He cocked an eye, silently questioned my having checked into his past. "I quit after eight months of that crap. Decided the weight I carried, my father's reputation, was easier than facing an attorney in the mirror every morning. Know what I mean? I dropped out. I picked up enough undergraduate hours to certify myself for the police exam."

"Put the arm on Carpona yet?"

"What'd the Treasure Salvors used to say? 'Today's the day.'"

"They said it for years," I said.

Dexter stuck his little finger in his ear, wiggled it. "They found the gold."

Chicken Neck Liska was in the last booth on Harpoon Harry's east wall. He glanced up from his newspaper. "Another bacon and eggs down the toilet."

"I can't stay, thanks." I sat opposite him. "What's a typical murder count, per year, in the Lower Keys?"

"Two." He lifted his coffee cup, sipped gingerly, as if it was boiling.

"The past four years, total?"

Liska overplayed the care with which he set down his cup. "Twelve."

"The national rate on solved versus unsolved?"

He looked toward the kitchen door. "Six-, seven-to-one. Maybe better."

"And . . ."

"Fifty-fifty. That answer your next question?" He finally faced me. "We got a flake doing life in an upstate jail, he wants to admit to two. That'll help. Our stats on all other major crimes are lower than the national averages."

I said, "You know things about the unsolveds that no one who's not a cop knows, especially the press. Has the killer copied non-public details? Or could there be a bad cop somewhere?"

Sheriff Liska screwed up his face, looked at me oddly. I sensed the flicker of a distant lightbulb. He said, "Go the fuck away."

"One more question. Any chance Jemison Thorsby's a car thief?"

"You're still hoping there's a hot-vehicle ring on Stock Island."

"Could be anywhere."

"That's right," said Sheriff Liska. "Could be anytime, too. But not now. Go away."

"Yep," I said. "Gotta read some newspapers."

I rode the bike down Margaret. The sun a gentle pastel, fresh sounds of birds, an odd absence of power tools. Morning people on foot, on bicycles. Everyone not jogging looked to be running errands, going to jobs. Morning people in Key West are different than night people. Or even noon people.

It wasn't really Hayes who looked bad, I thought, with all the unsolved murders being copied. Dexter was a newcomer focused on adapting to the department, the city. He's had no time to spend on old cases. It was Liska who'd left behind unfinished business. A reasonable man might suspect that the murderer had multiple purposes. In copying unsolved cases, someone was trying to drag Liska's reputation in the dirt. And Liska didn't care?

At the house, a message from Heidi Norquist: "Could you call me back, please, Alex? I want to see if you have information I don't have."

I hoped to hell I did.

I called Sam's dock. A man at the weather bureau, Marnie, and I were the only people who knew the number. Sam picked up.

"Can I bum a ride up the Keys?"

"My client's on the boat. I'm out of here," he said. "I'll leave the Bronco keys under the floor mat. What's wrong with the Shelby?"

"It's perfect. I'm talking your boat, to Summerland, after

dark. We need to know what Jemison Thorsby's doing. The deputies aren't interested."

He waited a moment. "Why is it up to you?"

"I'm stringing beads of knowledge. Bug attacks me where a murder victim is later found. Bug's body's in a car that chases me. The second victim's head shows up in Marnie's Jeep. I visit Jemison on Tuesday, and an hour later my motorcycle's a cinder. Heidi's car is stolen. Teresa's car is stolen. On Sunday I saw Jemison driving a forklift on Stock Island, following a stolen car. All this overlap in names and victims, I want to finish the puzzle."

"Knowledge is good," said Sam. "This angler's a full-day ride, but he'll jump enough fish to quit early. We can go anytime."

"Trailer?"

"Pain in the butt. The time it'd take to put a hitch on Marnie's Jeep, I'd be halfway there. Lemme think." The line went silent for a few seconds. "Stay by the phone," he said. "Call you back in two minutes."

I knew him well. I didn't even go to the kitchen for a glass of OJ.

The phone rang ninety seconds later. "I'll drop off my client at three," said Sam. "Then I'll load gear and take the backcountry to the east side of Cudjoe. Johnny Baker's on Blue Gill Lane. I'll stash the boat in his canal, Marnie'll pick me up. They've still got her Jeep in impound. She borrowed a car from a woman she works with. We'll go back tonight, start from there. You want us both to go ashore?"

"No. You're already risking your boat. I can slip onto the beach, check out the dock, check out those sheds."

"Once we leave Thorsby's, we can't go back to Baker's. We might lead bad people to his house. We can weave our way through the bottom end of Kemp Channel, run back here full-tilt. Ninefoot Shoal to Pelican Shoal is no more than a half hour."

The phone rang. Please, don't let it be Heidi.

I gave it the morning gruff: "Rutledge."

I recognized Teresa; she inhaled before she said, "Hi." The exasperation in her voice expressed a dozen emotions. Twelve shades of frustration.

"You okay?"

"I'm okay," she said. A quivering voice. "We were the last people to see him alive."

"I don't think so," I said. "But don't repeat that at work."

"Salesberry wants me at the county. They've arrested Donovan Cosgrove. He wants me to watch the sheriff's media rep in action."

"Arrest? Or just in for questions?"

"He threatened to kill one of Mercer's tenants a couple of months back. Weird timing, but they arrested him for it forty minutes ago."

"Perfect timing, but it's weird policy," I said.

"What're you going to do?" said Teresa.

"Get out of here, away from distractions. Go read some old newspaper clippings. Maybe hide in the library."

What had I said? *My house, my terms, and the rough parts lump by lump.* Great macho, but I hadn't considered my evil telephone.

"Use my condo," said Teresa. "I've got the line forwarding to my cell."

"You are my dream woman."

"Alex, you laugh when you dream."

I rode my bike down Southard, thought about my trust in Sam Wheeler. He'd always clammed up when people on the docks or in bars began to spin tales of Southeast Asia. I knew he'd been in combat, been awarded a medal for action that required courage beyond imagination. He'd explained it once, without detail. He'd said that bravery resulted from planning and reflexes. And clear focus when the brain is overloaded.

Overload I could claim. Focus, no chance.

26

A simple question, phrased as a statement in 1989.

"One of my clients, a doctor from Savannah, wants his sailboat delivered this week to Bimini," Sam had said. *"I'm a motorboat guy. Sailboats, bow and stern I'm okay, but nothing in the middle. Like Noah in that Cosby routine, asking God, 'What's a cubit?' I need a man of your talents."*

"When?"

"Thinking we could leave tomorrow morning. WX-2 says three-foot chop, light southeast winds through Wednesday. Possible storm formation in the Gulf, likely to move northeast. We motor out of Key West Harbor, four miles due south. Then we shut down the iron genny, cruise to the Bahamas. We've got a dock spot at Brown's and a room at Bimini Big Game."

"No Compleat Angler?"

"Full. We'll drink with Ossie in the bar. We'll play the ring-and-hook game, go back to Big Game, wake up to scrambled eggs and grilled snapper. Milk it for a couple days, fly home on Chalk's."

I packed two pairs of shorts, spare underwear, four T-shirts, one pair of jeans, and my foul-weather jacket. I brought the ditty bag I'd prepared for sailing transits: sunblock, extra shoelaces, a referee's whistle, an eyeglass-

repair kit for my shades, a "church key"—style can opener, single-edged razor blades, a corkscrew, two tubes of Tums, six stainless U-bolts in varying sizes, a rope weaver's fid, a pair of needle-nose pliers, a packet of No-Doz, Visine, and floss. I'd strung the whistle on a thick strand of nylon. I wore it around my neck at sea. If I fell over the side, it'd be louder than my voice, take less energy than yelling for help.

The beamy, Luders-design Cheoy Lee 48 cutter ketch displaced fifteen tons. It probably had set its owner back the value of my house. We sailed from the Key West Re-development Agency Marina, the wharves of the old Sub Base with its huge bollards and pilings. Sam brought along his powerful portable radio—for backup—and a plastic bag full of sunblock and aloe gel. He brought less clothing and good reading: Briarpatch, *a new one by Ross Thomas, and* The Neon Rain *by an author named Burke. He let me take the departure helm.*

"We'll take a running fix, line of sight, and confirm that the stream's pushing us," he'd said. "Then we'll steer zero-five-five for twenty hours. By then we pick up the South Bimini beacon and keep heading south of the RDF bearing. Gun Cay, south of Bimini, has a ten-second white flasher, twenty-three-mile visibility. Worst thing, we go too far north, find Great Isaac, have to beat back against the current to make the slot between North and South Bimini."

The storm from the Gulf of Mexico did not go northeast. It swept across the Everglades and hit us two-thirds of the way across the Stream. We had seen it coming. We'd checked Miami weather radio, secured our topside gear, swapped out the genoa for a storm jib, and dropped the mizzen. We wolfed down sandwiches and a couple of Cokes. We attempted a LORAN reading, to pinpoint our location. The signal became weaker as we moved east. We wouldn't be doing much navigation during the weather. We'd have to estimate our speed and, factoring wind, current, and maneuvers, our overall direction.

The sky became dull, dark at first, then ugly, though we

stopped taking time to look. The wind picked up quickly, blew up to thirty-five or forty knots before the seas became rough. Storm-driven mist soaked us, worked inside our waterproof jackets. We were three hours out of Bimini. We had six hours of daylight ahead of us.

Sam went below to secure loose gear. I heard clatter, slamming cabinet doors. He shouted from below: "I'm not believing this."

"Weather sneaks up all the time," I called back. "It happened to me on that Mariel trip nine years ago. Monster storm. We'll do fine in this boat."

"I don't mean the weather," he said. "I just broke my fucking ankle."

I lashed the helm to hold a rough attempt at our course, went below to splint Sam's lower leg. Two spatulas wrapped in dish towels, duct-taped to his ankle. He asked me to lash him into a berth adjacent to the radio and electrical control panels. He emphasized square knots, easily untied.

"You're the sailor," he said. "What do we do next?"

"If it gets hairy, we throw a sea anchor, shorten sail, and play the waves to save the boat."

"Sounds good," he said.

"So, let's go to Bimini. I can taste that rum in the Angler."

He sneered. "Don't worry about land. Worry about saving the boat from ugly waves. It's going to feel like the storm'll never end. The boat's in okay shape. We'll make land eventually. Too many people mess up boats trying to make a harbor."

Sam was right. My inclination had been rookie-stupid. Sam viewed the dilemma with a focus on survival. We knew that Bimini should not be entered during a strong west wind, especially in someone else's boat.

He added: "I'll be okay."

Then the storm turned mean.

Two months earlier I'd read Joshua Slocum's Sailing Alone Around the World, *the story of his 1895–1898 voy-*

age aboard his sloop Spray. *No crew, no radio, no modern equipment, navigating treacherous latitudes. Each time I thought waves would pound our Cheoy Lee to pieces or rip the rudder, or the wind would knock us down, split the mast, I put myself aboard* Spray, *in forty-foot waves for hours, then days. A man had survived worse, in tougher times, for weeks on end.*

The waves began to show what Slocum had called white teeth. I allowed the craft to head up, luff into the wind, then took a final reef in the main. I thought at one point that bare poles would give us controllable headway. I threw a sea anchor, tried to approximate our planned course, but played the waves to save the boat. Fierce wind bellowed, the hull shivered and pounded into compound waves that I fought to keep ahead of midships. I envisioned cracks in the fiberglass, shorted-out bilge pumps, a snapped bow sprit. I knew that each shudder of the keel sent shock waves into Sam's splintered anklebone. Sam had been correct about feeling that the storm never would end.

Sam called from below: "Problems?" It was reassuring to hear his voice.

Yes, I thought. The constant taste of sea water in my mouth. I had to shout over the wind roar: "No beer!"

Sam became mailman. He delivered gifts to the cockpit. He'd crack the cabin hatch, flip out items for comfort and safety. The first of several cans of beer rolled toward me, bounced around, fizzed on opening. Then candy bars. And, sure as hell, music on the exterior speakers. A new Little Feat album—without Lowell George—but hot.

Three times I heard the boat's generator kick in. I couldn't imagine why Sam needed it; radar wouldn't tell us much with the seas tossing. Sam knew as well as I did that running an engine is dangerous when the boat's heeling to one side. Oil flows to the sump's low side and doesn't circulate properly.

Three hours into the storm, the music was with me. I noticed that one CD had played again and again when I heard a Traveling Wilburys tune, "End of the Line," for the third time. I hoped it was not prophetic. I assumed that Sam, somehow, had managed to fall asleep.

But the hatch opened again. Sam's hand flipped out a spare harness. I knew what he thought. I needed to be double-harnessed to the helm. If a rogue wave struck, caused one harness to snap, I'd still be attached to the yacht rather than overboard with no one to know, no one to assist. Good thinking, with slight risk during the seconds I unhooked my primary harness so I could reach the extra one. I freed the pelican hook, abandoned my post for an instant.

Quick as the snap of an ankle, I was hit by water from the port quarter. My momentary glimpse registered a wave at least fifteen feet high. By the time I grabbed, I was sliding over the cabin roof, falling to starboard, salt-blind, scraping my belly on nonskid with the ocean pulling my legs.

No way Sam could know. No way to grab the whistle without losing my grip. I felt the boat head into the wind, heel farther, lee waves to my armpits. A big roller would knock me loose in a flash. I'd float in my life jacket, bob for hours in pitching seas while the ocean trashed the boat without a helm. Sam, helpless below, would have only a radio to save himself, only as long as the yacht held together. My hands fought slippery surfaces. Strength drained from my fingers. I tried to fashion a mental image of the cabin top—handholds, vents, porthole frames. The man-overboard kit, to be tossed in by someone who remained aboard—a short flagpole, a horseshoe float—lay two or three yards aft. If I could leg-lock a stanchion, somehow grab a winch—

As sudden as the rush of water that first tossed me, a breaking wave hit. A thousand hammers, a whack in the eye, a mouthful that never ended. I slipped, felt the water get colder, watched the sailboat's stern disappear over a crest.

An odd silence took over, even with spilling waves forcing me under the surface. I managed to pull the whistle out of my shirt. After wasteful seconds, I turned it upside down so that water would not fill it as I blew. Eddy currents pulled my legs. Each time I whistled I felt myself pitch forward. The harness felt tighter. My jeans weighed a hundred pounds, my shoes two hundred. How the hell, I wondered, does anyone get their money back if a life jacket doesn't work? Why the hell do I hear "The End of the Line" like I was in a room next to a stereo system?

The yank twisted me completely around. I didn't need to be force-fed more sea water. My shoulder struck something hard as a rock. My head bounced backward but I still couldn't see a thing. Then I felt the hull, felt myself become heavier. Felt myself being hauled from the ocean.

Literally, hauled aboard.

Sam had heard me hit the cabin top. He'd untied himself, crawled outside to the cockpit, spotted the trailing strap of my safety harness. He'd known that he didn't have strength or the leverage to hold me, to pull me back into the cockpit. He'd used the line that I'd used to tie him in place. He'd connected it to the harness strap, then managed to take two turns on the starboard mizzen winch. Then I'd gone in the drink. It had taken him four minutes to haul me aboard. It had seemed to me like five hours.

My life had been saved by my disabled teammate.

When the storm broke, after dark, the winds settled. We still had four hours of pitching seas. It would be a long night, tacking north-south, waiting for first light to approach Bimini Harbor.

I went below to help Sam into an aft bunk. But with calmer winds we could hear each other talk. He must have thanked me ten times that night. The man who'd saved my life was thanking me for my help.

"If I hear you say that once more," I said, "you're going over the side. Along with the Traveling Wilburys."

It wasn't until we arrived at the Bimini dock that I learned why Sam had turned the generator on and off. He'd spent the storm's peak hours directing the the Coast Guard to two disabled sailboats south of Gun Cay. He'd heard an

SOS on a UHF frequency and knew that the Coasties were out of UHF range. He'd used his portable UHF, the boat's longer-range VHF, and the boat's radar to coordinate the rescues. One was an older couple, seasick in a sailboat without a mainsail or rudder, in danger of grounding near Cat Island. The other was an ocean tug with four men aboard. It had lost power just before the squall hit.

We arrived in Bimini to heroes' welcomes. Ossie Brown, bless his soul, had monitored the UHF broadcast. After an island doctor had fitted Wheeler with a proper cast, Ossie sponsored a night's drinking in the Angler bar. It ended after the second rum. I was told I fell asleep with my forehead on the bar rail. Ossie sponsored the next night, too. That one went until the following morning.

27

Marnie had stuffed the newspaper photocopies into a manila file pocket. Four years' worth of unsolved cases. She hadn't attempted order. I couldn't fault her. She'd had a rough week and she'd come through with the favor.

I arranged the article pages by date, spread them across Teresa's bed. The case coverage overlapped in chronology, so I sorted again by victim. Each of the six began with a front-page headline. Two of them stood out: SEVERED HEAD FOUND and SUICIDE RULED OUT. I doubted that Marnie had written the first one. I read the second and mentally reran the chat that Teresa and I had shared with Holloway twelve hours earlier. He'd begun by mentioning the world's "universal death wish." I wanted to think he'd meant the rest of the world. He also had said that his son's death four years ago had ruined any happiness he might have found in the future.

I wanted to break my rule this once, put stock in simple coincidence. He was dead. I couldn't change that. But I'd rather it was murder than despair.

A selfish notion, not wanting him to have suffered depression. But I also needed to think that I hadn't missed a classic tip-off that someone was intent on suicide. The fact remained: I hadn't made up my mind about the man. I knew one thing. For all his faults, Mercer Holloway had treasured the old Key West as I did. I knew two things, deep down. Someone had killed him.

I'd forgotten to turn on Teresa's air. I hit the switch, took a Coke from the fridge, settled into a wicker chair, began to read.

It worked out almost exactly to one unsolved every eight months. The last one had been less than a year ago. Melvin Hale, trussed up, dressed up, decorated with sex toys. Jimmy Boyle, headless, the head found apart from the body. Mike Waters, garroted, found in his car. Quentin Toth, the hanging "suicide." The two that hadn't been mimicked were Faye Pratt, a woman shot in the head, and Sherman Lurie, stabbed in his outdoor shower.

I decided to shower at Teresa's before I left.

Forty minutes' reading had convinced me that I didn't have enough information. I wished I'd read the police files instead of settling for Dexter Hayes's synopses. I wish I knew what Liska knew. Without true scene descriptions, I couldn't tell if any factors were common to the unsolved murders and the attempts to duplicate them. I stopped reading, then asked myself what I could learn if I had every detail available.

Two things. Did the killer of the four recent victims have inside info about the earlier murders? And could anyone predict the circumstances of potential murders from the two yet to be copied? If the killer wanted a clean sweep, death by knife and death by bullet waited for two unlucky souls.

Liska was holding out. Did he have good reason to distance himself? Or had he become a true politician?

I looked up and dialed Dexter Hayes at the city. It wasn't a direct line. The first voice prompt offered a choice of three detectives. I pressed the "3" and wondered about Dexter's level in the hierarchy. Clicks and a short delay revealed auto forwarding.

Dexter's voice: "You aren't in the office?"

I said, "She's at the office."

It took him two beats. His cell phone's caller ID had

lied to him. He said, "What now?" A droning background noise. Was Hayes in a machine shop?

"I'd like to read the old case files."

No response. The droning fluttered and echoed.

"The ones I was going to see on Wednesday morning."

"You've quit photography, right? You want to be a cop?"

"I'm just being selfish, Detective. People are getting popped right and left. I'd like the next one not to be me."

"No can do."

I said, "By policy or jealousy?"

He clicked off.

"Thanks, asshole," I said to the dead line. So much for budgeting time to research. Dexter knew something, or was hiding something.

If I had to guess, I'd say Dexter had been on an airplane. But the carriers prohibit cell-phone use.

Before I left her condo, I called Teresa's office. She answered: "Teresa Barga's desk. How can I help you?"

"Wrap your legs around me like a circle 'round the sun—"

"Yes, I am," she interrupted. "I'll be in this meeting for a while. Let me get back to you later this afternoon."

"Can I borrow your point-and-shoot camera?"

"Sure," she said. "For a few days could we call it something else?"

I rode past a woman on Whitehead kicking a bus-stop signpost, venting her anger at a tardy driver. Key West went on with its day-to-day existence, oblivious to crimes it couldn't see firsthand. Near the courthouse, I passed through an invisible cloud of fresh Cuban bread odors. Down beyond Eaton a woman sat near the sidewalk on a tripod chair, her large canvas on an easel, painting foliage and old architecture. A man carried a single-sprocket bicycle rear wheel down Eaton. Farther up, nearer Duval, an old bum and a frail-looking young girl huddled in the doorway of a vacant storefront. Proof that Key West attracts your higher-class wino: they were sharing a bottle of Clos du Bois Merlot. Fausto's would have to write down another 750-milliliter heist. The girl had jet-black hair and skin so white it was almost blue. Blue lips, probably stained by wine. She couldn't have been more than eighteen. How had Marnie described that girl on Sunday night, "very Goth"?

I didn't check them out for long. I looked away—the guilt of the sober—before the juicers spotted me staring.

"Yo, Rutledge?"

I recognized Wiley Fecko's high-pitched tone immediately. I turned. He wasn't getting up. But he didn't look drunk. I assumed he didn't want to lose his premium seat.

"Mr. Fecko," I said.

"Been meanin' to swing by your pad, grab my stuff."

"It's safe in my shed. No inconvenience," I said.

"This lady here, Cilla, she knows all about this shit going down." Fecko's speech clear, articulated to conceal an old pro's drunkenness.

I looked at her again. Purple fingernail polish, a little silver circle looped in one eyebrow. Marnie had said, "Retro-punk," and "She looked dead as the man on the floor." Cilla fit the mold, but she was one of thousands.

I said, "Did you know Richard Engram?"

Nothing moved except her eyelids. They rose to open halfway. A hateful, evil leer, out of focus. The world was her enemy, and I represented humanity.

She said, "Fuck."

I looked to Fecko for guidance. A side-tick of his head. A finger wiggled, hidden behind his knee. He was telling me to be patient. I stared at the top of her head. Brown roots under the black dye.

Cilla rolled her head to one side and slurred, "The motel guy was a totally fucked asshole, you hear what I'm sayin'?" A slight Spanish accent.

Clear as mud. I ask about a murder victim, she expounds upon some imaginary beef. Strike one.

"Did a cop come on to you?" I said.

She pondered that one, then said to her right shoulder,

"What cop would do me?" She turned her head the other direction, sneered at Wiley. "The Feck won't even do me."

Strike two.

Then she said, "I never saw that black cop before."

Home run.

Bring it back to the playing field. I said, "Aren't all motel guys assholes?" A meaningless question, out of context. Sometimes being off the wall induces loonies to talk straight.

Cilla reached for the Merlot in Fecko's hand. A car's tires screeched at the Duval-Eaton intersection. Fecko looked in that direction. Cilla ignored the noise, took a slug, half-raised her eyelids to check me again.

I waited.

"Asshole gave me fifty fuckin' dollars to make that fuckin' speech to the cop. Two twenties and a ten and five hits of Ecstasy."

"Asshole got a name?"

She looked around the sidewalk, trying to decide if my question was worth an answer. Shook her head.

"Motel got a name?"

"Course. But I don't know it. He had it on his shirt. His cute little preppy fuckin' polo shirt." She extended her arm, offered me the wine bottle. Shook it, insisting I remove it from her hand.

I took the Clos du Bois. Cilla leaned to her right, supported herself on both hands, and vomited on the sidewalk. Fecko scrambled to move the girl's small, greasy backpack from the growing purple puddle. Cilla hocked and spat, then said, "Watchtower." She spat again. "The fuckin' Watchtower."

Fecko and I swapped glances. I said, "That's a motel name?"

She blew her nose onto the cement, flipped her fingers, freed them of snot. She said, "Fuera de aqui." I understood its tone. I was ready to leave, anyway.

I'd never heard of the Watchtower, or anything similar.

I asked Wiley to stick close to the young woman, and to introduce her to Dubbie Tanner.

"Tell you, brother," said the Feck. "Dubbie knows her good."

I'd already figured that.

I started toward home. Traffic on Duval waited for the light to change. Eight vehicles, all on two wheels. Three motorcyclists and three mopeds, their drivers enjoying the breeze without helmets. The helmet law had changed in June 2000. Two bicycle riders wore mandated head protection. What was wrong with this picture?

A new balloon-tire bicycle leaned against the front of my house. Butler Dunwoody sat on my side porch. A thirty-two-ounce bottle of malt liquor sat on the table. Marijuana smoke hung low in the yard.

Party time. Any time, any afternoon, everybody parties in Key West.

I rolled my Cannondale around back, snapped its Kryptonite lock to the stainless-cable I'd strung around my mango tree. I tossed the weather tarp over it. The neighbor's springer spaniel whimpered through the fence, stuck its nose out for a forefinger scratch, five seconds of friendship. Its eyes more alive, more intelligent than the Goth girl's. More alive than many downtown. The poor dog worried about the pot fog.

I stepped onto my porch, slung my helmet onto the porcelain-top table. "Problem, Butler?"

"I'm everybody's bum. You're everybody's hero." He tilted back the malt-liquor bottle. A half dozen drops leaked out the side of his mouth, dribbled down his shirt.

"Self-pity's an ugly ride, Dunwoody. You look better in a red convertible."

"My main backer is pulling out. The convertible's on the block, along with my project, my home, my other vehicle, my ass, and my future. It's all toast."

"Why's it so special, every damned day, to be on top of the world?"

"The rest of the world sucks," he said. "Better to be above it all."

"The bank give a reason?"

"She thinks I can't do it without Mercer Holloway's blessing, or without Donovan Cosgrove running interference with the locals. She thinks I'm useless without somebody else's horsepower."

I knew who he meant, but didn't want to let on. "She . . . ?"

"Tits on Sticks, the eighth wonder of her own little world."

Butler had failed the sensitivity-training course.

"Reason?" I said.

Another hit of the sauce. "She said I was ordering her up like a Happy Meal. She wants to cut her losses."

"With you or the project?"

"She begged me to write her into this thing. I could've done it without her. Halfway into final structuring, I said no to two banks in Jacksonville. They got offended. They won't come back on. I let my dick sign a contract. Now it's about to get chopped off."

"Why's it so easy for her to pull out? Doesn't she lose big?"

"She writes a check every week. She stops writing checks and somehow the job gets completed, she gets everything back, a pro-rated chunk of future profits."

"Pro-rated on her contribution until she quits writing checks?"

"Right," said Butler. "Smart deal, eh?"

"If it folds up, everything stops forever, what happens?"

"She loses everything."

"So she's banking on the idea that you'll bring in another investor?"

"Like I said, cutting her losses. Who can blame her?" Butler slugged one more mouthful of malt liquor. "She's playing it safe."

"I heard in a movie one time, 'Playing it safe's the most dangerous thing a girl can do.' Something's screwy."

"Righto," said Dunwoody. "My brain when I agreed to the crap."

"When she came over here that day—if you'll allow me to bring up the subject . . ."

"No problem. I have fond memories of the event . . ."

". . . I got the impression she'd go to the edge for you. She loved you, the money be damned."

"She worships money," he said.

"I don't think so. I think she just wants to kick you in the ass."

"At this stage I'm supposed to find another investor?"

"Do the damned thing," I said. "The way it's set up now, it might be an unenforceable contract. If you brought in another investor, Heidi could recoup. But you could stipulate that she be shut out of future profits."

"Not bad for starters. Now all we need is a deep pocket."

"Mercer's daughter."

"My boy Donovan's in a serious tight. She'll be spending all her money on lawyers."

"The other one," I said.

"Married to dipshit? No, thanks."

"A lot of investors are married to unpleasant people. Why should it make a difference?"

"It just does. That fucker gives me the willies."

On one hand, with Mercer's horsepower gone, Heidi's departure from the deal made sense. On the other hand it was weird timing, taking into account the fact that Donovan drove down Caroline Street last Sunday, past Heidi on her Rollerblades, and me about to be jumped by thugs.

Had I just implicated Heidi in a convoluted plot?

The phone rang. I left Dunwoody to his last six ounces of malt liquor. It was Teresa: "Can you meet me at Blue Heaven? I found a guy from Boynton Beach you might want to talk to."

The cop, Dexter Hayes's ex-partner. The owner of the hot Maxima, Bug Thorsby's last ride.

"I want to talk," I said. "But I don't want to go to Heaven for a few days."

She covered the phone mouthpiece. A silent moment.
She came back on. "How about P.T.'s?"
I said: "Five minutes."
I returned to the porch. Butler Dunwoody had left his
empty bottle and a half-inch roach. A few years back I
would've recycled both objects. I cleaned up, checked my
two messages. Tommy Tucker said he'd call back. Sam
said: "Pick you up at nine-thirty. Pack a bag. Wear darks.
If you want the skeeters to leave you alone, don't take a
shower today or yesterday or the day before. If you want
the bad guys to leave you alone, bring your knife collection."

28

Dexter Hayes's ex-partner owned the stolen Maxima.

Hayes, with his shifting moods, had told me to take a hike, to quit playing cop. Then his ex-partner, the car owner, had agreed to sit with me, to answer questions. Why the mixed messages?

One other thing. The Maxima had chased us with a body in its trunk. Then it showed up on a hot sheet. How many vehicles are reported stolen after their use in a crime gone sour? For every time I'd heard the story, the police had heard it a hundred more. The ex-partner knew that. He either thought we were rubes, or he was playing it straight. No middle ground.

I wasn't ready to buy his tale, but I wanted to hear the man talk.

I locked the house, unlocked the bike, rode against traffic to Grinnell and turned north. A light breeze, heavy traffic—tourists en route drive-through culture—and heavy dust. How many times will they dig up the east end of Eaton? Some genius, decades ago, plait-braided the water and sewer systems and laid their rust-prone pipes into salt-permeated coral rock. Job security for future backhoe drivers. Key West is like every other city in the nation in only one way. More supervisors than laborers.

P.T.'s is near the old shrimp docks, the 600 block of

Caroline. It occupies the building where, for years, the Big Fleet saloon had hosted Navy chiefs in working khakis, straight from the Naval Air Station or the submarine tender, petty officers in dark denim trousers and light denim shirts, Caroline Street sweethearts and deployment widows. The place would be packed from nine A.M. until closing time. There was a long-standing truce between the aviation and seagoing ratings. Strangers in civvies might enter but would sense the chill, leave before finishing the first draft beer. Today's bar was more welcoming. The last time I'd been in P.T.'s was for emergency food after a long night of carousing with a writer friend and a New York book publisher. The publisher had looked too screwed up to win at the pool table. He'd played perfectly until daybreak. He'd enjoyed his food and drink at my expense.

I chained the Cannondale to a news-vending box. I checked the chalkboard in P.T.'s walkway. Black bean soup, barbecued chicken breasts or pork chops with rice and veggies, ribs and black beans, blackened grouper with pineapple salsa. Blue-plate specials from lunch hour straight through to five or six A.M., depending on customer attitudes. Home for people who'd rather be in a bar than at home. The Thursday Special was roast turkey. If we had time for food, I was good for the grouper.

Leaving brightness, entering the cavern, all I could make out was the huge aquarium—three noise-resistant butterfly fish—and four TV screens. Baseball on one, hockey replays on the others. "Hearts and Bones" by Paul Simon on the sound system—at a level that allowed conversation without vocal strain. Near the door a dozen old photographs of neighboring streets. Shots from forty and fifty years ago. Most noticeable were vacant lots, true relics of days past. Two basketball jerseys had been framed and mounted on the pine-paneled west wall—Celtics 33, Bulls 23—along with a medium-sized sailfish and a huge bull dolphin.

I arrived first. I bought a bottle of beer.

The bartender, a stocky woman in her mid-thirties with a twinkle in her eye, whipped a chrome bottle opener from her rear pocket, popped my beer. She put my change on the bar, then went back to checking ashtrays, facing-out bottle labels, restocking glassware. "You want a show?" She pointed at a television.

"You pick," I said.

She pointed at the clock. "Usually, somebody walks in, three minutes to the hour, it's for a certain game. Anything you don't want to watch?"

"Best of the Great Racing Accidents."

"I'm with you there."

I claimed the northwest corner table. The booth floor elevated, foot-tall mirrors at shoulder level. A middle-aged couple leaned on the pool table in the adjoining room, mashed faces like teenyboppers to "Slip Slidin' Away." I shifted to the opposite bench, faced the kitchen. It worked out fine. Teresa arrived ten minutes later and introduced Jim Farmer. Jim wanted to face the wall. It took me a moment to figure out why. The mirrors offered a surround-view of one room, and he could face the other room. Security for the career law officer.

Farmer had developed style to counter the rural suggestion of his name. He was about five-ten, solid, with perfect posture. His T-shirt read FINS TO THE LEFT, FINS TO THE RIGHT—Key West had put Farmer in a relaxed mode—but his military bearing declared his belief in the daily workout, the weekly haircut. Some cops are like men I knew in the Navy, so caught up in spiffy uniforms, they lose all taste in street duds. It's hard for jocks or military trainees in great physical shape to look laid-back. Farmer's face was blotched from too much first-day sun.

He said, "Who's gonna win?"

I didn't get it. He pointed at the tube. A Super Bowl Preview Show.

"I forget who's going to play."

"Been that bad a week, eh?"

I nodded.

"Ms. Barga, here, tells me we're all car-theft victims,

except for your near-miss. You almost lost your car to the bums that got mine."

"They were more than car thieves. And I got a flaming motorcycle."

"I got the whole rundown."

"Where'd they take your Maxima?" I said.

"Shopping center on Congress Avenue in Boynton. Broad daylight. Right under the nose of a security weasel. The idiots wear American flags on their shoulders, patrol in little pickups with wimpy-ass roof lights. They couldn't catch a buggy thief. Type of guys who go for news coverage when they collar a purse snatcher. Most of them failed the cop qualifiers."

A longer answer than I needed. And he knew it.

"What day was that?"

"Week ago today. Thursday."

"You driving the car?"

"Yep. Usually drive the Xterra, but I took the wife's car."

"Go to the mall straight from home? Or did you come from work?"

He gazed at the table, pulled a long inhale. "Why you asking?"

Into the quicksand already. Think fast. "Whoever stole your car tried to kill us," I said. "He carried a body in the trunk. I'm trying to get inside his mind, trying to understand. Figure out if he followed you, targeted your car special, or picked it at random."

"Dexter said you were a wannabe detective."

"Not true. Certain things I take personally. Others I let go."

"Great. I'll take your word for it."

I needed to change the subject but keep pushing. "You trust Hayes's judgment, every time?"

"Every damn time," he said.

"How about his decision to come to Key West?"

"That's his business."

Almost every damn time.

"They must've totaled the car. Don't they just send you a check?"

"This is really enjoyable. Can I buy you folks another round?"

Teresa became peacemaker. "Alex didn't sleep well last night, Mr. Farmer. But he's buying this afternoon, and I could use another wine, Alex. I'd rather not wait for a server."

My cue to make a bar run. When I returned, Teresa and "Jim" were best pals. They were dishing the dirt about Hayes and his funny mannerisms, his oddball sense of humor. Farmer launched into an anecdote about the time Hayes was imitating Madonna in the squad room, mocking a dance from her then-current video. Dexter tripped over an extension cord, fell against a desk, sprained his wrist. He missed four days of work and claimed the injury on workman's comp. The day he returned to work he was called to a meeting in the squad room. Every officer present wore a pointy brassiere.

The ice had broken. The bartender delivered a plate of munchies that I'd ordered at the bar. Farmer loosened up, bought the round he'd facetiously suggested a few minutes earlier. He grinned slyly, pointed out the athletic bag that held his Rollerblades. "You might've thought I was carrying a semiautomatic weapon . . ."

Cops joke about weapons. I laughed to humor him.

Farmer admitted that his trip to the Keys was a schmooze deal. He'd come down with his insurance broker, a free vacation to "identify" the waterlogged Maxima. He'd inventory the car for personal belongings and agree to the totaling of it. That way, the broker claimed, the company could save the expense of transporting junk back up the Keys.

"Service with a smile and a tan," I said.

"I stop vehicles for traffic infractions, they've got out-of-date insurance cards. I turn some biz his way. I don't jeopardize my job. I don't invite kickbacks. The motorists appreciate my leniency. But, hell, they're not criminals.

Most of them forgot to clip the card, put it in their glove box. A few failed to renew. So I come here. Helps keep insurance costs low. Yours included."

Teresa kicked my ankle. She'd probably spent all morning on the phone with her insurance company. I didn't offer an opinion of Farmer's freebie trip. I wanted to get back to my questions. I was in dead-end territory, with Dexter refusing me access and Farmer defensive about my queries. I tried an end run, phrased as a joke: "All the headlines down here lately," I said, "you might be better off with a weapon than Rollerblades."

He smiled, shook his head. "Dex turned down a promotion to come here. You believe that? Crazy man. It's like his whole career's on standby."

"He told me he wanted the wife and kids off the Gold Coast," I said. "All the crime and traffic."

"Oh, horseshit. He owned a damn mansion in Parkland. Tall wall around the subdivision, you pay dues, every house has the same lawn service. With the promotion, those kids could've gone to private school. They could go months without seeing Federal Highway, the riffraff of Delray or Pompano."

"I've never met his wife."

"I think that deal's around the corner, too. When he married her she was down-to-earth. Natalie grew up wealthy— her dad founded the third-largest black-owned company in the state. They're metal fabricators. They make mailboxes, toasters, computer cases, garage doors, rack systems, you name it. Natalie didn't act rich, at first. Maybe the kids changed her. She turned into Ms. Yuppie Suburbia. She made Dexter sell a two-year-old Explorer and buy a new Ford Expedition because it was easier to get the kids' bikes in it. I mean, the new vehicle minus the trade-in whacked him for eighteen thou. If you add up the extra minute or two it might take to deal with bikes, every time she carried them for the life of the car, that trade-up was worth about five thousand bucks an hour."

Teresa said, "Next time he offers to buy lunch, I'm accepting."

P.T.'s sound system played "Diamonds on the Soles of Her Shoes."

"So he got homesick and came down here?" I said.

Farmer sneered, gave it a one-shoulder shrug. "How many people our age get homesick?"

Sam Wheeler was homesick for a town that didn't exist anymore.

"Screwed me up, too," added Farmer. "Good partner. He'd cover my ass in a tight. The toad I got now, scores are top of the class, no demerits, no write-ups. The book says he's a wizard. I wouldn't trust him to put coins in the meter."

I suddenly wondered about his trust in Hayes. My thoughts spun to a wild tangent. Why this sudden outpouring of info about Dexter? Farmer had jumped from a total reluctance to criticize the man to a total indictment of his moving to Key West. I never trust a changing story.

What else was flaky? Dexter had turned his back on the good life and a promotion. He'd moved to Key West for a tougher job. Had he been drawn by a desire to be close to Julie Kaiser? Was he capable of murder, for revenge or ambition or any other reason? Had Jim Farmer been driving the Maxima? Had Dexter sent him after me, to chase me up the highway at ninety miles an hour? Were they over-the-top cops with a sick agenda? Or was Jim Farmer piecing off the blame on Dexter? Setting him up for a fall?

Was I building a new pyramid of paranoia?

We became more aware of the sharp clatter of colliding pool balls, the constant drone of bar conversation. The bar had filled as mid-afternoon became Happy Hour. Eight or ten construction laborers crowded the bar, let off steam. One wore a T-shirt that said SOUTH FLORIDA VIAGRA TESTING TEAM.

Teresa said, "Been to Key West before?"

Farmer nodded. "Used to come down a bunch. Not anymore. College buddy of mine was here, I'd come down, go fishing, party in the bars. I talked him into quitting his job selling cars, following his dream. He became a city cop. One time I was down, I tried to hire on with the county. Had a chat with the sheriff and bagged the idea. What a dipshit."

"Tommy Tucker?" I said.

"That's the one. Any job—hell, private security—any damned thing'd be better than working for that doofus."

I asked his cop friend's name.

"Officer Monty Aghajanian. Now he's got himself into the FBI. He moved to New Jersey. This is my first time back since he left."

"I know him well." And I respected Monty's judgment, trusted him.

"Give him a call sometime. He's a lonely boy up there. Understand the wife's okay with it, but he's praying for a reassignment."

I would call Monty within the next thirty minutes. For the moment, my opinion of Jim Farmer had shot upward. I wasn't sure about the man, but Monty's words would make up my mind.

A server offered us another round. I'd had enough beer. Teresa needed to get back to her office before five o'clock. Farmer wanted to skate around Old Town. I thanked him for his time.

Teresa and I stood outside, watched more afternoon drinkers stream into the restaurant. "Your eyes told me," she said. "Your mind was going a million miles an hour."

I said, "Please say you talked him into this."

"Dexter had to leave the office in a hurry. He sort of abandoned Farmer in the coffee room. I explained myself, and told him I'd been in the car that his Maxima chased. He was very sympathetic. I asked him if he'd talk to you. Were you thinking that he set this up? As a distraction or something?"

"Or that he and Hayes set it up. Did anyone identify the bullets I found in Mercer's hallway wall?"

"I heard someone say they were nine-millimeter slugs."

"They could have come from your stolen pistol?"

She said, "I want this all to stop."

"Sam and I are going to visit Thorsby this evening. By boat."

Teresa looked more upset than pissed. "You are not a cop. Take care."

I went straight to Carmen's house. I wanted something with a waterproof lining. I asked to borrow her daughter Maria's rainy-day backpack. Carmen had just arrived home from work. She invited me in. "You can get your jollies, watch me change into my comfort clothing."

"My threshold for jollies is extremely high today," I said. "Maybe if you got naked and danced the dirty boogie to an old Fats Domino record . . ."

She gave me a look. "Shame about Holloway." She peeled off her Postal Service blouse, pulled on an old Miami Dolphins jersey. "I bet his daughters are devastated."

"You think Dexter Hayes would move his family down here if he wanted to be closer to Julie Kaiser?"

Carmen narrowed her eyes. She led me to her kitchen, offered me iced tea, poured two glasses. She finally shook her head. "It was too long ago. We fantasize about high school sweethearts, we all do it. But we're past thirty. Reality makes the rules. That romance was half their lives ago. There've been too many changes since then. There are too many obstacles today."

We took our tea to the front room. She heard something and said, "Here comes the male." Her boyfriend pulled up in a Dodge Ram pickup—the man in the VIAGRA TESTING TEAM T-shirt. The group in P.T.'s must have been Butler Dunwoody's crew. She introduced me to Nick. No last name.

"Rough place you're working," I said.

"Working until today," said Nick. "We got pulled off early."

"Any idea what's going down?"

"Nope. I mean, hey. Nothing weird ever happened until that Donovan character started hangin' around. Before that,

some other guy was around, checking on things, taking Po-
laroids. His brother-in-law, I guess. Then the first guy
stopped comin' by, and it was this Donovan and the next
thing you know Dick Engram's dead. The next thing, Donovan gets arrested. Now we got a stop-work order from the
boss."

"Any idea when you'll start back?"

"Dunwoody told us, 'Tomorrow or never.' "

Maria had left her backpack at school. Carmen gave me
a belly-pack with a plastic lining. I went home, called
Monty Aghajanian at the FBI's Newark office. Voice mail.
Goddamned voice mail. I asked him to call me back anytime. If he didn't get me tonight, or get the message tonight,
early morning was okay. I popped a beer—as if I needed
another—and began to sort items I'd need for my boat ride,
my onshore excursion. I sat on the bed to think about everything that had happened in twenty-four hours.

At eight-thirty the phone woke me.

Sam said, "Pick you up in ten."

I brushed my teeth, put on Levi's and a black long-
sleeved shirt. Sam had suggested I wear a black ball cap.
I'd never worn dark hats under the tropical sun. The only
one I owned read PARROT HEADS IN PARADISE. A freebie
from Lou, a bartender in Margaritaville. I found an old pair
of black high-top sneakers in the closet, then folded in a
fresh Ziploc bag.

Marnie and Sam rolled into the lane nine minutes later.
She'd borrowed a boxy old Buick Century. Sam looked
dressed to kill. Black pants, black shirt, a black knit watch
cap, ankle-high nylon brogans, a knife strapped to his calf.

We drove out North Roosevelt. I'd forgotten to call
Monty Aghajanian. Marnie had her cell phone, but I hadn't
brought Monty's number with me.

When the county jail came in sight, Sam said, "The more
I think about it, no matter who else is involved, Donovan
Cosgrove is weird. I say he did in Richard Engram."

Marnie argued the other way: "Donovan Cosgrove
doesn't have enough beans in his jeans to pull it off. His

bitchy wife, she's another story. If a girl could have brass balls, they'd hear clanging in Cuba."

They waited for my opinion. I finally said, "I've added up all the evidence and I've narrowed it down to nine possible suspects."

Sam asked Marnie to pull into Sugarloaf Key Resort's parking area. He pulled two black Motorola transceivers from his duffel. Palm-sized UHF units. "Captain Turk and I use these in the backcountry. We share information, but not with the world. Once in a while an angler will ask me to drop him on a mangrove spit. He'll want me to get lost, let him fish in peace. I'll go behind another island, chill out until he calls."

Sam matched the transmission channels, plugged in tiny earpieces and remote condenser mikes. He pointed out the microphone key and squelch control. Showed me how to set it for voice-activated transmission.

I got out of the car. Sam chattered the whole time Marnie drove him to the far end of the parking lot, U-turned, and came back. Every word came clearly through the pinkie-sized plug in my ear. Marnie drove another loop while I held the contact mike against my throat, chattered on constant-key. She looped again while Sam and I exchanged four or five quick messages.

When she dropped us off at Johnny and Laurel Baker's place, Marnie said, "Make it a success."

Always the reporter.

I said, "If I find what I think I'll find, you'll get your exclusive."

"That's not what I meant. I've written too many dead-people stories this week. Why don't you both come back alive?"

29

Sam coiled his dock lines, stowed them under the center console. I held the wheel, motored the canal at idle speed behind the homes of Blue Gill Lane. Sam had covered his gauges with a fitted foul-weather cover. Small flaps with Velcro closures shielded the illuminated dials. The sky was clear, the January night air crisp, close to sixty, with low humidity.

We looked like overdressed dope scammers heading for an offload. I wondered what the hell I'd dealt us.

"We'll go north," Sam said, "hang by Little Knockemdown, wait a few. Then run south, find our markers with the spotlight."

I steered the dogleg toward Kemp Channel. "Why all that?"

"Someone sees us exit this canal and run to Summerland, they might come back to Johnny Baker. We'll go north, shut her down, and wait. Then come back south, pretend we're lost, shut her down again. See if anybody comes out to help. No Samaritans means no witnesses. We go in."

"I go in. You're in the boat."

Sam looked into the water. "You said that before. You're the boss."

"Gimme a break. My learning curve has been bent for

years. I'll need you to come ashore and save my ass if they glom on to me."

He said: "Done."

"How about Customs? How about Marine Patrol? A reasonable cop would take us for Commie infiltrators."

"It's too shallow to scuttle hardware," said Sam. "We go to the backcountry and outrun them."

"They'll put a spotlight on your F-L numbers and trace the boat."

Sam opened a mini-duffel that he'd carried from Marnie's Jeep. I heard tools rattle. He pulled out a roll of two-inch black gaffer's tape, stripped a couple lengths, lay belly-down on the bow to cover his Florida registration numbers. He tore another piece, maybe three inches long, pasted it over my ball cap's Parrot Head insignia. "So much for that bull's-eye," he said.

Sam took the wheel, exited the canal, steered around four or five shallow water stakes. Only someone who'd seen them in daylight could've navigated without running aground. He pointed us north to deeper water. We stopped three minutes later. Sam killed the motor, let us drift.

"I don't get this far up the Keys much lately," he said. "Marnie told me a speeder hit a key deer on Big Pine this week. But the table got turned."

"How so?"

"Motorcycle, in excess of eighty in the special slow-down zone. The deer lived. Two broken legs. The bike rider went ass over teakettle. Hamburger on the highway. Killed instantly."

Justice, in theory, for an animal.

Six cold-case murder victims never got theirs.

Sam pulled more gear from the duffel. A small-caliber rifle, a night scope, a net bag full of tubes and tiny jars— a jungle survival kit. He handed me a four-inch rubber-handled stainless skinning blade in a nylon sheath. And a three-inch lockback to stick in my pocket.

I looped the belly-pack over my right shoulder, under my left armpit. Sam dropped in the radio, extracted the ear

and microphone wires. He used dark adhesive tape to attach
the ear wire to my neck, the mini-earphone inside my ear.
He taped the remote mike to my Adam's apple. "Now, in
case you sweat and fuck up the adhesive . . ." He wrapped
a short Velcro belt around my neck to hold the mike in
place. He clipped the other radio to his belt, rigged his
wires the same way. We stood apart, checked volume levels. With the voice-activated circuitry, we didn't have to
press buttons. "These are good for two miles," he said.

Sam pulled one more piece of equipment from the duffel. A Walther PPK pistol. He snugged it into my belly-
pack, said, "Safety on." Wheeler had called himself a
"qualified coconspirator." He was more than qualified. He
was an equipment freak. I was amazed at how little time it
took law-abiding citizens to turn themselves into vigilante
commandos.

Sam cranked the motor, popped us to a plane, sped to
Kemp Channel Bridge. We slowed a hundred yards south
of the overpass, raced our wake another ten yards. Sam
adjusted his throttle to mimic a sputtering engine, then shut
it down. We drifted, kept an eye on channel markers. Sam
sang softly, Vietnam humor to squelch his nervousness:
"The Magical Mystery Tour is coming to take you
away . . ."

We studied the shore, discussed lights in homes and on
poles. "The tide's coming in. I don't see any rescuers. Let's
start talking through the radios. I'll pole in and drop anchor.
You kneel on the bow. Be my eyes. You're looking for
rocks."

"Favor that Environmental Center," I said. "I don't want
to crawl ashore in the mobile-home park. Some land-
owner'll freak out, pop me with a twelve-gauge."

In my ear: "You think they guard the coastline like the
Cuban Army?"

"No, but they watch for Cubans. You can bet that."

"My point, exactly. Anymore, a boatload hits the beach
and a pack of starving people come ashore. They wander
through yards, grateful to be on dry land. Maybe swipe fruit

off the trees. My buddy on Grassy Key doesn't donate old clothes to Goodwill anymore. He hangs them in the yard. They're gone by morning. The refugees leave behind salt water–soaked rags. They're not a threat once they hit land. They're glad to be in America."

"Your point?"

Sam used his pole to slow our progress. "Define your threat. If shotguns pop, they'll belong to your target, not the neighbors. But don't think about it now. Just remember that Scott Kirby lyric." Sam spoke as if reciting gospel: "If you're walkin' on thin ice, you may as well dance."

"Mambo till the sea cows come home."

"If I see action ashore that's not you," he said, "I'll give you a *di di*."

"DeeDee lives in Indiana. She's a sweet one."

"This one's Vietnamese. Means hurry your ass out of there." He pointed to a moored sailboat. "If your boys shine a spot, I'll hide behind that."

"Time to go for it."

"Get off the south side of the boat, in case you splash," said Sam. "Think about noise, not hurry. Go slowly. If you trip, don't try to stay standing. Roll with it, into the water. Land on your knees. Come up slowly."

Sam was repeating words he'd heard over thirty years ago. Words he'd memorized going into enemy turf. Words that may have saved his life.

I went in. The thigh-deep salt water was warmer than the night air.

I heard Sam through my earphone: "Check in with me every couple of minutes. I hear the word *panic*, I'm on the beach."

I said, "Okay," into the microphone. "Did you hear that?"

"Don't worry. The radio works."

I eased through the water, aimed for a house between the study center and the Big Crab Fish House. I wanted to hit the beach just west of Thorsby's dock. The shallows were rocky. I stubbed my feet, scraped an ankle, felt grateful for my old basketball sneaks. I found a rhythm. I'd go a dozen steps, crouch, count to ten as I scoped the shoreline. I'd stand, repeat the process. I scanned the waterfront, memorized lights ashore. Lights turned on weren't so bad. Lights gone out might mean an observer. For now, no lights changed. Only two boats at Thorsby's dock.

Closer to land, I felt like my skin glowed, made me a walking target. I hit calf-deep water, wanted to hurry but minded Sam's warning about noise. Every reflection was a warning shot. Chunks of broken Styrofoam net floats spooked me. I wanted to sort night sounds, judge each threat. I sensed that a rustling of lizards in the ground cover was prelude to a billy-club whack. Each time I stopped to listen, a truck on the highway, many yards distant, would drown out every other sound. I thought, Do real commandos worry about waterlogged shoes that squish when they walk?

"I'm on solid ground," I said.

"I see you. Nothing else moving." Sam had his night scope on me. "You get your pack wet?"

"Dry."

I moved east toward the lobster boat I'd seen Tuesday. I tripped over a six-inch concrete footer. The foundation for a shed that never was built. The cat spray was either good or bad. Good, if people nearby were accustomed to prowling sounds. Bad, because I saw no cats. Perhaps, like the area birds, they'd been served for supper.

At the edge of Big Crab's property, a motorcycle graveyard in a mangrove clump. Frames, bent wheels. No fenders, no engines. Light reflected off a few pieces. New items, their paint not yet dulled by sun and corrosion.

I crouched under the dock, held still. No sounds except for the soft slap of inshore waves. I moved east, angled inward. What I'd taken to be a mobile-home park was five shabby trailers. The rusted one close to the water stood alone. The next three formed a U. I couldn't be certain in darkness, but they appeared to be connected. Light and voices and TV sounds came from the open windows of the

fifth unit, the one closest to the highway. A tall slat fence
blocked my view. It also blocked the highway's view of
Thorsby's compound. The sliding gate was wide enough to
bring in a boat on a trailer. Or a stolen car. A faint two-
track of flattened weeds ran from the gate to the triple-
trailer U.

I heard a solid *thunk* in the occupied trailer. I froze,
heard drink cans pop open. The refrigerator. Beers for three
people. I heard an exaggerated moan and canned music. A
porn-movie sound track. I couldn't have hoped for a better
diversion.

I followed the dirt track to the U, kicked something
small and hard in the dirt. Shit. A trip wire, a silent alarm?
I held still, waited for a scramble in the porn theater. I
quickly looked down, caught a glint of chrome. A fresh
Master lock, with no corrosion. I checked the rear wall of
the nearest trailer. A false wall, a lift gate disguised as the
ass end of a trailer, and a side-hinged metal door. On the
door, an unsecured hasp. I pocketed the lock so no one
could find it and lock me in. I opened up. A stink of grease
and mildew.

"Going inside," I radioed, almost whispering.

I heard: "Okay."

I stepped up. A sticky wood floor. The door swung shut
behind me.

"You hear me now?" I said.

"Yes."

I pulled the small camera from my belly-pack, hung the
string around my neck, flicked on the penlight. In the dim-
ness I could see most of the large, U-shaped room. I wondered if Navy Security missed their F-150 pickup truck. In
front of it, Teresa's Grand Am. Then Heidi's Jaguar roadster, Bug Thorsby's low-slung pickup truck, a bright red
Mustang Steeda Cobra, and a twenty-four-foot SeaRay
powerboat. I didn't know why they'd bothered to swipe the
moldy Pontiac Sunbird convertible. It had belonged to a
former bartender, Jesse Spence, now a boat builder in Fort
Pierce. Maybe he had abandoned it. I walked slowly to my

left, to check the far trailer. At least thirty mopeds. A Conch Train Jeep. Two of Paul's Portable Potties. Norby would be pissed. I moved back to the doorway. Hanging from the mirror of Bug's truck: an upside-down crucifix cut from a compact disc.

I said to Sam, "They could open a used-car lot."

I played the penlight along the walls to check for windows. I didn't want my flash to draw attention. The windows had been covered with flattened grocery sacks and duct tape. I wanted front shots and license tags of each vehicle. I quickly shot three photos. After the fresh meat—Teresa's car, the pickup truck, and Heidi's Jaguar—I found no more license plates. I checked the Jaguar's glove box. I pictured myself plopping pictures and registration slips on Liska's desk in the morning. There was no paperwork in the truck, the Jag, or Teresa's car. Liska would get only pictures.

A sound, outside. Oh shit, the fence gate sliding. The lock isn't hung on the hasp. The bad guy's going to know someone's in here. I pocketed my mini-flash, replaced the camera, and palmed the pistol in my belly-pack. Leave the gun alone, I thought. Too much noise, a pistol shot. Sure to draw a crowd. I didn't relish a knife fight in the dark. I didn't know how good he was. I didn't want to lose my only silent weapon.

I needed something quiet and solid. I took a chance, shone my penlight on the floor. Nothing. I shone it in the pickup bed. Nothing there, no two-by-four, no tire iron. Like the iron in Teresa's trunk. Four months ago I bought her a decent NAPA jack and a four-armed lug wrench so she could toss the factory-supplied can opener.

My brain sped into high gear. Teresa had complained that the remote release lever didn't work. She'd put a spare trunk key under the rear floor mat. Could I open the car door, shine the interior lights long enough to get the key? If shitbird walked inside the trailer and saw the light, all hell would cut loose.

I was walking on ice. Time to dance. I shuffled side-

ways, popped the door, reached down. I found the key
wedged in the seat track. I held tight, released the seat-
adjustment lever with my other hand. The key slipped free.
I popped the trunk. One more stroke of luck: I had offered,
then forgotten, to replace Teresa's burned-out trunk lightbulb. I reached under the old carpet she kept so things
wouldn't slide around in there. The tire iron, fresh as new.
The store's bar-code sticker still on the arm I grabbed. Now
. . . close the lid without alarming the man. No way. Too
much noise. Leave it open.

Suddenly the shed's door swung open. A man's voice:
"Yo, Douglas?"

We weren't twelve feet apart. I smelled the man's cigarette, or secondhand stink from his clothing. He didn't see
me. He left the door ajar, went back outside. I watched his
shadow in the moonlight. He was looking for the padlock.
I crouched, hustled toward the wall, froze again. The door
swung shut on its own. I slid along the wall to get close to
the door. If he came back in, walked in far enough, I could
bolt through the door. I could lock him in, make a run for
it. No, I thought, that won't work. If I locked him in, he
could climb into the pickup and lean on the horn. They'd
be all over my ass. Then I thought, he could be rounding
up the troops right now. Even if he came back in alone, I
was in trouble.

The door opened slowly. A strong flashlight beam
jumped wall to wall. The hand that held the light was attached to an arm as big around as my calf.

He aimed the light at the open trunk lid. He whispered,
"What the fuck?"

I slid behind him, poked my blade in his ear. I pushed
him forward. The door swung shut behind me. "Say one
peep, fuckhead, I'll stick it through your voice box. You'll
drink your own blood."

Sam was listening. He said in my ear, "Hang tough.
Remember the code word."

The man stopped, stiffened. He was my height, but outweighed me. His wrist swiveled, the flashlight came back

at my forehead. I dodged it, poked with the knife, slapped the light with my left hand. It clattered into the pickup truck bed, remained lighted.

"Don't do what you're thinking," I whispered. "You kick me in the balls, you'll never talk again. If you live."

He tried, anyway. He snapped his right calf upward. His ankle cracked into the tire iron. "Shit," he said. The iron fell on my foot. At that point, pain was better than noise. The knife had remained in his ear. I'd felt it puncture skin.

I reached into my pocket with my other hand, grabbed the Master lock, fitted one finger through the loop, a solo-brass knuckle. I rapped the man upside the head. "No shit, no talk," I said. "Walk to the open trunk."

He smelled like a boiled-down vat of greasy chicken soup.

I edged him forward, felt power in his back and shoulder. I kept myself alert. He could spin away in an instant, grab me, pluck the knife, toss me out the door, fillet me like a sea bass in the pea rock.

"Get in," I said.

"Bullshit."

I pressed the knife into his upper ear, felt it break skin again. He jumped. The knife stayed with him. I pushed on his shoulder. "I'll slash your face, fucker. Or that fat blood vessel in your neck."

He began to roll in, muttered, "Shit."

I rapped his ankle with the lock. "You kick, and I'll make that bone popcorn."

He was in. I pushed down the lid. He fought back. I was in no mood for a shoving contest. I jumped up, sat on the damned lid. His resistance quit. The latch snapped shut.

I turned to make sure no one else had joined us. Stood in place for a few seconds to make sure no one had heard the commotion. I said to Sam: "One down, two to go. I'm fine for now."

He responded: "Two neck arteries, called carotids. Also, jugular veins."

"That's good info. Thanks."

I went to the pickup and flipped off the man's eighteen-inch flashlight. I still needed pictures. I turned on my small flashlight, hurried around the oblong rooms, grabbed shots as quickly as the flash would recycle. The mopeds, the boat, the vehicles. The man in Teresa's trunk began to kick and shout. I thumped the lid, told him I'd open up and come in slashing. He shut up. I hoped he didn't make a personal mess in there.

The flash batteries went south. I took the large flashlight, flicked it off, pushed open the metal door. No one out there. I eased the door shut, fixed the padlock onto the hasp, snapped it. Listened again for observers, then retraced my steps to the dock. I couldn't see squat on the path. I knew Sam couldn't see me until I reached the waterline. I suddenly formed an image of Thorsby's knife-throwing ace just missing me two days earlier.

My feet hit the beach gravel. "Got me?" I crouched by the property edge, sealed the camera in the Ziploc bag.

"Yes. And no one else. Come back the way you came. The long way. You walk straight from there, you'll hit a dredged slot, be over your head."

"I've been over my head for twelve minutes."

Four minutes later I was in Sam's skiff. He tilted his engine halfway down, started it, noise be damned. He let the partially submerged prop counter the tide. I used the flashlight I'd swiped to search for channel markers. After I found the first marker, Sam hit the tilt button, then the throttle. Neither of us looked back.

Twenty minutes later Sam pulled back the gas lever. We were south of the Saddlebunch Keys, near West Washerwoman Shoal.

"My man," he said, "you need to learn the true essence of yachting."

He switched off the ignition, reached into a small plastic carrying case, pulled out two iced bottles of beer. We sat on opposite gunwales, rocked on the waves, soaked up the quiet night sea air. Sam had risked his boat. I didn't know how to tell him that I wasn't in the mood for celebratory beer. I wanted to put my photos to good use. I wanted to put a stop to Thorsby and learn his connection to the murders.

"Find what you needed?" said Sam.

"What I thought I'd find, except more of it. Teresa's car. Heidi's Jaguar. Like Jemison had a small operation that suddenly got bigger."

"Why now?"

"I've been trying to shape that thought. You got recent thefts that tie into a pattern of murders and attacks. And an odd business link between Butler Dunwoody and Mercer Holloway . . . The link is like an umbrella over all of it."

"Wasn't that in the back of your mind?" said Sam.

"It was there."

"Which is why we're right here, right now."

I mumbled, "Yep."

"Tone of voice check," said Sam.

"All day long, every time I heard his name . . . I still can't believe Mercer's dead. I mean, what a bundle of conflicts. He loved Key West, warts and all. But when I met with him Monday morning, he got incensed because a funky old Ford van parked in front of his beautiful house. Said it parked there all the time. Hated it. Like old cars shouldn't be part of paradise."

Sam stood, finished his beer, and restarted the motor. "The red van with the Vietnam stickers?"

"That's the one."

"Good man. The scars up and down his legs look like zippers. He walks funny because his ankles don't work. He's never been able to let it go."

"Speaking of ankles," I said. "I was thinking this morning about our trip to Bimini in '89. This is dumb, but I don't think I ever asked. How'd you break yours?"

"I slipped."

"That's it?"

"The bottom rung of the cabin ladder," said Sam. "I slipped."

"Now I know."

"Let's get ashore," he said. "I'm reading you like a book. You're so damn anxious to get that film in the soup, I'm surprised you're not swimming."

30

Compare a full-tilt night ride on a fishing skiff to jumping on a trampoline for eight hours. The fifty-minute ride to Key West had worked muscles in my belly and back that I'd been ignoring. Wheeler's fishing trips had conditioned him. He couldn't believe that I felt discomfort.

I called Duffy Lee Hall from a coin phone on the dock. Five rings, then a machine. At the beep I begged Duffy Lee to pick up.

Sleep in his voice: "Why, why, why?"

"You name it, I'll pay," I said. "One roll, right away, to help stop a killer."

"You are too much, Rutledge." A pause for effect. "Bring it on by."

Duffy Lee answered his door in bathing trunks.

I gave him the film. "Two sets of prints?"

"How about ten? Make it worth my while." He looked over my shoulder, winced at the sight of Sam's funky Bronco. "It'll take some time to set this up. Don't come back before seven."

I asked Sam to drop me at Sunbeam Market. I needed a six-pack of sedation, with rum back. I could barely get out of the Bronco.

Sam said, "Teresa's car, does it have a remote trunk release?"

"It doesn't work," I said. "Shit. I left the key in the trunk lock."

Sam thought a moment, then shrugged it off. "Let's hope Jemison's team goes to jail before they come find us."

"A stupid mistake. Tell Marnie I'll have prints before she goes to work."

A typical midnight Sunbeam. A wary clerk and one other customer. A big guy with bloodshot eyes carried an armload of munchies like a day-old baby. I bought the beer and walked toward the lane. On the dock I'd felt peace of mind, mission accomplished. But Sam was right. The presence of Heidi's and Teresa's cars defined the teams in conflict. Leaving the key in Teresa's trunk lock was an invitation for revenge.

The vaporous glow of Fleming Street's crime lights cast green tint into Dredgers Lane. Three steps brighter, it could melt paint off the house. Pale green pavement, humid green haze. Everything fuzzy and hard to see. Nick's Dodge Ram truck sat next to Carmen's house. She'd be dancing in the morning, hot-stepping the Bone Island Mambo, or recovering from it.

I grabbed the porch door handle, suffered brain fade. No chance a mail delivery had arrived during the past three hours. But I leaned to check my mailbox. I heard a sharp whack above me. I thought a door hinge had seized. I looked up, saw the knife in the door frame. I dropped the six-pack, ducked low, rolled from the stoop. A second blade bounced off the framing, ripped through the screen door, hit something on the porch. I kept rolling, trying to scoot through the croton hedge. I couldn't find space wide enough. The first blade had been like the one that just missed me Tuesday at Thorsby's dock.

I was stuck prone against the hedge, a large target in plain view. I waited for incoming, tucked my elbows inward to protect vital organs. My hip ached from rolling on the belly-pack and camera. I heard a thump, a loud "Uhhh" from across the lane. Glass rattled on the pavement.

Hector's voice huffed: "Coño, these bums."

I didn't move. I waited for another blade to hiss.

Hector said, "Alex, boy. You in the dirt."

"You okay, Hector?"

"I hate bums, Alex. Get off the burrs. Come see this bum sleep."

Hector held a bottle neck, jagged and lethal. "I bust that brandy," he said. "You can pay me back."

I nodded agreement. I'd just busted a six-pack of beer. But our watchman had scored a slam dunk. The man on his back was Jemison Thorsby's blade ace. Dressed like a New England fisherman—long pants, knit cap, waterproof boots. A pool of blood under his neck. I didn't want Hector in trouble if the knife man died. We needed to call 911.

I'd been warned on Sunday about a man who kept an ice pick in his boot. I checked the zonker for weapons. A dagger strapped to each ankle. I could start a collection. I pulled them, tossed them into my yard.

"Too damn many bums in the lane, Alex," said Hector. "I run a bum off your garbage this week. Trash-pickin' bum."

"Picking *my* garbage?"

Hector grunted, which meant yes. "Ran his short, fat, shitty boongie down the lane. I tell that fuck'emup not to come here. He's a dumb bum."

My paint-stained camera strap had been swiped from the garbage. The strap found around Bug Thorsby's neck in the Maxima's trunk. Hector's description of short and fat could mean that Robbie Carpona, my original attacker, had killed Bug.

I left Hector to guard the swamp rat. I went inside to call 911, heard the electric air cleaner's white noise. I flipped on a light. Teresa stood at the bedroom door with her pistol aimed at my chest. She'd been asleep, still fully dressed, and had heard the six-pack hit the porch steps.

She lowered the gun. "Did you get caught?"

"Somebody chucked a knife at me. Hector Ayusa saved my life for the second time in six months."

Her sleepy face looked bewildered, a mix of worry and

frustration. "Why does it need saving so often?"

Good question. Best answered in daylight.

My first call went to Carmen. "You need to be out in the lane," I told her. "Run interference for your father. He just got me out of a jam. There'll have to be some explaining."

"To my mother or the police?"

"The police."

"At least there's that." She hung up.

I pulled out my wallet, found the card that Bobbi Lewis had given me. She answered on the first ring: "Yes?"

I said, "Rutledge. Sorry to bother you—"

"Happens all the time."

"I got a situation here, on Dredgers Lane. Some asshole threw a knife at me, in my yard. My neighbor clocked him, then told me about a trash picker he'd chased away a couple days ago. It might explain how someone got the camera strap that went around Bug Thorsby's neck."

She said, "City on the way?"

"I called you first."

"Call the city. They'll go aggravated assault. If they upgrade to attempted murder, Liska may take it away. Did you walk outside, or were you coming from somewhere?"

"Just getting home from Summerland. I took pictures of stolen cars."

Bobbi Lewis said, "Oh, my."

"This is my guess. The cars are tied to the murders."

"I want picture copies."

"You were first on my list. My processing man already has the film. I'll have prints by breakfast."

"I'll be in touch."

I dialed 911. A blue light flashed in the lane. The city was on scene. One of the neighbors had heard the breaking glass. I recradled the phone.

Teresa ruffled her sleep-mussed hair, walked to a front window. I went to her, put my arms around her. "The people Sam and I creeped on Summerland Key must have figured us out."

"How would they do that?"

I explained about finding her car wedged in among the others.

"Not to diminish the idea that someone tried to kill you, but was my car in okay shape?"

Except for the guy in the trunk? Dodge the truth: "It looked fine, what I saw with a penlight."

"Thank you for finding it."

"We'll get it back," I said. "Go to bed. There won't be any reporters."

"To celebrate the fact you're alive, I'll take your word." She gave me a quick half-asleep hug to answer mine, then returned to the window.

"Can I ask two favors?" I said. "Please call Sam and tell him what just happened. And that gun he gave you? Keep it close."

"You had a message from Julie Kaiser. It's still on the machine."

"I'll check it when all this gets settled down."

Teresa walked to the bedroom, unbuttoned her blouse. "Hurry to bed."

Carmen saw me come off my porch. She ambled my way and whispered, "Play dumb. It shouldn't be hard."

"Love you, too," I said.

The punk from Thorsby's stable sat sideways in the backseat of the prowl car. The scowling face of Juvenile Evil, in handcuffs. No danger of his passing away.

Carmen had spun the magic perfected by many bilingual Conch women. Two cops were utterly confused. One was convinced that Hector spoke no English. The other—a Latin-looking youth with brand-new biceps—knew that he'd better keep his mouth shut. Through Carmen's translation, the officer in charge understood that Hector had walked to his porch for his nightly cigar, had spotted a prowler throwing knives at my house. He'd challenged the man, had been jumped, and had won the battle.

The officers asked Carmen if they could take Hector somewhere to write out his statement; in Spanish.

Carmen said, "He can't go downtown. His blood pressure, he may die in the office. And my mama will have to sue the city. They always fire arresting officers when the city gets sued. It shifts the blame. But it hangs you out to dry. We should go inside and take a pressure reading right now."

"We can get his statement in there," said the cop.

"No statement is worth waking my mother," said Carmen. She offered to write out his statement in the morning and deliver it to the police station. After I agreed to press charges, the officer in charge agreed.

A minute later the city cops were gone. I waited while Carmen ushered Hector to his front door, then walked her home. She passed the dark green Dodge truck, patted its fender. "I may have been wrong about this boy. He's not like the others," she said. "He gets better as time goes by."

"You're telling this to a man who loves you. What's that awful noise?"

Carmen paused at her door. "I know what you're thinking. It's as useless as trying to win someone's heart with sarcasm. There's no way to steal wind chimes without making them chime louder."

Teresa was wide awake when I came inside. "Sam wants you to call," she said. "Don't worry about waking him."

We both heard two short, sharp hissing sounds, then two light taps on the screen door. Teresa pulled the pistol from under the sheet. I raised my hand to calm her. I knew the hiss signal. I didn't want Sam dusted with his own gun.

He still wore his black clothing. He carried a Heineken and the duffel he'd had on *Fancy Fool*. "Looks like we declared war."

"I was right about the trunk key drawing the idiots. But it's over. Hector gets an award."

"But I know Jemison Thorsby. He knows it was you, and he probably knows it was me. He knows you've taken pictures. He's not going to wait around for the sheriff to raid him. He takes revenge, or he takes the road to Miami."

"You left Marnie alone?"

"Her brother's there, with Heidi. He's got some kind of .357 that'd turn a man into shredded wheat."

"Thorsby can find us quicker than we can find him," I said. "You won't like this question. Do we hunker down and wait?"

"We play like we played at Jemison's mobile-home museum. Lights out and radios. You sleep two hours. I'll take the first watch." Sam pulled a pistol and the Motorola UHF units from the duffel.

"You going to sit on my porch with night-vision goggles?"

"I'm going to sit on Hector's porch with two more Heinekens. We'll take turns wearing earphones and microphones."

"I'll call Hector and warn him."

Sam said, "It's taken care of."

"Give me three minutes to rinse off salt?"

"Take two. You're in a combat situation."

I couldn't wait to go prone and close my eyes. I used a flashlight to scout the yard. Palmetto bugs, but no invaders. I showered, drank a beer, brushed my teeth.

I remembered to check Julie Kaiser's message: "Hello, Alex. It's a little after eight. I wanted to check with you about the photos my father wanted done. I'm sure that my sister and Donovan and Philip will want to follow through with my father's charitable trust. But the attorneys say that we'll need valuations on the property even sooner, so they can start to settle his estate. The sooner we can transfer the property titles, the sooner the foundations can reap the benefits. I still would like you to do the photos. If you get home before ten-thirty, please call." She left her number and closed by thanking me for being a friend.

Holloway had planned to give his real estate to charity. He hadn't been blowing smoke when he'd talked about letting children fend for themselves, make their own fortunes. It was the sort of situation that generated murder motives as big as an ocean. Donovan Cosgrove must have disagreed with Mercer's plan. If any of Mercer's other heirs disagreed, we probably could identify a co-plotter. Or two. Or three.

In bed my brain spun like a boat propeller. After an hour of no sleep, I keyed the UHF radio. I offered to spell Sam on Hector's porch.

His voice came through clearly: "No way. I'm good for sunrise."

I tried not to toss and wake Teresa. Finally, around six, I put on shorts, shoes, and a long-sleeved T-shirt, and unlocked the bike. Chilly out there. I radioed Sam, told him it was time to pick up the photos from Duffy Lee Hall.

I rolled across Frances toward Hall's home on Olivia. The last of the wee-hour bike cruisers were out and about. Dreamers, loadies, and drunks ride mindlessly, fight insomnia, cure blahs, speculate about lovers back in their beds. They ignore stop signs, breathe vegetation instead of motor fumes, and burn off extra energy.

I tapped my fingernail on Duffy Lee's front door. Thirty seconds later he stood there, still in his bathing trunks. He held a small paper sack. He looked beat. "One set for you."

"I needed two, Duffy Lee."

"A lady deputy came by an hour and half ago. Said she'd save you a trip to the county. I don't mind waking up five times in one night."

Bobbi Lewis. She'd called Liska, found out who processed my film.

"Thank you for all this. Do you bill wake-ups equal to film runs?"

"This time I do." He slowly closed the door.

I rode home on back streets, better to dodge vehicles that might want to swoop out of the dark and flatten the bike. I found Carmen Sosa on Fleming, waving to her daughter as the school bus departed. She said, "Sam and my father were drinking coffee on my father's porch. Did they sit up all night?"

"As far as I know, Sam did it alone. We're worried about more visitors."

"Hector's a lonely man," she said. "He loves company."

"We need to buy your father a chrome badge."

Carmen shook her head. "Or a black shirt that says MIR-ADOR. We could build him a tall platform, put him in the watchtower."

Watchtower. The name slurred by Cilla, the barfing baby wino.

"What's mirador?" I said. "Spanish for guard?"

"El mirador—like the old name of that motel, over to United Street. What's it called now, the Key Breeze Suites?"

"What's mirador mean?"

"Sometimes 'spectator.' Usually, it's what I said. 'Watchtower.' "

"Do you recall who owned the El Mirador Motel when you were growing up?"

"Vernon Kaiser," she said. "Philip Kaiser's father. The family lived in the suite above the office. That's where Philip grew up. Then Mr. Holloway got ahold of it."

"So Mercer bought it? Like a retirement package for Philip's folks?"

She shook her head. "I'm not so sure about that. After Mercer took over, Vernon worked at that radio station on Stock Island. I don't think Holloway bought El Mirador. I heard that he loaned money to the Kaisers. He didn't get paid back, so he foreclosed. Vernon worked radio to keep food on the table."

"Mercer put his daughter's in-laws out of business?"

Carmen shook her head. "It happened many years before the wedding."

I asked Carmen to pay attention to traffic in the lane.

I blipped Sam on the radio. I told him to go home and sleep. Hector could watch out for our welfare. Sam said he'd be over in a few minutes. He'd bunk on my couch after Teresa went to work.

Inside, I smelled coffee and buttered toast. Teresa was starting her day in the shower.

I looked up Monty Aghajanian's number. Monty had been a fine Key West cop. When the FBI accepted him for agent training, he'd gone for it. The FBI had posted him to Newark. Monty and his wife had bought a ranch-style home in Flemington, New Jersey, almost in Pennsylvania. He'd said that the commute was better than living a rat race close to Manhattan.

He knew it was me when he picked up. "Seven A.M., Alex. Real damn early. This better not be rock-and-roll trivia questions."

"It's murders out the ying-yang."

"I heard that Mercer Holloway hung himself."

I said, "I think someone killed him. There've been three others you don't know about."

"I'm glad my office is in quiet little Newark."

"I met Jim Farmer yesterday."

"I know," said Monty. "He called me already. He wanted to know if you were legit. I told him you couldn't be trusted around Barbancourt rum. Other than that, you were okay."

"How about Farmer?"

"Anything he said, you can take to the bank."

"You're a clearing house for character. Remember Philip Kaiser?"

"Oh, boy, do I. We were on the force together, as long as he lasted. Talk about a guy in the wrong occupation."

"Why was that?" I said.

"He wasn't a great cop like some people aren't good ice skaters. We've all got certain things we're better at. He was a lousy police officer. I always thought he had a screw loose. He made mistakes. A couple of big ones."

"You ever have any run-ins with Jemison Thorsby?"

"Why do you ask that?" said Monty.

"He's moving stolen cars down here. I think it's tied to the murders."

"Jemison Thorsby was Philip Kaiser's biggest mistake. And vice versa, to start with."

"I've got to hear this."

"Jemison Thorsby was drunk in the Half Shell one night. The place was full of tourists. Officer Kaiser went in to

chill him out. Thorsby sprung bad on him. Kaiser called in
an 'officer down.' The watch supervisor raced in. Jemison
went for Kaiser with a broken beer mug. They busted
Thorsby for attempted murder of a police officer. It went
to trial, with a public defender. Somehow, in his testimony,
Kaiser screwed the pooch. Whatever he said opened the
door for a lesser charge. Thorsby got convicted, but he went
away for a much lighter pull."

"Why would Kaiser have messed up like that?" I said.

"Right then, nobody knew. Later, I heard rumors. Stolen
motorcycles, fenced parts, a big conspiracy. It all fit.
Thorsby would steal anything not nailed down. Kaiser,
when he was a kid, was a champion off-road dirt biker. His
folks would take him to mainland Florida. He'd compete
all over the place. But he had to stop racing when his family's finances went sour. His folks were always up and
down, feast and famine. His dad was a bad boozer."

I said, "Did Kaiser quit the force?"

"Chicken Neck Liska fired him after the freeze-up in
court. Some cops didn't agree with it. But that's how it
went down."

"Was Kaiser bitter?"

"Stands to reason," said Monty. "But he was a true
small-town boy. He was smart enough never to mouth off."

I said, "Does he still have friends on the force?"

"Oh, I'm sure there's one or two. Maybe a couple more.
I gotta go. I hear you're seeing the lady who replaced me."

"Yep, I am."

"Make sure she doesn't get wacky. You wouldn't think
there'd be a lot of pressure in a small town. But I'm here
to tell you, I'll take this FBI job any day over the old one."

"Thanks for your help, Monty."

The pieces were coming together.

Philip Kaiser's parents had been forced to sell the El
Mirador Motel to Mercer Holloway. Holloway had renamed
it Key Breeze Suites.

Chicken Neck Liska had fired Kaiser.

In each case—the forced sale and the firing, maybe the renaming, too—Kaiser still could hold a grudge.

Someone was copying Liska's unsolved murder cases. The ex-cop Kaiser had access through friends to unsolved case files, to details the public didn't know. Through old friends, the ex-cop also could have access to the FDLE computers. Enough access to generate two Richard Engrams. And Kaiser the construction liaison had access to Dunwoody's site, where the real Richard Engram's body had been dropped.

The jealous Kaiser probably viewed Dexter Hayes as the main threat to his marriage. A man wearing an EL MIRADOR polo shirt had paid Cilla the punk to accuse Dexter Hayes of infidelity and corruption.

The name El Mirador had been changed at least fifteen years ago. Not many people still would own an EL MIRADOR shirt. Maybe Kaiser thought he'd inherit his folks' old motel. The place where he grew up. Maybe he thought that, by thwarting Holloway's charitable plans, he wouldn't lose out. He'd get the old home place.

If Jemison Thorsby had called Kaiser after my Tuesday visit, Kaiser the off-road champ could have rolled out of town on his dirt bike, passed me on the highway, and followed me to Fecko's camp.

Why wonder? Kaiser had burned my Kawasaki.

The least of his offenses.

I wondered if Donovan Cosgrove and Philip Kaiser, the brothers-in-law, were partners in crime, in murder. Julie's message led me to think that she approved of the charitable trust. Suzanne was anyone's guess.

Jemison Thorsby must have found the key in the trunk of Teresa's car. He must have sent the knife thrower after me. I had to believe that he'd also called Kaiser.

Sam and I needed to watch for Jemison Thorsby and his wharf rats. We needed to watch and listen carefully for a dirt bike. Or any other move that Philip Kaiser might make.

31

"In a trance?" Teresa stood at the porch door. Fresh from the shower, towel-wrapped. The day's first sunlight sifted through the screening.

I stared at her from the sofa. "Philip Kaiser is a bad guy."

She stepped into the living room, leaned against the wall, ready to listen.

"Do I call Dex Hayes?" I said. "Try to convince him a maniac is on the loose? Or is he going to shoot me down one more time?"

"Did Kaiser kill Mercer?"

"Probably."

"And the other three?"

"He, or Jemison Thorsby, or his band of gypsies, or Donovan Cosgrove. It's a package deal. It's all tied together. They've been killing each other, too."

I explained Carmen's translation, the call to Monty. Everything I'd mulled for the past few minutes. The connections.

I stood as Teresa came to me. She put her arms around my waist. Pressed her hand into the base of my spine. She said, "Maybe it'll stop soon."

I pulled on her shoulders, held her tighter. "If it had ended yesterday, we could go in the other room."

"You've lost a lot of sleep."

"That wasn't on my list."

She kissed me. We held each other. A moment of peace, too short.

"You should call Dexter," she said. "His home number's logged in my cell phone."

She tightened her hug for an instant, then went to dress for work.

A drowsy woman told me that Dexter had left a half hour ago. "Can I have him return your call if he checks in?"

His wife was a champ, businesslike while still asleep. She did not offer Dex's cell phone number. I told her my name, told her that I'd try his office. I hung up, checked Teresa's digital directory, keyed Dexter's cell number. It shunted me to voice mail. I turned off the phone. Just as well. If I pitched my story face-to-face, Dexter couldn't hang up on me.

A car stopped out front. Marnie Dunwoody, in the borrowed Buick with squeaky brakes. She walked to the porch and checked me out. "If you don't mind my saying so, you look like forty cubic yards of trash."

Sam had walked across the lane. He stopped behind her. "Alex learned that look from me. It draws cheap sympathy from expensive women."

I ducked inside to call Bobbi Lewis. Another voice-mail message. I said, "Rutledge, one more time. No solid proof, but circumstance out the wazoo. We should think seriously about Philip Kaiser behind these murders. Along with Thorsby."

Teresa exited the bedroom. Sam and Marnie overheard my message. Marnie looked at Teresa to confirm my words.

Teresa shrugged and nodded. "Alex put everything together. He talked to Monty about it."

"You know," said Marnie pensively, "at Holloway's— what, Wednesday?—after the bullet went through the door, Philip had this look . . ." She looked at Teresa. "You were standing there with me."

"When he and Suzanne had their heads together?"

"Like lovers planning a nooner."

"Right," said Teresa. "They saw us and they moved apart."

Marnie said, "Of course, brother- and sister-in-law, in this town . . . Pretty tame stuff."

I said to Marnie, "Last night you thought that Donovan Cosgrove didn't have the cojones to murder people. But his bitchy wife was another story."

"I'll stick to that opinion."

We heard a shuffling in the lane. We all looked, then eased. Cecilia Ayusa, picking up fronds.

I kept two photos to show Dexter, gave Marnie the rest of the pictures for the *Citizen*. She drove away in the dusty Buick loaner.

Sam said, "Humor me." He held a UHF radio, a microphone on a wire, and a safety pin.

"You going to be awake to monitor?"

"Just humor me. Put the radio in your pocket. Pin this mike inside your shirt."

Ten after seven, light traffic, no dust in the air. I promised myself, if the nightmare ever ended, I'd take the same ride, the same time of day, with no destination or deadline. I'd do it ten times in ten days. Personal paybacks.

I did a quick radio check with Sam. He came back immediately, "Clear as mud. Just make sure it's on 'voice-activated.' "

Dexter Hayes stood in the Simonton Street parking garage. His rear end against his city Lumina, a phone to one ear, a finger in the other. His grim expression didn't change as he watched me lock my Cannondale. I stood aside to let him finish his call. He clicked off a half minute later.

"What the fuck are you doing, calling my home?" he said. "First you sit down with Jim Farmer. Then you bother my wife."

"I solved your mystery."

"Right. And I'm forever indebted."

"Philip Kaiser," I said. "You want details?"

Dexter checked his watch. "You get thirty seconds.

Don't worry about facts. Spin me a web of allegations and suppositions and conjecture and invention."

I said, "Sometimes you talk like Mercer Holloway."

"Bad start," he said.

"You wouldn't still be standing here if you didn't already think Kaiser was weird."

He considered his answer to that. He opened his car door, unlocked the glove box, pulled out his weapon in its snap-top holster. He clipped his badge and holster to his belt. "Julie just called, from Mercer Holloway's house. She asked me to come by." He pointed to the street. "Let's walk. I don't want to go alone."

"There's no one in the station with officer backup training?"

"This isn't city business. Julie hasn't seen her husband for thirty hours. Her father's dead. Kaiser never came home to console her. Donovan got out of the county lockup at dawn, went home, and caught his wife in bed with Kaiser. I think Julie wants comfort I'm not ready to offer."

I said, "Why the weapon and badge?"

"An official approach cuts out the personal aspect."

We began the short hike to Holloway's. I explained Thorsby's operation, my call to Monty Aghajanian, the link between Jemison and Kaiser from the past, the dirt bike rider who torched my Kawasaki. I let him know that Cilla had been paid to accuse him in public. Paid with cash and drugs.

"Someone once told me that most murders stem from jealousy, revenge, or money," I said. "Liska fired him. A reason for revenge. You and Julie are still friends. Good reason for revenge, at least in Kaiser's sick head. The copycat kills make you and Liska look bad. Especially Liska. It would have been easy for Kaiser, as an ex-cop, to gain access to the files and, maybe, the FDLE database. Why kill Mercer? I don't know. Maybe inheritance. Probably inheritance. Why Engram at the construction site? I don't know. But—"

"Too many 'I don't knows,' " said Dexter Hayes.

"You ever find Robbie Carpona?"

Hayes shook his head.

"Then I'm not the only one with an occasional dead end. Did Julie say anything else?"

He hesitated but said: "She's a mess. Her sister wasn't returning calls. Julie's been making all the funeral arrangements herself. She's started to pull Mercer's estate together, keep his financial plan alive."

"Some kind of charitable trust?" I said.

He nodded. "She told me the morning they found him that Mercer had arranged to split his property into two groups, and donate it. Two trusts or foundations, whatever. I don't know squat about that kind of stuff. But one is local, for the natural environment. The rental income would cover upkeep, taxes, legal fees, and salaries. Essentially make the foundation self-funding. The other group would benefit the National Trust for Historic Preservation."

"Do you realize what you just said?"

"What?"

"Historic and natural preservation means *no* inheritance. It especially means that Kaiser wouldn't be heir to his parents' motel, the old El Mirador. I'd say we're stacking up motives like crab traps."

Disgust on Hayes face. "Who's we?"

"So I guessed right?"

"What?" he said.

"That you'd blow off my logic."

"Well, I guess you were right about something after all."

"Who told you that Bug Thorsby jumped me?"

"When it happened, some woman offered you her cell phone? Go back to the police station. Look in the office two doors down from mine."

"Am I off your list of murder suspects?"

"On the word of Ms. Barga. She said that you'd wanted to go kayaking on Sunday morning, and she chose to work at home. I knew you had an alibi."

"You run hot and cold," I said. "You're a son of a bitch, then you act the good guy. You blow off my help. Now here I am, walking up the street about to help cover you with an ex-girlfriend."

"Ex-girlfriend?"

I said, "I've known for a few days."

"Where are you at with that?"

"I was never that lucky in high school. The pretty ones went after football players. I was a swimmer. How did Donovan Cosgrove walk?"

"His credit card got him out of jail. He borrowed a friend's station wagon Sunday morning. He drove to Home Depot in Marathon, bought materials to renovate a walk-in closet. His charge records verified his alibi."

"Why did they keep him in jail so long?"

"They didn't want to drop charges, in case he was indirectly involved. He had to wait for a judge to set bond."

We'd reached Holloway's front walk. Dexter Hayes's cell phone rang. He identified himself, listened a moment. He motioned for me to continue up Southard with him, past Mercer's house. He said, "Yes," a couple of times. Then: "Oh, Jesus, both?" Then: "Thanks for your quick work on this."

He hung up, stared at me, stunned. "The FDLE's Crime Lab in Tampa."

"And?"

"That remark you made the other day? About me picking through piss and shit to find evidence?"

"I recall that one."

"You were trying to mess with me. I took it as good advice. We got to the portable potties before they got cleaned. We found wadded-up duct tape in one of them. Stuck halfway down the bucket. The nasty crapper chemicals left us some usable images. I took the tape to Tampa yesterday. I flew up on the sheriff's Bonanza."

My opinion of Dexter Hayes skyrocketed. Not just because he'd taken my advice.

"Positive fingerprints?" I leaned forward for Hayes's next words. The microphone inside my shirt tickled my chest. I wanted Sam to hear who'd killed Richard Engram.

Hayes kicked a small chunk of loose sidewalk. "Kaiser and Thorsby."

32

The morning sun had lifted the temperature to the low seventies. Dexter Hayes and I stood four houses east of Holloway's home on Southard, staring at the street, checking out bike riders headed downtown. Hayes's mission to assist Julie Kaiser had shifted from a personal favor to pure law enforcement. Courts require strict procedure. Duty demands that friendships fall aside. Dexter was shifting gears, recalculating priorities. The chill in his eyes spoke of loathing and duty.

"Call for backup?" I said.

"Two things first." Hayes punched his phone keypad. After a moment he said, "Is he there?" He paused, then said, "Okay. Tucker, Donovan, and you?" He pressed two buttons. I watched him key another sequence. I recognized Detective Bobbi Lewis's cell phone number.

"Tallahassee called," he said to Lewis. "You were right. Hats off . . . Oh, I thought that . . ." Dexter made a face like someone had pissed in his coffee, then looked at me. Lewis must have given me credit for my contribution. Hayes took a deep breath, went back to business: "If Thorsby called Kaiser, he could be anywhere."

I shook my head. Dexter waved me off.

I insisted: "If Cosgrove caught him in his wife's bed, Kaiser never heard from Thorsby."

Hayes winced, nodded slowly. He said into the phone, "One of us has to go to the judge." He nodded again, and said, "I appreciate it." He clicked off, pocketed the phone. We started back to Holloway's.

I said, "You still need me along?"

"You think you're hot shit, don't you, Rutledge?"

"A man of your talents should have no use for jealousy."

Hayes spat, "Now it's you talking like Mercer Holloway."

"Let's shut up and go inside. Maybe we can figure how to put his killer in jail. Before the man notches his gun one more time."

The steely look again. "Let the police take care of that."

"Okay, Dexter. I'll head along home."

Hayes studied the long walkway to the stately veranda. I guessed he was pondering his history with the Holloway family. "I can't go in there alone."

"That makes no sense," I said.

"Neither do murders."

"Where's Bobbi Lewis?"

"The sheriff's special enforcement group is on Summerland, raiding the chop-shop compound. Their operation began forty-five minutes ago. Plenty of vehicles, plenty of evidence. No humans. They caught three of them at a roadblock north of Key Largo. They think Thorsby made it to the mainland before they set up."

Donovan Cosgrove answered our knock. He strained his neck to look up Southard, then let us in. He showed us into Mercer Holloway's office. Julie Kaiser sat in the chair behind Mercer's desk. Bloodshot eyes, no makeup, rumpled clothing. Tommy Tucker stood next to a front window. He held an MP-5 semiautomatic rifle. He glanced our way, then went back to squinting through the blinds. There were no scents of leather and elegance. The room smelled like an all-nighter—a college dorm or a hospital vigil suite. Hours-old coffee, stale munchies, several variants of body odor. All the blinds canted to keep daylight outside where it belonged. No one questioned my presence.

Dexter ignored the men and stared at Julie. He was stuck for words.

Julie's face showed no emotion. "My sister drove the Infiniti on Sunday morning. Donovan knows that for sure. She probably knew there was a body in the trunk. Mr. Tucker thinks my husband killed my father. My husband is screwing my damned sister. Thank you for coming to the house. Have you got anything that might surprise me?"

"You know what I know. The county's issuing an arrest warrant."

Tommy Tucker backed away from the window. "Donovan's car is pulling to the curb."

Dexter went to the other window, peeked through the slats. Over his shoulder I saw the silver Infiniti. Philip Kaiser sat low in the driver's seat. Someone, undoubtedly Suzanne, was slumped in the passenger's seat.

Dexter turned to Julie. "Why did you call me?"

"I needed a friend. I could use a hug."

Hayes took a deep breath. They stared at each other, but he stood still. The desk phone rang. Julie checked the caller ID, scowled, and let it ring.

Donovan lifted the receiver. "I want to talk to her," he said. A moment later he said, "Hold on," pressed a button on the phone base, and replaced the receiver.

Philip Kaiser through the speakerphone: "Am I meeting with everyone?"

"No one who wants to hear you," said Julie.

"I'll bet you're wrong. I'll bet Dexter wants answers to questions. I'll bet Rutledge wants to ask a few himself. And, yes, I was late arriving. I watched Donovan hurry you two through the door. I didn't have a chance to speak to you directly, out here on the street. By the way, Detective Hayes. If I see one single uniform or squad car, Suzanne Cosgrove gets a bullet up her nose."

With the knife attack on me, the only unsolved murder that hadn't been copied was the woman who'd been shot in the head. Kaiser's threat was not hollow. No one spoke.

I looked at Dexter. He stood in a far corner, whispering into his cell phone.

I said aloud, "What comes next?"

Kaiser said, "Hello, Rutledge. Let me put it this way. Remember that cop, thirty years ago, the one who shot his wife in Dennis Pharmacy?"

"I'm not sure I recall the story."

"Break of day, he gets a tip she's eating breakfast at the counter with her boyfriend. He goes to the station, drops his badge on his boss's desk, quits his job, drives to the pharmacy. He walks in, pulls out his service revolver, starts firing away. He wounds them both. He runs out of bullets, goes back outside to reload. On his way back inside he almost tramples a little old lady hurrying out. She looks up at him and says, 'Don't go in! There's a crazy man in there shooting a gun.' He thinks to himself, Shit, I'm the crazy man. What the hell was I thinking? So he goes home, empties the bullets out of the gun, sits down at his kitchen table, drinks a beer, waits for the police to arrive."

I said, "Your point?"

"I'm like he was, after the old lady spoke up. I'm standing outside myself, looking at a crazy man. The last week or so—"

"How was this week different from the last eight years?" barked Julie.

Kaiser said, "It's more fun to talk to Mr. Rutledge."

"Okay," she said. "After you've killed my father and I've interrupted, I'm supposed to apologize?"

"I'll get back to you. Anyway, whatever the confusion that made me kick ass all week, it's about spent. Of course, the last six days, every move I made, Rutledge was my roadblock."

I said, "Why didn't you kill me instead of burning the motorcycle?"

"I almost did. But I had a great day on the water Tuesday. My best day in three years. Captain Turk and I remarked, It was a considerate boater who pulled up short

before spooking my fish. There your ass was, in that boat.
I appreciate that."

"What else?" I said.

"I had some warped idea about sticking to my game
plan. By the time you went back to Stock Island, it didn't
matter what the bum had witnessed. Bug Thorsby was already dead, and you were pissing up a rope. I spooked the
reporter lady with that head in her Jeep. I tried to spook
you with a flaming Kawasaki. But, looking back, you made
this week more fun. Chicken Neck and Dexito were too
stupid to get the point. Somebody had to come after me.
You were the smart one."

I glanced at Hayes. He was off the phone. He sneered.
The killer had praised me. What was this crap, the brilliant
criminal respects the lucky amateur?

"Back to my first question," I said. "What next?"

"I'm in the mop-up stage. I'm not crazy, but I'm not
done."

"Your parents got screwed out of their lifelong dream?"

"When they sold out to Mercer," said Kaiser. "Like they
had a choice."

"What'd he do, loan money, then come back and demand payment?"

"You got it," he said. "Hit 'em in the off-season."

I said, "Is that why we're here right now? You're trying
to make a point?"

"I've pretty much made it, haven't I?"

"You must have planned it for a long time."

"That's correct," said Kaiser. "For twenty years. The
gritty details, maybe only three or four months. But don't
think it's been plain old revenge. I've played this little pup-
pet show out of honor."

"How would you like to honor your parents?"

"I took care of that Wednesday night, with a rope. The
man danced and his feet never touched the ground."

Julie put her face in her hands, rocked forward. Donovan
Cosgrove looked hypnotized. He stared at a wall sconce. I

heard Tommy Tucker's weapon click. He'd switched from semi- to full-automatic.

Kaiser said, "Maybe I'll go on over to the Key Breeze Suites. Shoot those people, too."

"Shit, Philip," I said. "Those people are tenants. They leased the motel from Holloway. They've got the same dream your parents had. They're little people, powerless. They pay rent, they struggle."

"You're good, Rutledge. You just saved their lives."

"Oh, fuck," Tommy Tucker whispered softly.

I looked over Tucker's shoulder. Through thin slits between the blinds I saw the funky red Ford van pull to the curb fifteen feet in front of the silver Infiniti. The van that had parked there often, that had so riled Holloway.

Change the subject, I thought. Keep it moving. I said, "I know why you did Mercer, Philip. I understand why you copied Liska's unsolved murders. Why Richard Engram?"

The van's left-side door opened slowly. A lanky man with a scrawny salt-and-pepper beard stepped to the sidewalk. He calmly extracted a half-smoked cigarette from a wrinkled pack, lit it, and walked toward Simonton.

Kaiser said, "There's an innocent man. I could take him down right now. I could play the irony because he survived a war but not the island."

"Mercer hated that man for parking there," I said. "I heard the speech Monday morning."

"I heard the speech fifty times," said Kaiser. "How the wrong people are populating Key West. But you're right. He pissed off Holloway. That's a good reason not to shoot him. You've saved three lives in two minutes."

He'd taken four in one week. I said, "What happened to your game plan? You're getting sidetracked, talking about popping people. I thought you'd spent your craziness."

"Right you are. I'm getting blabby."

"Why Engram?"

"That horseshit project, that big wart on Caroline. I couldn't burn it. The insurance money would bring it back even bigger. I had to make it a dead issue, an ugly reminder that anything can fail in Key West. Butler Dunwoody is nothing but a future Mercer Holloway. I wanted to scare him right the hell off the island. Make his failure a lesson to anyone who thinks they can take this town by its balls and screw the little guys."

"Killing him would do that?"

"I tried to bribe Engram into leaving town. I knew from the way they were operating he was important. If he went away, it would skunk the works. The fool refused, threatened to tell asshole Dunwoody what I was doing."

Dexter Hayes said, "Where are we now, Mr. Kaiser?"

"One more detail and I'm out of here," said Kaiser. "I'm through using Suzanne. Like I've used the other daughter for all these years."

Julie reacted: "How about it, Philip? Is my sister a good lay? Did she help you with your performance problem? I heard years ago she liked to get tied up. Is that still her thing? Is the whore worth the price?"

Kaiser's voice dropped. "The price she's about to pay? I'll peel the duct tape off her mouth and stick the gun where I stuck something else two hours ago. To answer your question, my lovely wife, you're more inventive in bed. You two, your positions and likes and dislikes, the way you get off, all your passion, all her hatred, no one would guess you were sisters."

Julie looked at Dexter Hayes. Dexter looked away. Donovan stared at the floor, slowly shook his head.

Kaiser continued: "But none of that matters. The first time I had sex with you, I felt like a traitor."

"Was that when you started your revenge?" said Julie. "The first time we had sex?"

"Long before that. I had a plan with no shape, from the night my family moved out of El Mirador. That wasn't just a setback. That was a high-wind, high-water hurricane in my life. Then I had to witness my old man's affair with Seagram's 7. And my mother plain gave up. But, to answer your question, my plan didn't take shape until Suzanne told me that your father was giving it all away. All of it, including El Mirador. Suzanne knew that Donovan didn't care. I knew you'd never complain."

Julie said, "The trusts were in place a month ago, Philip. When you killed my father, you made your loss of El Mirador a sure deal. All this killing got you nowhere."

"No," said Kaiser. "You're wrong. It also killed some of the hatred inside me. Now I'm taking down your family like your father took down mine."

I said, "Is that cop who shot his wife still in prison?"

Kaiser forced a laugh. "That guy quit his job, so it wasn't like he was a cop shooting a civilian. His wife and the boyfriend refused to testify. The case got rolled into a minor firearm-in-public charge. A misdemeanor, eventually wiped from his record. Last I heard, he was a detective in St. Pete Beach."

"You planning to skate that easy?"

"No. They'll strap me into Sparky."

"More like a chemical injection," I said. "The whole process has lost its drama. Instead of a big power zap, it's bedtime stories and warm milk."

Kaiser said, "Whatever. Maybe Jemison Thorsby'll get me first. He hated Bug. Now he hates me worse for taking him out. Wasn't that pretty good, planting his corpse in Jim Farmer's trunk? I'm proud of that special touch."

"You missed your calling," I said. "All these cable networks are looking for script writers. They'd have paid you so much in Hollywood, you'd have forgotten El Mirador."

"First of all, I'll never forget. Second, that remark you just made offended me greatly. Miss Suzanne, who, by the way, is not into rope but she's into handcuffs, will have to pay for the insult."

Suzanne, an accessory, was as guilty of murder as Kaiser. Perhaps she'd even helped with the slayings. But this was not the time to be judge or jury. I said, "Why is Suzanne less innocent than the motel owners, Kaiser? Or the Vietnam veteran? She didn't choose her father."

After a few seconds Kaiser said, "You're right again, Rutledge. So I'll make you folks a deal. You and Dexter

Hayes can decide who it'll be, but I want one of you to walk out the front door right now. If that happens, I won't hurt her. And no dawdling around. You've got thirty seconds to show a face. Dexter, if it's you, you can even carry your little pistol."

"What, *High Noon*?" said Hayes. He looked me in the eye. "Maybe I will."

"Good comparison," said Kaiser.

Tucker shook his head. He whispered, "When that front door got shot, I thought about it later." He wiggled his MP-5, pointed his free hand at the clip. "I heard a burp, not a pop."

Someone on Kaiser's team—or Jemison Thorsby's—owned a semiautomatic weapon. No reason why Kaiser couldn't be holding it right now. Dexter and I stared at each other. I felt no compulsion to trade my life for Suzanne Cosgrove's. I was sure that, deep down, Hayes shared my misgivings.

Julie whispered, "Oh, God, no!" She stood, pointed out the window.

None of us had seen Donovan Cosgrove leave the room. He'd already gone out the front door. Through slits in the blinds we watched him stomp across the porch, start down the steps into the yard.

I checked the Infiniti. The driver's-side power window descended. Kaiser stuck a pistol out the window.

Tommy Tucker ripped away the blinds, hip-aimed his automatic rifle. He was too slow. As he triggered a burst, a bullet shattered the upper window. Tucker went flat on his back. I heard Dexter Hayes bolt toward Julie Kaiser, heard him knock her to the floor.

I watched Cosgrove walk slowly, like a slow-motion movie, toward Philip Kaiser's gun. Kaiser slowly swung his aim toward his brother-in-law. No hurry, no rush. The slow aim. Donovan would die within seconds. I picked up the MP-5, edged closer to the busted window.

Suddenly a rear door of the red van swung open. I heard three gun shots. The Infiniti windshield cracked into a dense web, small chunks held together by safety laminate. The Infiniti's driver's-side door opened. Philip Kaiser fell out to his knees, bleeding from both shoulders. He looked up. Donovan Cosgrove was gone. He looked at the house, swiveled his wrist, squeezed a shot in my direction. A porch column exploded six feet in front of me. I was a deer in Philip Kaiser's headlights. I lifted the MP-5, fitted it to my shoulder.

So much happened in the next five seconds, I didn't register a fraction of it. The first thing I saw was the long spear that entered Philip Kaiser's back, pinned him to the inside of the car door. I glimpsed a motorcycle behind the Infiniti, a blur of acceleration, the quicker blur of the van rear door farthest from me as it swung outward. The motorcyclist struck the red door. First with his front wheel, then with his head. No helmet.

Sam Wheeler, pistol in hand, leaped from the van, hurried to Kaiser, swatted the weapon from his hand. I wondered if it was the gun Kaiser had stolen from Teresa Barga's apartment. I watched Sam Wheeler tuck his own pistol under his shirt and walk east on Southard Street.

A moment later Dexter stood next to me. No longer on the floor, shielding Julie.

"It's over," I said. "I think Jemison Thorsby just shot Kaiser and wrecked his motorcycle. That looks like him in the middle of the street."

Dexter radioed a quick message, then hurried to ex-Sheriff Tommy Tucker. Tucker was on his back, stunned, eyes open. His Kevlar vest had saved him. He probably had broken ribs. The hired security man had come through, loyal to his deceased friend and employer. I smelled alcohol on his breath.

I said, "It's over. How you doing, hero?"

"Fine." Tucker tried to reach up, tried to scratch the back of his neck. He winced and lay still. Dexter opened his shirt and vest so he wouldn't sweat to death before the wagon came with a stretcher and pain pills. Months from now

Tommy Tucker would stop hurting. I doubted that he'd ever feel fine.

Uniforms and city cop cars swarmed Southard Street. Someone covered Kaiser's body with a green sheet. A minute later Dexter Hayes determined that Thorsby, indeed, had killed Philip Kaiser with a spear gun. Thorsby had died instantly when his head struck the red van's rear door.

Dexter used a master key to free Suzanne Cosgrove from the ankle cuffs that held her to the Infiniti's front seat track. Near-catatonic, she had aged twenty years. Philip Kaiser's blood spattered her clothing. A detective in a plain black sedan took her away.

We waited on the porch for the EMTs. Tourists gathered, were herded by police officers to the far sidewalk, then to the nearest intersection. A silence took over, a surreal stillness in the trees and among the gawkers. A cluster of helium balloons—six of them—lifted above the street, floated upward, angled by the shifting wind. An old James Taylor song came from a radio up the block. *Damn this traffic jam . . .*

Teresa arrived on her motor scooter, parked it halfway up the block. She checked on us, then went to deal with reporters from the *Herald* and the TV stations and wire services. She said that Marnie already had the scoop, had picked up the scanner traffic, and had gone to the *Citizen* offices to file her story. I knew that Marnie had an inside story. I wondered how she'd word it.

The EMTs came and went. The FDLE's scene investigators showed up with their swagger and jargon. I sat around, watched the detectives seal the crime scene, then begin their work. Finally Dexter told me to go home. I had no argument for him.

"Your words. The problem's over," he said.

I tried to end it on a lighter moment: "All set for the Super Bowl?"

He shook his head. "Mercer's funeral. Scheduled for kick-off time."

*   *   *

I walked to the city garage, unlocked my bike. As I rode Simonton and Fleming I mentally reran the start of it all. If Suzanne had driven the Infiniti last Sunday morning, she had seen me with Julie, and seen my camera. I had to assume that she'd told Philip Kaiser and he'd called in the services of Bug Thorsby. They'd needed to remove me as a possible witness to the placement of Engram's body.

Thinking that far into the nightmare wore me out. I pledged to learn more in days ahead. Get it straight in my mind as quickly as possible, then spend the rest of my life trying to forget it.

Back home I locked the bike, communed with the neighbor's springer. Easy gig. Scratch the quivering nose, watch the eyes return unquestioning love. Somehow I found the strength to walk to the porch. City Electric had left a note on the door. I'd neglected to pay my intermittent power bill. Three days to make good, or they'd discontinue service.

If they shut off my power, how would I know the difference?

Keep reading for a compelling excerpt from
Tom Corcoran's next Alex Rutledge mystery:

THE OCTOPUS ALIBI

Coming soon in hardcover from St. Martin's Minotaur!

The air inside the taxi could have fertilized a Glades County
cane field. Stale curry and clove gum fought the driver's
body odor. A nicotine haze on the windows gave the sky,
trees, and buildings around me a sickly mustard tint. I
wished I was back in Key West, packing for my week-long
photo job on Grand Cayman Island. I had been hired to
shoot stills for a five-star resort's promo package and web
site. My southbound flight was forty-eight hours away, and
I'd let too many pre-trip details slide.

My wish to be elsewhere passed quickly. Sam Wheeler
had done me a lifetime of favors in the past few years,
favors hard to pay back. This was a chance to chip away
at my debt. I needed to be right where I was, in a smelly
taxi in a stamp-sized parking lot in Lauderdale. Sam, too,
was doing what he had to do. In the room where Sam now
stood, it was forty-five degrees colder than anywhere else
in South Florida just before noon.

The cabbie acted unnerved by our nearness to the
morgue. A GMC van departed, and he changed spots, from
open sunlight to the sparse shade of a bottle-brush tree. He
shifted into Park and flipped on a small orange radio he
had duct-taped to the taxi's dashboard. The box was tuned
to a talk show, a meeting ground for people whose opinions
outran their smarts. Someone had glued a religious icon to

the dash below the radio. I wanted to invoke its powers to make my day end better than it had begun. I doubted that I was tuned to its wavelength.

The man tapped his finger on a dashboard gauge. "We lose this cold air, mon, or I got to go."

He was wise to worry on a ninety-degree, late-April day. He was idling his motor with the air conditioner cranked to full blast. Most cars, it wouldn't take ten minutes for the engine to boil over. I leaned forward, checked his temp needle. It was dead center normal. Engine heat was not his problem.

Sam had been inside the sand-colored building for only seven minutes. I had no idea how long he would be in there. I slid the man twenty bucks—a third of it his tip. Better to sweat in the open air than to melt into vinyl seat covers, forced to listen to radio drivel. Sam's housemate, Marnie Dunwoody, had loaned us her cell phone. We could call another cab when Sam was free.

A damp heat hit me as I climbed out. The driver backed away, spun his steering, went full throttle. He almost hit a Sheriff's cruiser at the entrance apron. The deputy sneered, shook his head, and drove calmly to a parking slot as if near-misses happened all the time. He got out and slammed the county car's door. He was about five-eight, with a crew-cut, huge muscles, a thick neck and broad chest. He wore a red polo shirt, a gold badge clipped to his belt, a weapon in a hip holster. He ignored me as he strode to the building. A lawman on a mission. I could've been dancing on stilts, juggling hand grenades. He would have ignored me.

Broward County's a tough beat.

Sam had shown up on Dredgers Lane at seven-thirty that morning. He knocked on my porch door and whistled through the screen. Teresa didn't hear him. She was dressing with the bathroom door shut. That was strange in itself because she usually performed a get-dressed tease in front of me.

I heard Sam's knock with my head under the pillow. It

was too early for a social visit, and Sam never came by without calling first. He looked whipped, puzzled. He skipped the salutations. "You got a busy day?"

I thought about the legal pad list, chores I'd put off, bills I hadn't paid, quotes I should have mailed days ago. I pictured my last-minute scramble, getting from the house to the airport two days from now. Then I thought about everything Sam had done for me.

He said, "I mean, if you're busy, Alex . . ."

"Nothing I can't ignore."

"I need to be in Lauderdale for a couple hours. I bought two tickets for a turnaround. I'll buy us a good lunch. We'll be back on the island by five."

With the constant easterlies, the past couple weeks of twenty to twenty-five knot winds starting to abate, I'd have guessed that Sam would want to spend his day fishing, catching up with regular customers. He was dressed for work. He'd become sensitive to sunlight in recent years, and always wore lightweight long-sleeved shirts and long trousers. But I noticed that he wore sneakers instead of his leather boat shoes. I couldn't imagine a fishing guide and Vietnam veteran needing a traveling companion. I decided to let him explain when he was ready.

I said, "Is there time to brush my teeth?"

"Take a shower. The flight's not till eight-twenty. I'll make coffee."

Sam spoke softly as he drove his old Ford Bronco to the airport. "Not really my business, but is Teresa that unpleasant every morning?"

"She does her major thinking when she wakes up. That brain whips up to speed before the coffee hits. Plus, she worked late last night."

He shifted his cup from one hand to the other so he could shift gears. "She doesn't like dawn distractions?"

"Especially when she clocks out at midnight. I keep my distance."

"The woman in the bubble?"

I laughed. "With me outside, looking in."

"Tell me again that apartment deal."

"Her landlord went to monthly rentals, on short notice. He jacked up the rent more than double. It's gone from being an apartment to a condo, then a residential atrium. They'll probably advertise it as a two-bedroom, two-bath estate."

"So, you got a roomie?"

"Hell, for eight months we've been living together in two places. We've had to commute ten blocks back and forth. This should be easier."

"So far?"

"Three days. Too soon to decide."

Sam drove another block, then said, "I got a call an hour ago from a deputy medical examiner in Broward. They found a dead woman up there, beat up bad, dumped on a tree lawn in a ritzy community. They say it's my sister, Lorie. They want me to go through the formalities, sign the positive piece of paper."

"The sister you'd lost track of?"

"Since the mid-eighties." Sam paused, then said, "The same month the Challenger blew up, Lorie went poof, too. She'd sent me a photograph, she was holding a snook she'd caught in Chokoloskee. I called a few days later, and the phone was disconnected. I never heard from her again. My sisters up north, Flora and Ida, never did either." Sam went silent a moment, then added, "Lorie had problems back then with abusive boyfriends. Strange, she was still in Lauderdale."

"How did they track you down?"

"An old picture of me in her wallet. I mailed one to each sister from Fort Benning during Jump School. Lorie probably couldn't read yet. Florence was about to start school. Little Ida, come to think of it, I don't know if she was born. I signed the backs of the photos, 'Love, Brother Sam,' with my service number under my name. I was one gung-ho son of a bitch."

Sam was quiet on the flight. It's not easy to talk on a

droning commuter plane, anyway. This one was full of sunburned Spring Breakers, leaving the party early. We'd bought the *Key West Citizen* and the *Miami Herald* before boarding, and swapped sections during the flight. Several articles normally would have drawn comment from Sam. He'd had nothing to say. Not even a wisecrack about toasted college kids. Our friendship had endured because we could survive silence in each other's company. But this deflated mood was not reflective or pissed-off quiet. In the years I had known Sam, I'd never seen a silence of sadness.

Sam nudged me, pointed as we descended over the Everglades on final glide into Lauderdale. Months ago he'd described the huge highway cloverleaf below us. The Interstate had wiped out Andytown, the crossroad where Sam had grown up. He still could claim Muncie, Indiana, as his home town. But his sisters at home, all born in Florida, had lost their roots to the road planners, the graders and cement mixers.

After we touched down, Sam said, "Lorie was so damned stubborn, like my old man. She and the old man were going at it in the car one time, back when 441 was in the Everglades. He was snarling and she was snapping, arguing over nothing. He pulled to the shoulder and told her he wasn't going to have her damned sass. She could change her tone or walk home. She got out and slammed the door. A mile down the highway I realized he wasn't going to stop. He was going to let a nine-year-old girl hike ten miles on a rural two-lane. I told him to let me out, too. He did, and drove away. I'd walked maybe two minutes back in Lorie's direction. The next thing I knew a big Oldsmobile sedan pulled over to pick me up. She'd thumbed herself a ride. We damn near beat the old man home."

"How did he react to that?"

"He never said a thing. She never did, either."

"Tough little girl."

"I guess not tough enough."

*   *   *

The sun stared down at me as if I was on trial. I found shade next to a drainage culvert, stood under a tree hung with flaming crimson blossoms. I checked my watch, then told myself to quit checking my watch. The cabbie was halfway back to the airport hack line. I still smelled of clove gum and curry.

The Broward Medical Examiner Lab was typical of Florida single-story bureaucracy. I suspected that a county architect, in a hurry to get to happy hour, had whipped out the plans on a Friday afternoon. A landscaper had saved his ass with shrubs and trees. I found it strange that Broward had set the laboratory in a Dania Beach neighborhood of upscale trailer parks and mid-scale condos. A trump of all flags at half-mast, an empty flagpole, stood near the building's entrance. Its hoist ropes fluttered in the breeze. Heavy hooks slapped against the hollow pole.

None of this had diddly to do with my upcoming job on Grand Cayman. But the setting brought to mind the conflict in my career, the fact that I dealt with a weird blend of beautiful and gruesome, of fulfilling assignments and a few that had been draining and dangerous.

Three years ago I had thought that part-time forensic work would simply boost my finances and fill unproductive time. I had started with the Key West Police Department, jobs that didn't require science or complex procedures. My name got passed around. Within months, Monroe County's detectives were calling, when their full-timers were overworked or on vacation. I had been reconsidering my sideline for over a year. The only good thing was having extra bucks to put toward my bills. The bad part was how close I'd come to tragedy, how crime jobs had dragged me into a realm I'd avoided most of my life. I still managed to work regularly, mostly out of town, doing journalism, or ad agency shoots, or magazine features. But those gigs didn't promise me anything for the future. Within the past few months, two ad clients had been bought out. Their assignments had vanished along with their corporate names. Even with the Grand Cayman job, my year could be as hollow as the empty flagpole. Unless I hit a jackpot, I still had seven more years of mortgage payments. My short-notice forensic jobs could make the difference between eating and going hungry.

Sam once wisecracked, "If you or I ever go broke, we can blame domestic taxes and imported beer."

His one-liner was going south. Along with my bank balance.

At ten after twelve a white cab rolled into the parking lot. The woman at the wheel yelled, "Yo, Rutledge?"

I nodded.

"You're on the clock, honey. Your buddy watched your cab leave, so he called me. Damn, you're a tall one. Your buddy got a relative in there?"

"That's what they told him."

She shut off the motor, dropped the keys in her shirt pocket, and pulled out a box of Benson & Hedges. She was dressed twenty years younger than her face, fighting time. She had spent a few years on the beach, too, or else smoking had parched her skin.

"Cross your fingers," she said. She fired a cigarette, and held it high so the smoke wouldn't blow my way. In her other hand she held the cigarette box and a Bic pinched between her thumb and two fingers. She waved that hand toward the building. "They've been wrong in there before."

"You don't look as nervous as the man who brought us here."

"Black man?"

"Yes."

"They're immigrants from the voodoo league of nations. They're afraid their spirits will escape inside the morgue, or their souls will be gang-banged to the sound of a hundred batá drums. Or dead people walking—zombies and fire-hags—will dance a *rada* in their rearview mirrors. This is the tissues and sympathy hack. I get sent here a lot."

"You deal with it okay?"

She waved again. "I used to work inside a door that's inside that door right there."

"For the county?"

She nodded. "I saw what came through the back, the messes they offloaded. I never got used to it, but it didn't weird me out. When I was inside, I taught myself not to react, not to have feelings. I don't know how I did that. Looking back, I worry about that part of my personality. I worry about it more than ghosts or bad luck or whatever."

"So it's immigrants fighting their imaginations?"

She nodded and inhaled hard. Sucked smoke down to her knees.

I said, "Imagination can be more powerful than reality."

"They'd be shitless for sure, if they ever saw the real thing." The smoke leaked from her lungs as she spoke. She patted the taxi's roof. "The heat of the day, the nutso Gold Coast traffic, this job is heaven. Take my word."

"Heaven?"

"Well, raw heaven."

Sam stepped out of the building, flinched, and put on his sunglasses. He walked toward us without expression. His walk carried more resolve than before, as if he had promised himself a course of action.

"You hungry?" he said.

"Was it bad?"

"Yep, bad," he said. "But it wasn't her. You hungry?"

I wasn't, but I shrugged.

Sam asked our driver to take us to Ernie's Restaurant.

"Eighteen-hundred block of South Federal," she said, then looked me in the eye. She had told me that people behind those doors sometimes got it wrong. She wanted to win her point.

I nodded, silently gave it to her.

Twelve minutes later, the taxi driver pulled into the restaurant lot. She turned to Sam. She had an unlighted cigarette tucked behind her right ear. "Be careful, buddy," she said. "I used to work back there in that county lab. Six years, and I seen it all. The news you got sounds good, but it's not like you won the lottery. I'll tell you why. Unless you're one in a thousand, you went into the grieving process. Coming out unscathed isn't automatic."

Wheeler pulled out his wallet. "I don't feel this way because I skipped breakfast?"

"Was your sister's I.D. on the body?"

"Yep."

"Current I.D., photo of the victim?"

"Nothing current. Her Social Security card, a certified copy of her birth certificate, a few photos and personal papers."

"No valid driver's license, no unexpired credit cards?"

He shook his head.

The woman bit her upper lip and nodded. "You look like the kind of guy, you can handle straight talk. Take it from an old hand, for what it's worth. This ain't scientific, but it's up here." She tapped her forehead. "The doctors call it empirical evidence. Better than fifty-fifty, your grieving might be right on. You follow me?"

Sam looked her in the eye, paid the fare, and opened the door. "You mind if I ask your name?"

She pointed to the license on the passenger-side sun visor. "Irene Jones. Unique handle, eh? The assholes at the morgue used to call me 'Goodnight Irene.' I guess that's not the most sensitive thing to say to you right now."

Sam waved it off.

"And your name?" she said.

Sam told her.

We walked past a row of eight newspaper, real estate flyer, and coupon pamphlet boxes. Sam said, "Let's hope the place smells like grease."

"To boost your appetite?"

"To get the stench out of my nose."

Just inside the restaurant's door, a dozen people waited for tables. Sam gave the greeter his name. She ignored the line behind us, led us to a remote booth, asked for our drink order. Sam ordered us two beers apiece.

"Preferential treatment?" I said.

Sam said, "We've got a meeting, when the local fuzz gets here. Macho boy, said he'd buy our food, which is unlike a cop. I have no idea what he wants. He said try the conch chowder."

We watched a server spritz a vacant table with Windex. The mist floated our way, made us grateful our drinks and food hadn't arrived yet. I let Sam have his quiet, his time to consider what might come next. I decided he also was pondering the "straight talk" from the woman in the taxi.

Detective Odin Marlow showed up four minutes later. I spotted the red polo shirt and muscular build immediately. He was the deputy I'd seen in the morgue parking lot. He clutched a box of Benson & Hedges in his hand. The pack and a Bic, just like Irene Jones. Sliding a breath mint around in his mouth, Marlow introduced himself as "B.S.O., C.I.U.," as if initials meant big stuff to us. He wore a badge, and that said it all. The greeter appeared with an iced tea, made special with two straws and two lemon slices on the rim. She put the glass down, gave the deputy a flirtatious sneer.

Marlow took his tea, then said, "Mister Rutledge, you mind sitting over there? I'm a lefty. I'll bump your arm fifty times while I'm eating."

He didn't give a crap about arm bumping. He wanted to face us, and not worry about his gun being next to my hand. Sam slid over so I could fit on his bench. Marlow placed his cigarettes and lighter on the table as if they were ceremonial objects, and settled into the booth. He smelled like a sniff sample in a fancy magazine. He wore a diamond pinky ring, and an antique Gubelin watch on a leather strap. One more piece of jewelry and his department's internal team would be on his butt. The men at the top don't like to see their boys display wealth. Perhaps Marlow had shown his supervisor a receipt for Zirconium. Maybe that's how they all dress in Lauderdale.

The server took our food order, and Marlow started right in. "We found her out in District Eight, in what we call the I-75 Corridor, the extension of 595. You got your housing developments popping up like palmettos, your wealthy folk from south of the Gulf Stream, most of them from south of the equator. Where they come from, you know, they're kidnap targets. They can't shop, can't spend their money. It's low profile for survival. This is the comfort life. They got their Expeditions, their cable TV, slate tile floors, the built-in vacuum cleaner systems, the malls, red tile roofs. They also got public schools, no more political strife, and no more family security guards."

Sam said, "This has to do with a dumped murder victim?"

"The last thing they want in their new neighborhood is a body. I got no proof, but I say no way this was Latino connected . . ."

Neither Sam or I had suggested such a connection.

". . . and that improves our chances of solving this thing. Bumps it up from one percent to, say, three percent. So we know it's not your sister. All we got is fingerprints and a dental imprint which, with women, who are less often in jail and rarely in the military, drops our chances back to two percent. Take into account, women change their names when they get married, we're back below the one percent chance."

"That relates to the victim," said Sam. "Let's go sideways. What're the odds my sister's alive?"

"I hate to use the word 'zilch,' but here's how it works. Criminals working credit scams swipe names from the living. People who want new identities grab names from the dead."

"And here we've got . . ."

"New identities go to people hiding from the law, or hiding from partners they've screwed over, or hiding from abusive spouses."

"So, if I found old dental records for my sister . . ."

"Don't even think about it. It's bad enough looking for a name to match a body. Working backward don't cut it. Hey, I know where you're coming from. The M.E.'s investigators called you in, got you all jacked up, put you on a mission. Before you knew it wasn't her, you were thinking 'eye for an eye' to even the score. Am I correct?"

"Was it a robbery?" said Sam.

Marlow shook his head. "You'd find high-end clothing. Tan lines where the watch is missing, rings are gone. This victim, she was a Wal-Mart customer. She was small change. She was a poor target. I'd guess revenge, or she knew too much about bad people. Or, like I said, spousal abuse."

Sam shrugged, wandered off in his thoughts.

No one spoke as our food arrived. We began to eat. Marlow shifted gears. "Tell me about that island of yours," he said. "You really like Key West?"

Sam didn't look up from his food. "Other than your military, very few people live there because they're forced to."

"It's been years since I've been south of Florida City. Key West was full of fags and people smoking dope on the beach. That still the deal?"

"It's strange down there," said Sam. "And loud. Chain saws, cockatoos, straight pipes, roosters, sirens. You'd probably hate it. Don't waste your gas money."

The detective gave Sam a minute of silence, then said, "I'm reading your mind."

"It's blank," said Sam.

"You were thinking of ways, and don't tell me it ain't true. You're riding revenge energy. Nine times out of ten we appreciate that type of reaction. It reduces our job load. Ten times out of ten we bust you for it."

"I'm not the violent type."

"You're the right age to be a Viet Nam vet. You may not be the type, but it's my guess you were trained for . . . what did they call them, contingencies? So you find out it ain't her. You shift your mission, you try some freelance snooping. We like that about the same as two-bit vigilante work."

"Think what you want."

Marlow pulled a ballpoint and a tiny Spiral pad from his trouser pocket. "When's the last time you saw her?"

"Eighty-six."

The detective stared at Sam. "All these years, could she have found you? How long you lived in the same place?"

"Since eighty-one, the same place. My number's in the book."

Marlow stared at his pen, then began to snap it back and forth between the two bottles in front of Sam. The pen was not for writing. It was a prop, and the cop had taken notice of Sam's desire for two beers. "So if she had gone online, clicked 'People Search,' and typed your name, you'd have popped up on her screen?"

Sam nodded, shrugged again.

He said, "You got pictures of her?"

"Nope."

The pen went to the edge of the table, its use as a prop expended. "We wanted to let you know, ask your cooperation. We're gonna run a squib in the *Sun-Sentinel*, announce that the body was ID'd as your sister. It could work for both of us. I'll maybe learn something about the victim, and you'll maybe connect with a lost relative. The squib won't show up in Miami. It won't show in the Keys. We plan to keep it strictly local."

Marlow went to a vacant expression, waited for Sam's reaction. I didn't look at Sam, but I knew he wasn't showing emotion, either.

Marlow found another prop, a subtle distraction. He used a french fry to trace designs in his remaining ketchup. "Your own sister," he said, "and not a single photo? Can I ask why?"

Sam looked him in the eye. "You have your methods. I have my limits."

"Nifty answer. What's it mean?"

"You want to blow her out of the weeds. I'd like to coax her out."

"Look at it this way," said Marlow. "Her fifteen years to find you goes the other way. You've had fifteen years to find her. I take it you haven't tried."

Sam shrugged.

"And you're worried about her picture in the paper?"

Sam nudged me. "What do you think, Alex?"

"There's more to gain than lose," I said. "But if she's alive, could it put her in danger?"

Marlow leaned toward Wheeler. "This guy your roadie?"

Sam said, "No, my witness."

"You got a business card?"

Sam pulled out his wallet, and handed one to the man.

The detective read the card, stood, snatched his cigarettes. "Do yourself a favor, Captain Wheeler," he said. "Do like you've been doing since Ron and Nancy was in Washington, wait for her to call. Thanks for the club sandwich. You'll find a taxi out front in five minutes."

Marlow sucked in air, tensed the muscles in his chest, then walked from the table. Ten feet away he hesitated, then looked back at me. "The watch was my father's," he said. "Right to the day he died, he was the police chief in Greenwich, Connecticut."

Marlow exchanged patter with two waitresses as he left.

I said, "His next smoke was more important than our talk. He neglected to ask if you had other brothers or sisters."

Sam said, "Right. The type who promises what he wants you to hear and delivers what he wants you to believe. Finish your beer."

We walked outside to find Marlow still there, leaning against his county car, smoking a cigarette. He said, "I'm curious, Mr. Wheeler. How's fishing in the lower Keys this month?"

Sam shook his head. "Constant east wind, just like here. Messed things up good."

Marlow agreed, "When the wind blows, fishing sucks."

"Let me put it this way," said Sam. "Yesterday and the day before were my first all-day charters since the third week of March."

Marlow got a distracted look in his eyes, as if he'd gotten smoke in one of them. "I was thinking of running my Mako down there this weekend. It's been eight weeks since I ran that Yamaha 225."

"You need to run it more often," said Sam. "Your carb jets'll get clogged, your water pump'll go south. Anyway, the fish are hungry, but the wind's a bad enemy. If the shore trees are bending, you'll be skunked."

Marlow nodded, still distracted. "Speaking of not catching fish," he said, "you decide to snoop around up here, this is not a quaint beach town. You'll get yourself in a world of hurt. Hire yourself a private eye. We got 'em for all budgets and needs."

Sam didn't talk in the cab. He stared at the urban sprawl and reacted to nothing around us. He called Marnie from the airport, caught her before she left her office. I heard him say, "False alarm. I'd rather see Lorie dead than looking like that woman must've looked when she was alive."

The flight back to Key West was bouncy. Late afternoon heat played hell with the air mass above the heated land and cooling sea. A misty haze covered the Keys, obscured the horizon. If the pattern held, it would be seven months before tropical winter's cool, dry breezes returned. But there was still a chance that the northeast wind might stick around.

In forty-eight hours, I wouldn't care about Florida. I would escape to an island where I knew no one. I'd begin solid, income-producing work, would wallow in Grand Cayman's perfect weather.

Sam remained quiet during the trip, consumed by another man's jargon and his own frustration. Throughout our fifteen-year acquaintance, the past six or seven in close friendship, Sam and I had not been constant confidants. But around me, even in his worst moods, Sam never had failed to express himself.

The engines' buzzing zoned me out. I fled to a half-hour nap. I dreamed about my father chasing me into the house, in a rage. I don't remember why we argued, but I recall my mother screaming his name as he caught me in the kitchen and hauled off to slug me in the face. I ducked in time. The dent in the refrigerator door could not be repaired, so my mother got a new fridge. My father's hand was in a cast for at least two months, and he got off my case for the rest of the school year.

After I woke, I thought about squeezing five days' errands into my next forty-eight hours. And whether every smoker in Fort Lauderdale used the same brand of cigarette.

Sam woke, and stared out the window.

I said, "You ever wish your father was still alive?"

"Yep, twice," he said, "but only for those two reasons. He would unplug my radio whenever he heard 'What'd I Say?' or Buddy Holly's 'Peggy Sue.' I wish he'd been around to see Ray Charles perform at the White House. I'd have loved to stuff that in his racist face. And I wish he could've been at that football game in Lubbock, Texas, when 49,000 people made *The Guinness Book of Records* by singing 'Peggy Sue' in unison."

The pilot made his seat-backs-and-tray-tables speech. Sam poked me with his elbow. "Before I hung up, I asked Marnie to fetch us at the airport."

"Your Bronco's at the airport."

"Yep, it is. Somehow that fact departed my mind while I was talking. So we won't tell her it's there, and hope maybe she won't see it. I can't have her worrying about me. She gets neurotic."

"What's happened to your memory?" I said.

"I keep forgetting to take my ginkgo biloba."

"Can I ask the main distraction?"

"No cop would go to all that trouble to talk about immigrants. No big city detective would ask me if he could plant a phony squib in the *Sun-Sentinel*. Also, not many cops can afford a boat big enough for a Yamaha 225. Unless he inherited that, too."

"Why lunch?" I said. "He thinks you know the dead woman?"

Sam shrugged.

"He suspects you of something? Doesn't make sense."

"That's his cop job coming through. He thinks, 'Arrest them all, let the courts sort it out.' "

Had I heard a Vietnam echo in that phrase? "Arrest for what?" I said.

"He'll find something."

"What's that look in your eye?"

"I'm thinking I'll find something, too. With Odin Marlow attached."